THE WOLF AND THE RAVEN

By

H A Culley

Book seven about the Anglo-Saxon Kings of Northumbria

Published by

Orchard House Publishing

First Kindle Edition 2018

This novel is a work of fiction. The names, characters and events portrayed in it, which sticking as closely to the recorded history of the time and featuring a number of historical figures, are largely the product of the author's imagination.

TABLE OF CONTENTS

List of Principal Characters

VIKINGS

Ragnar's Family

Ragnar Sigvardson – Nicknamed Lodbrok (shaggy breeches). Son of King Sigvard of Agder (Southern Norway)
Thora Borganhjort – Daughter of Jarl Gutfred and Ragnar's first wife
Agnar Ragnarson – Their elder son
Eirik Ragnarson – Their younger son
Lagertha the Shieldmaiden – Ragnar's second wife
Fridlief Ragnarson – their son
Ragnhild Ragnarsdóttir – their daughter
Aslaug – A Norse princess and Ragnar's third wife
Ivar the Boneless – Their eldest son
Bjorn Ironside – Their second son
Sigurd Snake-in-the-Eye – Their third son
Halfdan Ragnarson – Their youngest son, also called Hvitserk (white shirt)
Åløf – Aslaug's daughter

Other Vikings

Agði – Olaf's eldest son and Ragnar's closest companion in his declining years. The name meant man from Agder
Eystein Beli – King of Uppsala in Sweden and father of Aslaug
Finnulf – Jarl of Gotland in Sweden
Froh - King of the minor Swedish kingdom of Alfheim
Gedda – Lagertha's brother
Gutfred – Jarl of Lindholm and the lands bordering the Limfjord in northern Jutland
Grimulf – A Danish hersir; later Jarl of Lindholm
Guthrum – His son and successor, later King of East Anglia
Harald Klak – King of Denmark
Hákon- Eystein Beli's nephew

Horik – King of Denmark after Harald Klak; also the name of one of his sons
Ingólfr Arnarson – The man credited with settling Iceland
Kjarten – Froh's brother
Olaf – Ragnar's closest companion
Osten – Eystein's brother
Sitric – A helmsman
Thorkel – A hersir
Torstein – Ragnar's godi
Yingvi - One of Ragnar's hirdmen

NORTHUMBRIANS

Kings

Eardwulf – 796 to 806 and again from 808 to 830
Ælfwald – Usurper. 806 to 808
Eanred – Son of Eardwulf. 830 to 854
Æthelred II – Son of Earnred. 854 to 858 then deposed. Restored 858 to 862. Murdered
Rædwulf – Usurper. 858. Died in battle
Osberht – 862. Deposed but still recognised as king by many
Ælle – 862 – 867. Ruled in competition to his brother Osberht

Ealdorman of Bebbanburg's Household

Eafa – 796 to 840. Son of Octa (d. 793) and Cynwise (d. 800)
Breguswid – His wife from 820 to 840
Ilfrid – Their eldest son. b. 821. Ealdorman 840 to 841
Edmund – Their younger son. b. 825. Ealdorman 841 to 880
Burwena – Edmund's wife and Rædwulf's sister
Osgern – Their daughter. b. 849. Married King Ælle in 862
Ricsige – Their son. b. 852, later the last Anglo-Saxon King of Northumbria
Garr – Captain of Eafa's warband
Cynefrith – Captain of Edmund's warband after Garr
Erik – Eafa's body servant
Laughlin – Ilfrid's body servant, later Edmund's

Drefan – A boy serving as a scout with Edmund's warband
Hrothwulf – Drefan's elder brother, also a scout

Other Northumbrians

Bishops of Lindisfarne

Heathwred – 821 to 830
Ecgred – 830 to 845
Eanbert –845 to 854
Eardulf –854 to 899

Archbishops of Eoforwīc

Wulfsige – 808 to 837
Wigmund – 837 to 854
Wulfhere – 854 to 900

Other Ealdormen

Anson – Islandshire during Edmund's banishment
Iuwine - Luncæstershire
Kendric - Dùn Barra and Dùn Èideann
Rædwulf – Cumbria from 836 to 858, when he seized the throne
Siferth – Jarrow and Tynedale

Franks

Bastiaan – Viscount of the coastal region of the County of Arras
Louis – His father, Count of Arras
Joscelin – Louis' daughter
Charles the Bald – King of West Frankia, later Holy Roman Emperor

Place Names

(In alphabetical order)

Many place names used in this novel may be unfamiliar to the reader. Where the Old English name is known I have used it and these are listed below, together with places in Scandinavia and on the Continent that readers may not be familiar with:

Alfheim – The coastal region of south western Sweden on the Kattegat, bounded to the north by Vestfold and to the south by Halland. It corresponds roughly to the modern Swedish province of Bohuslän
Agder – Modern Sørlandet. The southernmost region of Norway, bounded by the kingdom of Vestfold (q.v) and the Skagerrak (q.v.) to the east and the North Sea (German Ocean) to the west
Arendal – Capital of Agder (q.v.)
Bebbanburg – Bamburgh, Northumberland, North East England
Bernicia – The modern counties of Northumberland, Durham, Tyne & Wear and Cleveland in the North East of England and Lothian, now part of Scotland
Berwic – Berwick upon Tweed, Northumberland
Bohus – Capital of Alfheim in Sweden
Caer Luel – Carlisle, Cumbria
Caracotinum – Harfleur in France
Châlons sur Marne – Châlons-en-Champagne, France
Conganis – Chester-le-Street, County Durham
Dalriada – Much of Argyll and the Inner Hebrides
Deira – Most of North Yorkshire and northern Humberside
Duibhlinn – Dublin, Ireland
Dùn Breatainn - Literally Fortress of the Britons. Dumbarton, Scotland
Dùn Èideann - Edinburgh
Eoforwīc - York

Frankia – The territories inhabited and ruled by the Franks, a confederation of West Germanic tribes, approximating to present day France and a large part of Germany
Frisia - A coastal region in what today part of the Netherlands
German Ocean – North Sea
Gotland – Large island off the east coast of Sweden
Kattegat – The sea area bounded by Jutland in the west, the Skagerrak (q.v) in the north and Sweden in the east. The Baltic Sea drains into the Kattegat through the Danish Straits
Loidis – Leeds, Yorkshire
Luncæster – Lancaster, Lancashire
Lundenwic – London
Mercia – Roughly the present day Midlands of England
Neustria – Part of Frankia, lying between Aquitaine and Burgundy to the south and the English Channel. Roughly north-eastern France, excluding Brittany
Northumbria – The north of England and south-eastern Scotland
Orkneyjar – The Norse name for the Orkney Isles
Pictland – The confederation of kingdoms including Shetland, the Orkneys, the Outer Hebrides, Skye and the Scottish Highlands north of a line running roughly from Skye to the Firth of Forth
River Derventio – River Derwent in Northumberland; Derventio means valley of the oaks in the Brythonic tongue
River Twaid – The river Tweed, which flows west from Berwick through northern Northumberland and the Scottish Borders
Skagen – Now Denmark's northernmost town, it is situated on the east coast of the Skagen Odde peninsula in the far north of Jutland
Skagerrak – The strait running between the southeast coast of Norway, the southwest coast of Sweden, and the Jutland peninsula of Denmark, connecting the North Sea and the Kattegat (q.v.)
Snæland - Iceland
Strathclyde – South west Scotland

Uppsala - The main pagan centre of Sweden and the capital of the kingdom of the same name, lying on the east coast between Geatland in the south and Kvenland in the north.
Vestfold – The coastal kingdom on the Kattegat lying between Agder and Alfheim

Glossary

ANGLO-SAXON

Ætheling – Literally 'throne-worthy. An Anglo-Saxon prince

Birlinn – A wooden ship similar to the later Scottish galleys. Usually with a single mast and square rigged sail, they could also be propelled by oars with one man to each oar

Byrnie - A long (usually sleeveless) tunic of chain mail

Ceorl - Freemen who worked the land or else provided a service or trade such as metal working, carpentry, weaving etc. They ranked between thegns and slaves and provided the fyrd in time of war

Cyning – Old English for king and the term by which they were normally addressed

Gesith – The companions of a king, prince or noble, usually acting as his bodyguard

Geats - A Germanic tribe inhabiting what is now called Götaland (Land of the Geats) in the southern tip of Sweden

Hereræswa – Military commander or general. The man who commanded the army of a nation under the king

Knarr - A merchant ship where the hull was wider, deeper and shorter than that of a birlinn

Seax – A bladed weapon somewhere in size between a dagger and a sword. Mainly used for close-quarter fighting where a sword would be too long and unwieldy

Thegn – The lowest rank of noble. A man who held a certain amount of land direct from the king or from a senior nobleman, ranking between an ordinary freeman and an ealdorman

Settlement – Any grouping of residential buildings, usually around the king's or lord's hall. In 9th century England the term town or village had not yet come into use

Witan – The council of an Anglo-Saxon kingdom. Its composition varied, depending on the matters to be debated. Usually it consisted of the ealdormen, the bishops and the abbots

Villein - A peasant who ranked above a bondsman or slave but who was legally tied to his vill

Vill - A thegn's holding or similar area of land in Anglo-Saxon England which might otherwise be described as a parish or manor

VIKING

Bóndi - Farmers and craftsmen who were free men and enjoyed rights such as the ownership of weapons and membership of the Thing. They could be tenants or landowners

Byrnie - a long (usually sleeveless) tunic of chain mail

Godi – A pagan priest

Havnesjef – Harbour master (modern) or port reeve (medieval)

Hirdman – A member of a king's or a jarl's personal bodyguard, collectively known as the hird

Hersir – A bóndi who was chosen to a leader of warriors under a king or a jarl. Typically they were wealthy landowners who could recruit enough other bóndi to serve under their command

Jarl – A Norse or Danish chieftain; in Sweden they were regional governors appointed by the king

Konungr - King in old Norse; similar words were used in the rest of Scandinavia

Lagman (pl. lagmän) – Literally a lawspeaker. In Scandinavia where there were few written records, if any, a lagman was a respected individual who could recite the law from memory

Nailed God – Pagan name for Christ, also called the White Christ

Norns – The three goddesses who control the fate of all beings, including humans and gods

Thing – The governing assembly made up of the free people of the community presided over by a lagman (*q.v.)*. The meeting-place of the Thing was called the Thingstead

Thrall – A slave. A man, woman or child in bondage to his or her owner. Thralls had no rights and could be beaten or killed with impunity

Völva – A female shaman (meaning spirit medium, magician and healer) and a prophetess

NORSE GODS AND MYTHOLOGY

Asgard - Home to the Æsir tribe of gods, ruled over by Odin and Frigg

Frey – Son of Njǫrd. God of fertility

Freyja – Daughter of Njǫrd. Goddess of love, sex and sorcery

Frigg – Odin's wife

Hel – Goddess of the underworld (Helheim *q.v.*)

Helheim - One of the nine worlds where all who die from disease, old age or other causes without having accomplished something worthy go in the afterlife. Unlike the Christian Hell, it is place of icy coldness

Loki – The mischief maker, father of Hel

Midgard – The place where men live; one of the nine worlds

The Nine Worlds – Asgard (*q.v.*), Midgard (*q.v.),* Helheim(*q.v.*), Niflheim, Muspelheim, Jotunheim, Vanaheim, Ljosalfheim and Svartalfheim. The nine worlds are inhabited by different types of being (gods, mankind, giants, the dead etc)

Njǫrd – God of the sea and of wind, fire and prosperity

Norns – The three female beings who control the fates of men

Odin – The All-Father. Chief of the gods. Associated with war, wisdom and poetry

Ragnarök – A great battle sometime in the future when the gods Odin, Thor, Týr, Freyr and Loki will die. This will lead to various natural disasters and the subsequent submersion of the world by water. Afterwards, the world will be reborn

Rán – Goddess of the sea

Thor – Odin's son, god of thunder, armed with Mjolnir, a magic hammer. An emblem depicting the Mjolnir was worn around the neck by most Vikings, which they touched for luck

Tyr – Lord of battle

Valhalla – An enormous hall located in Asgard (*q.v.)*, ruled over by the god Odin. Chosen by Odin, half of those who die in combat travel to Valhalla upon death, led by valkyries *(q.v).* Those not chosen go to the goddess Freyja's meadow, Fólkvangr

Valkyries – The choosers of the slain. They decide who dies in battle and who lives and then choose whether the dead go to Valhalla or Fólkvangr

LONGSHIPS

In order of size:

Knarr – Also called karve or karvi. The smallest type of longship. It had 6 to 16 benches and, like their English equivalents, they were mainly used for fishing and trading, but they were occasionally commissioned for military use. They were broader in the beam and had a deeper draught than other longships.

Snekkja – (Plural snekkjur). Typically the smallest longship used in warfare and was classified as a ship with at least 20 rowing benches. A typical snekkja might have a length of 17 m, a width of 2.5 m and a draught of only 0.5 m. Norse snekkjas, designed for deep fjords and Atlantic weather, typically had more draught than the Danish type, which were intended for shallow water

Drekar - (Dragon ship). Larger warships consisting of more than 30 rowing benches. Typically they could carry a crew of some 70–80 men and measured around 30 m in length. These ships were more properly called skeids; the term drekar referred to the carvings of menacing beasts, such as dragons and snakes, mounted on the prow of the ship during a sea battle or when raiding. Strictly speaking Drekar is the plural form, the singular being dreki or dreka, but these words don't appear to be accepted usage in English

Prologue

September 808 AD

Sigvard, King of Agder, stood at the prow of his drekar as his small fleet entered the fjord which led to his capital at Arendal. He had good reason to be pleased. He had spent the summer raiding the coast around the Baltic Sea and, on his way home, the Swedish coast in the straight known as the Kattegat. He had avoided the Danish coast on the west side of the Kattegat for the simple reason that his wife's brother was jarl of the area around the Limfjord in Northern Jutland.

He wasn't the only king or jarl to be raiding in the Baltic that year and many of the settlements he came across had already been raided. Plunder had therefore been limited and, as his jarls and their warriors followed him because of the rewards to be gained, morale on the voyage home had been low.

That was why he decided to pillage the east coast of the Kattegat. It was risky as a sensible man doesn't defecate in his own neighbourhood; it's too easy for those raided to retaliate. For that reason they didn't take any prisoners to keep or sell as thralls in case they escaped and identified their captors. So they slaughtered everyone in the five places they attacked. They also took the precaution of rowing into shore, even if the wind was favourable. Sails could be seen from a distance and they were painted with the owner's device - in Sigvard's case a black raven on a red sail - or dyed in distinctive stripes of colour.

Even the infants were killed, but such callous behaviour didn't seem to bother him or his men. Life in Norway was tough and they were unable to survive on what they could grow or catch in the sea. Raiding was a way of life.

He had left his wife pregnant and the baby would be due about now. They had children before this one but they had all died in infancy. This time the godi had sacrificed several animals to ensure that the child survived. Furthermore Sigvard's sister, who was a völva, had predicted that the baby would be a boy whilst in a trance. He would grow up favoured by Odin, the All-father, and become a great hero.

Sigvard was sceptical - his sister had been wrong in the past – but the prediction that this child would survive had prevented him from disposing of his wife and taking another to his bed.

As was usual when the longships returned from months away, the whole population of Arendal came down to the jetties that stuck out from the steeply sloping shingle beach like the talons of an eagle to welcome their men home.

All five ships followed him in, even the three belonging to his jarls. This evening the spoils would be divided and everyone would drink themselves unconscious in celebration of a successful summer's marauding.

That evening Sigvard had more reason than anyone else present to get uproariously drunk. The day before he returned his wife had given birth to a lusty boy. The child was named Ragnar and in due course he would acquire the nickname Lodbrok – hairy breeches.

PART ONE - RAGNAR LODBROK

THE RAVEN

Chapter One – The Raid

Summer 821

Ragnar felt as if his lungs would burst as he struggled to swim through the icy waters. His limbs were so cold that he couldn't feel them and still he was a long way away from the ship which represented safety. All Norse boys were put through a tough regime from the age of ten onwards and not all survived to start their training as warriors a few years later.

The games they played as children were intentionally rough. Broken bones were common and those who gave up under the harsh training system would never become warriors. They could remain as bondi but they would have to hire a warrior to fight in their place when necessary.

That wasn't even an option for Ragnar. As the king's only son he would rather die than fail. How could he expect men to follow him in due course if he couldn't do everything they did, and excel at it?

He struggled against the numbing cold and his failing limbs which, paradoxically, felt as if they were on fire. He gritted his teeth and struggled to cover the final hundred yards to the waiting snekkja. Now he could faintly hear the encouraging cries of a few of his friends who had reached the longship ahead of him and he put renewed effort into his strokes. Exhausted, he reached the side of the snekkja and willing hands reached down to pull him from the water.

He collapsed onto the deck and someone wrapped a sheepskin around his shoulders. After a minute or two he felt a bit better and glanced up and saw another boy being helped aboard. There were only two left in the sea now; one was only ten or so yards from the ship but the last one, a close friend of his called Gunnar, was struggling. As Ragnar watched, the boy disappeared beneath the waves. He came up again only to vanish moments later.

Still shivering with fatigue and cold, Ragnar got to his feet and, before anyone could stop him, he dived over the side and started to swim to where he'd last seen Gunnar. When he reached what he thought was the spot he dived down with his eyes open and scanned the clear water for his friend. He was about to give up when he saw him struggling to reach the surface again.

By now Ragnar was close to blacking out due to lack of air and his limbs felt as though they weighed a ton. Making one last effort he reached Gunnar and, grabbing the belt that held up his trousers, he hauled him to the surface. They both sucked in lungfuls of the icy cold air whilst they struggled to tread water. Thankfully the crew of the snekkja had hauled up the anchor and rowed towards them. A few minutes later both boys were pulled aboard and they fell into blissful unconsciousness.

Far from being praised for his heroism, Ragnar was roundly chastised by Thorkel, an old warrior who everyone called 'uncle' and who was responsible for training the boys.

'You put your own life in danger to save someone who wasn't strong enough to pass the test. Now Gunnar will have to do it again tomorrow and without you there to help him.'

'Tomorrow? But he won't have recovered sufficiently.'

'Do you think that a foe will give you time to recover? There is no such thing as fairness in battle, Ragnar. It's time you learnt that. Furthermore, tomorrow I'll anchor the ship a little further out from the shore, and you will stay well away. Gunnar must pass the test on his own.'

However, unbeknownst to anyone, Ragnar stole some goose fat that evening and before dawn he covered Gunnar's body in it. As the swimming test had to be done in the clothes a warrior normally wore on board ship, his thick woollen tunic and trousers would cover the whiteness of the fat.

This time Gunnar just managed to reach the snekkja unaided. When he was pulled aboard Thorkel lifted his tunic and saw the remains of the goose fat that had coated his back. He knew that the person responsible was Ragnar and for a moment he thought of telling his wife that Ragnar had been pilfering her larder. He would be soundly beaten as any instances of theft were taken seriously, but he admired the boy's initiative and his loyalty to his friend, so he said nothing.

As was common amongst boys born to jarls and kings, Ragnar had left his father's hall when he was ten and had gone to live with Thorkel. Whereas King Sigvard's hall was a large longhouse capable of housing himself, his wife, his hirdmen and his many thralls, Thorkel lived with his wife, boys he was fostering and his thralls in a much smaller hall. He himself had been a member of Sigvard's father's hird until he married. Now he was called uncle by all; a term reserved for the elderly warrior who was regarded by all as their mentor and example.

Thorkel was a hersir – a leader of warriors – and a wealthy landowner, but he preferred to live in the main settlement of Arendal. His eldest son managed his extensive estate for him and collected the rents from the various bóndis who leased their farms from him. His other son looked after the flotilla of small knarrs he also owned, which were mainly used for fishing.

He was the shipmaster of the second largest drekar in Arendal - the largest being owned by the king – and could usually find the seventy men needed to crew it from the bóndis who acknowledged him as their hersir; that is his tenants, their families and those involved in the fishing business who were not thralls.

Unlike many hersirs, he owed no fealty to a jarl, but only to the king.

The last test faced by Ragnar was the games organised to celebrate the end of winter and the start of summer. To a Viking there were only two seasons – the one where the cold and snow made mere survival something of a struggle and the one where they could go raiding. He was now thirteen and he was determined to prove himself as a warrior so that he could be taken on as a member of a longship's crew.

The fact that he was the king's son was no guarantee of that. Some kings and jarls favoured their sons but Sigvard didn't believe in spoiling Ragnar. If he was accepted as a warrior after the games he didn't suppose for one minute that the king would take him with him; he would have to find another shipmaster. Only once he'd proved himself during a raiding season would Sigvard consider letting him join him.

In truth, Ragnar thought of Thorkel as more of a father than Sigvard.

Whilst the men celebrated the end of winter with a marathon session of feasting, drinking and wrestling bouts, the boys who were on the point of leaving their childhood behind were expected to display their stamina in running races and their skills as swordsmen.

The latter consisted of a knockout contest with the winner of each bout proceeding to the next round. A boy won his fight by either disabling his opponent with a blunt sword or disarming him. Ragnar sized up his first adversary as they circled one another, looking for possible weak points. The boy he was pitted against was six inches taller and had a longer reach than he did. He hadn't practiced against him before because he was the son of a rich bóndi, a hersir, who lived in a farming settlement some distance away.

He hoped that, being bigger, the boy, whose name was Eyjolf, would be slow but he quickly learned that he wasn't; he was fast and agile. It was nearly all over in the first minute. Eyjolf attacked unexpectedly and, banging his shield against Ragnar's, he sent the king's son sprawling onto his back. Eyjolf's sword came down with enough force to have cracked Ragnar's skull had he not rolled away just in time.

The crowd roared their approval. It wasn't that they disliked their king's son, it was just that they appreciated a good fight where there was every chance that one or other of the fighters would be seriously hurt.

As he rolled away Ragnar brought his sword around in a scything motion, still lying on the ground. He was lucky. The blade struck Eyjolf's right shin hard and he howled in pain. He hobbled around testing his injured leg, giving Ragnar enough time to scramble to his feet and bring his shield back in front of him.

This time Ragnar attacked. He feinted with the point of his sword, aiming at the other boy's eyes. Neither wore armour; it was expensive and would have been a waste of money for boys still growing fast. Eyjolf did as Ragnar expected: he brought his shield up to protect his head. Ragnar swiftly dropped onto one knee and stabbed the other lad hard in the thigh. The sword might have been blunt but it was still heavy and the momentum of the thrust was enough to momentarily cripple Eyjolf.

He fell to one side and Ragnar stamped on his left arm, trapping his shield. He batted away Eyjolf's feeble attempt to hit him with his sword and thrust the point of his blade into the other boy's throat. Ragnar pulled the blow at the last moment so that he bruised his throat instead of crushing his windpipe. Eyjolf was sufficiently disabled for the adjudicator to award the bout to Ragnar.

He helped the loser to his feet and Eyjolf gave him a rueful smile.

'I was told that you would beat me but no-one ever has in the last two years so I didn't believe them,' he croaked through his damaged throat. 'Good luck in the next round.'

Ragnar watched the boy hobble off to be teased by his friends and went to watch another bout, wondering who his next adversary would be. In fact none of the next few rounds were as difficult to win as the one against Eyjolf had been. That changed when he reached the final.

He had watched Olaf Sigurdson carefully as he won his four bouts. It was obvious that the boy, though small, was very fast and he was clever. Ragnar was fairly certain that of all the boys who won their first round, Olaf would reach the final.

Both boys were somewhat bruised and battered by the time it came to the final bout. Ragnar had taken a blow to his right biceps, which had weakened his sword arm, and one eye was swollen and closed after the rim of someone's shield had connected with it. Olaf was limping and his shield had split from the rim to the metal boss during the last fight. However, Ragnar wasn't entirely sure that the limp wasn't being exaggerated in order to fool him.

Ragnar attacked first, smashing his shield repeatedly against Olaf's, forcing his opponent back and denying him the chance to take the initiative. It wasn't popular but he ignored the odd insult and derogatory comment from the watching crowd. He used his greater weight against Olaf until the latter managed to side step his next push and bring his sword into play. Ragnar had been expecting it though and he turned in time to intercept the blow with his shield.

Olaf's sword glanced off it and Ragnar grunted in triumph as he thrust at where the Olaf had stood a split second earlier. However, he was no longer there and Ragnar was only just in time to parry his opponent's cut at his head from somewhere on his blind side.

He whirled to face Olaf but he was now standing several paces away, grinning mockingly at him. For an instant he was furious because Olaf had made him look a fool and the crowd were laughing and cheering. Then he remembered what Thorkel had told him.

'Never lose your temper. Your opponent wants the red mist to descend because then you won't think clearly and it'll be easy for him to kill you.'

Ragnar took a deep breath and nodded his head at Olaf, forcing himself to smile. The other boy looked annoyed and the crowd hushed in anticipation, wondering who would attack first and what move he would make.

Olaf ran at Ragnar and then, just as Ragnar was bracing himself for the impact of shield against shield, Olaf let go of his damaged shield and leaped high in the air, bringing his sword down onto Ragnar's head. It was totally unexpected and, although Ragnar started to raise his own shield he only got it up far enough up to absorb some of the sword's momentum. The impact of the blow was lessened so that, when it struck his head, it only made him dizzy instead of knocking him unconscious – or even killing him.

Olaf's body came down on the disorientated Ragnar and the two fell to the ground with Olaf on top. The wind was knocked from Ragnar's lungs and for a moment he was helpless. What saved him was the fact that Olaf had lost his grip on his sword when he fell.

Olaf rolled away and grabbed it again as he rose to his feet. Ragnar still lay on the ground, struggling for breath, but he still had his sword and his shield. He managed to cover his body with the latter and raised his sword to deflect Olaf's second attempt to strike his exposed head.

As the frustrated Olaf tried once more to attack the prone Ragnar the latter kicked out at the other boy's foot – the one at the end of the leg with the limp. The foot shot back and, from the cry of pain Ragnar gathered that the limp wasn't feigned. The leap in the air must have damaged it further.

Olaf collapsed beside Ragnar but he quickly rolled away, his face contorted with pain. Ragnar struggled to his feet just in time for Olaf to pull his shield out of the way and strike him hard in the stomach with the blunted tip of his sword. As Ragnar's head came down in reaction, Olaf raised the knee of his injured leg, catching Ragnar's chin as he doubled up.

Blackness enveloped Ragnar and so he wasn't aware until much later that Olaf Sigardson, the youngest son of a poor tenant farmer, had beaten him.

Ragnar did his best to contain his excitement but, at thirteen years of age, he was embarking on his first raid. Thorkel had accepted him as a member of his crew and this time they wouldn't be just raiding in the Baltic; they were heading to Orkeyjar as their base for the summer and from there Thorkel planned to raid the west coast of Pictland and even possibly the north coast of Ireland.

Ragnar would be one of four ship's boys. Boys on the verge of puberty weren't strong enough to row for any distance, although they each took a turn at the oars for short spells to toughen them up, so they were responsible for other tasks, such as hauling up and trimming the mainsail, preparing and distributing food and drink, keeping the longship clean and, when the warriors were on land, guarding the ship with the helmsman, an old man called Jorun. He didn't mind the menial tasks but he was annoyed that he wouldn't be involved in the actual raiding.

The other three ship's boys were Olaf, who had beaten him in the final bout at the games, and two fourteen year-olds: Gorm and Hakon. Gorm was friendly and taught the two juniors what to do and how to do it. Hakon was the opposite. He was the elder and liked to throw his weight around. He seemed to delight in belittling Ragnar in particular and made derisive remarks every time he made a mistake.

Ragnar was by nature hot blooded and he only kept his temper in check through self-discipline but, by the time that the coastline of the main island of Orneyjar came in sight on the third day out, he decided that he'd had enough. When Hakon made yet another of his sneering remarks about the younger boy's prowess, Ragnar went for him. Fortunately Gorm and Olaf grabbed him in time and held onto him until he'd calmed down. Had he struck Hakon he would have been whipped. Dissention amongst a crew could be fatal and wasn't tolerated.

Of course Thorkel and Jorun were well aware of the animosity between Hakon and the two new hands. His solution was to keep both Ragnar and Hakon at their oars far longer than he would have done normally in the hope that mutual suffering would solve the problem. It didn't and both boys blamed their raw and bloody hands and aching muscles on the other.

It was Olaf who put an end to a difficult situation. The drekar was large but with seventy four men and four boys on board there was no opportunity for him to do anything about Hakon. However, the first night ashore the men had gathered in groups around campfires whilst the boys brought them ale and cooked food. Finally, with sentries posted in the rocks above the beach where their drekar and a snekkja , whose shipmaster was another hersir called Øystein, lay beached, everyone settled down to sleep.

The four ship's boys and their fellows from the other longship had shared a fire and lay down around it. Hakon had continued his verbal abuse of Ragnar and Olaf during the evening, despite being scolded by the senior boy from the other ship.

Later, when the sound of snoring convinced him that everyone was asleep, Olaf slowly crawled over to where Hakon slept wrapped in his cloak. He woke with the point of Olaf's dagger pressing into his neck hard enough to have drawn a few drops of blood.

'If you don't keep your filthy trap shut, Hakon, you won't find my dagger at your throat; I'll use it to cut off your balls.'

Like many bullies, Hakon was a coward at heart and he bolstered his self-confidence by disparaging his juniors. Although Olaf couldn't see the wet patch in the crotch of the other boy's trousers he caught the faint tang of urine and grinned.

'And I'll tell the others you pissed yourself like a baby.'

He left Hakon shaking with fear and wondering how he was going to get the tell-tale yellow stain out of his cream coloured trousers by morning.

A few score Norsemen had settled on the main island of Orkneyjar over the past few decades and had enslaved the original inhabitants. They eked out a living by farming and fishing but they also traded with the Picts and the Irish. Now other Norsemen had started to arrive, some to settle with their families, but most wanted to use the islands as a summer base from which to raid. There were over seventy islands and skerries that made up Orkneyjar and only a few of these were inhabited. Skerries were too small to be of use but that still left over twenty uninhabited islands for Thorkel to choose from.

Raiders weren't popular with the permanent settlers as raiding had meant that those they normally traded with were now frightened of all Norse ships. Some could tell the difference between the knarrs used by merchants and the longships used for war, but not all, and some Orkneyjar traders had been killed as soon as they landed. Thus Thorkel avoided them and set up his base on an uninhabited island lying north east of the one with the major settlement. It had a deep inlet on the north coast that provided shelter from the prevailing westerly winds and had a large sandy shoreline on which to beach the two longships.

Ragnar had noticed almost immediately that Hakon had suddenly become quiet and withdrawn. He thought it strange that the boy had gone swimming in his trousers first thing the next morning; everyone else had stripped off completely before running into the sea to wash the sweat and grime of the voyage from their bodies. Perhaps he's shy because his manhood is like a shrunken worm Ragnar thought and nearly teased the other boy about it. However, he told himself that would be to sink to Hakon's level, so he didn't.

Two days later they set sail again heading south. Thorkel had been told that the northernmost part of the island of Britain was inhabited by poor people with nothing worth taking so he continued down the east coast until he encountered a coastline ahead of him which ran horizontally from west to east. As the wind was coming from the west, they turned and sailed eastwards along this coast.

The sky was blue with a scattering of white and grey clouds and the wind was just strong enough to turn the crests of the waves white. Apart from the odd fishing hamlet they saw nothing of interest on the first day. They found a sheltered cove in which to spend the night and they continued to head east until the land turned south west. After turning the corner they had to tack to and fro as they were now heading south west. The wind gradually grew in strength and veered as the day progressed and the relatively calm sea became agitated with waves five or six feet high crashing into the ship, spraying those inside her with cold, salty water.

'Get the sail down and put two reefs in it,' Thorkel yelled, telling Jorun to put her broadside on to the wind at the same time.

The ship rocked as waves crashed into her side as the four boys held the sail side on to the howling wind and lowered the yardarm from which it was suspended. Jorun let her run before the wind whilst they were gathering in the bottom half of the sail and tying it to the yardarm using the reefing points. Then, broadside on again, they struggled to haul it into position up the mast and secure the halyard. A second later Jorun leant on the steering oar to bring her back on course whilst the four boys trimmed the ropes attached to the ends of the yardarm to achieve maximum speed from the lithe craft.

Ragnar was exhausted but exhilarated. Now the drekar flew before the wind again, but without the risk of tearing the mast out of her. As suddenly as it had arrived, the squall passed and, although the swell continued to make hills and valleys for the ship to climb and skate down, the wind had died enough for the reef to be shaken out again.

That done, Thorkel looked around for the other longship but there was no sign of her.

'Either she's over the horizon or she's foundered,' his helmsman said unhelpfully.

Then his attention was drawn to the four boys.

'What are you standing there gawping at? Get bailing!'

It was only then that Ragnar and the others became aware of the sound of water sloshing around in the bilges where the ballast lay. Three of them formed a chain and passed leather buckets full of foul smelling water up to Olaf who threw them over the side to leeward. By the time that Jorun was satisfied they were beyond exhaustion and collapsed where they stood.

Two hours later the wind died and the men unshipped their oars and started to row. Shortly after that they spotted a cluster of buildings on top of a cliff. Most were built of timber or were timber framed with infill panels of wattle and daub, but one was built of stone. There was what looked like a watchtower near it and they could vaguely hear the monotonous pealing of a bell. At first Thorkel thought that they had been spotted but then he saw a line of men clad in long brown robes heading into the stone building.

'They're going to pray to their god. They call that building a church.' Olaf told the other boys. 'My father told me about what he called monasteries. Their priests live there without women.'

It seemed an unlikely story to Ragnar but he said nothing. Even at thirteen he'd had more than one tumble with a willing thrall. He couldn't imagine living without sex.

'Perhaps they enjoy each other,' Gorm suggested with a grin and the others laughed, even Hakon.

The steep cliffs continued for miles and the drekar sailed on, looking for somewhere to land. Presumably the monks thought themselves safe from the Vikings in view of their position, or perhaps their lack of alarm was because they hadn't spotted the ship without its sail raised.

Then Hakon, whose turn it was to climb the mast and act as lookout called down that he could see a shallow bay with a sandy beach on the larboard bow. Thorkel calculated that they were some ten miles south of the monastery they'd seen but it was only a few hours until nightfall so he told Jorun to steer for the bay, then yelled for the men to unship their oars.

As they were now heading into the wind the boys didn't need to be told to lower the sail and, as soon as Hakon had climbed down from his perch and rushed to the prow to resume his duties as lookout, the other three undid the halyard and carefully lowered the yardarm to which the sail was attached. It wasn't an easy exercise especially with the wind backing the sail, but they managed to get it down, secur the flapping sail and stow it without making any mistakes. Thorkel smiled to himself. They were improving. By the end of the voyage they might even be able to call themselves sailors.

The next morning Throkel and most of the crew set off to walk the ten miles or so north to the monastery. He left three of the older men with Jorun and the four boys to guard the ship and sent out a pair of men to the low hills that shadowed the path along the coast. They and the two scouts in front of the main body would protect them from a surprise attack.

Ragnar watched them depart wistfully. He wondered when he would be allowed to join the men. He was shaken out of his reverie when Jorun yelled at him and Gorm to deploy as sentries on the rise to the west of the beach.

Ragnar sat with his back against a rock watching the empty scrubland inland and occasionally looking down at the men on the beach playing knucklebones and drinking. Suddenly he thought he saw movement in the trees off to his left. He watched intently but, after a few minutes, he came to the reluctant conclusion that he must have imagined it; or perhaps it was just an animal. He looked over towards where Gorm was sitting a few hundred yards away but he didn't look as if he had seen anything.

Something made him look back towards the small wood and, to his horror, he saw about a score of half-naked warriors running towards the beach. They were further away from the ship than he was so he started to run and yell a warning at the same time.

Gorm started up from his position and joined Ragnar in slithering down the sandy slope to where the others were rushing to arm themselves. Ragnar scooped up his bow and bent it to fix the string in place. By now the Picts were about three hundred yards away; too far for an arrow to do much damage from where he was. He ran back to the ship, ignoring Hakon's cry of coward, and climbed aboard. He raced to the prow, where he was about ten feet higher than the others.

His first arrow struck a Pict in the thigh and the next killed one with a hit in the centre of his torso. He downed three more before they were too close to Olaf and the others to risk another shot.

The Norsemen might be outnumbered two to one but they were disciplined and well-trained, whereas the Picts were a disorganised mass. Jorun and the other three men formed a shield wall with the three boys behind them armed with spears which protruded over the men's shoulders. Instead of flanking them, the Picts charged directly at them and five of them were killed or wounded before the first Viking fell.

His shield had been pulled down by one Pict whilst another stabbed him in the throat. Both Picts were quickly killed but this wasn't a rate of attrition that the Vikings could stand for very long.

One more of the Norse warriors was killed and Jorun was fatally wounded before the Pict's frenzied attack ceased and they withdrew. Ragnar had leapt down from the prow, having exchanged his bow for a sword and shield, as soon as the close quarter fighting started. As the Picts withdrew he ran after them and managed to slice through a hamstring before the red mist cleared from his eyes; he realised with a start that he was isolated and about to face nearly a dozen Picts on his own. He turned and walked unhurriedly back towards the one remaining warrior, a man called Fiske, and the other three boys. The Picts were arguing amongst themselves as Ragnar re-joined them.

'What do we do now?' Hakon asked. 'They still outnumber us by over two to one.'

Fiske shrugged. 'Fight them until either we're all dead or they are.'

Ragnar grabbed Hakon's shoulder and pulled him around to face him. Although he was three inches shorter than the older boy he pushed his face up close to Hakon's. The latter jerked back, thinking that Ragnar was going to butt him in the nose.

'The next time you call me a coward I'll kill you myself,' Ragnar told him through clenched teeth.

'For Odin's sake, haven't you got enough people to battle against without fighting amongst yourselves?' Fiske asked.

Ragnar let go of Hakon and both took their place in the shield wall, still glaring at each other.

'Right, we've got three spears' Fiske continued. 'They're useless now we're all in the front rank so throw them at the bastards and make sure you each hit one of them.'

Olaf, Gorm and Hakon took aim and two warriors tumbled to the ground, one with two spears in him. The five stood with shields overlapping and swords poking above or below the shields as the Picts crashed into them. They tried to hack at them with axes, swords and long thin daggers with a sharp point but their opponents pushed forward to limit the Picts' room for manoeuvre. The Vikings' swords stabbed into exposed flesh and Fiske, the only one wearing a helmet, banged it into the face of an opponent, breaking his nose and cheekbone. A moment later and another Pict thrust his spear into Fiske's neck and the old Viking collapsed.

Ragnar was at the end of the short shield wall and he sensed rather than saw a Pict to his right. The man was about to thrust a spear into the boy's side when Ragnar sliced sideways with his blade, cutting the point off the spear. He rolled his wrist and the tip of the sword entered the Pict's eye and he collapsed screaming.

Hakon was to Ragnar's left and, as he turned his attention back to his front he realised that the other boy had moved away from him to fill the gap left by the death of Fiske. A Pict took advantage of his exposed position and brought an axe down towards his unprotected head. Ragnar just managed to lift his shield to meet it but the blow felt as if it had broken his left hand. He gritted his teeth and resisted the urge to let go of his shield.

The axe was embedded in the limewood shield and the Pict tried to pull it out. Ragnar was jerked forward and lost his balance. As he went down on one knee he stabbed upwards into the axeman's groin. He leapt to his feet, only to discover that it was all over. The three remaining Picts had fled.

Ragnar darted to where he'd dropped his bow and quiver and scooped them up. He took careful aim and let fly. As soon as the arrow left the bowstring he replaced it with another. The first Pict fell forwards onto his face with an arrow in his back just as the second one reached the top of its trajectory and started to descend. The twang of the bowstring indicated that a third one was on its way.

The other boys watched as the second one caught a Pict in the calf and he was reduced to hobbling. However, the third one only grazed the shoulder of the last man.

'Quick, after them. They mustn't be allowed to summon reinforcements.'

'Who are you to give orders?' Hakon asked, not moving. 'I'm the eldest.'

'There's no time for your stupidity Hakon. Come on.'

Ragnar started to chase after the two Picts and Olaf joined him. Gorm hesitated for a split second and then ran after them. Hakon was left fuming but, after swearing and calling Ragnar every name he could think of he too started to run.

It took no more than a few minutes to catch the limping Pict and Olaf dispatched him with a chop into his other leg followed by a thrust into his bare back. The other Pict disappeared into the tress but he left a trail of blood from the arrow wound in his shoulder.

Ten minutes later Ragnar caught him up and the man turned to face him. He thrust his spear at the Viking boy, which Ragnar easily evaded. He had long ago thrown aside his shield so he was vulnerable as the Pict brought it back in a slashing movement. Had the spear slashed across his belly as intended, his innards would be tumbling out at his feet by now. Ragnar realised that the man was too far away for him to reach with his sword so, instead, he made a grab at the spear and was lucky enough to grasp it. He pulled with all his might and the Pict, caught by surprise, was pulled forward onto Ragnar's sword. As it slid into his belly, the Pict spewed out the contents of his last meal all over Ragnar. The boy let go of his sword in disgust and pushed the dying man away from him.

Just at that moment the other three arrived. Olaf and Gorm stopped, bending over to try and recover their breath now that it was all over, but Hakon leapt at Ragnar calling him a filthy turd as he aimed his sword at Ragnar's head.

Ragnar turned as he heard Hakon's voice and his foot slipped in the Pict's entrails. He lost his balance and fell on his back, Hakon's sword cutting though empty air where he'd been standing a split second earlier.

The momentum of his attack nearly unbalanced Hakon but he recovered swiftly and went to stab Ragnar as he lay on the ground unarmed. Suddenly Hakon arched his body and fell on top of the Pict, Olaf's dagger protruding from his back.

When Thorkel and his men returned laden with plunder and bringing seven monks and a dozen novices to be sold as thralls, he found his ship guarded by just three boys. The Picts had been left for the buzzards and carrion crows to feed on but Jorun and the other Norse dead had been piled on top of a funeral pyre made up of deadwood and wood chopped from the nearby trees using the Picts' axes. Hakon had been laid there with the four men; there was no need for anyone else to know about the ignominious manner of his death.

Chapter Two – Northumbria

821

Thorkel appointed an experienced sailor called Sitric as the new helmsman and, to sail the ship efficiently, as well as to even up the number of rowers, he had told the youngest warrior to join the three ship's boys. The young man, whose name was Ketil, had protested, but Thorkel had given him a choice: become a ship's boy or swim to shore and take his chances amongst the Picts.

When Ketil tried to throw his weight around, the other boys told him to back off. Olaf pointed out forcefully that Ragnar had killed more Picts than anyone else, so he was their leader. Ketil was sixteen and a warrior; quite naturally he refused to accept a thirteen year old ship's boy as his senior, but when Olaf pricked his neck with the tip of his dagger, he accepted the situation – for the moment. He was furious with Olaf and Ragnar, but most of all with Thorkel.

The drekar turned into the entrance to the wide fjord that had opened up to their right and, with the easterly wind behind them, they made good progress. There were several settlements, both on the north coast and to the south, but they were close together and the mighty fortress on the rock a little way down the fjord, which Thorkel later found out was called the Firth of Forth, convinced him to look elsewhere for easier pickings. When several small ships put out from both shores he decided he needed to retrace his steps, and quickly.

The smaller birlinns had no chance of catching the much larger drekar and they left their pursuers behind well before they reached the open sea again. The Vikings turned south and passed another inlet, probably the mouth of a large river, but it too was guarded by a fortification on the north bank a little way down the river, so they raised the sail once more and pressed on southwards.

'There's what looks like a monastery on an island ahead,' Ragnar, whose turn it was as lookout, called down. 'No, wait I think it's connected to the mainland by a strip of sand.'

'Lindisfarne,' Thorkel muttered to himself.

'There should be a bay on the south side if we're where I think we are.'

'Yes, there is,' Ragnar confirmed as they rounded the tip of the island where a large conical mound of rock rose up from the low lying land around it.

At that moment smoke began to curl lazily skywards before being whipped away by the wind.

'They've lit a warning beacon by the look of it.'

'Much good may it do them,' Thorkel laughed, thinking that monasteries were seldom defended, and even if this one was, there wouldn't be many guards and he had seventy warriors.

Ragnar was about to descend, the need for a lookout having ceased as they prepared to beach the longship, when he looked to the south. He could just make out what looked like a fortress on another, much larger, rock shimmering on the horizon. Then he faintly heard what sounded like the pealing of a bell coming over the water.

-ᛉ-

Ealdorman Eafa was playing with his three year old son, Ilfrid, when he heard the alarm bell being rung. His wife, Breguswid, looked at him in alarm. They both knew that the most likely cause was another attack on Lindisfarne. After the disastrous raid of 793, there had been two more, the most recent being three years ago.

The monastery complex was now defended by a palisade and the members of the fyrd amongst the islanders could hold off a small raiding party until help from the fortress could reach them. Eafa hoped that he could make it in time, if what he feared was true.

It was. From the ramparts he could see the Viking longship turning to run before the wind and then head towards the beach. Monks who had been fishing or working in the fields outside the enclosure were running for the gates, together with the local inhabitants. A few monks stood ready to close and bar them as soon as the last person was inside.

Those who lived too far away from the monastery to reach the safety it offered were heading for the path over the sand to the mainland. Luckily the tide was ebbing and Eafa was confident that they would make the crossing safely. The Vikings had yet to beach their ship and they would most probably concentrate on the monastery first.

He ran down the steps, only pausing to let Erik, his body servant, help him to don his byrnie, helmet and spurs. A stable boy came running with his horse and, mounting, he took his shield and spear from Erik before kicking the animal into a canter. His fifty men followed him out of the sea gate and, once through it, they upped the pace to a gallop as they made for the jetty in Budle Bay, the natural harbour that lay to the north of the looming bulk of Bebbanburg on the rocky outcrop above it.

They piled aboard two of the birlinns tied up alongside and cast off. Once clear of the bay, the men shipped their oars and hoisted the sail. The wind was coming directly from the east and they hauled the sail around so that they were sailing on a broad reach as they headed across the six miles that separated them from the beach below the monastery complex. Although they were making a good four knots through the water, it seemed very slow to Eafa. At this rate it would take them an hour and a half to get there.

Ragnar glanced across the sea towards the imposing stronghold on the horizon when he reached the top of the shallow cliff above the beach.

'There are two ships heading towards us,' he called out to Thorkel, pointing towards them.

'They're half the size of ours,' the hersir muttered, more to himself than to Ragnar. 'Perhaps fifty men, sixty at most. Still, I can't afford to lose men for no purpose.'

He looked at the tall wooden stakes that formed the palisade in front of him. Given time, his men could capture the place but time was the one thing he didn't have.

Egbert, the Bishop of Lindisfarne, appeared on the walkway above the gates at that moment and held up a gold cross on a pole. He was cursing the Vikings in Latin, not that they understood a word of what he was shouting, but they got the gist of it. Ragnar strung his bow and took careful aim. At a range of eighty yards it was a difficult shot but when he saw the arrow strike the prelate in the centre of his chest he knew that Odin had guided his aim.

Egbert fell backwards off the walkway to crash onto the hard earth inside the compound. The bishop was dead before he hit the ground. A great cheer went up from the Norsemen, matched by the wail of despair uttered by the monks.

'Well done, Ragnar,' Thorkel called across to him.

Ragnar beamed with pleasure whilst Ketil gave him a venomous look. It conveyed all the hatred he felt for the younger boy but nobody noticed it, except for Olaf. He was about to warn Ragnar when Thorkel shouted.

'Back to the ship! If they're looking for a fight we'll give them one; we'll kill the turds and then come back to kill the rest of the White Christians.'

The men cheered and headed back to the drekar. Thorkel's words had been ones of encouragement, but he had no intention of losing warriors to no good purpose.

Eafa sighed with relief as he saw the Viking raiders head back to the beach and push their ship back into the sea. He had achieved his purpose and saw no point in trying to fight the big longship at sea. Vikings had a fearsome reputation for maritime warfare, and deservedly so. Although he had two ships, he knew that the Norsemen would outnumber his men and Northumbrians weren't used to fighting on ships being rocked by the waves.

Once it was afloat, the men who had pushed her off the beach swam out to the lowest part of the gunwale and were hauled aboard. The oars were pushed through the small holes that served as rowlocks and Eafa counted thirty a side. That meant sixty rowers and probably at least ten more in her crew.

'Spill a little wind from the sails' Eafa called and his ship's boys ran to obey, relieved that their lord evidently wasn't intenting to fight.

His two birlinns slowed by about a knot and he watched as the big Viking ship turned and her crew rowed her into the wind. He was still a good three miles away when it turned to the south-east and hoisted its sail. He could just make out the device on the faded red sail. It looked like a black raven. He glanced up at his own sail. Once it had been a bright yellow but it had now weathered to a dirty cream. Nevertheless, the black wolf's head stood out quite clearly.

The Viking longship would pass them well out to sea. Even if he wanted a fight, which he didn't, Eafa didn't think that he'd be able to intercept them before they'd be out of reach.

'Farewell Raven. The next time you come raiding I will have a big longship like yours. Then we may be able to engage in a fair fight.'

Eafa turned and headed back to Budle Bay wondering how he could build a larger ship than the birlinns. He knew it wasn't just a matter of building bigger; the structure of the hull wouldn't be strong enough to stop it flexing and letting water in. He supposed that it was a matter of either capturing a longship and studying its design or travelling to where they were constructed. An Anglo-Saxon would stand out, but then he thought of Erik and an idea began to take shape in his mind. However, in the event it wasn't necessary.

The Vikings had spent the night on a deserted beach several miles south of Lindisfarne. Thorkel had studied the stronghold sitting high on its impressive lump of basalt rock rising high above the sea as they sailed past it and realised how difficult it would be to attack. A banner with the black wolf's head on a yellow background flew from the top of the watchtower, the same device as the one on the sails of the two small warships and he wondered idly whose it was.

He'd seen another birlinn and two knarrs moored in the bay to the north of the fortress. That told him that, whoever the local lord was, he didn't have enough warriors at hand to man more than two ships.

The next morning the fine weather had gone and they woke to find that they were enveloped in a thick sea mist. Only a fool would put to sea in such weather, especially as they weren't familiar with the coast. It looked like a day of make and mend.

The ship's boys were kept busy removing the rust from helmets and byrnies. At least they weren't expected to clean and sharpen weapons. Whatever his status, a Norseman looked after his own weapons, even the kings. A man depended on them in battle and they were treated with almost reverential care.

Ragnar found broken links in one byrnie and he went in search of its owner to see if he had any spare links with which to effect a repair. Only kings, jarls and the richer bondis could afford to pay an armourer to make them a byrnie, so most had been taken from a captured or a dead enemy. In this case the brown stains around the broken links weren't rust, they were dried blood. Whoever the byrnie now belonged to hadn't bothered to have the damage repaired after he'd acquired it. Ragnar imagined that the owner wasn't a man who took a pride in his appearance, unlike most Norsemen.

Despite the scars that many bore and their fearsome appearance, hygiene and appearance were important to the Norse. Most washed at least once a week and everyone owned combs to groom themselves with. Men grew a beard as soon as they were old enough and they wore their hair long. That meant that they had to spend time each day combing out the tangles and ridding their hair of lice and fleas.

Ragnar eventually found the owner of the byrnie. It belonged to Leif the skáld. Although he was a warrior and took his place on the rowing bench with the rest, his real purpose in life was to compose and recite sagas. None of the Scandinavian nations had much in the way of written records. They were all verbal.

Whereas the lagmän recited the law, skálds narrated stories about the gods and heroic deeds.

As a child, Ragnar had learned about Norse history, literature and mythology from the skálds. They were the main source of Norse history and culture but, as he grew older, Ragnar learned that skáldic poems could be reverent or boastful, humorous and boisterous, witty, defiant or even obscene, and they weren't necessarily an accurate record of what had actually happened. Skalds were valued for their ability to entertain as much as for their role as the repository of history and myth.

Poetry was regarded as a gift from Odin, the All-father, and many poems were reverent and respectful, if a little exaggerated. However, skálds could also compose mocking stories of unworthy actions and mischance, so it didn't pay to make an enemy of a skáld. Ragnar therefore approached Leif with some trepidation.

'Your byrnie needs some new links to repair it, Leif.'

The skáld looked at him with an expressionless face for some time and Ragnar found himself getting nervous. The silence dragged on and the boy didn't know whether to turn and leave the man or say something else. In the end he got angry.

'Well, for Odin's sake, say something Leif. Do you want me to repair it or not? If so, I'll need some spare links and the tools to do it with.'

To his surprise the skáld smiled.

'I was interested to see how long you'd just stand there. A lesser man would have just walked away. It's alright, I've got a better one. You can keep it and, when we reach somewhere with an armourer, you can get it reduced to your size. Make sure you get the mail links he takes out back though; you'll need them to enlarge it as you grow.'

Ragnar couldn't believe his luck. By rights he should have had his share of the weapons and armour taken from the Picts, but all he got was a mediocre sword and a little silver. Picts didn't seem to wear chain mail – or at least their attackers hadn't – and the few helmets they had were too large for him. One that kept falling down over your eyes was more dangerous than not wearing one.

He didn't have enough money for an armourer and, in any case he was impatient. There wouldn't be an armourer's shop he could visit this side of Norway. So he spent the rest of the morning using some borrowed tools to remove a section of links down each side and to repair the bloodstained hole. When he tried it on it reached below his knees and the sleeves, which would have come down to cover half a man's upper arms, came to below his elbow, but he didn't care. At thirteen he had his own byrnie.

Needless to say Ketil was livid. He had a poor quality helmet and a quilted cotton over-tunic but he coveted a byrnie above all things. Even Gorm was a little jealous of Ragnar's good fortune, but Olaf was delighted for his friend. If the byrnie still looked too large on Ragnar, it would have dwarfed the other boy's small frame. A byrnie was also heavy and it took some getting used to before you could fight properly in it.

Like the men, Ragnar would wear his on land but he would stow it in an oiled leather bag when at sea. He might be able to swim fully clothed well enough, but the weight of the chainmail would drag even a strong man down to a watery grave.

Just after midday a gentle breeze began to clear the mist. Soon it had strengthened enough for Thorkel to think about putting to sea but, as the last strands of vapour cleared from the tops of the tall dunes that lined the bay, he saw that the crests were lined with hundreds of armed men, some fifty of them mounted.

As soon as Eafa saw that the Norse longship was heading south he knew that his intervention had only diverted their search for plunder to somewhere further down the coast. As his shire stretched as far as the River Tyne, he determined to shadow the Vikings and attack them when they next landed.

Once back at Bebbanburg he sent out messengers to summon the fyrd from the surrounding vills and also to his thegns further down the coast, telling them to muster at Alnwic. Meanwhile he sent out scouts to shadow the drekar, keeping out of sight as much as possible.

'Lord, they've beached their ship in a deserted cove a few miles north of where the River Aln meets the sea. My companions have stayed to keep an eye on them, but I'm sure that they will still be there at dawn. The wind had died and already wisps of fog are appearing.'

Eafa's plan was to attack them as the sun rose above the horizon to the east but the sea mist put paid to that idea. Even though he knew the coast between Bebbanburg and where the Aln ran into the German Ocean as well as he knew his wife's face, fog was disorientating. When it settled over his encampment that night he decided to stay at the muster point for now and, in the morning, follow the river to its mouth before turning onto the path along the coast.

It wasn't much of a path and his scouts had to continually ride to and fro along the column to make sure no-one took a wrong turning. He was relying on the inevitable sounds that came from any armed camp to locate the Vikings. He wasn't disappointed. The problem was that in the mist he couldn't tell where the sounds were coming from. It was frustrating but they would have to halt where they were and wait for better visibility.

At last the mist inland started to clear, but it remained over the coast. Finally the sun burned it off just before midday and the scouts left behind came in to guide them to the small cove where the longship was beached. Just as the last tendrils of mist vaporised his men reached the sand dunes overlooking the beach and took up their position. He had managed to muster one hundred and fifty members of the fyrd to supplement his permanent warband of fifty mounted warriors and, although the fyrd were inferior in terms of equipment and training, they were nevertheless quite capable of fighting effectively in basic formations such as a shield wall.

Eafa watched as the Vikings quickly donned their byrnies and helmets and grabbed their weapons and shields. However, it wasn't his intention to fight these raiders unless it was absolutely necessary. He knew that they were tough fighters and, although he might well annihilate them, they would take many of his own men with them.

With Erik on one side of him and his banner bearer on the other he rode down to the beach. The sand shifted under their mounts' hooves as they descended and all three had trouble in controlling their horses. He was glad when they arrived on the gently sloping beach without suffering any loss of dignity. He walked his horse forward and stopped a hundred and fifty yards away from the Norse shield wall.

For a moment he thought he would end up sitting there looking foolish, but then the tightly packed line of shields parted and three Vikings walked forward until they were within fifty yards of the Northumbrians.

'What do you want Saxon?'

When Erik had translated for him, Eafa nearly pointed out that he was an Angle rather than a Saxon, but he realised that to these northern barbarians it didn't matter whether he was an Angle, a Saxon or even a Jute.

'I want you to stop trying to raid my lands. Now, we can come to some sort of arrangement and you can sail back whence you came, or you can die here. Either way you will not plunder and pillage Northumbria.'

'Ah, so you want to offer me gold and silver to sail away?'

'No, I'm not like others who think that they can buy peace. That just encourages you to come back again next year and try to extract an even bigger bribe from me.'

The man's reply wasn't what Thorkel had expected. To buy himself time to think he changed tack.

'I'm puzzled. Who is the Norseman who acts as your interpreter? Did you buy him as a thrall?'

This time Erik answered for himself.

'I'm no thrall. My father was a bondi, but I was captured during the first raid on Lindisfarne nearly thirty years ago.'

'I see. Where did you come from?'

'To be honest I don't remember the name, but it was somewhere up the west coast of Norway.'

'Ah. We come from the southern tip. Nevertheless, do you want to join us?'

For a moment Erik was tempted. He had never forgotten that he was a Norseman but he was now in his early forties and he was sure that his parents must have died years ago. There was nothing left for him in Norway. Besides he had a wife and three children at Bebbanburg and they wouldn't want to go and eke out an existence in a foreign land.

'I may have been born a Norse pagan but I'm now a Christian. These Northumbrians are my people now.'

Eafa was getting impatient with the exchange in a language he didn't understand.

'What are you two discussing?' he demanded.

'He wanted to know what a Norse speaker was doing here.'

'What did you say?'

'I told him the truth. I also said that I'm a Northumbrian now.'

Eafa grunted. He hadn't expected Erik to want to join these barbarians, but they were his people after all. He was pleased by Erik's response though. They'd been together for too many years for him to want to lose him.

'Tell him I will buy his prisoners off him for a fair price if he swears by his gods that he will leave Northumbria and not return.'

'He says that he wants more than that. You can buy his slaves but he wants fifty pounds of silver as well.'

'I've told him I don't bribe pirates to go away; I'll only buy his captives in return for his departure from these shores. You can also tell him that more men are on their way. When they get here I will attack if he's not agreed to my terms.'

When Erik had translated this Thorkel went back to his men and explained what had happened. Whilst they were arguing - the majority being in favour of fighting – another thirty horsemen arrived to join Eafa.

'I'm pleased to see you, Turec,' Eafa said with a broad smile.

The Ealdorman of Berwic nodded towards the seventy Norsemen on the beach below.

'There's another hundred men from my fyrd coming up behind me. They should be here by nightfall.'

'These barbarians will slip away in the dark. We need to resolve this before then.'

'Do you want to attack now then?'

'I told him that I would do so if he didn't agree to go peaceably; after giving me his oath that he wouldn't just go and raid elsewhere in Northumbria, of course.'

'And you'd trust his word?'

'If he swears to do something, he'll do it. Norsemen do not break their oaths, unlike the Danes and the Swedes,' Erik cut in.

'Aren't they all the same? All Vikings?'

'All Vikings? Yes. All the same? No.'

At that moment Thorkel strode out of his men as they formed into a shield wall once again and Eafa, Turec and Erik rode down to meet him.

'Well, have you decided? Another hundred of Lord Turec's men will be here shortly.'

'We'll sell you the monks for a hundred pounds of silver and I'll give you my word not to raid here again this year.'

'For seven monks and a handful of young Picts? That's an insult.'

'No, that's just for the monks. If you want the boys as well, it'll cost you two hundred pounds of silver.'

'Fifty pounds of silver for all of them and that's my final offer.'

'You'll lose a lot more men than I will and we'll slit the throats of the Picts.'

Eafa shrugged. 'So? They're Picts. Go ahead and kill them; at least it won't be on my conscience, whereas leaving Christians in the hands of pagans would be.'

Thorkel had been watching the faces of both Eafa and Erik during this exchange but he couldn't tell whether the ealdorman's indifference was feigned or not. The other ealdorman's face was just as impassive.

'What are we waiting for, Thorkel? Are we going to fight or just stand here clacking like a load of old women?' one of the Norsemen called out.

'One hundred pounds,' Thorkel said. 'My men are eager to kill you so make up your mind quickly.'

'Fifty,' Eafa said obdurately.

The Viking must have learnt what the word fifty meant by now so, without waiting for Erik to translate, he turned on his heel and re-joined his men. The shield wall waited for the Northumbrians' charge, which never came.

Eighty horsemen disappeared behind the dunes whilst the fyrd advanced down onto the beach then stopped. Suddenly the horsemen re-appeared, half with flaming torches in their hands. They galloped around the bewildered Vikings and threw the torches into their longship. The tar soaked cordage caught fire almost immediately and the crew watched helplessly as the flames spread to the mast, then the pitch in the caulking between the strakes of the hull began to smoulder.

The Vikings prepared to sell their lives as dearly as possible. However, the Northumbrians still didn't attack. Instead dozens of archers walked forward and, once they were within range, they sent three volleys of arrows into the Norsemen, who were now hunkered down behind their shields. Most arrows hit the latter or else pinged off helmets but a few found chinks in the linked shields and half a dozen Vikings were wounded.

Meanwhile the monks and the captive Picts had been freed by the horsemen. They ran around the Norsemen and into the safety of the massed fyrd, blessing their saviours as they went. There were two priests with the small Northumbrian army and they took the rescued captives to the camp in the sand dunes to give them food and water. Thankfully they were uninjured apart from a few bruises, minor cuts and abrasions from the ropes with which they'd been tied up.

The horsemen now lined up and charged the rear of the Norse shield wall, throwing their spears into their foes' unprotected backs. Over twenty men were killed or wounded before the Vikings managed to change their formation into a circle. Thorkel was in despair. He knew that his men would die bravely in the expectation of spending that night feasting and drinking in Valhalla, but he feared that, having lost his ship and crew, Odin's skálds would mock and deride him, making the afterlife a misery for him.

He therefore stepped out of the circle of shields and, throwing down his weapons, he walked towards where the two ealdormen were sitting on their horses.

'Very well, Saxon. You can have your precious monks back for fifty pounds of silver.'

Erik roared with laughter at the hersir's impudence, as did Eafa and Turec when he translated the offer.

'Perhaps you didn't notice, Viking. I already have the monks safe and sound. You no longer have a seaworthy ship and you can't really expect me to allow the rest of you to roam the countryside raping and pillaging, now can you?'

'Then it seems as if we will have to die, but I promise you, Saxon, that we will take many of you with us.'

'It doesn't have to be that way,' Eafa said. 'You are traders as well as pirates, I think?'

'When it suits us.'

'Well, I too am a trader, a merchant. I trade with Frankia and other lands across the German Ocean. However, it is getting more dangerous as the cursed Danes attack my knarrs. I send my birlinns to protect them, but they are smaller than their ships. I need to build longships like yours to protect my trading vessels.'

'That's your problem. What has it got to do with me?'

'If you help me to build two longships I will let you repair yours so that you can sail home.'

Thorkel took a little time to think the offer over. It wasn't what he'd been expecting. At first he thought it might be a trick to disarm and enslave his men, but the explanation had the ring of truth to it.

'I'll need to talk to my men,' he said abruptly and returned to them.

Ragnar had watched the meeting with narrowed eyes. He was determined not to become a thrall of the cursed Northumbrians and he'd managed to acquire a better sword and a shield from one of the fallen Viking warriors. If necessary he would charge the enemy and die with a sword in his hand.

Beside him Olaf was also carrying a shield. It was the one which, unbeknownst to him, had already saved Ragnar's life.

Ketil had pulled the spear from the back of one of the Vikings slain by the Northumbrian horsemen and, in the confusion when they had reformed the shield wall as a circle, he'd thrown it at Ragnar. Only Olaf's quick thinking had saved the boy's life. The spear pierced the shield and Olaf had used a small axe lying on the ground to chop the haft from the spear point. Then, without pausing, he'd sent the axe spinning towards Ketil.

The sharp blade had struck Ketil's forehead and lodged in his skull. Only Torstein the godi had seen what had happened and he smiled to himself. He had dreamt that Ragnar was destined for great things and he knew that Odin himself had guided Olaf's actions. He would say nothing about the incident, but he would keep a closer eye on Ragnar and Olaf from now on.

When Thorkel outlined Eafa's proposal to his men the majority, including Ragnar, were in favour of fighting on. However, Torstein spoke for the first time.

'I see the hand of both Odin the All-Father and Loki in this. There is one amongst us who is destined to become a great Viking hero, perhaps even greater than Bēowulf. He must live to fulfil his destiny.'

'You are certain of this? Who is he?' Thorkel asked sceptically.

'To name him would displease the Norns. He must create his own fame.'

'So he is young yet?'

'I didn't say that. Bēowulf was a warrior long before he sailed to Zealand to kill the giant Grendel and his monstrous mother.'

'Why is Loki interested in us?' Leif asked, already composing a saga in his head.

'Because to provide this Saxon lord with two drekars would discomfit the Danes. There is nothing Loki likes more than a bit of mischief making.'

Most of the men were convinced by the godi's reasoning but Ragnar was not. His mother was a Dane and her brother was a jarl in Jutland. However, he was a boy and had no say, even if he was their king's son.

Thorkel walked back to where Eafa was waiting.

'Very well, Saxon. We will build you two drekars – though they should properly be called skeids as I don't suppose you'll want the figurehead that gives our drekars their name - but you must swear on one of your holy books that you will allow us to repair our ship and allow us to return home as soon as we have fulfilled our part of the agreement. Furthermore you must treat us as free men, as artisans, not thralls.'

'I will so swear on our most holy of books, the Lindisfarne Gospels, which tells of Our Lord Jesus Christ's time on Earth before he ascended into Heaven.'

'Very well. Now get your men to help us put out the smouldering remains of the fire on board our ship.'

Chapter Three – The Return Home

822 to 823

Ragnar had sulked for some time after their arrival at Bebbanburg. The Vikings weren't housed inside the fortress itself but were allowed to build a timber hall some miles away beside the stream that fed into Budle Bay. Some of Eafa's warriors took it in turns to live in a separate hall beside the Norse one. Originally the two communities distrusted one another and there some fist fights. However, as time went on they became friendlier. When Eafa sent his shipwright and a few carpenters to learn how to build a drekar some of the Northumbrian warriors got interested and started to help.

Ragnar held himself aloof from all this at first but he too became intrigued with the construction process and made himself useful. In return he, Gorm and Olaf were allowed to make themselves practice wooden swords, blunt spears and shields and were trained by the men. In time he even became happy, but only because a return to Agder was getting closer.

Although Thorkel didn't have a master shipwright amongst his crew he had two apprentice shipwrights and a master carpenter. The two new drekars were built side by side. The first problem was sourcing the right wood. The initial item to be laid down was the oak keel, made up of several sections spliced together and fastened with treenails to give it weight and strength. There was no problem finding the oak but the other woods used for the hull and mast in Scandinavia, such as pine, didn't grow in Northumbria and the shipwright in charge had to experiment with other timbers.

Eafa was a frequent visitor and took a keen interest in the design and construction process. After the keel the stems, based on segments of circles of varying sizes, were added to the keel. The next step was the interior frame and cross beams. The frames were placed close together to stiffen the ship, but far enough apart to allow the rowers to place their sea chests between them. There were no rowing benches - the rowers sat on their chests.

Once the frame was complete the next stage was the strakes – the lines of overlapping planks joined endwise from stem to stern. Unlike the birlinns, where the strakes abutted one another and the joints were caulked, the strakes on a longship were clinker built with the bottom of the upper strake slightly overlapping the top of the next strake down. In section the strakes tapered from top to bottom and so it was a laborious task to trim each one to the desired shape.

As the strakes reached the desired height, the deck was added; planks being nailed to the cross bracing of the frames. Once finished, the hull and deck was waterproofed with animal hair, wool, hemp or moss drenched in pine tar and forced into every gap. The holes cut between the deck and the gunwale to take the oars were kept closed when sailing by plugs.

Once the two hulls were finished the masts were lifted into place and the side, fore and aft stays were rigged. The two mainsails proved to be something of a problem as they were woven in one piece and there was no loom big enough at Bebbanburg. Eafa therefore bought the sails needed from the Danes via a merchant in Frisia. He dyed his own sails yellow and Breguswid and her slaves sewed his device of a black wolf's head onto it. He also bought a sail for the Vikings' ship to replace the one lost to the flames. However, this was left plain as Eafa refused to pay for dyes or to get his women to make the pagan raven emblem.

The two new drekars took until the autumn of 822 to complete. As soon as work on the new ships was underway Eafa had agreed to Thorkel's request that the Vikings' drekar should be made seaworthy and towed back to Budle Bay. Left where left was it would slowly be broken up by high tides and people looking for an easy supply of timber.

However, it was kept covered and guarded until after the sea trials of the two new skieds were completed. As soon as they were ready, he sent them up to Berwic to remove the temptation for the Vikings to steal one of them. By the spring of 823 the work to repair and refit their drekar was finished and its crew took it out to sea to test it, but without the stores needed for a long voyage.

Eafa threw a feast for the Norsemen before they left. As usual everyone got drunk but, surprisingly, there were no serious fights. Eafa sat at the high table and invited Thorkel to sit with him, Breguswid, the local thegn and his wife. However, Breguswid was pregnant with Eafa's second child and once she and the other woman started to talk about babies the hersir got up and went to join his own men. If Eafa was affronted by his rudeness he hid it well.

By this time Ragnar and Olaf had turned fifteen and Gorm was sixteen. All three were accepted as warriors and took their places at the oars, though they still had to act as ship's boys and do all the menial work. The sky was overcast and the wind was blowing strongly onshore as they left the next morning. Eafa had brought his young son, Ilfrid, down to see the Norsemen depart and he watched them go with mixed feelings. In one way he was glad to see the back of a load of pagans, whose overt adherence to gods he knew were false continued to upset him; on the other hand he knew what doughty fighters they were and he would have employed them to guard his trading knarrs if he could. He'd mooted the idea to Thorkel but the man had laughed, telling him that they were men, not nursemaids.

With only three quarters of a full crew they had struggled against wind and tide to clear the bay and round the point at the eastern end of the Holy Island of Lindisfarne. Once there they could hoist the sail.

Once he had finished securing the halyard Ragnar went to talk to Thorkel.

'We're short of rowers as it is and you need us to play a full part at the oars. We need to find some ship's boys.'

'Don't you think I don't know that? I tried to get Eafa to let me recruit some of the poor orphan boys from the vill. They would have a better life with us instead of living by begging and thievery, but he refused to let Christians live with pagans.'

'We could raid the next settlement and take a few as thralls?' Ragnar suggested.

But Thorkel shook his head. 'No man of honour uses thralls to crew his ship. However, if we captured a few boys I could offer them the choice of becoming thralls or staying free and working the ship.'

He had given his word not to raid Northumbria on his way home and so he waited until they were north of the wide fjord that Eata had called the Firth of Forth. As the sun headed towards the western horizon Sitric looked for a bay with a beach where they could spend the night. The first one they saw was at the mouth of a small river with a fishing settlement on the north bank. Above it stood a small monastery built of timber with a palisade around it. Thorkel licked his lips. He calculated that they had a couple of hours before dark; time enough for what he intended.

Before they beached the ship on the sand Ragnar and the others pulled on their byrnies or leather jerkins ready to fight ashore. Ragnar had used what little money he had to pay the armourer at Bebbanburg to put back the rings taken out when he was smaller. Now the byrnie was a little large for him but it would fit him for a few years yet. He grabbed his sword, shield, bow and quiver and stood waiting with Olaf and the rest for the keel to run aground.

As soon as it did, he jumped from the side of the ship into the shallow water and splashed ashore. Then he was racing with the others towards the settlement as the local inhabitants ran about in panic, gathering up small children and grabbing a few precious possessions before heading up the path towards the supposed safety of the monastery.

A few men tried to oppose the Vikings with spears, hunting bows and axes but they were soon cut down. Ignoring the crude huts and the livestock for now, Thorkel led his men up the path to the monastery on the clifftop. They overtook a few Picts on the way, mainly the old and infirm and a few young children who had been abandoned by their mothers as they fled. These the Norsemen cut down without a second thought as they rushed past them.

Ragnar was caught up in the excitement as much as anyone but, when he reached a boy of about twelve or thirteen who had evidently pulled a ligament in his haste to get away and was now hobbling as quickly as he could, he refrained from killing him. Instead, Ragnar hit him on the head with the pommel of his sword and the boy dropped unconscious into a shallow dip beside the track.

The palisade proved little obstacle to the Vikings. It was about ten feet high, low enough for a man to grasp the top if he stood on a shield held at waist height by two others. Ragnar was the first to reach it, closely followed by Olaf and one of the younger warriors. Olaf was the lightest so Ragnar and the other warrior held the shield horizontally and bent their knees to take the weight as Olaf jumped onto it. They strained to lift the shield up so that Olaf could grasp the top of the timbers and then he was over the top and onto the parapet behind.

A monk was waiting for him, screaming curses at him as he swung a stout cudgel at the young Viking's head. Olaf ducked and grabbed the dagger he held in his teeth. There was no time to draw his sword and he'd dropped his shield and spear outside the monastery before springing onto the shield. As the monk made another swing at his head Olaf dropped his shoulder and rolled on it, coming to his feet a foot away from the monk. He was too close for the monk to use his club so he dropped it and fastened his ham-like hands around the young Viking's throat. Olaf struggled for air but he managed to stab his opponent in the stomach just as he was about to black out. The monk released Olaf's neck from his vice-like grip and tumbled off the parapet screaming in agony. He hit the earth below with a resounding thump.

Olaf saw several more monks armed with cudgels and staves heading towards him and he drew his sword, but then Ragnar was at his side and several more Norsemen appeared at various points along the parapet. From then on it was a massacre. Both Ragnar and Olaf did their fair share of killing. Their victims included women and young children as well as men who tried to fight back. Once the blood-lust was on them they just wanted to kill and go on killing.

It wasn't until Thorkel knocked Ragnar to the ground just as he was about to kill a young boy that sanity returned. All in all it was a good haul. Five young women would be sold as thralls together with a few monks and a dozen children. The monastery itself had yielded a gold altar cross, several silver cups, plates and chalices and a few ornately illustrated books that Thorkel knew would fetch a significant sum if he could manage to auction them in Frankia.

However, only three boys of the right age to serve as ship's boys had survived the massacre. Ragnar and the other ship's boys knew that they would have to train the young Picts and teach them Norse before they could take over from them. They really needed four though, and then Ragnar remembered the boy he'd knocked out on the way up to the monastery.

He raced down the hill ahead of the others but, of course, the boy was no longer there. Ragnar was a good hunter and the Pict's trail wasn't difficult to follow. He stood there debating what to do. He knew Thorkel would want to get away just in case the alarm had been raised and he would be furious if he had to wait for Ragnar. Anyone else he might abandon but not the king's only son.

However, it was nearly dark and so he would probably decide to spend the night on the beach in any case. His mind made up, Ragnar ran along the clear trail left by the young Pict. He had to hurry. As the light failed the boy's trail would be impossible to follow, however obvious it was in daylight.

Twilight was deepening and Ragnar was about to give up when he saw a lean-to built into the hillside ahead of him. Presumably it was a shelter used by shepherds and a likely place his quarry to hole up in. He approached cautiously and peered inside. In the failing light it was too dark to make out anything inside, but the sound of breathing meant that there was someone inside who was fast asleep.

The boy awoke with a start and went to sit up until the prick of a dagger at his throat persuaded him otherwise. Ragnar found his arm in the dark and pulled him outside. In the twilight he could just make out that it was probably the same boy. He looked to be about twelve or thirteen with a mop of dirty blond hair. Ragnar found this strange as he was under the impression that most Picts had dark or black hair.

'What's your name?' he asked, then cursed when he realised how foolish that was; there was no chance that the boy spoke Norse. However, he tried again in English. To his surprise the boy sullenly replied 'Leofstan'.

'How come a Pictish boy speaks English,' Ragnar asked curiously, then added, 'no, never mind, we need to get back to your settlement. Do you know the way?'

Leofstan gave him a pitying look.

'Of course. Even if I didn't, you could follow the light of the campfires.'

Ragnar looked down and could just make out three pinpoints of light where the ships' crew had lit cooking fires on the beach. He smiled ruefully to himself. He should have thought of that. At least it meant Thorkel was staying the night.

Ragnar thought that Leofstan might make a run for it in the dark, despite his pulled muscle, but the boy made no attempt to escape. As they descended the narrow path he told Ragnar his story. He was an Angle from near the great fortress of Dùn Èideann, the stronghold that the Vikings had seen on the south bank of the Firth of Forth.

He'd been captured during a raid by the Picts two years ago, when he was eleven. There was peace between the Picts and the Northumbrians but raids by both sides still occurred occasionally. His father had been a fisherman but his parents had been killed in front of him, as had his elder brother. He'd been kept as a slave to one of the Pictish shepherds and so exchanging one master for another didn't particularly bother him.

'Well, you might not have to be a thrall.' Ragnar explained what being a ship's boy entailed and Leofstan grew positively enthusiastic at the prospect. Ragnar thought that if Leofstan was used to working a fishing boat, then he should pick up his new duties quite quickly.

The other boys had all been fishermen's sons so they too were used to a life at sea. Their lives before they were captured by Thorkel's men had been hard. Every day they had helped their fathers to eke out an existence and they had grown inured to hunger and exhaustion. In contrast life as a ship's boy might not have been easy, but they were well fed and treated fairly.

After the young Picts had got used to their change in circumstance and picked up enough rudimentary Norse to understand instructions without translation by Ragnar into English and by Leofstan from English into their language, they readily accepted their new roles. The promise that they would not become thralls if they behaved made them positively enthusiastic to perform well.

'Have you noticed that Leofstan has become quite attached to you,' Olaf asked Ragnar one evening as they sat by a campfire back on the island in Orkneyjar.

Ragnar glanced over to where Leofstan was cooking a fish stew for them and their closest friends amongst the Norse Warriors. The light of the fire illuminated the grin that the boy gave him as soon as he was aware that Ragnar was looking his way. Ragnar laughed and smiled back.

'He's like a puppy, that's all.'

'Maybe, but I think he's got a bad case of hero-worship, Odin knows why,' one of the other warriors said. Ragnar went red and punched the other man on the shoulder so hard that he fell over. The others around the fire laughed but Ragnar wasn't sure whether it was at the man who'd fallen on his side or at the idea that he was some sort of hero.

The young boy's evident devotion to Ragnar drew the occasional lewd comment as well but only one man was foolish enough to tease Ragnar about it. KiǪtvi had sneered and called Leofstan Ragnar's bum boy. Not wanting to cause a fight Ragnar had pretended to ignore the comment but he didn't forget it.

He brooded over it and knew that he had to do something or his reputation would suffer, however unjust the accusation, so he started to treat the boy harshly. It wasn't something he was proud of but it had the desired affect; Leofstan stopped fawning over him but he became withdrawn and resentful. However, his ire wasn't directed towards Ragnar but at KiǪtvi. He was a bright boy and he was well aware what had caused Ragnar to change his stance towards him.

Olaf had watched what had happened with some dismay and thought less of his friend because of it. It wasn't the action of a man with a strong character and he told Ragnar so. It didn't help that he knew that Olaf was right; you didn't reward loyalty and devotion with scorn and derision. He bitterly regretted reacting to the comments of a bully like KiǪtvi, but he didn't know what to do now to correct the situation. However, he soon had bigger problems to deal with.

A week later the drekar entered the mouth of the River Søgneelva after an absence of over two years. They headed upstream to the settlement of Arendal, which was King Sigvard's base. However, as they rounded the last bend, Ragnar saw that, instead of his father's raven banner fluttering in the breeze before the king's hall, the one that flew there now was blue with a golden spread-eagle - the emblem of King Froh of Alfheim.

-Ꝩ-

King Eardwulf was not pleased.

'You mean to say that you captured a Viking crew and you let them go? Are you so stupid, Eafa, that you don't realise that they will only return and raid my kingdom again? Your action was not just irresponsible, it's akin to treachery.'

'I'm neither stupid, nor am I am traitor, Cyning,' Eafa replied, keeping his temper with difficulty. 'Their hersir swore not to raid Northumbria again and I believe him to be a man of honour. In any case, his was only one longship; there are scores more that raid the shores of Britain and Ireland. In return for his freedom he has built me two of the largest longships that I have ever seen. That ensures protection for my knarrs when they trade with the Continent and my craftsmen now know how they are built, so we can build them ourselves. How is that foolish or traitorous? I believe that I have done Northumbria a valuable service.'

'Your opinion is not shared by me.'

'There are other ealdormen with shires on the coast who have already shown an interest in my new longships. They seem to think the idea was a good one.'

'Are you trying to unite your friends against me?'

'No, of course not, Cyning. I am merely telling you the facts.'

Eafa looked at the ceiling in despair. The older Eardwulf got, the more paranoid he became. He'd been on the throne for ten years when he'd been deposed by Ealdormen Ælfwald and he'd defeated two challengers for his crown before that. He'd fled to the court of Charlemagne at Aachen, where he'd married one of the emperor's daughters, and had returned in 808 with an army of Frankish mercenaries to reclaim his throne. Ælfwald was killed and for the last fifteen years Eardwulf's rule had been unopposed.

'You are treading on very dangerous ground, Eafa. Because you were one of the first ealdormen who rallied to my side when I returned from exile, I'll forgive you this time. However, I'll be keeping my eye on you from now on. Now get out and send my son in to see me.'

Eanred was thirteen and his father doted on him. He was being schooled by the monks at the monastery of Eoforwīc, but his father kept sending for him, to the despair of both the Master of Novices and Eanred himself.

The prince was sitting by the central hearth in the new hall talking to the captain of the king's gesith. The previous king's hall had been built in timber and, although much larger, compared unfavourably with Eafa's stone built hall at Bebbanburg. However, unlike the latter, which had been built of rough cut stone, this new hall at Eoforwīc had been constructed using faced blocks.

The roof was impressive too. It was supported on square columns of stone running down each side of the hall and consisted of timber 'A' frames on top of which planks had been nailed and then any small gaps had been filled in much the same way as the hull of a ship was waterproofed. This would have been enough by itself to keep out the rain which dripped down on the occupants of most buildings, but Eardwulf's masons had covered the roof with overlapping stone tiles.

It was the most impressive hall that Eafa had ever seen. Nevertheless, the smoke and soot from the central hearth, which took the form of a fire trough, still tainted the interior with acrid fumes. The new roof beams were already darkened in the area of a strange structure that evidently served to extract the smoke – or most of it.

It consisted of a square hole at the apex of the roof above the fire trench, over which something that looked like a pyramid on stilts had been erected in wood. It was intended to keep the rain out whilst allowing the wind to suck out the smoke as it blew across the space under it. Eafa had to admit that it worked better than the hatch in the side of the sloping roof on his own hall.

However, stone buildings had one drawback, they seemed to suck the heat out of you and there wasn't even a brazier to take the chill off the air in the king's private chamber. Eafa therefore made for the hall's central hearth to warm himself up.

Eanred sighed and walked towards the door into his father's private chamber when Eafa passed on the message, his monk's habit making the lanky youth look like a beanpole.

'Like a few of our kings in the past, I think that he'd be more suited to the life of a churchman than a warrior prince,' the captain muttered as Eafa joined him to warm himself.'

The man was silent for a moment before changing tack.

'Eardwulf was furious when he heard that you'd released those Vikings you captured. He isn't alone either. Every shire with a coast has been raided this year. You're not popular.'

'Then my fellow nobles are short sighted idiots. Our coastline is too long and too vulnerable for us to defend it ashore. The answer is to tackle them at sea before they can land. That's why I did the deal with Thorkel for my two longships. Now I can patrol the coast and fight them at sea. At least my close neighbours have welcomed the idea.'

'Can you defeat them at their own game? I hear that they are experts at sea battles.'

'We can learn. Besides, if we give them a hard time they will seek easier prey; the Land of the Picts or Ireland, or even Mercia and Wessex.'

'I see. Perhaps it's a good idea after all. What did Eardwulf say?'

Eafa snorted. 'What do you think? Building a hall in stone is about as new as his ideas get.'

'Perhaps you ought to have a word with Eanred. If anyone can convince Eardwulf, he can.'

-Ꝟ-

Thorkel had hated the idea of using a plain sail but now it proved fortuitous. Vikings like to boast and have the skálds laud their deeds. Sailing incognito was anathema to them. However, had he arrived displaying the raven of Agder he would have had to turn tail and flee without finding out what had befallen Arendal. As it was, he decided to moor alongside one of the empty jetties as if he was a trader. In a way he was as he had several Pictish slaves to sell.

However, he and those of his crew who came from Arendal would have been recognised and that might have proved dangerous, given the obvious change in who now ruled the place, and presumably the rest of Agder. Although Ragnar had put on several inches and had filled out in the two and a half years they'd been away, he was still recognisable. Thorkel therefore sent Olaf with two men who came from outlying farms to find out what had happened to Ragnar's father and family and, more importantly to him, what had happened to his own wife and daughters. Other married members of his crew who came from Arendal were equally keen to discover the fate of their families.

When the official who collected the tax from visiting ships appeared Thorkel kept his face hidden and another man pretended to be the shipmaster, though Thorkel didn't recognise the man and he was evidently a Swede.

'How long will you be staying,' the man asked whilst the two warriors escorting him gave the female Picts lascivious looks.

'We've come to sell these thralls. When is the next market?'

'In three days.'

'Then we'll be departing as soon as we've sold them.'

'That'll be three pounds of silver then,'

'That's extortionate,' the supposed shipmaster said, pretending to look dismayed.

'That's the price set by King Froh. Pay it or leave now and sell your wretched thralls somewhere else.'

'Wait here. I'll fetch some silver and my scales.'

After the official and his escort had left Thorkel went to speak to Ragnar to see if he knew anything about this Swedish King Froh, but he couldn't find the lad anywhere.

'The bloody idiot has slipped ashore. If he's recognised we could all be in trouble,' he muttered to Sitric.

It didn't take Olaf and his companions long to find a tavern. They sat down in the crowded interior reeking of smoke, stale sweat and vomit and ordered three tankards of ale and a bowl of stew each. They were lucky to find a place where they could sit together but they had to share the table with a group of young men.

In due course they got talking to them and found out that were apprenticed to a blacksmith. All of them had been born in Arendal and would presumably know what had happened there.

'The last time we came here to trade the king was Sigvard, a Norseman, not a bloody Swede; what happened?'

One of the youths snorted. 'The old fool fell for a pretty face – the daughter of one of his jarls; I forget his name. The trouble was the girl was already promised to Froh of Alfheim.'

'I thought Sigvard was married?'

'So he was, but he divorced her. He forced his jarl to break off the betrothal to Froh and give the maid to him instead.'

Olaf wondered how he was going to break the news to Ragnar about his mother but worse was to come.

'Of course Froh wasn't best pleased and he assembled his jarls and their men to take his revenge on Sigvard. Our king was so besotted with his new bed mate that he ignored warnings that Froh was going to attack. After all, Arendal is a large place with many bondis and their families living within the stout palisade around it, and Sigvard had a hundred men in his hird. He thought that he was invulnerable.

'But Froh came by sea and at night. They swooped like the Valkyries collecting souls for Valhalla when everyone was asleep and killed everyone in Sigvard's longhouse; his hirdmen, the king, his daughters, his thralls; even the new queen and her predecessor too. Evidently Froh didn't want soiled goods back, just revenge.'

'So does Froh rule here now?'

'Yes, Agder is a more prosperous kingdom than Alfheim. He gave his old kingdom to his brother.'

'Didn't Sigvard's jarls contest his right to the throne?'

'Why should they? Sigvard was dead and his son Ragnar had never returned from Orkneyjar. The other drekar that went raiding with Thorkel – that's the ship that Ragnar sailed on – limped back badly damaged by a storm and they said that Thorkel and his crew had been lost. Besides, Froh paid the jarls well from Sigvard's chests of silver for their oaths to him.'

Whilst Olaf was in the tavern Ragnar had taken a more direct approach to find out what had happened. He went straight to Thorkel's hall and spoke to his wife. He had expected her to be relieved to find out that her husband was still alive but there was a complication. Believing herself to be a rich widow, she had married a young bondi and had no intention of returning to Thorkel.

It was only after he'd left to make his way back to the ship that he realised that he might well have put all of them in danger. If Thorkel's wife had used his money to buy herself a young replacement, she might prefer him to stay dead. If she went to tell Froh that Ragnar was back and could be found on Thorkel's longship they were all in peril.

When Ragnar told Thorkel what he'd found out the hersir was furious and, despite the risk, he set off with three of his closest companions to kill his wife and her new husband. In his anger he didn't even reprimand Ragnar for recklessly endangering them all.

Ragnar waited anxiously for Thorkel's return, and that of Olaf. For a while the settlement remained quiet but sound travels far at night and soon he heard the unmistakeable sound of fighting coming from somewhere in the centre of the settlement. Olaf and his companions arrived breathless ten minutes later and told him that everyone was saying that

Thorkel had returned and killed his wife and her lover, only to be killed himself by Froh's hirdmen.

'Ragnar, they'll come here next. We need to leave. Now.'

He realised that, with Thorkel and their king dead, the other men were looking to him as the obvious person to lead them. Much as he wanted to stay and avenge the death of his family and of the old hersir, his duty now was to his crew.

'Get to your oars and cast off.'

'Where are we going?' Sitric the helmsman asked.

'To visit my mother's brother, Jarl Gutfred of Aarlborg.'

'A Dane?' Sitric asked in surprise.

'Yes, a Dane. Hopefully he'll prove more trustworthy than my father's jarls and the accursed Swedes.'

Chapter Four – Toppenafdanmark

823

Several snekkjur pursued Thorkel's ship out of the river and into the Skagerrak but they soon gave up the chase as the larger drekar progressively increased the distance between them.

Once it was clear that they had outpaced their pursuers, the crew had to make a quick decision. With Thorkel dead they needed to elect a new hersir and shipmaster. There were several seasoned warriors who the others respected, but most either felt that they didn't have the brains to be a leader or they didn't want the responsibility. In addition all were still suffering from the shock of losing their homeland and that undermined their confidence. It was Olaf who proposed Ragnar.

'After all, he is the son of King Sigvard and should succeed him.'

'Except that he no longer has a kingdom to rule,' KiǫtvI pointed out. 'No, you need an experienced man like me to lead you.'

'No kingdom for the moment,' Ragnar corrected him vehemently. 'Do you think that I will rest until I have killed Froh and taken back what is mine? If so, you don't know me very well.'

His eyes swept around the warriors challenging them to contest his right to lead them. No one except Kiǫtvi met his eyes, though there was some quiet muttering about his youth and inexperience. He knew he would have to fight the other warrior to become hersir and he welcomed it. His reaction to the other man's snide remarks about his relationship with Leofstan had eaten away at him like a cancer for long enough and he welcomed the opportunity to cleanse it with blood.

'Very well, KiQtvi, we could settle this by a show of hands but you have challenged me and besmirched my honour in the past. We'll fight to decide the outcome. Sword and shield?' he asked.

KiQtvi was more of a troublemaker than a leader and had only challenged Ragnar out of mischief. Now he'd been put on the spot. He didn't want to fight Ragnar and he certainly didn't wish to become the hersir. However, he couldn't back down now. It was unthinkable.

Although fighting on board ship was something that Vikings were used to, there would be little room for a duel on an overcrowded longship. Sitric therefore steered them towards the northern tip of Denmark and beached the ship on the deserted golden sands. He drew a wide circle in the sand with his sword and the crew crowded round just outside the circle. The warriors all brought their spears, which they would use to jab at either contestant if he came too close to the boundary.

A few yelled encouragement to KiQtvi but most were shouting for Ragnar, Leofstan's unbroken voice as loud as anyone's.

As KiQtvi didn't possess a byrnie, Ragnar felt that it would be unfair to use his and so both men wore just a leather jerkin to protect their bodies. They fought bareheaded and were armed with just a sword and shield. The older man was the more experienced fighter but he was at a disadvantage because he didn't really want the prize he was fighting for. On the other hand Ragnar was angry at the insinuations that KiQtvi had made about him and Leofstan and what he really needed at the moment was a cool head.

Ragnar made the first move; jumping in the air and making a feint at his opponent's head, KiQtvi instinctively raised his shield and Ragnar landed in a crouch, bringing his sword around in a sweeping motion to cut at KiQtvi's legs. The other man jumped backwards just in time so that only the tip of the blade connected and made a shallow cut into the front of KiǫQtvi's right thigh just above his knee.

Dimly he heard Leofstan's high pitched cry of 'first blood' above the roar of the crowd. Ragnar fought to control his anger. Olaf had told him enough times that he was prone to impetuosity and he needed to be calm and think clearly if he was to beat the experienced warrior facing him.

This time it was Kiǫtvi who acted unexpectedly; he retreated but, when Ragnar went to follow him, the other man stepped forward so that he was inside the sweep of Ragnar's sword. Kiǫtvi had the pommel of his sword raised, ready to bring it down on Ragnar's exposed head. However, it met the rim of his shield instead and Kiǫtvi' wrist struck the thin metal band protecting the rim. His fingers spasmed in reaction to the blow and flew open, the sword falling to the ground.

Ragnar could have thrown away his own shield and used his left hand to pull the other's out of the way so that he could end the fight with his sword, but he didn't. He stepped back and allowed Kiǫtvi to retrieve his sword. It was a foolish but magnanimous gesture and the crowd loved him for it; all except Leofstan who had yelled for Ragnar to kill Kiǫtvi. Olaf cuffed the boy hard around the head and he shut up, rubbing his head and giving Olaf a hurt look.

'You don't understand, boy,' Olaf hissed at him quietly. 'By that act of generosity to his enemy Ragnar has won over all those who doubted him. Now no one is shouting for Kiǫtvi.'

The latter had picked up his sword and was circling Ragnar warily. The right leg of his trousers was now dark red with the blood that had flowed out of the flesh wound to his thigh and his right hand hadn't recovered fully from striking the rim of the shield. He was also tiring. In contrast Ragnar was unmarked and was breathing easily. He had all the appearance of enjoying the duel.

The sun was low on the horizon now and Ragnar was anxious to finish the fight before dark. He lunged forward with his sword held horizontally and KiQtvi went to knock it away with his shield. At the last moment, just before the shield would have made contact, Ragnar lifted the point. The shield missed it and KiQtvi was momentarily off balance. He had begun to stab forward with his own sword but Ragnar twisted to the side and raised his right hand, tipping the blade down to strike over KiQtvi's shield. The point entered his neck and Ragnar thrust with all his might so that the point emerged the other side.

He worked the blade to and fro, half severing the head, and KiQtvi crashed to the ground as the last of his life blood pumped into the sand. Everyone rushed forward to clap Ragnar on the back and congratulate him. He felt euphoric but he was dimly aware that someone had grabbed him around the waist and was hugging him. He looked down to see Leofstan grinning up at him. He laughed and tousled the lad's mop of fair hair before picking him up and throwing him in the air and catching him.

They set sail again the next morning but the wind was fickle. When it did blow in the right direction it pushed them along at barely two or three knots and they spent most of the day rowing. Ragnar didn't mind. After the adrenalin rush of the fight with KiQtvi, he found the effort and monotony of rowing strangely soothing. They had erected a pyre the previous evening and burnt his body as a mark of respect. Whatever his faults, KiQtvi had died a warrior's death.

Finally in the middle of the afternoon the wind picked up and the rowers thankfully shipped their oars as Leofstan and the three Pictish boys rushed to haul up the sail. As dark descended the ship's boys shortened sail so the drekar slid over the calm sea at a mere two knots. Ragnar didn't want to risk overshooting the entrance to the Limfjord, especially as he only had a vague idea where it was.

Dawn found them in that part of the sea known as the Kattegatt which was the straight between Sweden and Denmark.

Suddenly the Pictish boy who was acting as lookout called out in broken Norse that there was land dead ahead.

'It looks like an island,' he added.

'Probably Læsø,' Olaf, who was standing beside Ragnar at the prow, suggested.

'Læsø?'

'Yes, according to Sitric it lies in the middle of the Kattegat just north of the entrance to the Limfjord.'

Ragnar cursed. He should have thought to ask the helmsman what he knew of these waters. Evidently Sitric wasn't a man to offer advice if he wasn't asked for it.

'Do you know the entrance, Sitric?' he called back towards the stern.

'We pass to the west of Læsø, lord. It's only about another four hours sailing from there before we turn into the Limfjord,' he replied from his position at the steering oar.

Ragnar remained at the prow as the drekar left the Kattegatt. The ship's boys hauled down the sail and his crew rowed it into the mouth of the Limfjord. It wasn't a fjord as he understood the term. The land on either side of it was flat, unlike the mountains that lined the Norwegian fjords. However, unlike Norway, it looked to be good pasture land with large herds of livestock eating the lush grass. He later found out that the narrow waterway widened out beyond the major settlement in his uncle's domain of Lindholm into a series of connected lakes and inlets. The fjord eventually ran out into the Nordsee, which the Anglo-Saxons called the German Ocean. It made the northern part of Jutland effectively an island.

His uncle Gutfred was Jarl over the area to the north of the Limfjord and to the south as far as the Marianfjord, another inlet from the Kattegatt. In Norway or Sweden he'd call himself a king as ruler of such a large domain, but Denmark had been united as one kingdom by Angantyr Heidreksson more than a hundred years previously. The present king was called Harald Klak, though he was lucky to have retained his throne.

He'd been restored earlier in the year with the help of Louis the Pious, the son and successor of the late Charlemagne, who ruled Frankia, Frisia and Saxony. One of the conditions for his help had been the baptism of Harald as a Christian and the establishment of a church at his capital, Hedeby, near the border between Denmark and Saxony. This had increased his unpopularity with his pagan subjects and weakened his power base. Gutfred might be called jarl, but he ruled his lands independent of much control from Hedeby. He hadn't even paid any taxes for the past few years.

He was therefore pleased to see Ragnar. The addition of nearly fifty trained warriors and a drekar to his forces was welcome at a time of such turbulence in Denmark. Furthermore it meant that his forays to plunder his neighbours could be extended. Danish longships were designed to sail in the shallow waters of the Frisian coastline and the Baltic, unlike Norse ships, which could cross oceans with their deeper keel and high freeboard. However, he hid his pleasure well at their first meeting.

'Well, nephew. If you've come here in the belief that I'll help you against Froh and the Swedes you're mistaken. He and his brother rule the lands across the sea to the north and east of mine and I need to keep the peace with him.'

Ragnar had indeed expected his uncle to help him avenge the murder of the latter's sister, if nothing else, and he said so.

'Do you intend to let the murder of my mother and your sister go unpunished then?'

'Don't sneer at me, you whelp. Your accursed father divorced my sister in order to take some twelve year old child into his bed. It's him I blame, not Froh, who only acted as I would have done in the same circumstances.'

Ragnar kept his temper with difficulty. He needed a safe haven for the moment and it would do no good to antagonise Gutfred.

'I, er, I suppose I can understand you thinking like that. I too was furious with my father when I found out what he'd done. Perhaps Froh was provoked, but I cannot forgive his killing of my mother or of the hersir I was pledged to serve until I became a man.'

'If you want to stay here and serve me you will forget all about seeking to avenge yourself on Froh. Is that clear?'

Ragnar took a deep breath and bit back the retort on the tip of his tongue.

'Yes, uncle. Very.'

He paused for another moment before continuing.

'If I and my crew are to serve you, what can we expect in return?'

'A place to sleep in the warriors' hall, a free berth for your longship and half of whatever the proceeds are from raids that I send you on.'

'So you get the other half? The jarl's share is normally a tenth.'

'And the king's share is a quarter, which you won't have to give him if we keep quiet about your raids, so I'm not asking for much more that you are bound to hand over, are you? In any case it seems to me that you have little choice but to agree to my terms, or I will see what price Froh will give me for your head.'

Ragnar regarded his uncle through narrowed eyes. It seemed that their relationship meant nothing to the man; he was only interested in what he could squeeze out of the situation.

'Not nearly as much as you'll get from the proceeds of my raiding,' he said, trying to keep the derision out of his voice. 'However, I want more than you are offering. My men and I need farmland - a place to settle and spend the winter when we're not away raiding for you.'

Gutfred sucked his teeth and thought about what Ragnar had said. It was during the silence that followed that Ragnar was conscious of a pair of eyes studying him from a corner of the hall where women were sewing and embroidering clothes. From their clothes Ragnar assumed that they were members of the jarl's family, or perhaps of a rich bondi. The girl who was studying him was probably about twelve or thirteen, a few years younger than he was. Ragnar realised with a start that she was extremely pretty. He was captivated by her and was still returning her bold look when his uncle spoke again.

'Land in Jutland is scarce; that's why so many people left in the past and settled in England.'

Ragnar recalled hearing that it was the Jutes who had conquered Kent and part of the south coast of England from the Britons who used to live there.

'However,' the jarl continued, 'few want to live on the exposed northern peninsula, known as Toppenafdanmark. There is one small settlement at Skagen but the bondi who lives there owes me taxes for the past ten years so I would be justified in confiscating his land and giving it to you.'

So it was that Ragnar sailed north again and beached his ship on the broad white sandy beach behind which he could see a few huts and a small longhouse. He was expecting trouble and so he and his men donned their armour and helmets and picked up their shields and weapons before jumping down into the shallow water.

They had mounted the dragon's head on the prow of the drekar to make it clear that they didn't come in peace. Armed men and boys started to gather in the dunes above the beach as they waded ashore.

Ragnar stood and looked at the opposition once he reached dry sand and smiled. There were barely a dozen men and about the same number of boys, ranging from eight to fourteen, facing him. Then, to his dismay, a load of women and a few girls joined their menfolk. They brandished knives, pitchforks and other everyday items that could be used as a weapon. However, he had no intention of making war on women.

He strode up the beach accompanied by Olaf and Sitric until he was near enough to the people confronting him to be heard.

'Which one of you is Aksel?'

'Who wants to know?' a large man with red hair called back in a low booming voice.

'I'm Ragnar, nephew of Jarl Gutfred. You owe him taxes for ten years or more and have forfeited this land as a result. You may leave with your family, but not your tenants or your thralls, or you may stay here and die on this beach.'

'Leave? And where would I go?' he snorted in derision. 'This land is mine and I'll kill any man who says otherwise.'

'Well, I say otherwise, Aksel. If you don't wish to go then at least save the lives of your tenants. Fight me in single combat.'

He heard Olaf hiss 'no' and sensed Sitric start in surprise. He could only imagine Leofstan's reaction.

'Fight you? But you're a mere slip of a boy. It would hardly be fair. No, nominate one of those hairy-arsed warriors behind you to be your champion and I'll kill him instead.'

'I've killed more men in my short life that you have, you bloated belly of lard and piss.'

The insult enraged Aksel, as it was intended to do. With a roar of rage he ran down the sand dune on which he'd been standing and headed for Ragnar. The comment about his belly was justified but the man had arms like tree trunks and legs to match. He stood a good six inches taller than Ragnar and was armed with a large axe in addition to the sword at his waist.

This would be a very different fight to the one against Kiǫtvi. Ragnar knew that one blow from that axe would cleave his shield in two and so he threw it away and drew his dagger instead. Then he waited with sword in his right hand and his dagger in his left. Olaf and Sitric withdrew to a safe distance but Torstein the godi stepped forward from the rest of the crew and walked calmly towards the running giant.

'Come to meet your doom Aksel,' he yelled. 'Ragnar is destined by the Norns for great things and the Valkyries are already circling to cart you away to Valhalla.'

The godi's doom laden prediction had no noticeable effect on Aksel but it gave Ragnar encouragement. He waited calmly until the bondi reached him and then he sidestepped. The axe came down with such force that it would probably have split Ragnar's head in two and continued on to embed itself deep in his torso had he still been there.

As it was, the absence of any resistance unbalanced Aksel and, before he could recover, Ragnar's sword had carved into his unprotected side, followed swiftly by a stab from his dagger into his right biceps. Blood spurted out of the big man's side and Ragnar knew from the numbness in his sword hand that he must have broken a rib or two as well, despite the covering of fat.

Aksel roared in rage and spun around surprisingly quickly for such a heavy man. He dropped his axe, which he needed two hands to wield effectively, and drew his sword with difficulty before changing it to his left hand. Ragnar realised that he must have cut tendons in his biceps, rendering his right arm useless.

Ragnar faced Aksel, balancing on the balls of his feet, as the man brought his sword around in a slicing blow aimed at his young opponent's neck. When he ducked the sword did no more damage than dent the very top of Ragnar's helmet. Once again he managed to get a counter blow in, this time slicing his sword into Aksel's calf. The giant staggered but managed to stay on his feet. However, he could only move by hobbling now and he was getting weak through loss of blood.

'Come on Ragnar, stop playing with him and finish it,' someone called from the semi-circle that had gathered around the two fighters.

The crowd watching from the dunes had also come down onto the beach, but they stayed a hundred yards away from the combatants.

'Do you concede me the victory?'

'Go to Helheim, you bastard spawn of a Norseman,' Aksel replied, gritting his teeth against the agonising pain in his side, arm and leg.

'Very well.'

Ragnar's sword moved too quickly for anyone to follow it as it chopped through Aksel's wrist and his sword fell onto the sand, still clutched in his severed hand. A split second later Ragnar leaped into the air and thrust his dagger into the big bondi's neck, severing both carotid arteries. The former lord of Toppenafdanmark fell into the sand and, just like KiQtvi, his blood stained it red until his heart stopped pumping his blood out of his body.

Wild cheering brought Ragnar out of the momentary stupor he'd fallen into as soon as he realised he'd won. The adrenalin that had coursed through his system during the fight drained away leaving him feeling sick and exhausted.

'You need to act before the crew massacre those who are now your people,' Olaf whispered in his ear.

Ragnar glanced up the beach towards the folk gathered there, who looked as if they were about to flee. If they did that his warriors would chase them and mayhem would ensue. Olaf was right; these were his people now.

'Stay here,' he barked at his crew, a new authority apparent in his voice.

He walked alone towards the nervous group of Danes with a forced smile on his face.

'Don't be afraid. You have nothing to fear now. It was Aksel who had displeased the jarl. You are my tenants now and no harm will come to you; on the contrary I swear to protect you.'

The men came forward and introduced themselves whilst the women took the children home. He noted that the older boys went unwillingly, wanting to stay and meet the youth who had defeated the mighty Aksel. Of course their fate had been to work the land, whereas they doubtless dreamt of becoming warriors. That would now change.

When Ragnar inspected the longhouse and the hovels in which the inhabitants lived he was appalled. The whole place stank of human and animal faeces, rotting straw and urine. The overriding impression was one of poverty, decay and lethargy. The area around the settlement was full of blown sand, salt water bogs and scrub. What areas of soil there were had been cultivated but the crops and vegetables they produced were of poor quality. The few sheep and cattle were scrawny and the three horses looked as if they were about to expire. They'd been worked almost to death. Even the oxen used to pull the two ploughs that the place possessed looked weak and undersized.

Only the pigs looked as if they could provide a decent meal and Ragnar bought two of them to give his men and the inhabitants a decent meal. It was obvious why Aksel hadn't paid his taxes to his jarl; he had nothing with which to do so. Gutfred must be laughing into his ale, Ragnar thought sourly. Who would want such a hell hole?

-V-

However, Ragnar had something that Aksel didn't: a drekar and the crew to man it. There was three months left before winter made raiding hazardous and he intended to take full advantage of the time. He decided to raid Sweden and he didn't intend to seek permission from his uncle to do so.

First, though, he toured his new territory with Olaf and Leif the skáld. He had been tempted to take Torstein as a godi tended to frighten most people out if their wits, but he wanted to enlist the support of these people, not make them afraid of him. On the other hand, the skáld would entertain folk and earn him support. At the last minute he decided to take Leofstan as his servant and the boy couldn't be more pleased if he'd been made a warrior. The presence of a young lad would advertise the fact that he came in peace too.

There were ten farmsteads in all in Toppenafdanmark, in addition to those on the peninsula around Skagen. The coastal area on both coasts was much the same as it was on the narrow peninsula but inland there was good pasture, areas of woodland and even some rich soil that produced good crops.

'Why on earth would Aksel choose to live at Skagen when he could live here?' Ragnar wondered aloud.

As he toured the area he learned that Aksel was a lazy bully. His father had chosen Skagen because he was paranoid and wanted to be away from people and Aksel had been too idle to move elsewhere after the old man died. He hadn't even bothered to collect all the rents due from his tenants and seemed content to live in squalor and poverty.

Initially Ragnar's reception was mixed. Now his tenants would have to pay him the proper rents as their landlord, which was unpopular, but he let them off what they owed from the past, which helped. Leif's sagas and Ragnar's promise of plunder and wealth under his leadership won the bondis over and he gained a grudging acceptance as their hersir, despite his youth.

He calculated that, between the outlying farmsteads and the settlement at Skagen he could raise another fifty warriors; enough to fill his empty rowing places and protect his land whilst he was away. There were also enough fishermen and eager boys to crew a knarr to carry the plunder. First he would have to build it though.

At the end of his tour he found a better place for his hall. There was a large curved bay called Fladstrand twenty miles south of Skagen. There was a wooded hill south of the bay and Ragnar decided that the hill would be the perfect place for his new hall. It was much more defensible, was surrounded by good arable land and wasn't too far from the sea where he could keep his ships. To protect them he would build the warriors hall where his hirdmen would live close to the shore. The shipbuilding yard he planned would be located there as well.

At first the bondi who currently rented the land from him was reluctant to give it up, but when Ragnar told him he'd reduce his rent as compensation, his tenant reluctantly agreed. Privately he thought that he'd secured a good deal because he didn't have the thralls to farm the land properly in any case.

Chapter Five – The Rise of Ragnar

823 to 824

When Ragnar returned from his raid on the south-east coast of Sweden he brought with him four horses, a small flock of sheep and half a dozen calves as well as a quantity of silver and a few slaves. They had to fight for some of their plunder and they had lost three men, but everyone was elated by the success of the venture. Admittedly the return journey with so many animals on board had been unpleasant and Ragnar was even more determined to build a knarr before his next raid.

During his absence the hill near Fladstrand had been cleared of trees and work had started on his new hall, the palisade to go around it and the longhouse to house his hirdmen to guard the port that was taking shape in the bay. One jetty was complete so he could tie his drekar up instead of beaching her and sheds for the shipyard were well underway.

It was going to be a race to finish the hall and the longhouse before the cold and wet weather set in and, in the end, Ragnar decide to concentrate on the longhouse. Living with his men until the spring would be no hardship, or so he thought.

What he hadn't expected was the gales that continually struck the low lying land once October arrived. He was lucky that his longship hadn't torn free of her moorings during the first of these. After that they hauled it well up the beach, out of possible reach of the storm driven sea.

Spring came as a great relief. Food had grown short and they had even been reduced to eating the tough old horses that they'd found at Skagen. Once the warmer weather arrived they quickly discovered that there wasn't much to hunt in that part of Denmark, so increasing the herds of livestock became even more important.

Work on the hall, palisade and shipyard recommenced in mid-March and by early May they were ready to start work on the new knarr. Ragnar was now sixteen and had the beginnings of a beard on his face. He decided to wait until the knarr was ready before raiding again. This time his target would be Frisia, he decided. However, all that would change.

At the beginning of June he had a visitor. Jarl Gutfred had sailed up to Skagen and became concerned when he found the place deserted. No-one had spotted the new settlement at Fladstrand because they had been struggling with a squall when they rowed past it. When they sailed back down the sky was blue and visibility was excellent.

'Jarl, there's new buildings over there,' the lookout called down as they cleared the point north of the bay.

Half an hour later Gutfred's snekkja was tied up on the other side of the jetty from Ragnar's much larger longship and the jarl cast envious eyes at it. Ragnar had seen the snekkja approaching and had walked across from the shipyard to the jetty to welcome the jarl.

'Welcome to Fladstrand, uncle.'

'You didn't tell me you'd moved from Skagen,' Gutfred said without acknowledging the greeting.

'I didn't know I had to, but I did intend to visit you once my new knarr is ready and discuss raiding this summer. I'd have told you then.'

'This summer is well underway and it's time you earned the land I've given you.'

He looked around him with pursed lips and Ragnar guessed that his uncle hadn't realised that Toppenafdanmark included such good land. No doubt he thought that it was all like the area around Skagen.

At that moment Ragnar spotted the girl he'd first seen in Gutfred's hall and who had seldom been out of his thoughts ever since.

'I see you have brought someone with you,' he said, trying to hide his interest.

'What? Oh, yes, my daughter Thora. She insisted on coming with me, Odin knows why; normally she hates the sea.'

'May I be introduced to my cousin?'

'Why? Don't tell me you're interested in her. She's destined for a much better match than the exiled son of a dead king.'

'Oh, is she betrothed then?'

'No, I'm not. Nor will I be sold off to the highest bidder like some thrall,' Thora said with some passion.

'You'll do as you're told, girl.'

'No, I won't. If you make me wed against my will I'll kill my husband and involve you in a blood feud.'

Ragnar laughed, which earned him a furious look from Thora.

'You'd make a good shield maiden, cousin,' he told her.

Shield maidens existed only in Scandinavian mythology as far as Ragnar was aware but Thora's eyes seemed to light up at the idea. She smiled at him and then looked demurely down at the ground. Ragnar thought that she might be as interested in him as he was in her. Her obvious feistiness was an added attraction. He didn't think life with her would be boring.

'Don't encourage her, Ragnar. She's bad enough as it is. I'll be glad when she's married and off my hands. But that's not why I came here. The raiding season has started and I want you to join me in a raid on Austrasia.'

'But that's part of Louis the Frank's kingdom isn't it? I was under the impression that he and your king, Harald, were allies.'

'That's why my ships will be displaying a plain sail, like yours.'

They had been walking up the path to Ragnar's new hall as they talked but now Ragnar stopped.

'My sail has now been dyed in red and white stripes and displays the raven symbol of my family.'

'Well, you'll have to get another plain one from somewhere, won't you?'

'No.'

'What do you mean no?'

'I'm not creeping around like a thief in the night. I want my enemies to know who I am and to tremble at the sight of my ships.'

'You'll do as I say or I'll take back these lands. In fact, I'd never have given Toppenafdanmark to you if I'd known it contained rich lands like this.'

'If you remember you didn't give me this region, I had to fight for it, and I pay taxes for it, which is more than my predecessor ever managed to do.'

Gutfred looked Ragnar in the eye and then grunted before continuing to climb the slope towards the hall.

'By Thor's hammer, boy, I thought your father was pig-headed but he was a model of amenability compared to you. If I let you go raiding on your own where would you go?'

'Ireland.'

'Ireland? Why?'

'Because few have ventured that far as yet so there should be richer pickings, but not until next year. I need to leave early to make the most of the summer and I need to take my knarr to bring back everything I manage to steal; half of which will be yours, of course.'

'And this year?'

'The area around Uppsala.'

'Uppsala? On the east coast of Sweden? Why?'

'Because their warriors will be busy raiding the land of the Rus. I need more livestock and more thralls to work the land.'

'They're no use to me, I want silver.'

'There'll be some of that too.'

By now they had reached the palisade around the hall and Gutfred nodded in approval at the depth of the ditch and the height of the ramparts. The top of the earth bank was ten feet above the bottom of the ditch and the palisade stood twelve feet above that. It would be a difficult place to assault.

The hall itself was a typical Norseman's hall, built to keep out the weather rather than for comfort. The roof trusses were supported on a colonnade of straight pine trunks that ran all the way around the hall. Inside it planks had been set up vertically to make the walls and then the gaps had been plugged with dried mud. There were windows with shutters, one main doorway and the roof was of turf laid on more timber planks. The protruding roof edge and colonnade beneath it gave some protection to the walls and allowed the windows to be open in all but the foulest weather.

Despite the windows the interior of the hall was still dark. As Gutfred entered the hall he noted the usual features – the beaten earth floor covered in rushes, the tree trunks down each side of the hall supporting the roof trusses, the partitioning between those columns and the outer wall and the benches in each alcove that served as a place to sit during the day and as sleeping platforms at night.

The central hearth was round and had a pig slowly roasting over it. A boy stripped to the waist was slowly turning the spit, the sweat glistening on his thin body. The jarl noticed the lad's badly scared back and assumed that he needed punishing to keep him in line. He was therefore startled when the boy grinned at Ragnar who punched the boy lightly on the arm as he passed.

'Are you that familiar with all your thralls?'

'No, of course not, but that's Leofstan. He's not a thrall; he's my body servant. He's a Northumbrian who I rescued from the Picts to become one of the ship's boys on my drekar. He's also got the knack of cooking pork to perfection without burning it. All my thralls either char the outside or leave the meat half cooked inside.'

Gutfred looked around at the number of thralls busy cleaning the hall and laying out refreshments on the table at the end of the hall.

'Where did you get all these thralls from? Are they Northumbrians as well?'

'No, Ragnar smiled. Thorkel was in charge then and he gave his oath not to raid Northumbria in exchange for our freedom. No, there are a few Picts and the rest are Swedes.'

'Swedes? You've raided Sweden? Did I know about this?'

'Don't worry, it was two day's sail from here and I have a chest of silver to give to you as your share.'

Gutfred was going to rebuke his nephew for going raiding without permission but the mention of a chest of silver mollified him. Ragnar sat down at the table at the far end of the hall and invited the jarl and his daughter, who had followed them into the hall, to sit either side of him.

Thora seemed a little miffed at being ignored so far, but she soon thawed when Ragnar started to talk to her. Now it was Gutfred who was feeling a little ignored until Olaf came and sat beside him.

'Aren't you a little young to be a hirdman?'

The jarl had made the natural assumption that Olaf must be one of Ragnar's household warriors; no-one else would come and sit with their hersir.

'Ragnar and I are the same age, jarl. Oh, I know that I'm small for sixteen but I've killed my fair share of men.'

Ragnar stopped talking to Thora and turned to her father.

'There is no-one I'd rather have beside me in a fight. Olaf and I met when he defeated me in the final round of the boys' swordsmanship competition at Arendal.'

'You do seem to have the knack of inspiring loyalty, Ragnar,' he said, a trifle enviously.

'I suppose so. At any rate I seem to have attracted enough young bondis looking to blood their swords to fill another longship. I'll be leaving enough men behind when I go raiding this summer to guard my hall and to start building another drekar.'

Gutfred narrowed his eyes at that. As jarl he had several snekkjur and knarrs, but only one drekar, and that was smaller than Ragnar's. With two drekars and a knarr Ragnar would become his most powerful bondi; so powerful that in Norway or Sweden he could have called himself a jarl.

He listened to Olaf with half an ear whilst he watched Thora and Ragnar deep in conversation. They obviously got on well together; perhaps he should bind his nephew closer to him by offering him his daughter in marriage? He pushed the thought to the back of his mind and turned his full attention to what Olaf was telling him about Ragnar's plans for raiding that summer.

-ᛉ-

Leofstan was excited. Once again he'd be going to sea and this time he'd be the senior of the four ship's boys. He wasn't the oldest but his position as Ragnar's body servant gave him precedence over the three Picts and the young Danish boy who made up the rest of the crew.

As a youngster in Northumbria his father had made his life a misery; it wasn't just the beatings he gave the lad when he was drunk, which was much of the time, but it was the mental torture that Leofstan had hated the most. The man made him feel more unworthy than the meanest cur in the settlement. Life as a Pictish slave had been no better. It was only Leofstan's resilient nature that enabled him to survive.

During the tour of his lands the previous year Ragnar learned something of the boy's background and, unlike most Vikings, he felt a growing responsibility for the lad's welfare. It wasn't just that he felt sorry for him - servants were beneath his notice generally – but the boy's eagerness to please and his lively sense of humour made him stand out.

He soon found out that the boy wasn't just a good servant, he was a good raconteur, making the most mundane tale amusing. Had the boy been Norse or Danish he would have made a good skáld when he grew up. He could be cheeky at times but, as the months wore on, Leofstan never once stepped over the line and became too familiar. He even took his turn on the roasting spit with good humour; something none of the household thralls did.

It was when he first took a turn at the spit and took off his homespun tunic because of the heat that Ragnar saw the matrix of scars on the boy's back; the scars that later Gutfred had seen and which had led him to assume that he was a troublemaker. But it wasn't Ragnar who had disciplined him, it had been the boy's father. He'd been whipped repeatedly with something like a leather belt and, judging by the depth of the welts on his mutilated body, he was lucky to be alive. From that day on Ragnar's respect for the boy grew and they gradually established a relationship that was as close to friendship as was possible in their respective circumstances.

-V-

The drekar bumped gently as its prow hit the sand. Leofstan and three of the other ship's boys leapt ashore and ran up the beach with two anchors and embedded them securely in the sand. The knarr came to rest fifty yards away and was similarly secured. There was no tidal rise and fall in the Baltic Sea so, baring a storm, the two ships wouldn't move.

Leaving the ships' boys and the crew of the knarr as guards, Ragnar led his seventy warriors off to explore. The island of Gotland, where they had landed, was the largest Swedish island in the Baltic. Its main settlement, Visby, was an important trading centre and Ragnar believed that its warehouses would be full of furs, iron bars, fleeces and, of course, silver and gold. They had landed in a deserted bay ten miles south of Visby and, as the bay was surrounded by woodland, he hoped that their ships would remain undiscovered.

Once clear of the wood they cautiously traversed the undulating countryside with scouts out to the front and the flanks. Apart from a few sheep and the occasional bird, the place seemed bereft of life. At the sun neared its zenith it blazed down on the column of warriors sweating in leather jerkins, byrnies and helmets.

Suddenly one of the forward scouts came running back, keeping to the hollows.

'There's a party of mounted warriors ahead, Ragnar,'

'How far and how many?'

'About half a mile and there are about ten or so.'

'Do you think they know we're here?' Olaf asked in a low voice.

'Hopefully not, it's probably just a routine patrol. We'll stay in this hollow and hope that they don't notice us but pass the word for everyone to get their shields ready to use, just in case.'

When on the move warriors kept their shields slung on their backs.

The sixty men of the main body clustered into the depression in the ground and waited, clutching their heavy ash spears. The ten men with bows strung them ready for use and selected their best arrow, wetting the feathers with their lips to give them the best chance of flying true.

Olaf crept to the rim of the hollow and cautiously peered around the bottom of a bush. He could hear the muffled sound of horses' hooves on the hard packed earth of the nearby trackway but the Swedes were hidden from sight in another undulation in the ground. Then he saw a helmet appear swiftly followed by the man's torso and another head. He counted a dozen men coming towards them before slithering back down to join Ragnar and the others.

'There's a dozen of them, some in byrnies, but most in leather jerkins or quilted tunics. They're two hundred yards away - nearer now – but they're on the track so we should remain undetected,' he whispered.

Ragnar shook his head. 'I can't take the risk of them finding the ships,' he mumbled quietly, almost as if he was talking to himself.

Olaf was about to point out that the beach where they were was well hidden from the track when the sound of someone's spear point clattering against a helmet broke the silence. The patrol came to a halt looking around in alarm for the source of the sound. He cursed the idiot who'd made the noise, but the decision had now been made for him.

Ragnar signalled frantically for the archers to get ready, then pointed at Yngvi, one of his most experienced warriors and gestured for him to take half of the warband to cut the horsemen off. He beckoned the other half to follow him and then he called out 'now!'

The Vikings swarmed out of the hollow, one group heading left and the other right as fast as their legs could carry them. The archers halted at the rim and taking a couple of deep breaths to calm their breathing, they let fly with their first volley.

The Swedes sat there for a moment, shocked by the sudden appearance of so many armed men. Then their leader kicked his horse into motion, but it was too late. An arrow struck it in the rump and another pinned the rider's calf to its side. The horse reared in surprise at the agonising pain and the horseman fell off, tearing the arrow in his leg free in the process. His horse bolted with blood streaming from its rear and chest before collapsing a hundred yards away.

Ragnar saw this out of the corner of his eye and swore; he had a use for the horses. Fortunately most of the other archers were better shots and, apart from one who missed his target entirely, they managed to hit five more riders, killing three and wounding two more. That left half a dozen who looked around them in panic.

The Vikings were rapidly forming a semi-circle ahead and behind them, cutting off any escape along the track so they did the only sensible thing and headed for the scrub to the right of them. As they fled the archers brought down two more with arrows in their backs but four escaped before the circle could close. A well thrown hand axe brought another down and a third volley of arrows at long range hit the thigh of another Swede, but it didn't unseat him.

'Odin's blood, they can't get back to Visby and warn them,' Ragnar cried in alarm.

He ran and vaulted onto the back of a surprised stallion, who was calmly eating grass after the death of his master. Olaf and two other warriors grabbed other horses and set off behind him as he galloped off in pursuit of the escaping Swedes.

It soon became apparent that horses carrying warriors weighed down by byrnies were unlikely to catch ones ridden by men in padded tunics, except for Ragnar's stallion which was proving to be much faster than any of the other horses. However, the man with the leg wound was evidently feeling faint from loss of blood and two of his companions came alongside him to support him. It was a mistake as it slowed them down.

Ragnar caught them up but he ignored them and continued after the fourth man, leaving the others for Olaf and his companions to deal with. Now the fourth man was a mere two hundred yards ahead. He glanced behind him and, seeing only one pursuer, he pulled his horse to a sudden halt and turned to face Ragnar.

In leaping onto the stallion Ragnar had dropped his spear and shield so he now found himself facing a man armed with both when he only had his sword and dagger. He didn't draw either, however. As the Swede lunged at him, Ragnar ducked then launched himself into the air, barrelling into his opponent's body and knocking him out of his saddle.

They crashed to the ground, Ragnar on top. He was slightly winded but his adversary was struggling to breathe. The Norseman recovered first and thrust his dagger into the other's neck. Hot blood spurted up soaking his face as the Swede convulsed once and then lay still. Ragnar stayed where he was for a minute recovering then struggled to lift the corpse onto his own horse.

Leading it he retraced his steps until he found Olaf and his other two men. The three Swedes were dead but they hadn't died quietly. Olaf had wounds to both legs and his left arm and, although no more than nasty flesh wounds, they would need washing in sea water to stem the blood flow, sewing up and binding. He therefore sent him back to the ships on one of the horses.

They buried the dead Swedes in a shallow grave away from the track so no-one would find them until it was too late to matter and they continued on their way towards Visby.

'What are you plans, lord?' Yngvi asked him as he rode beside him.

Ragnar was dressed in the clothes and padded tunic taken from the smallest of the Swedes whilst Yngvi wore the polished byrnie and helmet taken from the leader of the patrol. All the other riders were also dressed in the Swedes' clothes and one carried aloft the red and green pennant that one of the patrol had been carrying.

They stopped behind the last ridge before Visby and Ragnar crept forward with Yngvi. The settlement was quite large and they estimated that it probably had about three or four hundred adult inhabitants. There was a large longhouse surrounded by a palisade that had to be the jarl's hall, and two other longhouses. The rest of the buildings were huts and down by the quay there were five warehouses of varying sizes. Three jetties jutted out at right angles to the wooden quay to which there were moored three knarrs and a snekkja.

One of the knarrs was being loaded and another unloaded. They could see four warriors on guard duty on the quay and another two stood in front of the open gates in the palisade which ran around the whole settlement. There didn't appear to be any guards patrolling the palisade itself but just behind the warehouses there was a tall tower with a lookout in it. However, his attention appeared to be directed out to sea.

Next Ragnar studied the lie of the land. It was too flat to offer any hope of concealment, but there was a wood which was only a hundred yards from the main gates at the closest point. Ragnar smiled to himself. Had he been the Jarl of Gotland he would have made sure that the perimeter was clear of any undergrowth out to at least three hundred yards.

'Come on, Yngvi. I think we've seen enough.'

But the man grabbed his arm and pointed.

'That must be the warriors' hall,' he said, pointing at the larger of the two longhouses outside the jarl's enclosure.

Three men had just come out of it armed with shields, spears and wearing helmets. They proceeded to change places with the men at the gate and the lookout. Ragnar nodded.

'Well spotted. We'll need to take care of the warriors living in the longhouse before attacking the jarl's hall,' he said.

He studied the settlement again carefully, expecting to see at least some of the off duty warriors training, but there was no sign of anything except the inhabitants going about their normal business. He smiled to himself. Such indolent behaviour indicated to him that the warriors in Visby wouldn't be very well trained.

A little later one of the sentries at the main gates nudged his companion.

'Jarl Öjulf is returning. I wonder why? I thought he was meant to be away until tomorrow.'

'Ours is not to reason why, boy,' the older man said and the pair drew off to one side to allow the horsemen to pass. 'That's funny, there seems to be fewer of them than left this morning. I wonder if they ran into trouble.'

'What sort of trouble?'

'Shhh, lad. Best not to be seen chatting away by the jarl when we're meant to be on duty.'

Had the sentries continued to examine the approaching horsemen they would have realised that they looked nothing like Öjulf and his men, apart from their borrowed clothes and helmets. However, the Swedish jarl didn't like his men staring him in the face and so the sentries stood with their eyes to the front as the cavalcade reached them.

As Yngvi drew level with them he drew his sword and chopped down into the elder warrior's neck. The man dropped like a stone. The younger man, who was scarcely old enough to have a proper beard yet, stood paralysed by shock. Before he could gather his wits one of the other horsemen stuck a spear into his unprotected chest.

Yngvi took off the Swedish jarl's ornate helmet and tossed it away, taking his own helmet from one of the other men. Ragnar rode forward and congratulated them before riding on towards the warriors' hall. Thankfully the lookout was either dozing or looking out to sea and no alarm bell rang as they trotted through the busy streets, not wanting to seem in too much of a rush.

People stared at them, wondering who these strangers might be. The subterfuge had ceased at the gates when the banner had been discarded along with the jarl's ornate helmet. It was useless to pretend that they were Öjulf and his men in the narrow streets. The deception would never stand up to scrutiny at close range; far better to be a band of visiting strangers.

Odin was with them it seemed. The warriors' longhouse was unguarded and there was a carpenter's workshop nearby. Ragnar had intended to kill those inside but now he saw a better alternative. Beside the one door, there were two windows on each side of the long building. Both had two shutters either side of the opening to keep out the wind and rain when necessary, but today was warm and they were open to let in what breeze there was.

Sending men to grab hammers, nails and lengths of timber from the carpenter's yard, others slammed the four shutters to and it was the work of moments to seal both the windows and the door. Now he wouldn't have to worry about the men inside, at least for a while.

As they were doing this, the rest of the Vikings had reached the open gates before the jarl's hall and poured in through them. If the sealing shut of the warriors' hall hadn't alerted the inhabitants of Visby the screams of those near the gates and the belated ringing of the alarm bell did.

Ragnar cursed. Now the residents of the jarl's hall would be alert. However, that wasn't his prime concern. He sent Bjarke and the first of his men who arrived on foot down to the quayside to secure the warehouses and prevent any of the ships from leaving.

It didn't take him long to persuade those in the hall to surrender. Once she knew that her husband was dead, Öjulf's wife agreed to surrender the hall and its contents in exchange for the lives of herself and her three young children. The eldest, a boy of ten named Finnulf, swore to avenge his father's death but, as no one knew who the raiders were – apart from the fact that they were a mixture of Norse and Danes – Ragnar ignored him. Had he suspected that the boy had the remotest chance of carrying out his threat, he would have killed him on the spot.

-V-

Ragnar sailed around to the beach in the captured ship to find that it had been Leofstan who had sewed Olaf back together again, a skill he had learned from the female thralls at Fladstrand. He was a little surprised to find that Olaf didn't seem at all grateful to the boy. For the first time the thought crossed his mind that his closest friend might be jealous of the bond between him and his servant. However, he dismissed the idea as preposterous.

He arrived back at Fladstrand with more ships than he could moor alongside the jetties. In addition to the knarrs and the snekkja he had captured at Visby he had come across another drekar as he rounded the southern tip of Sweden. He would have left it alone – he had enough of a problem as it was manning all the ships he'd captured – but its mainsail proclaimed the fact that it belonged to King Froh, the killer of his parents.

Shouting for the four knarrs to stay well clear, he made a course to intercept the Swedish drekar. It was a little smaller than his own ship and it was rowing into the wind whereas

Ragnar's two longships were sailing with the wind behind them. The Swedish ship immediately turned and hoisted its own sail in an attempt to make a run for it, but it was slower than either of Ragnar's longships.

When they drew level with it, one on each side, Ragnar ordered his archers to open fire. The Norns must have been smiling on him because the Swedish steersman was killed in the first volley and the ship slewed to one side until it was broadside on, the wind spilling from its sail. Minutes later Ragnar's ships threw their grappling irons and secured their prey. Warriors poured into the Swedish longship from both sides and trapped the crew between them.

The Swedes were as numerous as their enemy but they were hemmed in with little room to wield a sword, let alone an axe or a spear. They were butchered where they stood but they refused to yield. In the end only the wounded survived and Ragnar ordered them thrown overboard. He had lost ten men in the encounter and another fifteen were wounded, but he considered it a price worth paying to have taken the first step towards hitting back at Froh.

Rowing at any speed above a snail's pace with so many ships and so few men to crew them was impossible. It meant that he was at the mercy of the wind. It took twice as long as normal to get back but he eventually limped home at the beginning of July.

He had intended to sally forth for one more raid that year but his knarrs were weighed down with silver, furs, wool and captives who he'd either put to good use on his land or sell as thralls. He would have to give some of his spoils to his uncle, but perhaps not half. After all, he wouldn't know exactly how much he'd plundered. However much he gave Gutfred he was now a rich man. His warriors were more than pleased with their share and the skálds would sing of his exploits. That would attract more young men to serve him.

He was beginning to think that the year couldn't get any better. He was wrong.

Chapter Six – The Raid on Neustria

824 to 825

Ragnar had expected his uncle to come north as soon as he heard that he had returned in order to claim his half share of the plunder, but he didn't. Eventually Ragnar came to the conclusion that the jarl must be away raiding himself; then he heard what had happened.

Gutfred and his two sons had taken their four longships to go raiding along the Frisian coast, but they had been betrayed. The king, Harald Klak, had got wind of Gurfred's plans and had secretly plotted with Louis the Pious to ambush Gutfred. The jarl had two hundred and fifty warriors with him but Harald and Louis had mustered a fleet of ten ships and a thousand men on land.

Gutfred had escaped but he'd lost two of his longships and over half his men in the process. It was even more of a disaster because both his sons were among those killed. Now his only children were his three daughters, the eldest being Thora.

When Ragnar eventually sailed south with what he'd decided should be the jarl's share of what he'd looted from Sweden he had one object in mind: marriage to Thora. He sailed into the Limfjord in his drekar with two knarrs carrying his tribute to Gutfred and escorted by his two other longships. It might have been difficult to man them all but, as he'd hoped, a number of young warriors from Denmark and Norway had come to join him as his reputation spread. Of course, it meant that word would eventually get back to Sweden as well, but that couldn't be helped.

He couldn't afford to keep them all as his hirdmen but there was enough spare land for him to make those with families his tenants. As they brought the land under cultivation and bred more livestock to graze it, so his own income would increase. Nevertheless, he realised that he would need to be as successful at raiding next year as this if he was to keep on top of his outgoings. Not for the first time, he resented being expected to pay half of the proceeds to Gutfred.

Since he'd last seen her Thora had grown into a young woman and he could hardly take his eyes off her. With a jolt he realised that Gutfred was waiting for a reply to a question he'd asked.

'I'm sorry, uncle, I didn't hear what you said.'

'No, you were too busy ogling my daughter,' the man said sourly.

'What are your intentions for her?' Ragnar asked, quite unabashed.

He sensed that he'd said the wrong thing when Thora looked up from her needlework and gave him an angry look.

'King Harald has a brother, Hemming, who is his heir as things stand. His wife has just died and an alliance with him would be useful to me.'

'Huh, I'd rather die; he's as old as the hills,' Thora retorted.

'He's only in his late thirties, as you very well know, and he is the Count of Walcheren in Frisia. He has a lot to offer you.'

'The Frisians are our enemies, or at least they used to be,' she replied heatedly.

'Not since their king put Harald Klak back on the throne of Denmark.'

'And that's another thing, both Harald and Hemming are followers of the White Christ; we're not!'

'Why are you so keen to ally yourself with Harald and Hemming, uncle?' Ragnar interrupted. 'Klak is only king because Louis the Pious lent him an army to regain his throne. He's unpopular with his jarls and the people. It's foolish to ally yourself with someone whose days are numbered.'

'Who asked you?' Gutfred asked heatedly.

Ragnar shrugged. 'As I must now be one of your most powerful bondis, I thought my opinion might count for something, especially as I'm now your closest male relative.'

'Don't get above yourself, boy. I'm not dead yet and I can still sire more sons.'

'Father, be realistic. You're in your fifties and mother is beyond child bearing age.'

Her mother, who had studiously continued with her embroidery work on a new tunic for her husband up to this point, looked sharply at her daughter.

'Thora, that is not something to be discussed in the hall, or anywhere else come to that. I'm ashamed of you.'

'Why? It's the truth.'

'It may be,' her father said, a dangerous glint in his eye. 'But there is nothing to stop me taking a younger wife, who will give me sons.'

Both his wife and his daughter looked at him in shock. His wife sat there dumbfounded but Thora let out a wail and ran out of the hall.

'You are not thinking clearly, jarl,' Ragnar said. 'Even if you sired another son next year, you would have to live into your seventies for him to be old enough to be accepted by the Thing as jarl.'

What Ragnar had said was true. Although it was normal for a son to follow his father as jarl it wasn't necessarily always the case. The Thing was the assembly of all bondis held whenever necessary to resolve disputes, decide on policy, pass new laws or repeal old ones and, most importantly, elect their jarl.

Gutfred sat in his chair fuming for a while and Ragnar had the good sense to let the silence lengthen. Eventually the jarl's shoulders' slumped in resignation. He got up and, ignoring his weeping wife, sent men to find Thora.

She had no idea where she was running to when she left the hall, all she wanted to do was get away from her father. She was oblivious to her surroundings until she was nearly run down by a wagon. The carter cursed her roundly as he pulled his horse to a sudden halt.

'Get out of the way, girl. Why don't you look where you're going?'

The man evidently had no idea who she was or, if he did, he couldn't care less. Thora stood there shaking with emotion when she felt two strong hands on her shoulders. She started and whipped around to find herself staring into Ragnar's concerned eyes.

'Would you marry me, Thora,' he asked gently.

'Yes, oh yes, there is nothing I want more, but my father will never agree.'

'We'll see about that,' he said with a smile.

Gutfred hadn't gone looking for his eldest daughter himself, of course, but had sent his hirdmen to find her. When they saw that she was with Ragnar and heading towards the jarl's hall they called off the search.

Ragnar and Thora didn't go straight to the hall though, they went via the quayside so that, when they did reach the hall, Ragnar entered first followed by his men carrying bales of furs, sheep and goatskins, flax for weaving into linen and two sizeable coffers containing silver.

'Your share of my raiding this summer, uncle.'

Gutfred sat there open mouthed. Ragnar had made him a wealthy man. Now he could afford to replace the ships and men he'd lost in his abortive raid on Frisia. It would also mean that he wouldn't need to appease Harald Klak. His shrewd eyes narrowed. If this was his share he imagined that Ragnar had kept more than half of the plunder. He knew that he needed to keep Ragnar loyal to him now.

'What do you want in return, nephew?'

'Two things, jarl. The freedom to wreak my revenge on Froh and his brother. Once I have regained my kingdom I give you my oath that I will enter into an alliance with you and we will support each other.'

'Agreed. Try not to upset all of Sweden though. Even together we would never stand a chance in a war against the combined Swedish kings.'

He paused.

'You said two things?'

'Thora's hand in marriage.'

At that moment his daughter appeared in the doorway and went running up to her father, throwing herself at his feet.

'Please forgive me father but I implore you to agree. Ragnar is the man I wish to marry.'

Gurfred's instinct was to deny his wilful daughter but he saw how tense Ragnar was out of the corner of his eye. His answer really mattered to the seventeen year old Norseman. If he said no then Ragnar would probably turn against him, attack Froh anyway and, if he did regain the crown of Adger, he could prove to be a powerful enemy.

His furrowed brow cleared and he smiled.

'Nothing could please me more,' he lied.

-ᛉ-

The wedding took place on a bitterly cold day in January 825. Instead of wearing a thick woollen tunic or a long robe and a cloak made of oiled wool like everyone else, Ragnar appeared wearing a byrnie of steel rings polished by Leofstan until it looked as if it was made of silver. The servant walked behind him carrying a helmet with a gold band and a golden raven as a crest. But that wasn't what had surprised the bondis and other guests; he also wore trousers and a jerkin under his byrnie made of goatskin. The trousers were tucked into calfskin boots stained to match the dark grey goatskin. Over his armour he wore a cloak made from the skin of a large wolf. It was obvious to all that he was making a statement; he wasn't just a bondi and a hersir, he was a warrior in the mould of Beowulf.

The goatskin trousers were stiff and uncomfortable, though they would became suppler the more that Ragnar wore them. He later found them to be effective protection in battle and he continued to wear them as well as his byrnie when dressed for war. Thus he acquired the byname Lodbrok – hairy breeches.

Thora looked uncharacteristically demure as she entered the hall and stood beside him to watch the godi perform the ritual sacrifice and pronounce the omens propitious for their future together. They swore their vows to each other and then everyone present proceeded to get uproariously drunk.

Thora left once things began to get a bit unruly and Ragnar did his best to stay sober enough to make love to his bride later.

However, he failed, and when he was half led, half carried into the chamber they were to share he was far beyond doing anything except snore the night away – much to Thora's disgust and disappointment.

She made her feeling about his inebriation perfectly clear the next morning when she woke up and kicked him awake. He sheepishly apologised and found that he felt much better than he had any right to be. He turned her anger away with soft words and endearments, accompanied by kisses and caresses. Eventually she gave in and he proceeded to take her virginity, trying to be gentle.

However, there was no doubt that Thora enjoyed the experience and clawed at his back and bit his neck in her passion. Thus encouraged Ragnar stopped trying to be nice and gave way to his own animal lust. The experience left them exhausted and, after a suitable pause, eager for more.

He and Thora returned to his hall in the north and, by the time that Ragnar went raiding that summer, she was able to tell him that their passionate coupling had born fruit. She was expecting their first child.

'Stay with me this summer until our child is born, husband.' she said, not so much pleading as demanding.

Her own mother hadn't prepared her for the changes that pregnancy would bring and she became less sure of herself as a consequence. Instead of being her normal self-sufficient self, she wanted her husband to comfort her and help her through it. Ragnar didn't understand this, of course, and her imperious tone annoyed him.

'I'm sorry Thora but I need to gain wealth and ships and thus attract more warriors to my banner if I am ever to regain Agder.'

'You think more of that accursed place than you do of me,' she accused him, her eyes blazing.

His face grew cold and he left her without another word. The next thing she knew he had sailed without even saying farewell. She broke down and cried, more in frustration at her failure to bend Ragnar to her will than anything. He, on the other hand, felt no remorse. Thora needed to understand that being a husband was only part of who he was.

-V-

As the summer wore on Thora's resentment grew. Thankfully the birth of their son was straightforward but, instead of waiting to see what Ragnar wanted to call his first-born she went ahead and named him Agnar, meaning terror. It seemed a fitting name for the son of Ragnar Lodbrok.

It was a name that could be applied to the father rather more appropriately. Ragnar had raided all the way along the Frisian coast from the enclosed bay known as Jadenbusen to the end of the East Frisian Islands. However, the inhabitants had got used to Viking raiders and had built watch towers at intervals along the coast. As soon as Ragnar's men landed the locals fled inland taking their valuables and possessions with them.

Apart from burning settlements to take out their frustration, they had precious little to show for their efforts. Olaf threw a flaming torch into a hut as they left the last of them on the banks of the estuary of the River Ems and then trudged angrily back to the ships.

'What now?' he asked his hersir angrily.

From being something of a hero to his men Ragnar's stock had fallen and they were dispirited and feeling mutinous.

'Don't take out your resentment on me, Olaf. I'm as infuriated as you are. This coast has been raided too often, that much is clear.'

'Is it too late to try Sweden again?'

'Probably not, but it would be a mistake to repeat what we did last year. They'll be ready for us this time.'

'So do we just give up?'

'I can't afford to. Men follow a leader because they think he has the favour of the gods and because he makes them wealthy. I have to find somewhere new to raid.'

'Further along this coast then?'

Ragnar shook his head.

'I can't risk having the same problem in West Frisia. No, I think we're going to have to try even further west.'

'You mean Neustria?'

It was the heart of the Carolingian Empire ruled by Louis the Pious, but the emperor was currently busy trying to put down a revolt by his sons in the south. Consequently there were few soldiers in Neustria at the moment. It was reputed to be a prosperous kingdom with many wealthy monasteries, though no Viking had raided there as far as Ragnar knew.

'Yes, Neustria.'

The first place they landed contained a large settlement with a monastery standing on a high hill near a wide river estuary. As Ragnar's hundred and fifty warriors leaped into the sea and waded ashore the Neustrians gathered to oppose them. Ragnar was surprised how many there were but only thirty of them were properly armed warriors; the rest seemed to be some sort of local militia and, although some of them had spears, helmets and shields, most were armed with scythes, pitchforks and even broom handles with a knife strapped to the end.

However, they did have quite a few archers and they, coupled with a score of boys with slings, forced the Vikings to advance with shields raised. Even so one received a flesh wound to his shin from an arrow and another had his arm broken by a stone. This only served to enrage the raiders and they quickened the pace to close with the Neustrians as quickly as possible without breaking formation.

They crashed into their opponents and forced them back. Ragnar yelled for them to adopt the boar's head as they advanced and those on the flanks dropped back, allowing Ragnar and his hirdmen to form the point, or snout. They sliced into the armoured warriors in the centre of their opponents, forcing them apart and giving the warriors in contact with Ragnar's men little room to wield their weapons.

Once the Vikings had split the enemy in two, they continued to push the two halves apart. The Neustrians in the rearmost ranks had little idea what was happening and they lost their nerve. Those at the back always tended to be the timid and the least experienced; now they turned and ran. Flight became infectious and the militia routed, leaving the experienced warriors outnumbered and surrounded. About half of them had died or were badly wounded by the time that their leader – the local count – decided that the battle was lost and fled the field, his men streaming after him.

The monastery was deserted when they reached it. The monks had long gone, carrying as many of their treasures with them as they could. Ragnar decided that pursuing them wasn't an option; this was a populous land and it wouldn't be too long before more soldiers and militia arrived to attack them. They looted what was left behind, and that alone made the raid worthwhile, before ransacking the settlement.

They looked for freshly dug earth where the inhabitants had buried what valuables they couldn't take with them and Ragnar's men carried the chests and valuables they unearthed back to their ships. They were still busy doing this when one of the scouts rode in on a borrowed horse to say that a large body of men was approaching.

"How many?' Ragnar asked, puzzled by how quickly a new force had been mustered to oppose him.

'Difficult to say, lord. There are a few riders at the front but the rest are obscured by the dust they're kicking up; but there must be hundreds of them to raise that much.'

Olaf was about to give the order to fire the place but Ragnar stopped him.

'No, leave it be. That way they'll still be here when we return in a year or two's time and we can raid them again.'

As they sailed away a dozen horsemen watched them go. They congratulated themselves on their successful trick and untied the saplings they had dragged behind them to make the heathen raiders think that there were hundreds of them. Once they were satisfied that the enemy had really gone for good, they went to let everyone know that the coast was clear.

Ragnar looted two more places before he reached the mouth of the River Seine. He raided the two small settlements either side of where the wide estuary ran into the sea and was tempted to explore along the river itself, but it was late in the season now and so he turned for home.

He was well pleased with the outcome of the summer's raiding. Now he had enough wealth to recruit an army to take back his kingdom and exact revenge on those who had killed his parents.

Chapter Seven – Ragnar's Revenge

828 to 830

Thora looked up from where she was playing with her two sons, three year old Agnar and baby Eirik, as Ragnar walked into their bed chamber in the jarl's new hall on the island of Egholm in the narrowest part of the Limfjord. From there his men could easily control traffic along the seaway which linked the Germanic Ocean in the west to the Kattegat and the Baltic Sea in the east. The taxes he collected added to his wealth but, in truth, they paled into insignificance compared to the proceeds from his raiding.

Jarl Gutfred had died in 827, but by then most of his bondis already looked towards Ragnar as their leader. Unsuprisingly Ragnar's preying on the coasts of Frisia and Neustria had earned him the enmity of King Harald, allied as he was with the Emperor of the Franks, Louis the Pious.

However, Harald's unpopularity had increased, not only due to his association with Louis, but also because he had become a Christian. Horik, once King of Denmark before he was deposed by Louis and replaced by Harald Klack, had been reduced to being the Jarl of Fyn, the second biggest of the Danish islands in the Kattegat. A revolt against King Harald's rule had been simmering for some time and now the former monarch had approached him to join a plot to oust Harald.

'What will you do?' Thora asked climbing to her feet with difficulty; she was in the latter stages of pregnancy with their third child.

'I will go and meet Horik and the others to see what they plan. However, my priority remains to kill Froh and regain Agder, so I don't want to get involved in a prolonged internal struggle for the throne of Denmark.'

Thora sighed. She was quite content to remain the wife of one of the richest jarls in Denmark and had no desire to risk everything to become queen of a much more inhospitable land in Norway. However, Ragnar was not a man to be dissuaded from what he regarded as his destiny.

'I still say that our best approach is to row up the Schlei and attack Hedeby from the water,' Horik maintained. 'The landward side of the settlement is protected by a tall palisade on top of a steep earth embankment. There are no defences along the bank of the Schlei.'

The Schlei was the long, narrow fjord that led to Harald's capital at Hedeby.

'The problem is that there are two choke points along the Schlei which he could easily block once he had warning of our coming,' one of the other jarls pointed out.'

Of the thirty two jarls in Denmark, nineteen were present at the meeting called to plot Harald's overthrow. The other thirteen were either supporters of Harald or preferred to sit on the fence so that they could join the winning side. Many of those, and even some of those present, were worried that Louis was unlikely to sit idly by whilst his protégé was deposed.

However, Ragnar wasn't concerned about Louis and said so.

'He's got enough problems without bothering about Denmark,' he had said when the subject came up. 'His eldest son, Lothair, is disputing Louis' decision to make his youngest son, Charles, Duke of Swabia. I wouldn't be surprised if the dispute ended up as a war between Louis and Lothair. At any event, he's in no position to intervene in Denmark at the moment.'

Ragnar was well aware that, as the youngest jarl present by at least ten years, the others tended to disregard his views, however successful a raider he might have been over the past few years. However, he now took comfort from a few nods of grudging agreement and pressed on.

'You are all talking as if there are only two options, an attack by land or one from the fjord. There is a third: attack on land and along the Schlei. If we create a diversionary attack by laying siege on the landward side, we'll be able to row along the fjord without too much interference.'

'Even if they do put booms in place at the narrows we can land and lower them again. They won't be able to defend them in strength if they are being beseiged.'

Those who had been about to object fell silent as the unexpected support had come from Horik.

Ragnar went home elated by the adoption of his stratagem to depose Harald Klack. He also seemed to have made an ally of Horik, the next King of Denmark if all went well, and his head was full of plans to recover Agder. He couldn't wait to discuss them with Thora and Olaf. However, as his drekar approached the jetty at Egholm he had a premonition that all was not well.

His unease was reinforced when he remembered that Torstein, the godi, had sidled up to him at the feast the previous evening. He had whispered in his ear that the Norns were displeased with him and plotted to bring him low. Ragnar had dismissed it at the time, being too drunk to care much for the man's doom laden warning, but he recalled what he'd said now.

When he landed he found Olaf, who he'd left in charge in his absence, waiting for him on the jetty. His friend's face only confirmed that he was the bearer of ill-tidings.

'Ragnar, I'm sorry,' Olaf said when he'd walked with him a discreet distance away from the welcome being given to the crew by their families. 'There is no easy was to say this, the baby was born dead and Thora lost so much blood that she died the next day.'

Ragnar felt as if a horse had kicked him in the guts. He and Thora were both strong willed and they'd fought a lot, but he respected her and she had been there to guide and help him over the past few years. He wasn't sure that he'd loved her in the way the skálds portrayed it, but he would miss her advice, companionship and support.

He nodded his thanks and patted Olaf absently on his shoulder before walking away along the beach to be alone with his thoughts.

A worried Leofstan went to follow his master but Olaf grabbed him, by the arm.

'He needs to be alone with his thoughts and memories now, lad. He doesn't need comfort from the likes of you.'

Leofstan thought that was probably just what Ragnar needed right now but he didn't say anything. He glanced at Olaf and nodded but he was puzzled by the young man's expression. Leofstan had given Olaf no reason to dislike or distrust him, as far as he was aware, but the look the Norseman gave him was unmistakeably one of hostility.

-ꝟ-

In April 829 all was prepared and, whilst the majority of the jarls based on the Danish mainland marched south to Hedeby, Ragnar, Horik and the jarls from the other Danish islands sailed into the Schlei. Ragnar's task was to land his men on either side of the fjord near the choke points and secure them to allow the fleet safe passage.

He still missed Thora but he'd got over her loss faster that he thought he would. It had helped having the campaign to concentrate on. He had fostered their two sons out with one of his married bondi who had no children of his own. At first he visited them weekly, then monthly, but it had been nearly three months now since he had last seen Agnar and Eirik.

The first point where the waterway narrowed was located near a small settlement called Grödersby. The latter lay a little way inland from the peninsula which jutted out into the fjord, lessening the width of the fjord at that point to no more than two hundred and fifty yards. There was a lookout tower on the west bank, together with a large windlass powered by a horse who, at that moment, stood placidly eating grass. The animal was evidently used to raise and lower a cable to block the river, as required.

The rain had started as they entered the fjord and it was quite heavy by the time that Ragnar's drekar drew close to the shore below the wooden tower. He watched impotently as the lookout climbed down the ladder and made for the wood piled ready nearby. No doubt this was a warning beacon but the Norns, who weaved the fate of men, were with the rebels. The man tried frantically to light the fire but the kindling was too wet.

The shore was rocky so Ragnar pulled off his byrnie, goatskins and helmet before diving into the water. After a few powerful strokes he tried to stand and found to his relief that the water was only waist deep. He overcame the tendency to shiver and waded ashore armed with an axe and sword strapped to his back and gripping a dagger between his teeth.

The man was still trying frantically to get the sparks from his flint to set the shavings alight when he became aware of the young man heading towards him. He rapidly got to his feet and started to run away, but he wasn't quick enough. Ragnar's axe came down on the small of his back, severing his spinal cord and smashing his lower spine. The next blow stove in his head and Ragnar stood there for a moment, breathing hard whilst he recovered his breath.

He pulled his bloody axe free of the man's skull before using it to kill the horse which powered the windlass. Finally he severed the cable, although it took five blows to do so. Satisfied, he hung his axe on his back before swimming back to the ship, where he was pulled aboard to the cheers of his crew.

Dripping all over the deck, he grinned at them for a moment before barking out, 'well, what are you idle sods waiting for; start rowing and catch the others up or we'll miss all the fun.'

The next restricted channel ran for half a mile just before the entrance into the lake on which Hedeby stood. This was no more than seventy yards wide and was defended by a fortress on the west bank at the narrowest point. Once again there was a boom that could be raised to close off the channel but this one was made of heavy chain. There was a windlass similar to the last one, but larger. This one was powered by two horses because of the greater weight of the chain, despite its shorter length compared to last boom.

The archers on board killed the horses as they plodded around the windlass, raising the chain, and the boom came to an abrupt halt. Then they kept the defenders' heads down whilst the longships rowed over the half-raised chain.

'Stupid buggers should have put a defensive breastworks up to protect the horses,' Olaf muttered as they entered the large lake beyond the narrows.

'Their purpose is to collect taxes, not defend Hedeby,' Ragnar pointed out. 'Knarrs pull into the wharf, have their cargoes inspected and pay their dues. Then the boom is lowered and they sail on to Hedeby. I doubt that anyone thought that it would be attacked by a Danish fleet. Not until today, at any rate.'

The rain continued to lash down as they hoisted their sails to give the rowers some respite and they made their way across the lake to the southern offshoot known as the Hedeby Nor. Hedeby itself lay on the south western shore of this lake and, as the longships entered it, they could just make out the encampment of the besiegers through the falling rain. They headed for the various jetties jutting out from the quayside and, thanks to the poor visibility through the driving rain, were a mere hundred yards away before the alarm was raised.

By the time that they had come alongside and the warriors had disembarked, leaving the ships' boys to moor the ships to the jetties, Harald's own warriors had started to form a shield wall. However, it was obvious that they were outnumbered and a tall man with arms like tree trunks stepped forward and halted halfway between the two forces.

'There is no point in fighting,' he said calmly. 'Harald Klak slipped away in a small knarr as soon as he heard the alarm.'

He pointed to the small ship which was now halfway across the fjord and heading for the other bank.

Horik cursed. It was pointless chasing him. No doubt he would have horses waiting to make good his escape.

'They'll have crossed onto the emperor's territory before you could catch him,' the big man said with a grin.

'Wipe that smile off your face or I'll do it for you,' Horik snapped, frustrated that his enemy had eluded him.

He took a deep breath to calm himself before asking 'do you surrender then?'

'And acknowledge you as our king, Horik?'

The other man nodded but didn't say anything further.

'Very well, yes but on one condition. Some of us are Christians now and we have a church and priests here. Will you promise them your protection and allow those of us who wish to practice our religion freely?'

'Allow you to sully the name of Odin and the gods of our fathers? No. All I'll do is to permit the followers of the White Christ and their lily livered priests to depart Denmark. Any still here after dawn tomorrow will be killed.'

The leader of the inhabitants of Hedeby sighed and his shoulders drooped.

'Very well, I suppose I should have expected no better from a godless pagan like you, Horik. We'll leave tonight but our God is the true God and he will prevail in the end.'

Ragnar watched those who had gathered to oppose them disperse with mixed feelings. He was glad he wasn't about to lose any of his men in a fight where the outcome was obvious, but he itched to kill the followers of the man who had brought the hated new religion to Hedeby.

That night Horik was formally installed as king and his godi sacrificed a prize bull to Odin and the gods in gratitude for their easy victory. Ragnar got as drunk as the rest of them, but in the morning he went for a swim in the sea to clear his head and to think about recovering his birth right.

'Why attack Alfheim first? Won't that just give Froh warning that you are coming for him?' Olaf asked Ragnar as they sat together drinking back in the latter's hall at Egholm.

Ragnar had built a much bigger longhouse than the one back at Fladstrand. He could now afford to keep a total of eighty hirdmen, over half of whom were bachelors who lived in his hall instead of in a separate warriors' hall. It was long and relatively narrow with ten alcoves each side, each furnished with tables and benches. These served as places to eat and drink and, when pushed back against the wall, sleeping platforms.

There were two long fire pits in the centre space which kept the hall warm in winter. They also served as the place where the cooking was done. As the two friends spoke together two young boys were roasting a cow and a stag respectively on two spits above the fire for the evening meal. The boys' bodies and faces were bright red and they were sweating profusely from the heat. Their only solace was to count the time until they would be relieved by other young thralls.

As Leofstan refilled Ragnar's drinking horn with ale the latter glanced up and the two exchanged a smile. It didn't seem that long ago since he'd used any thrall as his body servant. Now Leofstan not only looked after him much better than anyone else ever had, but he also supervised the young thralls and ensured that they did their jobs properly. Effectively he was a combination of body servant and steward.

All of Ragnar's thralls were young Swedes and Frisians that he had captured during various raids in recent years. Girls as well as boys served him and his hirdmen and two of the former took it in turns to keep him company in bed these days. After Thora's death he was in no hurry to marry again. However, Leoftstan jealously guarded his privileged position as Ragnar's body servant and beat any girl who thought that her place in Ragnar's bed gave her a right to challenge his position.

At the end of the longhouse there was a spacious bedchamber shut off from the noise of sixty men and thralls sleeping, snoring and farting in the main hall by a stout wooden partition. He gestured for Olaf to follow him into this chamber. It was chilly in there compared to the main hall as the brazier had not yet been lit, but they could talk in private.

'If I launch an assault on Agder first, I give Froh's brother, Kjarten, time to raise an army to oppose me and perhaps re-capture Agder. Destroy him first and hopefully the Norse jarls will desert Froh and side with me.'

'It's been nearly seven years since Froh killed your parents, the jarls and the bondis may decide they owe him their allegiance now.'

Ragnar scowled. 'Are you trying to help me or dissuade me from killing Froh?'

'I'm just worried that we'll lose a lot of men in a fruitless attack on Alfheim, which has nothing to do with us, and that will prevent us from a successful campaign against Froh himself.'

'So you think I should kill Froh and take back Agder and then hope I can defeat the inevitable counter-attack by Kjarten?'

'Is it inevitable? Kjarten seems content with his kingdom; why should he risk it by an attack on Agder?'

'To avenge his brother and take back what he'll see as his family's land. Don't forget he has two sons whilst Froh has only had daughters. One of Kjarten's brood will see Agder as his inheritance.'

Olaf had to agree that Ragnar had a point, though he couldn't shake the suspicion that his friend had ambitions to rule rather more than his father's old kingdom.

It took Ragnar another year of ship building and recruiting men before he was ready for the invasion of Alfheim. He had raided Frisia again in the summer of 829 but the Frisians had learned their lesson and had fled with their valuables before the Vikings could land. He vowed that next time he went raiding along that coast he would try Frankia instead.

He had sunk all the silver and gold he had accumulated into the campaign and he was reliant on gaining significant plunder from Alfheim to meet some of his obligations to both his ship builders and his warriors. Nevertheless, he was confident and buoyant as he set out with his fleet of four drekars, six snekkjur and three knarrs to attack his enemy. In total he had over six hundred warriors as well as several dozen sailors and ships' boys. Only half of the former were his hirdmen and bondis; the rest were adventurers and mercenaries.

He might have sufficient ships but he didn't have enough experienced ship captains or steersmen. Many of his warriors had served as ship's boys and knew something about seamanship but too few had the necessary skill or had the right temperament to take charge of a ship.

Leofstan had stopped being a ship's boy when he reached sixteen, the age at which Vikings became warriors. Since then he had helmed Ragnar's own drekar.

'I'm going to make Leofstan captain of one of the new drekars,' he told Olaf one day, 'and I'd like you to take over another.'

If he'd expected Olaf to be pleased he was mistaken.

'So you put me, your oldest friend, on the same level as someone who is little more than a thrall, a Northumbrian to boot.'

Ragnar had anticipated that Olaf might prefer to stay with Ragnar on the latter's drekar but he hadn't expected him to be jealous of Leofstan.

'I'm making a gift of the drekar to you,' he said stiffly. 'You might at least thank me.'

'You expect me to be grateful? Well, I'm not.'

With that he stormed off leaving a puzzled Ragnar standing open mouthed. At first the jarl wondered how he could make amends but, as time passed, he began to find Olaf's attitude unacceptable. He didn't repeat the offer and he found someone else to captain the new longship. He hid his resentment well but the rift between the two old friends took a long time to heal.

Leofstan, on the other hand, was delighted at his promotion, but he insisted on finding a suitable replacement as Ragnar's body servant before he took over his ship. His choice fell on a young Swedish thrall called Lodvik. If Ragnar was surprised by this, when he could have perfectly well found his own servant, he said nothing. It was an indication of Leofstan's personal loyalty to him that he'd taken so much care to find the right boy to replace him.

The coast near the King of Alfheim's hall was pockmarked by small inlets and fjords bounded by low hills covered in pine trees. Ragnar had landed in a deserted cove a few miles south of Bohus, where the hall was located. Leaving his small army to make camp he took Olaf and two of his best warriors called Lars and Bjarke with him and set off to reconnoitre Bohus.

They made their way through the densely packed trees heading parallel to the coast. At that time of the year tiny biting insects swarmed in the shade of the trees and the four men cursed and swore at them, slapping at bare bits of skin and they hurried to reach the fjord they were looking for.

Ragnar had learned that the hall itself stood on a rocky promontory at the end of the southern branch of one of the longer fjords. Two hours later they crested a hill and stood at the edge of the trees looking at a hall standing a hundred feet above the surrounding settlement. Compared to the main settlement in Agder this place was small and insignificant and Ragnar could see why Froh had deserted it for Arendal. However, the hall – although undefended by a palisade – looked impregnable to assault.

On two sides cliffs dropped sheer to the water. The hall was located twenty yards back from the edge but they couldn't see the other two sides. They cautiously worked their way around the settlement until they could see the two landward sides. They were also protected by cliffs with a narrow path winding its way up one of them. This appeared to be the only access and it was scarcely wide enough for a man on a horse or two people on foot walking abreast to traverse it.

There was a strange apparatus hanging over the water which puzzled Ragnar until Lars suggested that it might be for lowering a barrel to collect fresh water.

'Won't it be saline?' Olaf asked but Lars shook his head.

'Not this far from the sea. That stream over there is bringing fresh water into the fjord all the time.'

Ragnar narrowed his eyes, lost in thought for a moment, before deciding that they'd seen enough.

-ᛉ-

They had come out of the trees at dawn. The few hundred men in the settlement of Bohus had been caught unawares and, disorganised as they were, proved no match for Ragnar's warriors. It was a massacre; a few people escaped but the majority of the men were killed and the women and children captured.

To everyone's surprise Ragnar let the old women go.

'Won't they spread the word about our invasion?' Olaf asked.

'That's the idea,' the enigmatic Ragnar replied with a grin.

However, that still left Kjarten and his hirdmen bottled up in his hall. Ragnar had no intention of wasting his men's lives trying to assault the place up such a narrow path and sat down to besiege it instead. The first time that the Swedes tried to lower their barrel to collect water they found a longship waiting underneath. The crew grabbed the barrel and cut through the rope it was suspended from. The same thing would happen every time they lowered a barrel – assuming they had spare barrels.

It was evident that Kjarten hadn't taken the simple precaution of storing some water on top of the plateau and, after three days, he asked to negotiate. Ragnar decided to let him stew a little, but that was a mistake. The weather for the past week had been fine but, by the time that he had agreed to meet Kjarten half way up the path that led to the top of the plateau, dark clouds had begun to gather. Ragnar waited at the bottom of the path but Kjarten didn't appear. When the first fat drops of rain hit his face he knew that he'd left it too long. That night several inches of rain fell and Ragnar realised that, unless he was a complete idiot, Kjarten would have gathered enough rainwater to last for days, if not weeks.

His men started to worry. The longer they remained at Bohus the more chance there was of a relief force from the rest of Alfheim trapping them there. It was even possible that Froh had now heard of his brother's predicament and was on his way as well. Morale in Ragnar's camp deteriorated rapidly, but Ragnar himself didn't seem at all concerned.

-ᛘ-

Øfden cast his net again as another fishing boat rowed past them heading from Arendal into the Skagerrak.

'You won't catch much there, my friend. You want to head further out,' a man in the other boat called across the water.

Øfden waved his thanks and he, his brother and their two sons started to pull in their net. They made a pretence at moving but as soon as the other boat was out of sight, they cast their net into the water near their original spot at the entrance to the fjord. From there they could see up it to the jetties of Arendal. It was the second day they had fished in these waters and Øfden was becoming concerned that someone would soon get suspicious.

As the afternoon drew to a close they were about to haul in their nets for the day and head for one of the small coves to camp for the night when three longships rounded the point to the west of them.

'Jarl Dagfinnr,' Øfden said quietly to the others, though the ships were too far away to hear him even if he'd shouted.

'Dagfinnr? Who's he?' one of the boys asked.

'He's the Jarl of Rørvik on the island of Vikna, though he controls much of the west coast of Agder. The symbol of a serpent on his sails is his. Presumably Froh has now got wind of Jarl Ragnar's attack on Bohus and is mustering his men. I wonder why Dagfinnr has only brought three drekar though.'

'Perhaps he's an unwilling adherent of Froh's and has brought as few as he thought he could get away with,' Øfden's brother suggested.

'In which case I wonder whether it's worth taking a gamble?'

'Do you know Dagfinnr? Is he likely to side with Ragnar against Froh?'

'I don't know. He used to be a close friend of Ragnar's father, so I can't imagine that he would have given his allegiance to Froh unless he had no other option.'

In the event the decision was taken out of Øfden's hands. The leading drekar passed quite close to the fishermen and Dagfinnr's steersman glanced their way and then suddenly stiffened. He pushed the steering oar away from him so that the longship came up into the wind and glided to a stop.

'What are you doing man? Are you mad?'

A Norsemen with a grey beard and dressed in a fine tunic strode aft to confront the steersman, but the latter was busy studying the crew of the fishing boat.

'Øfden, if that you? And your brother? I thought that you were both lost with Thorkel.'

'Thorkel wasn't lost at sea. He was killed by Froh's hirdmen. We escaped in his drekar to Denmark.'

'Who do you serve now then?

'Jarl Ragnar, King Sigvard's son.'

'What's going on?' Dagfinnr demanded when he reached the steersman, his eyes swivelling between him and the crew in the small boat.

'Jarl, I'm Øfden. I used to be one of Thorkel's crew. May I come aboard and speak to you privately?'

-ᛉ-

Half an hour after Øfden's fishing boat had sailed into Bohus, Ragnar gave the order to fire the settlement and get the longships under way. However, instead of sailing out to sea, they turned at the junction of the two branches of the fjord, lowered their sails and the crews started to row up the left hand branch.

The steersman put the oar over and the sail came swiftly down to be lashed to the yardarm on deck. After that it was swung through ninety degrees so that it could be secured fore and aft. At the same time the men unblocked the holes in the hull and pushed their oars through them so that they could start to row at the same time as the sail was being secured. It required skill and coordination if the ship's momentum was to be maintained, but Vikings had to be accomplished sailors as well as warriors.

Once out of sight of the junction between the two branches of the fjord the longships dropped their stone anchors and waited. Meanwhile Øfden and his crew started to fish in the shallows just south-west of the point where the two branches of the fjord met. From there they could see the fjord's outlet into the Skagerrak as well as Ragnar's fleet at anchor.

Whilst they waited the wind dropped and veered until it was blowing up the fjord. As soon as Froh's fleet hove into view Øfden's boat scuttled off to the western shore of the fjord; a not unnatural reaction to the sight of twenty longships heading towards them.

'By Odin's beard,' Olaf muttered to Ragnar when he saw the size of the enemy fleet. 'We don't stand a chance against that lot!'

'Have faith my friend. All is not as it seems,' he replied. 'At least, I bloody well hope that's the case,' he added quietly under his breath.

After the last of the enemy fleet had disappeared towards the smouldering ruins of what had been Bohus, Ragnar gave the order to hoist in the stone anchors and his crews started to row their ships back to the junction. Once there, they turned into the other branch of the fjord and the ships boys, helped this time by some of the warriors, hauled on the halyards to raise the mainsails as quickly as possible.

In such a light wind they were barely making two knots through the water, so Ragnar gave the order for the rowers to help propel his drekar and the rest of his captains did the same. Up ahead Froh, still oblivious to Ragnar's presence, also gave the order to start rowing. However, only the longships manned by his hirdmen and those of two of his jarls followed his example. The rest continued under sail only.

Then Olaf noticed something strange. The eleven longships nearest to them seemed to have dropped a sea anchor – a sort of sock with a wide mouth and a small heel - over the stern to slow them even further. It was obvious that Ragnar's fleet would soon catch them up. Standing beside Olaf at the prow of his drekar, Ragnar gave a sigh of relief and smiled at his friend.

'Now we shall have some fun. Twenty one longships against nine seems good odds to me,' he said with a broad grin.

'You knew that half of Froh's fleet would desert him and join you?' Olaf asked in amazement. 'Why didn't you tell me?'

'Two reasons; firstly I wasn't sure that Øfden had actually been able to persuade any of the jarls to join me and, secondly, you have a loose tongue when you are drunk, which is most nights. In the event Øfden talked to Jarl Dagfinnr but he needn't have bothered. It seems that they were already involved in a conspiracy with the jarls in northern Adger.'

As Ragnar caught up with Dagfinnr and his fellow jarls they pulled in the sea anchors and unshipped their oars. Now Ragnar led a fleet of twelve drekar and nine snekkjur against Froh's five drekar and four snekkjur. It wasn't long before someone in the latter's fleet spotted that there were ten more longships to their rear. The raven emblazoned on the red sails of ten of the following ships left little doubt as to whom they belonged.

Froh's leading drekar was now nearing Bohus. His brother and his hirdmen, waiting on the waterfront to greet their saviours, watched in bewilderment as Froh's ships now turned to face back the way they'd come. As the two fleets closed on one another Ragnar gave the order to lower sails. They would only be a liability in a sea battle. Two of his warriors sheathed their swords and picked up a grappling iron each and prepared to hook an enemy ship as they came alongside it. Ragnar's crew shipped their oars at the last minute, without bothering to block up the holes, and grabbed spears, axes, swords and shields ready to board the enemy vessel.

It was Froh's ship that they came alongside, but his men weren't quite so quick to unship their oars. Five were smashed by the impact and their rowers suffered broken arms and smashed ribs in consequence. Ragnar was the first over the side and he landed on the other ship's deck with Olaf and two of his hirdmen right behind him. He faced a ring of Swedes, who thrust spears and swords at him, and for a moment he was hard pressed to counter their attack with his shield and sword.

He felt several blows and a spear point strike his body but his goatskin jerkin and his chain mail byrnie protected him and he suffered nothing worse than some severe bruising, though the chainmail would doubtless need repair work later. He managed to chop off the hand of one assailant at the wrist just as a spear point slid off the fixed steel visor protecting his upper face and slashed open his exposed cheek. He was so full of adrenaline that he didn't even feel the wound and he proceeded to hack halfway through the spearman's neck.

As more and more of his crew piled in to the fight, the Swedes were forced back a few inches at a time until there was nowhere for them to go. The drekar belonging to Leofstan had latched onto the far side of the hull and its crew now attacked Froh's men from the rear.

At one point Olaf saw Leofstan fighting nearby with his back to him. All his old resentment at the bond between Ragnar and his former servant came flooding back and for a moment he was tempted to stab him in the back, then he saw a Swede about to strike Leofstan down from the side and Olaf stepped in to save him. Olaf couldn't have said why he'd protected the other man but he felt better for what he'd done afterwards. He still didn't like Leofstan, but from that moment on he was no longer jealous of the friendship between Ragnar and the former Northumbrian fisher boy.

The Swedes fought bravely but they were outnumbered and gradually Ragnar's men slaughtered them until the last dozen, including a wounded Froh, were forced back to the small aft deck.

'Surrender, Froh, and I will spare the lives of your men,' Ragnar called up to him.

'What happens to us if I do?'

'You will hang for the murder of my parents and your men will become thralls, what else do you expect?' Ragnar shrugged.

'We'd rather die,' one of the other Swedes spat at him.

'So be it.'

Ragnar had no intention of wasting his men's lives and it would be difficult to fight one's way up onto the small aft deck where the steersman normally stood. Instead his archers came forward. The Swedes had been taken unawares and didn't have time to put on mail byrnies or leather armour. Despite their shields, it didn't take long to wound or kill most of the remaining men with a few volleys of arrows.

Ragnar led the assault on the aft deck, running along the narrow gunwale and leaping down onto the deck. He slew the man who tried to protect Froh and then, at last, he was facing the man who'd killed his parents. Froh had an arrow protruding from his shoulder and another in his thigh, but he still stood tall and proud. Ragnar feinted towards his other leg and Froh dropped his shield down to protect it.

It was the move that Ragnar had anticipated and, instead of bringing his sword up as Froh had expected, he threw his weight behind his shield, smashing the boss into Froh's nose. The nasal on the king's helmet did nothing to protect it and it was squashed to a red pulp. The blow brought intense and crippling pain in its wake and for a moment Froh was unable to see. Ragnar brought his sword around as hard as he could and the sharp blade cut through the flesh, bones and sinews of Froh's neck. The head few sideways and over the gunwale to land in the sea a few feet from the longship.

With a roar of rage Froh's surviving hirdman, in spite of his wounds, brought his sword down hard onto Ragnar's helmet, using such force that it snapped the blade in half. The metal of the helmet had absorbed much of the impact before it split into two halves, but the jagged remains of the sword cut through the leather cap below and struck Ragnar's skull with enough force to kill most men.

PART TWO – EDMUND OF BEBBANBURG

THE WOLF

Chapter Eight – The Humbling of Eanred

830 to 832

Six year old Edmund was playing with his elder brother, Ilfrid, when the messenger arrived. Full of curiosity, the two boys rushed into their father's hall to find out what had happened, but were disappointed when the man handed their father, Eafa, Ealdorman of Bebbanburg, a letter and retired without saying anything.

'What's happened, mother?' Ilfrid asked Breguswid quietly as soon as their father left the hall.

'The king is dead and your father is summoned to a meeting of the Witan at Eoforwīc in three weeks' time.'

'King Eardwulf is dead? Who will succeed him? His son?'

'Probably, but that is for the Witan to decide.'

King Eardwulf had been an old man, so his death wasn't unexpected. However, after nearly a century of turmoil, regicide and civil war over the throne, his reign of thirty four years, albeit with a break of a couple of years when he'd been deposed in 806, had brought stability and prosperity to Northumbria. Eardwulf's son, Eanred, had been his father's hereræswa for the last decade or so, ever since he reached the age of twenty. However, thanks to his father's skill at maintaining peace with the Picts in the north and the Mercians in the south, his military prowess had never been put to the test.

Things were changing, however. The long running battle for power in the south of England had been won by Egbert of Wessex in 829 and Wiglaf of Mercia had fled into exile, albeit briefly. He had returned in early 830 and had been restored to his throne after acknowledging Egbert as Bretwalda. Only Northumbria stood against Egbert's mastery over all of England.

At least the new king wouldn't have to worry too much about his northern border. The Pictish kingdom had internal problems and both its king, Angus, and Domnall of Dalriada were pre-occupied with the encroachment of the Norse who had settled in Orkneyjar sometime previously. Now they had expanded south, capturing Skye and the northern Hebridean islands. At least King Riderch of Strathclyde had no such problems and he seemed content to rule his kingdom without interfering with his neighbours.

Edmund was too young to understand much of this. All he knew was that his father was going on a long journey and he was taking Ilfrid with him whilst he had to stay at home with his mother. Like most children, he was impatient to grow up and had bitterly resented it when he was told that he was too young to go.

Ilfrid had little patience with Edmund's tantrums. He was thrilled to be going with his father, though his excitement was somewhat tempered by the knowledge that, once they returned, he would be leaving for Lindisfarne to be schooled by the monks in reading, writing, Latin and Christianity. He would stay there for over three years before being sent to train as a warrior at the hall of another noble, perhaps even that of the king himself. Edmund didn't know that his playmate and idol was about to leave Bebbanburg for some years. Had he done so he would have been even more upset.

As they rode through the main gates of Bebbanburg Ilfrid rode beside his father. The warrior riding behind them carried Eafa's banner of a black wolf's head on a yellow field. Although, once they were out of sight of the fortress and the large settlement that had grown up in its shadow, it was furled and placed in one of the wagons until they approached Eoforwīc, when once again it would proudly proclaim the presence of the lord of Bebbanburg and Ealdorman of Islandshire. Eafa's domain stretched from the River Tyne in the south to the Twaid in the north. Beyond Berwic on the Twaid lay the province of Lothian, which was divided into three shires. Until a few years ago Lothian had been dominated by the Ealdorman of Dùn Barra and Dùn Èideann on the coast of the Firth of Forth, but the current lord was Kendric, a seventeen year old boy who was far from a powerful character. He and the other nobles of Lothian now looked to Eafa as their leader.

At the Tyne they met up with Kendric and the other ealdormen of Lothian whilst waiting for the ferry to laboriously carry them over the river, four at a time. Each lord had brought between eight and a dozen men with him as escort and it took hours for them all to be ferried across. By the time that the last few horsemen were on the south bank it was getting late and they decided to seek shelter at Jarrow Monastery for the night.

The guest accommodation could only house the four ealdormen and Ilfrid and so their men settled down for an uncomfortable night in the open. Ilfrid felt sorry for them when it started to rain heavily, but then the sentiment changed to smugness. He was in the dry whilst they would be wet and miserable, even inside their leather and greased wool tents. The storm raged all night but in the morning the day dawned bright and clear.

Unfortunately for Ilfrid the weather didn't stay fine and by the time they reached that night's stop at Durham Monastery, he was wet, cold and the inside of his thighs had been rubbed raw by his wet saddle. He didn't feel quite so smug now.

The infirmarian gave one of the Bebbanburg slaves some unguent to ease the soreness and two bandages to wind around Ilfrid's thighs to protect them from further chafing. As the slave gently rubbed the unguent into his raw skin Ilfrid felt an immediate respite from the pain he'd been suffering. When the slave had finished wrapping the bandages around his thighs, he became curious about him. He'd seen him around Bebbanburg but had never had contact with him before.

'Thank you. I'm very grateful for your thoughtfulness. How did you know I was suffering?'

'From the funny way you were walking when you got off your pony. Others sniggered, knowing what you were going through on your first long ride but I decided I should help you.'

Ilfrid looked at the slave thoughtfully. He guessed him to be about fifteen and, from his accent, Welsh or Cumbrian.

'What's your name?'

'Laughlin, it means servant in Gaelic.'

'You're not Welsh then?'

'No, master, Irish. I was one of nine children and my father was a poor shepherd who couldn't afford to feed all of us, so he sold me and two of my sisters as slaves when we were younger than you.'

Laughlin's plight left Ilfrid unmoved. It was a common story. However, he was impressed at the boy's initiative in seeking out the infirmarian and the way he had taken care of him. That evening he approached his father as soon as Eafa was alone.

'Father, am I too young to have a body servant of my own?'

Eafa was startled; it was a peculiar question coming from a ten year old.

'Yes, of course you are. Your mother's slaves look after you and Edmund at the moment and you'll be leaving for Lindisfarne as soon as we return. Why would you need a servant?'

'Well, there is no-one to look after me until then is there?'

'No, I suppose not.' He looked thoughtful for a moment. 'Do you want to share Erik with me?'

His son shook his head.

'No, Erik has enough to do looking after you.'

Ilfrid blushed; that hadn't come out quite the way he intended it to.

'What I mean is, that wouldn't be fair on him. What about Laughlin?'

'The Irish lad? He's a stable boy who drives one of the wagons.'

'I don't need him on the march, just when we camp. Others can look after his horses surely?'

'Why him?'

Ilfrid blushed again.

'I'm, er, a bit, um, sore. From riding. He got something from the monks to ease the pain.'

Eafa was somewhat surprised, but he supposed that Laughlin had some experience of lotions and poultices from looking after horses.

'You don't need him for that now do you? Presumably he obtained enough to last you for a few more days? In any case, you need to get used to riding all day, day after day.'

'Later, perhaps, father. But I won't be doing much riding on Lindisfarne. There's little point in getting thighs like leather now, is there? Besides, my clothes will need washing and drying and he can help me look after my pony. I'm sure she's developing a bit of a limp.'

Eafa laughed. 'Very well. I'll tell the head carter.'

Ilfrid discovered that Laughlin was more than a washer of clothes and the applier of healing lotions. He was a good hunter with his slingshot and a good cook. Instead of suffering the stew of dried beef - which still tasted like leather even after being boiled for an hour – and whatever vegetables the servants could find or buy, Ilfrid and Laughlin dined on small game basted on a makeshift spit over a fire, apples, cheese and a variety of berries. Laughlin obviously harvested the wild berries locally, but Ilfrid refrained from asking where the cheese and apples came from.

Eoforwīc came as something of a shock to Ilfrid, but not to Laughlin, who'd been sold in the slave market in Duibhlinn. It was far bigger than Ilfrid had imagined, sprawling outside the confines of the Roman walls, which were now in a serious state of disrepair. Once inside the city proper, the stench was overwhelming. The fortress at Bebbanburg wasn't immaculately clean, but most of the rubbish was put into the chute which dumped it into the sea. The wind kept the place smelling sweet too.

Here and there were all manner of detritus, dead rats, cats, and even dogs, littering the streets. Faeces lay everywhere and there was a distinct stench of urine. When they got to the Shambles – where the butchers plied their trade – the prevalent smell changed to the coppery tang of blood. Discarded bones and bits of intestine which couldn't be used lay everywhere, being gnawed by rats, picked at by carrion birds and sucked at by a swarm of flies.

Ilfrid wasn't the only one who was glad when they entered the comparatively clean precincts around the king's hall. Of course, there wasn't space for eighteen ealdormen and their retinues in the king's hall. The nobles and the few sons that they'd brought with them were housed there, in the monastery or in the Ealdorman of Eoforwīc's hall, but the others had to camp wherever they could find space outside the city.

Eafa and his son were lodged in the guest dormitory of the monastery. Gradually the original timber buildings were being replaced in stone, but their lodgings were a simple wooden hall with sleeping benches down both sides and a hearth for cooking in the middle of the building. Ilfrid was pleased to see that there was another boy there already, Rædwulf, the twelve year old son of the Ealdorman of Cumbria.

'Who are you?' Rædwulf asked brusquely as Ilfrid went up to him to introduce himself.

Ilfrid's eyes narrowed. He had thought that it would be nice to have another boy to talk to amongst all the adults, but Rædwulf's brusque question made him wary.

'Ilfrid of Bebbanburg. You?'

The other boy sighed. 'Rædwulf of Cumbria, not that there is much of the shire over which my father still rules.'

'Why? What's happened?'

'You haven't heard? The bloody Strathclyde Britons have invaded from the north and captured our home – Caer Luel. To make matters worse, the Norse started to raid along our coast and now they are beginning to settle there.'

'Couldn't you push them back into the sea?'

'No, my father is too busy trying to stop the Britons from encroaching further into his lands.'

'Surely the old king would have helped?'

'Huh! All Eardwulf did was to suggest that my father made peace with Strathclyde and with each of the various jarls of the Norsemen. He was too afraid to risk war. Let's hope that his son is made of sterner stuff.'

'You're certain that Eanred will be the next king?'

'Who else is there? Oh, there are plenty who claim to be descended from one of the many kings who have ruled Northumbria over the last century, but they would be at each other's throats if any of them were elected. The ealdormen are well aware of this and know that the only way that Northumbria will remain united is if they elect Eardwulf's only son.'

Ilfrid was impressed by Rædwulf's grasp of the situation and wondered, with some bitterness, why his own father hadn't told him all of this. He supposed that he thought that, at ten, he was too young to grasp the situation, but he had understood everything that the other boy had said to him.

'Why didn't you tell me about Cumbria, father?' he asked later that evening when he got Eafa alone.

'Cumbria? What do you mean?'

'I'm talking about the capture of Caer Luel by the Britons from Strathclyde and the Norse settlements along the coast. It's part of Northumbria; why aren't we helping to expel the pagans and push the Britons back where they came from?'

'Who've you been talking to?'

'Does it matter? Do you think that I'm still a baby to be shielded from bad tidings? Why did I have to find out from someone else?'

'Because it's got nothing to do with you, or me come to that. Eardwulf thought that the loss of Cumbria was a small price to pay for peace in the rest of his kingdom.'

'And do you think he was right?'

Eafa was beginning to realise that his son was growing up, and probably had a maturity well ahead of his years.

'No, I don't. If you appear weak, others stronger than you will prey on you.'

He paused and regarded his son thoughtfully.

'I brought you with me because I felt that we were growing apart. I wasn't going to take you to the Witan tomorrow because I thought that you were too young. I was wrong. Would you like to come?'

Ilfrid's eyes sparkled with interest and excitement.

'Yes please, father. Thank you.'

'Don't thank me. It'll be pretty boring. I expect we'll elect Eanred, swear loyalty to him and he'll appoint a new ealdorman to replace him in his shire, and then we'll all go and get drunk – not you, of course.'

As it turned out, Eafa was quite wrong.

Several ealdormen and a number of senior churchmen were already present in the king's hall when Eafa and Ilfrid entered, shaking the rain off their cloaks. The grey, dank weather matched the sombre mood in the hall. Ilfrid saw Rædwulf standing next to a tall, rather gaunt man with grey hair and a livid scar on his cheek, presumably Rædwulf's father. Unusually in these days when men grew long moustaches as soon as they were old enough, he was unshaven like the clerics.

Ilfrid nodded at the other boy and smiled but Rædwulf ignored him. Ilfrid felt his face flush with embarrassment and annoyance. Eafa had noticed and was puzzled by the boy's aloofness; he'd assumed that the Cumbrian boy was the source of his son's new found knowledge so his failure to greet his son seemed odd.

There was another boy in the hall – one that neither Eafa nor Ilfrid had seen before. He looked to be about fourteen and was standing beside Wulfsige, Archbishop of Eoforwīc, who was talking to the Bishop of Hexham. At that moment Kendric and the other two Lothian ealdormen joined Eafa and Ilfrid took the opportunity to slip away to approach Rædwulf.

'Are you ignoring me?' he asked the other boy bluntly.

'What? No, that is I've got a lot on my mind at the moment. Sorry.'

'Oh, you mean about the Britons and the Norse?'

'No, well yes, but I'm more concerned about Ælle and his brother Osberht.'

'Who? I've never heard of them.'

'Well, you will shortly,' the other boy replied curtly. 'That's Ælle over there talking to the two bishops. He's an ætheling, or so he claims. So is his brother, the older boy who's just entered the hall.'

Ilfrid turned and glimpsed a boy about Rædwulf's age enter the hall just before he disappeared behind a group of nobles. He re-appeared again as he joined Ælle.

'How is it that they are æthelings? I thought that Eanred was the only contender for the throne.'

Rædwulf snorted. 'They're not. At least no more than I am. They can trace their descent back to Ida, but only through the female line, just as my father and I and lots of other nobles can.'

'Including me. In fact one of my family was the king at one stage.'

'Who?'

'Eadwulf. It was a long time ago.'

'It must have been. I've never heard of him.'

'Ask your father. Anyway, forget about him; why are you troubled about Osbehrt and Ælle?'

'Let's just say that I don't like them and they don't like me.'

'And you're afraid that the Witan might acknowledge their claim to the throne?'

'Yes, not now obviously - they're too young – but their uncle, the Ealdorman of Luncæstershire, supports them, as do a few of the other nobles. Eanred isn't married and, if anything should happen to him in a few years' time, they could be elected if they can establish their claim now.'

'So that's why they are talking to the bishops and abbots?'

The two brothers had moved on from Wulfsige and were now talking to the abbots of Melrose and Ripon.

'Isn't Bishop Heathwred of Lindisfarne here?' Rædwulf asked suddenly.

'No, or he would have travelled down with us. He's seriously ill and likely to die soon. I expect that the Prior, Egfrid, will be chosen to succeed him. I hope so anyway, as I'm to be educated at the monastery as soon as we return and I rather like him.'

At that moment the archbishop, who was presiding over the meeting of the Witan, banged his crosier on the wooden floor and asked everyone to take their seats.

'Well, that was a surprise,' Eafa said to his son after the Witan was over.

'You mean the fact that Ælle and Osbehrt were accepted as æthelings?'

'Yes, that and Rædwulf standing up to oppose them, claiming that he and his father had more right to be regarded as æthelings. He was out of order and his father was right to tell him to shut up and sit down.'

'But wasn't he correct? I mean he belongs to a senior branch of Ida's descendants.'

'Perhaps, but that's not the point. His father doesn't want to be considered for the throne and I don't blame him. We have an even better claim to be æthelings, after all one of our ancestors was king, but I wouldn't accept the crown even if it was offered to me.'

'Why not? I would.'

'Are you sure you would want to be king? Eardwulf died of old age but many of his predecessors were assassinated, deposed and dispossessed of their lands or forced to become monks. Few ruled for very long. In any case it's a thankless task. Keeping your nobles happy and your borders safe isn't easy. '

'Well, Eardwulf didn't keep Cumbria's borders safe did he?'

'No, and I suppose that will be Eanred's first challenge now he has been elected king.'

'Are we staying for the crowing ceremony tomorrow?'

'Of course; it would look very odd if we didn't, especially as Eanred has named me as his hereræswa, a role I neither expected nor particularly wanted.'

'Why not? It's one of the most senior appointments the king can make? You're one of his inner council now.'

'Which means that I'll have to be wherever the king is, instead of being with my family at Bebbanburg.'

'Oh! I hadn't thought of that.'

'At least he's allowed me to travel back home so I can see you safely to Lindisfarne. I've already told Garr that he will have to look after Bebbanburg whilst I'm away.'

'Garr?' Ilfrid said looking over towards the captain of his father's warband. 'Won't mother take charge in your absence?'

'She'll becoming with me to Eoforwīc, as will Edmund.'

'Oh! Of course.'

Ilfrid suddenly felt that his whole world was changing. He hadn't minded the thought of moving to Lindisfarne when his family were only six miles away across the sea. Now that they were going to be far away in the south of Northumbria he felt very alone.

-ᛉ-

Eighteen months later, in the spring of 832, Eanred was at long last ready to lead the campaign to take Cumbria back from the Britons and the Norsemen. By then over two thirds of the shire had been wrested from the control of Rædwulf's father. The border with Strathclyde now rested on the River Derwent in the west and Ullswater in the east. Practically all the coast from the mouth of the Derwent southwards had been settled by the Norse and they had even made some inroads further south into Luncæstershire.

However, just as he and Eafa were about to set out something more urgent demanded their attention. Egbert of Wessex had marched north and was about to cross the River Ouse from Mercia into Northumbria. After Egbert had subdued the Mercians three years before, their king, Wiglaf, had fled into exile. He had returned just after Eanred had been crowned in 830 and acknowledged Egbert of Wessex as Bretwalda. However, Egbert wasn't content with being just the overlord of Mercia and had made Wiglaf kneel to him and give him his oath as his vassal. Now it seemed that he was intent on doing the same with the new King of Northumbria. Instead of marching north-west, the Northumbria army of three thousand men headed south-east to confront Egbert.

'He's no longer there, Cyning,' the chief scout told Eanred and Eafa as soon as they reached Selby.

'Well, where is he?' the king demanded.

'We don't know, Cyning. All the signs of a large encampment are there on the south bank, but there are no tracks heading east or west to find a crossing place.

'You're sure?'

'Of course,' the man replied curtly, affronted by the unnecessary question. He would never have reported to his king until he was certain.

'I suggest we send the scouts across the river to find out where he has gone, Cyning' Eafa said quietly. 'It could well be he has headed south to put us off the scent and then doubled back to cross the Ouse elsewhere.'

He had learnt from bitter experience that his king was a somewhat volatile character who needed handling carefully.

Eanred chewed his lip in agitation for over a minute.

'If we do that it is an act of aggression. No, I won't be the first to set foot in his territory. It may be that he was just testing our resolve.'

'It's more likely that he thought that we had already departed for Cumbria and sought to take advantage of an undefended land,' the Ealdorman of Catterick muttered, earning a sharp look from his king.

'I agree that would explain his sudden withdrawal,' Eanred said, 'but we mustn't jump to conclusions. We need to find out the truth.'

'How are we going to do that if we sit here like impotent old men, twiddling our thumbs?'

'Remember to whom you are speaking,' the king said, glaring at the ealdorman. 'If you want to retain the shire of Catterick, that is.'

'Perhaps I have a solution, Cyning,' Eafa interrupted before the exchange got any more heated. 'My servant, Erik, is Norse. He could follow the tracks of Egbert's army and see where they are headed. If he falls into their hands he's just one man, and a Viking at that. There's nothing to connect him to Northumbria.'

'Unless he talks,' Eanred pointed out. 'Very well, it's the best idea I've heard. We'll camp at Selby until he returns.'

'They have halted at Dore, a settlement on a hill above the River Sheaf. I heard rumours that Wiglaf and the Mercians have revolted against Egbert's rule, mainly because of the taxes he's imposed on Mercia.'

The truth of what Erik had reported was confirmed the next day when a small delegation of Wessex emissaries arrived to invite Eanred to discuss a truce at Dore.

'Do you think me a fool, to cross the border and place myself at your king's mercy?' Eanred responded. 'Let Egbert come here if he wants to talk to me.'

'Umm, he is unable to leave Mercia at the moment,' the ealdorman leading the delegation replied. 'However, he's sent his eldest son, Æthelwulf, to act as hostage against your safe return, Cyning.'

At this a young man dressed an expensively embroidered tunic and a finely woven scarlet cloak urged his horse forward and gave Eanred a half smile.

'Good day to you, cousin. I assure you that my father is the last person to play you false.'

He and Eanred weren't related. The use of cousin in this context was meant to indicate that both men were of royal blood.

'Very well. But I will take my warband with me and, should I not return within four days, my hereræswa will hang Æthelwulf and wreak revenge on Egbert for his perfidy.'

For late April the weather had been warm and fine but that changed as soon as Eanred left Northumbria. Grey clouds scudded in from the north-east and the wind turned chilly. That first night the rain started and, when he woke up the next morning, Eafa looked out onto black clouds and sheets of near horizontal rain. He knew that the farmers in the fyrd would be fretting about their newly planted crops but, to give them their due, only a few deserted and made their way home. Of course, they would be punished later but one of the problems with an army that was mainly made up of men who weren't primarily warriors was that their minds would always be back at home, especially when they were doing nothing, as now.

The rain had stopped by midday and blue patches of sky appeared. The wind was still cold, however. The next two days were a mixture of sunshine and showers, which infuriated the Northumbrians. As soon as they put their clothes out to dry, they'd get wet again.

All of this seemed to amuse Æthelwulf, who Eafa got to know reasonably well as there was little else for them to do except talk, drink and play dice or nine men's morris. He found him a congenial character who didn't seem in the least worried about the prospect of hanging if Eanred didn't come back in time. However, he must have been slightly relieved when the king returned, however well he managed to hide it.

Eanred was in a foul mood and stomped into the thegn's hall at Selby, which he had commandeered after kicking the owner and his brood out with scarcely a word of apology.

'Get out, Æthelwulf, you can return to your charlatan of a father. Just be thankful I don't hang you out of hand.'

The young man bowed and left with a smile on his lips and a nod to Eafa.

'What happened Cyning?' Eafa asked as soon as they were alone.

'I was tricked!' he shouted, kicking the table in his ire. 'Wiglaf hadn't revolted against Egbert. It was a false rumour, no doubt spread by that Wessex fox. They were both waiting for me with a combined army nearly five thousand strong.'

'What did you do?'

'I had no choice. I was forced to submit to Egbert. He made me swear an oath on the bones of one of his saints that I would become his vassal.'

'Oh, I see.'

Eafa didn't know whether to feel pleased that his arrogant king had been humbled or concerned about Egbert's growing power.

'Not that it matters,' Eanred continued. 'An oath sworn under duress isn't binding. I'll get Archbishop Wulfsige to release me from it as soon as we get back to Eoforwīc.'

Wulfsige did as the king asked but word spread about the humiliating way that Eanred had been forced to acknowledge the King of Wessex as his overlord and his reputation suffered in consequence. For the next few years he didn't dare embark on a campaign in the far north-west of his kingdom in case Egbert invaded, as well he might when he heard that Eanred had repudiated his pledge of fealty. Eanred also became paranoid that, having lost the respect of his nobles, as he saw it, they would depose or kill him. Of course, this just made that more of a possibility. However, Eafa remained loyal and the respect in which he was held did much to dissuade potential rebels.

Chapter Nine – The Cumbrian Campaign

839 – 840

Eafa was annoyed with King Eanred, and not for the first time. The situation in Cumbria had continued to deteriorate to the extent that the invading Britons were now struggling to hold back the tide of invading Norsemen and their families who were settling all along the coast.

Rædwulf had become the ealdorman when his father was killed in a skirmish with the Britons but his shire was now effectively confined to the south-east of what had been Cumbria. Luncæstershire had also come under pressure from Norse settlers, who were also colonising the Isle of Man and the area near the Irish settlement at Duibhlinn, mainly centred on the River Poddle, a tributary of the Liffey.

The Northumbrians on the west coast had to cope with the incursions by those wanting to settle as well as frequent raids from Man and Duibhlinn. In early 839 Eanred decided that he had to do something about the situation, mainly because of the increasing pressure from his ealdormen and the bishops, alarmed at the influx of pagans. However, he had more sense than to undertake the seemingly impossible task himself, so he claimed that he needed to remain at Eoforwīc in case of invasion by Wessex or Mercia.

It was a poor excuse. Although Egbert had continued to threaten to invade Northumbria in retribution for the breaking of Eanred's oath of fealty to him, he had recently died and his son and successor, Æthelwulf, was a very different character. He was seen by most as excessively pious and incompetent as a ruler. Certainly he was extremely unlikely to embark on a war of conquest against Northumbria.

It was obvious that Eanred's instruction to Eafa to conduct the campaign in the west on his behalf was driven more by fear of failure than by the need to defend his southern border.

However, Eafa decided that his strategy should be diplomatic rather than martial, at least as far as the Norse were concerned.

The inclusion of Bishop Egfrid of Lindisfarne, together with several of his priests and monks, didn't arouse much comment. Everyone assumed that they were there to look after the spiritual needs of the army and to tend the wounded. They were, of course, but they were also there to try and convert the Norse settlers to Christianity.

Ilfrid had remained behind to look after Bebbanburg and Islandshire. He was now nineteen and had pleaded to go with this father, saying that his mother and his brother Edmund could look after the shire. However, Breguswid was getting frail, even at the relatively young age of thirty seven, and Edmund was being trained as a warrior at Dùn Èideann. He had therefore had little option but to stay behind.

Eafa began his campaign in the south, sweeping along the coast, capturing Norse settlement after Norse settlement. He gave the invaders a choice: they had to become Christians and accept Rædwulf as their ealdorman, or they would be sold into slavery. Unsurprisingly many chose to be baptised, though Eafa wasn't so naive as to think that their sudden conversion was genuine. He just hoped that the priests that remained with them could convince them to become true Christians.

More importantly, they were fierce fighters and Rædwulf recruited a number to swell the ranks of his warband. Of course, they weren't accepted by his existing Cumbrian warriors, but that was Rædwulf's problem, not his.

As they moved northwards he found the Norse settlements deserted. For a while he thought that they had returned to Duibhlinn, but that proved to be a forlorn hope. They had banded together and near the promontory the Cumbrians called Saint Bee's Head he was confronted by a Norse army four hundred strong. Eafa had four times that number, but he wanted to avoid a conflict if he possibly could; he needed all the warriors he had for the inevitable battle against the Strathclyde Britons.

The Norsemen held the far bank of a small river that ran north to south across the headland. It wasn't much of an obstacle but it would put the Northumbrians at a considerable disadvantage as the far bank was quite steep and slippery. He formed those of his warriors who were afoot and the men of the fyrd just out of arrow range and waited whilst his horsemen rode off to cross the river further upstream.

Although the enemy saw his eighty riders disappear northwards it didn't seem to bother them. Eafa smiled grimly; he doubted whether the Norsemen had encountered warriors on horseback before – at least not ones who could fight from the saddle.

Once his horsemen were in position to the north of the enemy, he gave the order for his archers to advance, protected by a man with a shield. They sent flight after flight of arrows into the massed ranks of the Norsemen. Most struck helmets or shields but some found exposed flesh. Only a few of the Norse had bows with which to respond.

The man carrying his banner waved it to and fro – the signal for his mounted warriors to charge. Coincidentally Eafa gave the order for his warriors on foot to advance through the ranks of the archers and attack. Just as they reached the enemy shield wall the Norse became aware of the horsemen thundering towards them in a wedge formation. They crashed into the flank of the enemy, killing and disrupting the enemy formation like a wave crashing onto a beach.

The shield wall broke apart as the Norsemen turned to defend themselves against the horsemen and, with a cheer, those Northumbrians on foot hacked their way into the Norse ranks. The battle deteriorated into a series of individual fights and Eafa signalled to one of his warband with a horn to sound the pre-arranged signal for the horsemen to withdraw before they got too embroiled in the general melee.

The Norsemen were outnumbered, outmanoeuvred and disorganised. Within a short time they started to make a fighting withdrawal, but by then Eafa had sent the fyrd around their right flank to encircle them. Many fought on and were killed but eventually the survivors surrendered.

By the middle of the afternoon it was all over. The Norsemen had lost half their number killed or badly wounded and ninety had been captured. Those who had escaped were not enough to defend the rest of the settlements; the grip of the Norse on the south-west of Cumbria had been broken – at least for the foreseeable future. Now Eafa could turn his attention towards the Strathclyde Britons.

-ꝟ-

'How many did we lose?' Eafa asked his fellow ealdormen when they met the day after the battle.

'The pagans fought hard, Eafa,' Rædwulf replied. 'I lost forty two men killed and twenty too badly wounded to continue.'

The other ealdormen reported their losses in turn and, when they had finished, Eafa turned to the monk who had been writing down what each noble had said.

'The total is three hundred and forty two dead and another two hundred and ninety one badly wounded, lord,' the monk said after he had totted up the two columns of figures.

Eafa sucked his teeth. He was left with roughly one thousand nine hundred men, and that included the newly baptised Norsemen who were now part of Rædwulf's warband. They had fought bravely against their fellow countrymen, but Eafa still wasn't sure that he could trust them. Either way, they wouldn't be enough to take on the Britons if their king, Riderch, brought his main army south to defend Caer Luel.

However, he had one advantage: the impetuosity of the Britons meant that they were difficult to control and tended to fight as individuals or as small groups rather than a cohesive whole. It was therefore a matter of choosing ground which favoured the defenders over the attackers.

-ꝟ-

Eafa stood in the centre of the first rank of the Northumbrian army alongside Garr and his warband. A little way further down the line he could see Rædwulf's banner. Three other ealdormen and their warbands made up the first rank of the shield wall whilst the warriors of Iuwine of Luncæstershire, Kendric and three more ealdormen made up the second rank. The third rank consisted of the rest of the ealdormen and their warbands. Behind them stood the massed fyrd with the archers on the flanks. The banners of Northumbria and each shire flapped soggily in the wind driven rain above their heads as Bishop Ecgred and his priests went along the lines saying mass and dispensing bread and wine to give spiritual and physical sustenance to the men.

Eafa had chosen his ground well. He was defending a saddle high in the hills south of Caer Luel above a long lake. The summit of the two mountains to either side of his position were held by a mixture of spearmen and archers to prevent his position from being outflanked.

The Britons from Strathclyde appeared in dribs and drabs and started to hurl insults at the opposing army, occasionally bending over and exposing their naked backsides to the Northumbrians. Eafa and his men stood and regarded the capering Britons impassively. He began to wish that the enemy would attack, instead of taunting him, but he knew that was what Riderch wanted. A strong shield wall was difficult to break and, as he knew that Riderch had the advantage of superior numbers, for the Northumbrians to attack would be a disastrous mistake.

Just after midday two things happened. The Britons organised themselves into some sort of formation and just as the rain stopped falling Riderch sent in the first wave. What they lacked in terms of discipline they made up for in bravery. Many of them leaped clean over the first ranks of warriors and landed amongst the fyrd. Few of the Northumbrian peasants and artisans had encountered the fierce Britons before and they started to panic. It was only the fact that they were hemmed in by their fellows in the rear ranks that prevented some of them from fleeing. In the end most of the Britons were killed but they had wreaked havoc before dying and the morale of the fyrd had suffered a severe blow.

Meanwhile, the warriors in the shield wall were battling with the main body of the enemy and Eafa found himself hard pressed. Although he was wearing a helmet, a chain mail vest over a leather tunic and leather boots with metal bars sewn into them to protect his shins and calves, he still had a number of exposed areas. His large round shield covered his lower face down to his boots but his eyes were vulnerable, as was his head. A direct blow by an axe could split his segmented helmet asunder if delivered with enough force at the right angle.

He soon discovered that the Britons worked in pairs: one aiming an axe at his head, or else a spear or sword at his eyes, whilst the second man, often a young boy, tried to cripple him by wounding his legs below the shield. Not for the first time, he thanked the Lord God that he had gone to the extra expense of getting his boots reinforced.

The ground on which he stood was getting slippery with mud and blood, which made keeping his footing difficult, but the pile of bodies in front of the Northumbrian line now impeded the Britons' attack. He knew that he was tiring and was about to step back and let one of the warriors in the second row take his place when the Britons decided that they had had enough and withdrew just as suddenly as they had attacked.

For a moment Eafa rested on his sword to recover his breath. Then someone tapped him on the shoulder and he stepped back to allow another to take his place. He looked along the line as he did so and was dismayed to see that a significant number of the first rank lay dead in front of the pile of enemy corpses. They might have won the first encounter but it had been at a heavy cost.

Eafa took the opportunity to re-organise his army so that there were two ranks of ealdormen, thanes and warriors now, instead of three. The archers had managed to kill a number of the Britons as they advanced. They had gone to the rear before they became involved in the close combat, so thankfully their numbers were undiminished.

Now Riderch sent his own archers forward. They were mainly equipped with hunting bows, which had a short range, but a number of Britons had war bows which had greater range and power. The enemy bowmen started to fire over the heads of the front ranks, striking the unprotected fyrd in the rear. At the same time those with war bows shot at the front ranks. The hail of arrows from the sky started to unnerve the fyrd but those at low trajectory didn't do much harm to the armoured warriors behind their stout wooden shields, other than pepper them. One of two found unprotected feet or lower legs, but not many.

Then disaster struck. Eafa was watching through a narrow gap between the top of his shield and the brim of his helmet for any sign of a new assault against the shield wall when an arrow struck the metal rim of his shield and ricocheted off it before hitting the side of the nasal riveted to his helmet. It rebounded again and struck his left eye, the point entering his brain. As he fell, a groan went up from those who had seen him killed and the news of his death swept through the ranks of the Northumbrian army like wildfire.

If Rædwulf hadn't stepped in to steady the army it could have all ended in disaster. As it was, he took firm control, backed by the other ealdormen, who put aside petty jealousies about seniority, at least for the moment.

An arrow had penetrated Garr's shield and had injured his left hand, but he ignored it and rallied his warband. They had been the most shaken by Eafa's death but, just as he thought that the line had steadied, he saw Iuwine of Luncæstershire go down on one knee with an arrow in his calf. He yelled at Iuwine's gawping warriors and someone had the common sense to give the ealdorman his spear to lean on before helping him to the rear, where the monks had set up a makeshift infirmary.

With two ealdormen down things were not looking good, but at that moment Riderch's archers fled, having been severely mauled by their Northumbrian equivalents. For a while nothing happened and then the King of Strathclyde decided to gamble everything on one last attack en masse in the hope of breaking the shield wall. If that happened the fyrd would be massacred. This time he sent the Norse settlers from his part of Cumbria forward as the point of a giant wedge.

There were about two hundred of them, nearly as many as there were Norse warriors left in the Northumbrian centre. Rædwulf watched apprehensively, wondering whether Norse would fight Norse or whether his men would suddenly side with their fellow Scandinavians. He needn't have worried. It was the opposing Norse who suddenly switched sides and turned on the

Britons. For a moment chaos ensued and then the Britons found their centre being carved asunder by over four hundred Norsemen.

With the flanks also under pressure from the Northumbrians, the lightly armed Britons gave ground and then their whole army melted away. First a few fled, then more joined them and minutes later it became a rout. The Britons didn't stop running until they were back across the River Lyne north of Caer Luel.

Chapter Ten - Death at Whitby

842

Of course Ilfrid mourned the death of his father but, if he was honest, he was more upset by his mother's death a few months later. She'd been unwell for some time and her slow decline had been pitiful to watch. For the last two months of her life she was bedridden and, although he never admitted it to himself, subconsciously Ilfrid had found her death as something of a relief. However, he tried to put the loss of both his parents behind him as he began to think about the future.

Edmund had returned the previous year and, at the age of sixteen, he was now a trained warrior. He took over the duties of shire-reeve, a role that Ilfrid had carried out until their father's death. He had been home for the last few months of his mother's life and, although he put a brave face on it, Ilfrid knew that the gradual deterioration in her health had distressed his brother even more than it had him, if that were possible.

The two brothers had been forced to grow up suddenly and, at twenty, Ilfrid had been faced with the responsibilities of an ealdorman. He realised then what a shock it must have been for Kendric when he'd become an ealdorman at seventeen, only a year after he'd finished training as a warrior.

If King Eanred had been pleased by the recovery of Cumbria he never said so, not to Ilfrid at least, nor did he commiserate with him over the death of Eafa. He appointed the Ealdorman of Loidis as his new hereræswa, a man who hadn't even taken part in the Cumbrian campaign. More and more the king's attention was focused on the south of his kingdom and in more than ten years he had never come north of the Tyne. It was almost as if he were just King of Deira – the old southern kingdom that had united with Bernicia to form Northumbria two hundred years previously.

'I want you to go and visit our business in Paris,' Ilfrid told Edmund on a fine spring day in 842.

Edmund was glad of the break from what had become a rather boring and mundane life. All he seemed to do was collect taxes and deal with disputes between the thegns of Islandshire. He was also responsible for training the fyrd but, after the recovery of Cumbria, it was difficult to motivate freemen who were far more interested in tending their crops or carrying out their craft than they were in training for war.

He decided to take one of the skeids that Thorkel and his Norsemen had built for his father twenty years before. These were normally employed patrolling the coast of Islandshire and escorting the fleet of knarrs on their trading missions. The one he chose was named the Holy Ghost. It had just been re-caulked and the rigging had been renewed ready for the new sailing season. It required a crew of nearly seventy, but he had no trouble recruiting forty young men eager for an adventure to supplement the twenty warriors that Ilfrid had given him from his warband.

In addition to the crew who manned the oars and fought when necessary, there were six others: the captain - a man named Nerian, Ryce the helmsman and four ship's boys who varied in age from twelve to fifteen. It was the job of the latter to look after the sail, feed and water the rowers and generally clean and maintain the ship.

The weather changed the night before they set out and they had to contend with a strong hRicsiged and a heavy sea as soon as they left Budle Bay and the fortress of Bebbanburg behind. Even those who had rowed before found it hard work after a winter spent largely indoors. Those who were new to the sea were soon complaining about aching arms, sore backs and blistered hands.

Edmund, who had been standing in the prow by the crucifix, which had been placed there instead of the dragon's head typical of Viking ships, reluctantly stepped down and took the place of the youngest rower. He'd been enjoying the wind in his long brown hair and the salt spray on his face but one thing his father had drummed into him was the need to lead by example. When they saw their shire reeve pulling at his oar for all he was worth the moaners shut up, too ashamed to complain further.

Thankfully the wind backed from south east to north east after an hour and Nerian ordered the boys to pull up the sail. Ryce brought the Holy Ghost around so that the wind was abeam. That made it easier for the ship's boys to raise the spar to which the sail was attached. Two held the halyard around the cleat near the base of the mast whilst the other two pulled it out from the mast to create some slack. As soon as they let go the other two pulled a foot or two of the halyard in around the cleat. That way they sweated the spar with its flapping oiled woollen sail up the mast. It was slow work but eventually Nerian was happy that it was far enough up the mast for such windy conditions and the boys made the halyard fast before reefing the bottom of the sail.

That done, Ryce brought the ship back on course and they set off once more, this time travelling at twice the speed the rowers could manage. As they sped along, the bow cutting through the choppy sea, more than one of the new men began to feel queasy now that they didn't have rowing to concentrate on. The old hands called out ribald comments as several brought up the contents of their stomachs.

Most had the common sense to spew over the leeward gunwale but two of the younger men made the landsman's error of retching into the wind. They soon learned their mistake as their vomit blew back into the faces and soaked their tunics.

The wind held, albeit decreasing somewhat as time went on, until the third day. By that time they were off the coast of Kent. They were about to cross the open sea to the coast of Frankia at the narrowest point between England and the Continent when the lookout up the mast called down that three ships had emerged from the old Roman fortified port of Dovera and were heading their way.

Kent was under the control of Wessex and, although Northumbria and Wessex weren't at war, neither were relations between them all that friendly. However, the ships heading towards Edmund's skeid were smaller and he didn't regard them as much of a threat. With the wind now coming from the north east, the Northumbrian longship slowly pulled away from its pursuers. By the time that they spotted land dead ahead of them again the Kentish ships had given up the chase.

Nerian altered course so that they now had the wind directly behind them and, although the Holy Ghost wallowed a little, rocking from side to side as the waves passed under her hull, they continued to make good progress. After a while the Frankish coast turned and headed due west. Ryce put his steering oar over without having to be told and the ship's boys rushed to trim the sail for the new heading.

They had been travelling parallel to the coast for a couple of hours when the lookout called down again.

'Ships putting out from the Frankish coast.'

'How many?'

'Four, no, wait. Five.'

Edmund could now see the Kentish warships as they emerged over the horizon. That meant that they were only about three miles away as visual range from the deck was much shorter than it was from the masthead. He still couldn't see the Frankish ships and he asked the boy up the mast to point in their direction.

'Head where he's indicating,' he told the steersman.

Ryce nodded and put the steering oar over to take them south west again whilst Nerian yelled for the ship's boys to tighten the sail on the new course. Edmund had decided that, as he was heading for Paris, it made more sense to tell the Franks who he was than to try and avoid them.

As the Holy Ghost bore down on the five ships, they started to spread out into a line abreast, presumably ready to come alongside the longship and board it.

'They think we're Vikings,' Edmund said with a grin.

'Then they must be bloody blind,' Nerian replied. 'Can't they see the cross on our prows?'

'Probably not at this range.'

The five ships were now hull down on the horizon but making slow progress as they were rowing into the wind. In contrast the skeid was flying along under sail at six knots.

'Get ready to lower the mainsail,' Nerian yelled as they neared the other ships. 'Rowers to your oars.'

The warriors, who had been lining the gunwales to gawp at the strange Frankish ships, scattered and sat on their sea chests before picking up their oars from where they lay. They pulled out the plugs, which stopped the sea slopping into the ship when under sail, and thrust their oars out, holding them above the waves and waiting for the next order.

'Drop the sail, down oars and pull together,' Nerian called. 'One, two, three,' he called out with a long pause between each one.

The sail fluttered down the mast to be gathered up and secured by the boys whilst the rowers picked up the rhythm being called out by the captain. Once they had settled into it, he stopped calling it out. By then the approaching ships were no more than half a mile away.

Once they were within hailing distance Nerian gave the order to stop rowing and, apart from the odd adjustment to maintain the ship's heading, he let the longship drift towards the five Frankish ships. Now he could see them clearly, Edmund realised that they were similar to an illustration of a Roman galley that he'd seen whilst he was on Lindisfarne. They were almost float bottomed, having the shallow V shaped hull designed for coastal craft in the Mediterranean. They were quite unsuited to the rougher waters of the German Ocean.

'Greetings, I'm Edmund of Bebbanburg, a merchant of Northumbria, heading for our trading post in Paris,' he called across the water towards the central ship in Latin. 'We are Christians from Northumbria and we come in peace,' he continued as there had been no response to his first hail.

'How do we know you're not Vikings trying to trick us?' someone called back in Latin.

'How many Vikings do you know who speak Latin and display a cross as a figurehead?'

'I'm coming alongside. Don't do anything stupid or my other ships will attack.'

Nothing more was said until the galley came alongside and the ship's boys caught the two mooring lines that their counterparts on the other ship threw to them as well as a third rope to serve as a spring. This ran from the stern of one ship to the prow of the other to hold them together without one hull rubbing constantly against the other.

The man who clambered down onto the deck of the skeid was in his thirties. He was six inches taller than Edmund and broad chested. His carefully washed and combed hair and beard contrasted with the faded leather armour he wore. The way he smelled reminded Edmund of his mother; quite unlike the way he and his men did. Their prevailing odour was a mixture of sweat and salt.

'Greetings, I'm Bastiaan, the viscount of this coastal region and the younger son of the Count of Arras,' the big man explained.

Edmund knew that a count was a man appointed to govern a region, very much as an ealdorman governed a shire in England. A vice-count, or viscount, was a deputy who was responsible for helping the count by enforcing the law and collecting taxes in a sub-division of the province. In this case, it looked as if Bastiaan was also responsible for the defence of this section of the coast.

'I'm Edmund, the brother of the Ealdorman of Bebbanburg and the Shire Reeve of Islandshire in Northumbria,' the young Northumbrian replied.

'I thought you said that you were a merchant?' Bastiaan replied, giving a suspicious look around him. 'This doesn't look like a trading ship, more like a Norse raider.'

'That's because she was built for my father by a crew of Norsemen who he captured.'

'Are these them?' he asked in alarm, indicating the rowers.

Edmund gave a short laugh.

'No, that was twenty years ago. These men are all Northumbrians.'

'You still haven't explained why you claimed to be a merchant.'

'That's because my family own a warehouse in Paris where we trade items such as wool, jewellery, weapons and leather goods that we export from Bebbanburg.'

'Nerian, uncover the hold and show the viscount what we are carrying,' he ordered, switching to English.

The ship's boys lifted the wooden planking in the centre of the ship and brought up two of the bales from the dozens lying there. They undid the oiled leather covers to display a bundle of wool and a crate full of swords, byrnies, helmets and spear heads, all coated in lard to protect the metal from the corrosive sea air.

Bastiaan's eyes lit up when he saw the weapons.

'Are they for sale?' he asked in poor English.

'For the right price.'

'Come, follow me into the port. You are my guests tonight and, when your head has cleared sufficiently in the morning, we'll talk business. We have suffered a lot from Danish and Norse raiders in recent years, so you will forgive our suspicions.'

'You certainly seem to be prepared for them now.'

'Yes, but our ships are no match for theirs, and they come in increasing numbers so all we can do is try and convince them that there are easier pickings elsewhere.'

They followed the galleys along the coast and entered a broad estuary heading almost east. They turned into a harbour on the southern bank of the estuary. The port of Caracotinum was scarcely worthy of the name. It had evidently been much more important in Roman times, to judge by the extensive ruins, but the current settlement consisted of a few small warehouses, a hall, a church and a few dozen huts. There was a dock and a stone wall which separated the port from the estuary. The dock had room for all six ships to moor alongside, in addition to the two knarrs which were already there. It had obviously been built in more prosperous days.

The hall belonged to Bastiaan and, despite being small and built of timber, was quite luxurious on the inside. The first half was the communal area with one massive oak table and four chairs at the far end. The wall was lined with trestle tables and benches which would be erected for meals. The rolled up palliasses and chests presumably belonged to Bastiaan's servants and household warriors.

Through the door in a partition lay the viscount's own quarters, not that Edmund was invited to enter. His host's family came out to greet him instead. His wife was buxom and talkative, so it was a little while before he was introduced to the children – two boys of around four and seven and an older girl.

As soon as he saw her Edmund had trouble in tearing his eyes away from her. She looked to be about twelve, her breasts were discernible under her shift and surcoat, but were a long way short of the other woman's splendid endowment, which looked like two rather plump turnips encased in material that was struggling to contain them. The girl was also extremely pretty.

'I'm sorry, what were you saying?' Edmund asked, realising that he hadn't been listening to him.

Bastiaan gave his wife a meaningful look before he replied.

'I was saying that this is my sister, Joscelin, who is living with us to help look after the boys.'

Edmund was not yet eighteen and the last thing he was looking for at the moment was a wife. Not even Ilfrid, who was four years older, was thinking of marriage yet. However, as soon as he saw Joscelin he was infatuated with her.

The viscount laid on a feast for his visitors that night and Edmund found himself seated between Bastiaan and his garrulous wife with Joscelin on her brother's other side and the elder boy, who he learned was called Gervaise, beside his mother. The only one who wasn't competing for Edmund's attention, it seemed, was the one person he wanted to talk to. The mother wittered on, her husband tried to compete but soon gave up, whilst Gervaise kept plying him with questions about England.

It was something of a relief when the wife retired to let the men continue drinking. Unfortunately she took Joscelin as well as Gervaise with her. Both seemed reluctant to go, but for very different reasons. Throughout the evening Joscelin had kept glancing his way and then blushing and looking demurely at her half eaten meal as soon as she saw that his eyes were looking into hers. It was an encouraging sign.

He had no idea if she was betrothed or what plans Bastiaan's father had for his daughter but he had gathered during the evening that the viscount's elder brother was his father's favourite and would inherit when the old man died. Bastiaan and his brother didn't get on and he was obviously worried that he might lose his position when that day came. Neither the post of count or viscount was meant to be hereditary, nor for that matter was the position of ealdorman. All were officially royal appointments, but it was becoming normal for the son to follow the father unless there were good reasons for not doing so.

Once they had withdrawn the serious matter of drinking started. Edmund was used to mead and ale, but not wine and he made the mistake of thinking it was innocuous. He didn't recall passing out, nor did he remember what he and Bastiaan had discussed when he finally re-joined the land of the living late the next morning. However, he had a nasty feeling that he may have declared his undying love for the man's twelve year old sister at some stage during the evening.

He had, but he needn't have worried. Edmund was not a boastful youth but he had said enough about Bebbanburg and Islandshire for Bastiaan to realise that, not only was his brother an important man, but also that he and Ilfrid were close. The fact that Edmund would have his own hall at Alnwic when he decided to marry did much to commend the boy to Bastiaan. More importantly, although Edmund didn't remember it, was the fact that they had discussed building a warehouse at Caracotinum and moving his family's business base there. Bastiaan would then hire or buy barges to convey the goods up river to Paris.

This was much more sensible than sending ships designed for crossing the sea up the winding course of the Seine. It typically took five days to traverse the one hundred and forty miles from the sea to Paris; time which could be better spent at sea.

When Bastiaan reminded Edmund of their conversation, once he had sobered up sufficiently, he had a vague recollection of it but he was quick to point out that he would have to discuss the idea with his reeve in Paris and with his brother, who would have the final say.

At first Edmund had a suspicion that he was being taken advantage of, but the more he thought about it, the more he thought the idea a sensible one. His one concern was the Vikings. They had left Caracotinum alone so far but it was wide open to a raid. If the idea was going to work, the place would have to be made defensible. A simple chain boom across the entrance would protect that side but Bastiaan would have to make the settlement defensible from the landward side, and that would cost money; money the viscount clearly didn't have.

However, Bastiaan was no fool and he dangled the one bait that Edmund couldn't resist in front of the young man's eyes – betrothal to Joscelin. Of course, he had no right to do so. She was his sister, not his daughter, and her father, the count, would have the final say.

By the time that Edmund sailed down the River Seine two days later they had an understanding. The hold of the Holy Ghost was lighter by two crates of weapons, but they were replaced by a chest full of hack silver and coins of various denominations. Bastiaan could ill afford the cost, but now at least he could arm his warriors and his freemen properly.

-X-

Edmund returned to Bebbanburg in late August. He should have been back a month earlier but he had called in again at Caracotinum on the way home see Joscelin again. They managed to get to know each other rather better, despite her sister-in-law's incessant chattering whilst she was acting as chaperone. She seemed under the mistaken impression that Edmund was more interested in talking to her than Joscelin; something that Edmund quickly found intolerable, as he told Bastiaan.

The next time he was allowed to walk with Joscelin he was accompanied by Gervaise and a servant. The servant remained silent but not so Gervaise, who seem to have inherited his mother's ability to chatter nonstop. At least his questions were about Northumbria and Edmund was able to tell Joscelin about it at the same time. They were forced to converse in Latin at first but Edmund began to learn a few words in Frankish and he taught his two companions a few words in English during the time they spent together.

He kept sneaking looks at Joscelin and she would catch his eye and then look demurely down at the ground. Of course, that just excited Edmund even more. When she could get a word in on those rare occasions that her brother was quiet, her questions displayed intelligence and a genuine curiosity about a foreign land that Edmund hoped would become her home.

After four days he asked to see Bastiaan and asked for Joscelin's hand. The viscount beamed with pleasure and told him that he would strongly recommend the match to his father. He assured Edmund that he would agree; a confidence which was to prove somewhat misplaced.

'I hope that you will establish a warehouse here, as we discussed, and visit it often so that we may see Joscelin from time to time.'

'I will certainly recommend it to my brother. I will return as soon as I have his answer.'

Joscelin's feelings for the handsome young Northumbrian were plain for all to see. She wept at his departure and only his promise to return before winter set in enabled her to regain some composure as the Holy Ghost disappeared from view.

'You really think this idea could work?' Ilfrid asked him once Edmund had explained his proposal.

'I do, yes. It would shave nearly two weeks off the time that our knarrs are away and Viscount Bastiaan's barges are far more suited to navigating the River Seine.'

'What about these Viking raids. From what I've heard they are on the increase.'

'Yes, I agree that it's a risk but our goods would only remain at Caracotinum for the time it takes to unload them and load them onto the barges.'

'Yes, but inevitably they would have to remain in the warehouse at times whilst the barges are away upstream. No, if we are going make the idea work safely we need to improve the defences of the place. How much would it cost to build a palisade around the warehouse? Does the viscount have enough warriors to defend it?'

'I think it would be a question of enclosing the whole settlement. As to his warriors, he had enough men to man five galleys so I suppose that means a hundred or so.'

Ilfrid was impressed that the viscount could afford to keep so many warriors and said so.

'Of course, some are fishermen and townspeople who help man the galleys when the alarm bell is rung,' Edmund admitted reluctantly. 'I only saw about forty warriors in his hall.'

'Oh, I see. Just because they can row doesn't mean that they can fight. I like the sound of this less and less.'

'The Vikings haven't attacked Caracotinum so far.'

'That means nothing. If they are preying on that coastline they will do so sooner or later.'

Edmund knew deep down that his brother was right. His own judgement was clouded by his passion for Joscelin, but he refused to acknowledge this to himself. Before he could say anything more, his brother spoke again.

'In any case that's of no importance at the moment. What I haven't had the chance to tell you is that Eanred had summoned us both to appear before him.'

'What on earth does the king want with us? He hasn't shown any interest in this part of the kingdom before.'

'I've no idea, but I don't suppose it will be good news, whatever it is.'

'When do we depart for Eoforwīc?'

'The king's summons came three weeks ago. I've explained that I had to await your return as it's both of us he wants to see, but I daren't delay any longer. We leave tomorrow, but not for Eoforwīc. He's at Whitby at the moment.'

'Well, at least we can travel down by sea then.'

'Yes, and it gives us the excuse to take seventy men with us. If we turned up on horseback with that many it would be difficult to explain why.'

'You think he means us harm?'

'I don't know what he intends, but it's best to be prepared for trouble.'

-X-

Edmund was tempted to tell Ilfrid about Joscelin on the voyage south but he wisely decided that his brother wouldn't be in the most receptive frame of mind until this business with the king was sorted out. The weather was kind to them and they rowed into the mouth of the River Esk at dusk on the second day. The monastery on top of the East Cliff loomed above them as they moored alongside the jetty that served the small settlement on the other side of the river.

Leaving a guard on the ship, the crew managed to find accommodation ashore, although some had to sleep in stables. Ilfrid and Edmund shared a room in a tavern with Erik and Laughlin sleeping on the floor. Garr and three more of the warband occupied the room next to theirs.

That evening Ilfrid, Edmund and Garr sat at a table in the main room of the tavern drinking a tankard of ale each whilst they waited for their meal. Several of their warriors sat at other tables similarly occupied when the door banged open and six armed men barged into the room.

'Which one of you is Ealdorman Ilfrid,' the leader demanded.

'I am, why? What's it to you?'

'The king wants to see you and your brother now.'

'Now? Surely it can wait until the morning?'

'If you don't come with me willingly, my orders are to take you to the monastery by force.'

At that the fourteen warriors who had been sitting quietly at their tables got to their feet as one and drew their swords.

'And how exactly are you going to do that?' Garr asked quietly.

Ilfrid put a restraining hand on his arm.

'Sit down all of you and put your swords away, at least for now,' he ordered.

Laughlin slipped out of the door with the other patrons of the tavern, all of whom had suddenly decided to find somewhere else to drink.

'Now, what is the meaning of your threat to take my brother and me to see the king by force? Are we under arrest, and if so, for what offence?'

'I've no idea,' the man said impatiently. 'My orders are to take you into the king's presence now.'

'Well, I suggest that you go back to Eanred and tell him that I will come to see him at a reasonable hour tomorrow. I am a noble, not some bondsman to be ordered about, even if he is the king. If he wishes to bring some charge against us, then it must be done before the Witan. Remind him that the last king who tried to arrest ealdormen without proper authority lost his throne. Now get out; you're disturbing my meal.'

The man looked about him impotently. He was about to argue when the door banged open again and armed warriors flooded into the room, surrounding the members of the king's gesith.

'Thank you, Laughlin, but I think these men were about to leave anyway.'

The next morning Ilfrid and Edmund walked up to the monastery. They were unarmed save for a dagger at their waists but they were accompanied by fifty fully armed warriors. Ilfrid didn't trust Eanred and, if necessary, he would defy the king and return to Bebbanburg until the Witan could be called to hear the charges, whatever they might be.

The more he thought about it, the more puzzled he became. He might not like or have much confidence in Eanred as king, but he hadn't been disloyal to him, not so far at any rate.

They entered the monastery leaving the majority of their men waiting outside. Only Garr and Laughlin accompanied them. A passing monk said they'd find the king in the church and so they made their way there.

It was an imposing building constructed of stone, unlike the rest of the monastery. Inside they found Eanred seated on a chair with two people on either side of him. One was the abbot and the other the king's twelve year old son, Æthelred.

'Why didn't you come when you were summoned last night? Instead you threatened my men with violence; that's treason.'

'Good morning to you too, Cyning,' Ilfrid replied with a smile. 'The man was impudent and I couldn't believe that you would really want to see me in the middle of the night. I was certain that he must have misunderstood your orders. Anyway, my brother and I are here now, as you requested. What can I do for you?'

Ilfrid's urbane manner seemed to infuriate Eanred even further. Hearing Æthelred snigger at Ilfrid's words didn't help either. He gave his son an irate look and the boy looked suitably contrite. However, as soon as his father turned his head away, his son smirked. It was evident to both Ilfrid and Edmund that Æthelred didn't have a great deal of respect for his father.

'It has been brought to my attention that you have a trading post in Frankia from which you make a great deal of money.'

What the king said was true but Ilfrid still didn't see where this was leading, so he remained silent.

'Well, is that true?'

'We have a warehouse in Paris, yes. But I don't understand why this should be of interest to you, Cyning. My family has had a base there for a long time.'

'Ah, I thought so. And in all that time how much profit have you made as a merchant?'

Eanred said the last word as if it left a bitter taste in his mouth. Evidently he thought that involvement in trade was beneath a noble.

'I have no idea, Cyning. I would have to ask my reeve in Paris. May I ask why you are interested?'

'Because you need to pay taxes to me on whatever you and your ancestors have made from your sordid dealings on the Continent.'

'I'm sorry, but I already pay taxes on my profits in Frankia.'

'You do? To whom? Not to me.'

'No, to the emperor.'

'That's of no concern of mine. You are a Northumbrian and, as such, you must pay me the tax due on all your income; furthermore you must pay the Church their tithe as well.'

'I will pay what I owe but not to both you and to Louis the Pious. If you want me to pay them to you in future, then you will need to reach an agreement with Louis. No man can be made to pay the same tax twice.'

'Don't you dare tell me what I must do,' Eanred almost yelped. 'Your arrangement with the emperor is a matter between you. I will have what is rightfully mine.'

'I'm not the only one of your ealdormen who trade abroad, Cyning. Several trade with Mercia and with Ireland. Are they to be asked to pay you additional taxes too?'

'That's not your concern.'

'Isn't it? I think it is very much my concern. As a member of the Witan I am vitally interested in what amounts to a change in the law, especially if it is to be applied selectively.'

'Are you threatening me?'

'No, Cyning. Of course not; merely suggesting that this is a matter for the Witan to decide.'

'No, it is a matter for your king to rule on. You will return to Bebbanburg and obtain your ledger for the past one hundred years from your reeve in Paris. My clerks will then assess what you owe me. Once you have settled your debt I will release your brother.'

'Release my brother?'

'Yes, Edmund will remain with me as my guest until you comply with my commands.'

The king nodded to a monk standing by a side door and seconds later several of the king's gesith entered the church and surrounded Ilfrid and his companions.

'You needn't think that the men you left outside the monastery will come to your aid. They have already been disarmed by my warband. Now get out of my sight and do what I've told you to do. I'm afraid that your brother will be confined in uncongenial surroundings until you return, so I would hasten if I were you, or his health may suffer.'

Ilfrid stood there numb with shock for a moment and then, with a cry of rage he drew his dagger and lunged towards the sneering king. He never made it. With a yelp of fear Eanred leaned back to escape the dagger and his chair toppled over, taking the king out of Ilfrid's reach. The king's gesith were taken by surprise but Æthelred reacted quickly, throwing himself at the enraged ealdorman and locking his arms around him. It didn't take Ilfrid a moment to shake the boy off. But Æthelred's prompt intervention gave the king's warriors time to gather their wits. One of them thrust his sword into Ilfrid's back before he could attack Eanred again and Edmund watched in horror as his brother fell face down on top of the prostrate king, blood staining the back of his yellow tunic a dark crimson.

Eanred extracted himself angrily from under the dead ealdorman and he kicked the corpse several times before he recovered his composure.

'Traitor,' he spat. 'Take his treacherous brother outside and hang him.'

'Father, wait. Aren't you going to thank me for saving your life?'

'What, oh, yes. Thank you Æthelred. You did well.'

'I don't think it's a very good idea to kill Edmund out of hand.'

'Be quiet! You may have saved my life, but that doesn't give you the right to be impudent.'

'I'm not being impudent, father, just sensible,' the boy replied calmly. 'It will be difficult to explain to the Witan what has just happened here. Your enemies will accuse you of murdering the most important noble in the north and, if we aren't careful, that could inspire a revolt.'

'Who are these enemies you speak of,' his father asked suspiciously. 'What do you know of such matters?'

'I keep my ear to the ground, father. I speak of the ealdormen of Lothian, Bernicia and the western shires. They all admired Ilfrid and looked upon him as their leader. It's hardly surprising; you have never shown your face outside Deira.'

Eanred was about to rebuke his son when he realised that they were not alone. His first instinct was to order that Ilfrid's body be taken out of the church and thrown on the midden heap. However, what his son had just said made him realise that he might need to tread carefully. He looked at Edmund, who was weeping and struggling with impotent rage against the men who held him. Perhaps killing him wasn't the wisest move in the circumstances, but he knew that the youth would be his implacable enemy after what had happened. He needed time to think.

'Take this wretch and chain him up in one of the cellars whilst I think about what to do with him,' he ordered. 'The rest of you can leave us now.'

'What about the crew of Ealdorman Ilfrid's longship, Cyning,' his captain asked. 'We have them outnumbered and surrounded but they are hardly disarmed, as you claimed.'

Eanred looked at the man sharply. He wasn't certain but he thought that there was a hint of derision in the man's voice.

'Well, go and disarm them now.'

The captain looked uncomfortable and didn't move.

'Well, what are you waiting for?'

'I may have more men than they have but they will fight back if we try to disarm them. You are likely to lose a significant number of your warband in the ensuing fight.'

'And a battle with the Bebbanburg warband is hardly likely to improve the sticky situation you have got yourself into, father,' his son added.

Eanred bridled at their implied criticism of him, but he knew that they were right. He was normally a careful man and he quickly realised that his greed was likely to end up costing him his throne if he wasn't careful. He needed time to think.

'Very well, tell them that they are to return to their ship and wait there for their ealdorman to rejoin them. After all, they won't know that Ilfrid is dead.'

'It won't take long for word of what has happened here to spread, Cyning,' his captain pointed out.

'What about the body?' the abbot asked. 'Ealdorman Ilfrid deserves a Christian burial.'

Eanred nodded.

'Yes, thank you Father Abbot. See to it would you? But I don't want any fuss, just a quick internment in consecrated ground as soon as it's dark.'

'I want to take the body back with me to bury it on Lindisfarne with our ancestors,' Edmund stated forcefully.

'You're not going anywhere.'

'What about if I give you my oath to be faithful to you, much as it goes against the grain. My brother wouldn't want to see some royal favourite given Bebbanburg.'

'You expect me to believe that you would stay loyal if I released you?'

'I will never forgive you for what you have done, Eanred, but I'm not stupid. No-one need know what transpired here today. You will need to hang the man who killed my brother, of course, but I'll keep quiet about the reason behind his death. You can blame it on a man who went mad.'

Eanred looked dubious, but he gave what Edmund had said some thought.

'I need time to think,' he said again. 'Leave me for now. Edmund, you and your two men will remain in the church. Go and wait over there until I've made a decision. Father Abbot, you can get your monks to prepare this traitor for burial. Whether it stays here or goes to Lindisfarne, it needs to be purified and placed in a coffin before it begins to stink.'

The way that Eanred spoke about his brother infuriated Edmund even further, but a warning glance from Æthelred was enough to make him bite his tongue. He would bide his time, but he promised himself that he would have his revenge on Eanred.

PART THREE – RAGNAR THE KING

THE RAVEN

Chapter Eleven – The Shield Maiden

829 to 830

Ragnar lay unconscious for several days after the blow to his head. For a time Olaf thought that he was going to die but Torstein, the godi, cast his runes and predicted that he was destined for great things, so his death was hardly likely to be imminent. It reassured Ragnar's followers, but deep down Olaf was not convinced. He felt that Torstein would say what was necessary to keep the disparate warband that Ragnar had gathered around him from disintegrating.

When he did regain consciousness, Ragnar was desperately weak. However, he was not the sort of person to lie on his sick bed when there were things to be done. With the help of one of his hirdmen he managed to clamber to his feet. He stood on the aft deck of his drekar swaying like a drunk whilst the world seemed to be spinning around him. Suddenly he lurched to the gunwale and spewed bile and stomach acid over the side. He gripped the wooden rail under his hands tightly to stop himself falling forwards over the side of the moving ship and then he felt strong arms grab his shoulders and force him to lie down again.

'That was foolish, jarl,' he heard Lars say as he and Bjarke lowered him onto his bed of furs.

He was about to utter a stinging retort when the world went black and he slipped back into unconsciousness. When he awoke next it was dark and he lay there for a moment looking up at the stars and the full moon. There were a few clouds in the sky and, as he watched, one of them obscured the moon from view. The sea and ship beneath were plunged into darkness again.

'Are you awake, jarl?'

He didn't recognise the voice and the face was difficult to make out until the cloud moved on and then he saw a beardless boy crouched beside him offering him a leather beaker. He recalled that the lad was the youngest of the ship's boys, but at first he couldn't remember his name.

'Drink,' he croaked, indicating that the boy should give him the beaker he was holding.

He was pleased to find that it contained mead. The usual brew of fermented honey and water had been supplemented by herbs, a concoction of Torstein's which he claimed had healing properties. Ragnar slowly sipped the contents, with the lad's help, until the beaker was empty. He sighed with contentment and went back to sleep.

He awoke next when rain splattered down onto his face. The sky was grey and for a moment he watched the scudding clouds as he blinked the water drops out of his eyes; then someone erected a piece of oiled wool cut from an old sail over his makeshift bed. The ship's boy knelt by him again and helped him to drink another beaker of mead.

'Where's Lodvik?'

'Who, jarl?'

'My body servant.'

'Oh, the thrall,' the boy said dismissively. 'I believe that he was killed by an arrow during the battle.'

Ragnar was annoyed at the boy's casual indifference to the young man who'd been his constant attendant for some time and who he'd come to like and respect. But then he supposed that this boy wasn't to know that. To him he'd just have been another thrall – the lowest of the low.

'What's your name, boy? I've forgotten,' he managed to croak between mouthfuls.

'Gedda Bótolfrson.'

'Bótolfrson? Who is your father? Bótolfr is not a name I recall.'

'He was a bondi in Agder, a rich landowner, but one of Froh's hirdmen coveted his land and laid false charges against him. Naturally that bastard, Froh, found in his man's favour and so we were forced off our own land. My father went back to our hall and killed the usurper, for which he was hanged. My mother, my sister Lagertha, and I sought refuge with my uncle, who is a jarl in the north of Agder.'

Gedda was about to continue but he noticed that Ragnar was slipping into unconsciousness again and so he got up and went to help the other ship's boys to collect the rain and fill the water barrels.

'You were telling me about your family,' Ragnar said when he awoke again. The rain had stopped but his shelter had been left in place as the sky still looked ominous.

'Oh, well, Lagertha has always been strong willed and more of a warrior than most boys. When we were evicted she became a shield maiden and formed her own small warband from amongst our uncle's young warriors. They started to attack those Swedes who had been given land by Froh until she became such a nuisance that he offered a chest of silver for her head.

'Of course, this just increased her renown and more and more young men looking for adventure joined her. I wanted to as well but my uncle said I was too young. However, he allowed me to join one of the other jarl's as a ship's boy. When two of yours were killed in the battle against Froh, he sent me and another boy to report to your shipmaster as replacements. As I was the youngest, at twelve, I was tasked to look after you.'

He was about to continue and tell Ragnar what had become of Lagertha but the man interrupted him.

'And a good job you've made of it too. Right, Gedda Bótolfrson, get rid of this damned awning and help me to get to my feet again. This time I don't feel as weak as a new-born baby, so maybe I'll manage to stay upright.'

Ragnar made it to the gunwale without feeling faint this time and, although he was still quite feeble, he determined to get back to normal as soon as possible. In the meantime he needed to know what was going on. Why were they still in the anchorage at Bohus, for example?

'Where is Olaf, Gedda?'

The boy shrugged.

'Raiding, jarl. He and the other jarls are laying waste to Alfheim whilst you recover.'

Ragnar groaned.

'Are you alright, jarl?'

'What? Oh yes. I'm feeling much better, though my belly is rumbling as if the pipe between it and my mouth has been cut. No, that wasn't why I groaned. Never mind, just see if you can find me something to eat.'

In fact Ragnar had groaned because they were wasting time here when they should be heading north to secure his kingdom of Agder before anyone else did so. When Gedda came back Ragnar sat down and greedily ate the bowl of mutton stew that he'd brought him. After the first few mouthfuls he was sick again, so he learned to eat it slowly and not to try and consume too much in one go.

The next day Ragnar was feeling more like his old self, but Torstein warned him not to try and do too much at first. The one thing he did do was to send messengers, found from the force left behind to besiege the fortress on the top of the hill, to find Olaf and the jarls and get them to return post haste.

By the time that they set out two days later Ragnar was feeling much better. The fleet left the fjord behind and turned into the Kattegat before heading north-west into the Skagerrak, on the far side of which lay the Kingdom of Agder.

-ᛘ-

Lagertha Bótolfrsdotter had always regretted being born female. Growing up she had been able to outrun and outwrestle most of the boys her age. Of course, such behaviour earned her reprimands and the odd beating, but it made little difference to her behaviour. When she was twelve she started to badger her father to be allowed to join the boys in their training with sword, shield and spear. Both her parents were adamant that it would make them a laughing stock amongst their fellow bondis. However, Bótolfr did agree to let her have a bow.

Lagertha had become the best archer in their valley by the time she was fourteen. Then disaster struck. King Sigvard and his family were killed and the Swede, Froh, seized the throne of Agder. When her father was hanged Lagertha, her mother and her seven year old brother, Gedda, fled to her uncle, Jarl Magnus, at Lysebotn in the far north of Agder.

Magnus' base lay at the end of a fjord some twenty five miles long called the Lysefjord. It was surrounded by steep-sided mountains, whose summits were covered in snow for most of the year.

Magnus' bondis and their thralls existed by fishing and farming the flat land alongside the river behind Lysebotn. They were also a successful raiders. Because of its inaccessible nature, the settlement was the perfect base for Lagertha to use to exact her revenge on Froh and the Swedes who came to settle in their new kingdom.

Her first foray was against the Swedes who had occupied the nearby island of Rennesøy, whose jarl also ruled over a number of other islands on the south side of the Boknafjord. These islands guarded the entrance to the Lysefjord and, when a Swede and his hirdmen killed their Norse jarl and subjugated the people who lived on them, Magnus' bondis were furious. However, he was still dithering about how best to deal with the Swedes when Lagertha acted.

Taking two dozen warriors who acknowledged her, at least unofficially, as their hersir, she stole a snekkja one evening. In truth it belonged to the father of one of her young followers and so she regarded it as borrowing, rather than stealing. The night was relatively balmy with scarcely a light breeze to ruffle the dark waters of the fjord and they rowed silently westwards under the sporadic light of a new moon.

Clouds scudded along, obscuring the only source of light from time to time as they made their way slowly towards the mouth and on into the Boknafjord. At first Lagertha worried that it might be difficult to navigate when clouds intermittently obscured the moonlight, but such periods of inky blackness didn't last long. By the time that the main settlement of Vikevåg on the south coast of Rennesøy hove into view they had been rowing for some six hours. It was now only an hour before the sky would start to lighten but her men needed to recover after rowing all that way.

By the time they were ready, the tops of the mountains to the east had started to appear, silhouetted by the rising sun. The shores of the island were rocky and so they had no option but to land on the wooden jetty at Vikevåg where the other longships, knarrs and fishing boats were moored.

At that time of the morning there was no one around. There was a sentry in a lookout tower near the jetty but when they drew close they could hear the unmistakable sounds of snoring. Lagertha signalled to one of her men and he silently climbed up the tower. It seemed a lot longer to those waiting impatiently below, but within a minute the man reappeared and quickly descended. When he reached the ground he grinned at Lagertha and drew his hand across his throat.

Her warriors followed the shield maiden through the filth strewn streets of Vikevåg towards the jarl's hall. The only sound was the odd bark of a dog but no one seemed to pay any attention to it. Then, as they rounded a corner, Lagertha nearly bumped into a man with his trousers around his thighs as he relieved his bladder into the fetid mud outside his hut.

It took her barely half a second to recover her wits. The man had turned, still pissing away the ale he'd consumed the previous night, and stared at Lagertha and her followers as they came to a halt behind her. He opened his mouth but didn't have the chance to utter a sound before she brought her shield up so that the rim smashed into the man's throat, cutting off the yell of alarm before it started.

The warrior behind her jammed his spear into the unfortunate man's chest and the group moved on. Lagertha had regretted his death, and that of the sentry, as they were both probably Norse, rather than Swedes, but she didn't have much of a choice if they were to remain undetected until they reached their destination.

She studied the jarl's hall from the shadows of an alleyway. Two sentries stood on guard at the only entrance and, unlike the man in the lookout tower, they were awake and alert. Although the sky was getting lighter the sun was hidden behind grey clouds and, whilst she was wondering how to dispose of the sentries without waking the warriors sleeping within the hall, the first drops of rain started to fall, splattering on her face and bare arms. The two men on watch immediately retreated to the door in an effort to find shelter as the rain got heavier. However, it was blowing from the wrong direction and with a curse, they opened the door and slipped inside the hall.

'Lucky the Swedes don't like getting wet,' the man behind her whispered derisively.

'Who does?' she muttered. 'Come on, as quietly as you can.'

Her men followed her across the open ground to the hall. She took a deep breath and opened the door wide. The two sentries were standing just inside the door and it banged into them, knocking them off balance. One dropped his spear and, as he went to retrieve it, Lagertha kicked him hard in his side. He toppled sideways and, before he could recover, she stuck the point of her sword into his neck.

Meanwhile the other sentry had tried to use his spear, but it was the wrong weapon for such a confined space. Before he could thrust it at anyone someone had cut deeply into his neck with a sword and he dropped to the dirt floor of the hall where someone else made sure he was dead by thrusting a dagger into his heart.

The commotion by the door caused a few of those sleeping to wake up and there was some angry grumbling about being disturbed. The voices were slurred and the Norsemen assumed, correctly, that they were still suffering from the previous night's over-indulgence.

There were more than the new jarl's thirty hirdmen in the hall; a dozen female thralls were sleeping beside various men and several other servants, mainly boys, lay near the door. Now all was confusion whilst the inhabitants tried to work out what was going on. The quicker witted of the jarl's hirdmen grabbed their weapons but they wore no armour and had no shields.

Lagertha left her men to kill the rest - whether still asleep or not, armed or not - whilst she made her way to the back of the hall where there was a curtained off section. A man dressed in an expensive tunic and wearing an ornate helmet appeared through the curtains carrying both sword and shield. A woman and a young girl followed him. The former carried a byrnie and was imploring the man to stop and put it on.

He brushed her aside and strode to meet Lagertha.

'Who do you think you are?' he asked scornfully. 'Some shield maiden of legend?'

Although she was dressed like a warrior in a byrnie worn over a tunic and trousers with a helmet on her head, they didn't hide her pretty, beardless face, nor the long, braided fair hair which was twice as long as any man would wear it.

'Come and find out, you Swedish turd, born of a harlot mother and a bastard father.'

As she had intended, the insult enraged the jarl and he made a wild cut at her neck. She moved back swiftly before the blade struck and a spit second later she pushed off with her back leg and cannoned into her opponent.

Despite her much lighter body, the momentum of the impact forced the jarl to stagger backwards. He was off balance and his sword was in the wrong place to block her counter stroke. He was fortunate to intercept her sword with the rim of his shield before it struck him, but the defected blade didn't leave him entirely unscathed. The point sliced open his cheek and nicked his left eye, leaving him in pain and partially blind.

The Swede realised that his adversary was much more skilled at fighting than he had expected. Ignoring the battle going on around them he forced himself to calm down and studied the girl in front of him, trying to read her next move. Lagertha's eyes flickered towards the jarl's left leg and he dropped his shield to cover the expected cut. Instead she whirled her sword in a semi-circle and brought it down on his exposed right thigh, the sharp edge cutting through flesh, sinew and muscle until it struck the femur.

The Swede howled in rage, hobbling back out of reach. Blood streamed down his leg, which was scarcely able to support his weight, as pain gripped his whole body. Lagertha's sword was wrenched out of her hand, still stuck in the flesh of the Swede's heavily muscled thigh, leaving her unarmed for the moment. Her opponent saw his chance and, gritting his teeth against the agony, he lunged forward in one last attempt to kill her.

She contemptuously blocked the blow with her shield, batting the blade away. Then she smashed the boss of her shield into his face, reducing his nose to a bloody pulp. He instinctively closed his eyes as he fell backwards and landed on the foul straw that covered the hard earth floor, so he never saw Lagertha discard her shield, draw her dagger and plunge it into his left eye socket.

She rose to her feet, swiftly looking around her in case she was about to be engaged by another enemy, but the fighting in the rest of the hall was over. The woman and girl rushed to the dead jarl, wailing and embracing him as if they could will him back to life. She ignored them, spitting at them to show her contempt for their display of emotion.

Her men cheered her to the roof beams before hoisting her onto their shoulders and carrying her around the charnel house that once had been the Swedish jarl's hall. She had lost five men and a few more had minor wounds. The enemy hirdmen were all dead and she had captured sixteen thralls, if the dead jarl's wife and daughter were included, to show for the night's work. Her men found a hoard of silver which she distributed amongst them after taking half for herself. Leaving the Norse inhabitants to select a new jarl, she returned to Lysebotn richer than anyone else there, with the possible exception of Jarl Magnus.

Her success attracted new warriors to her banner, all seeking fame and fortune. She would have to keep up the momentum of her attacks on Froh's followers or they would vanish just as quickly as they had appeared. She had returned the snekkja she'd used for the raid on Rennesøy to its owner with enough silver to make him forget that it had been stolen, but she needed ships of her own. She used her share of the hoard from Vikevåg to pay Magnus' shipwright to build her two new longships, both drekars – one with thirty oars a side and one with thirty five.

It took time, but by mid-summer she had the ships and the men needed to man them. She also needed ship's boys, but she was inundated with lads too young to be warriors who wanted to sail with her. In the end she chose the best ten, one of which was Magnus' son, her thirteen year old cousin Tóki.

Her next target was Lauvvik on the Høgsfjord, which joined the Lysefjord from the south near its mouth. However, when she got there she found that its Swedish jarl had taken fright and had fled back to Arendal. She decided that Lauvvik would make a better base than Lysebotn as it was much nearer to the open sea.

'What will you do now, cousin,' Tóki asked her as he poured her a goblet of ale one evening.

The boy had attached himself to her and was eager to please her. It didn't seem to bother him that he was acting like a thrall. At first Lagertha thought that he had a bad case of hero-worship, but now she suspected that he fancied himself in love with her. She knew she should have put an end to his infatuation straight away, but the truth was she liked him and was enjoyed his attention, young though he was. After all, she was only a few years older herself. Her failure to nip his infatuation in the bud was a serious error of judgement.

Of course, Tóki wasn't the only male sexually attracted to the shield maiden, as her men now openly called her, but all of them respected her skill as a warrior and a leader and no-one overstepped the mark.

'Don't be impudent, boy, she retorted. 'You may be Jarl Magnus' son, but such matters are of no concern of yours. If you want to behave like a thrall and serve me, then do as the thralls do and hold your tongue.'

She had spoken more sharply than she had intended– after all Tóki was her cousin – but the truth was she didn't know the answer to his question and it vexed her. She didn't notice but the boy reacted like a whipped cur. He said nothing but he seethed with resentment at the way she had treated him. After that he avoided her, for which she was thankful. She had other, more important, concerns than lovesick boys.

The three jarls – Magnus of Lysebotn, Gedda of Rennesøy and the newly elected Liðsmaðr of Lauvvik bonded together for their own protection, certain that Froh would not accept losing control of the northernmost part of his kingdom without a fight. They were certain that any attack would come by sea as the mountains provided an impenetrable barrier between Arendal and the region known as Roga controlled by the three jarls.

Although not a jarl, Lagertha Bótolfrsdotter was acknowledged as a hersir by the three jarls and treated as such.

It was an important increase in her formal status but she considered herself better than any of them. However, she had to be content with that for now and, albeit reluctantly, she swore allegiance to her uncle Magnus.

Between them the jarls of Roga now had a dozen longships with which to defend their coast. As the king in Arendal had eight other jarls and a total fleet of nearly thirty ships, it wouldn't be nearly enough if they all came north to attack them.

There was one factor in their favour. Most of Froh's jarls in the south were Norsemen, not Swedes. Froh had installed the two Swedes on his northern boundary, partly to reward them and partly to defend his newly acquired kingdom from possible attack by the King of Hordaland to the north. The latter was Norse and had been alarmed by the encroachment of the Swedes across the Skagerrak. It had also frightened the King of Vestfold, whose kingdom lay between Alfheim and Agder.

Only two of Froh's remaining jarls were Swedes – both based to the west of Arendal to guard his eastern border – although he had replaced several of the wealthier Norse bondis with Swedes on one pretext of another.

'I still say that we should enlist the aid of Úlfrekr of Vestfold to attack Froh,' Jarl Gedda maintained.

'Úlfrekr has his own problems,' Magnus pointed out. 'Several of his jarls are in rebellion against him. He'll be lucky to hold onto his throne. In any case he's sandwiched between Froh in Agder and Alfheim, now ruled by Froh's brother. No, you can forget about any help from that quarter.'

'Then surely he would welcome the removal of Froh?' Liðsmaðr butted in.

'Yes, of course. But he is not a man to take risks. He is cunning and will bide his time before joining the winning side. Froh's days will have to be numbered before he'll risk helping us, particularly as his own position is precarious.'

'If they won't join us, what about the Norse jarls of Agder? They can't be happy being ruled by a Swede and there are six of them.'

'They have given their allegiance to Froh. Honour is as important to them as it is to us. They may want to get rid of him, but that's a very different thing to breaking their oaths and becoming his enemy.'

'Will they stay neutral if we attack Froh?' Lagertha asked.

'I suppose they might be persuaded to be a little dilatory in responding to a muster,' Magnus said, guessing what his niece was thinking.

'As I see it we have two alternatives; we can either sit here and wait until Froh attacks us, bringing the whole of the rest of Agder with him, or we can send messages to the Norse jarls and strike first.'

'Perhaps the first thing to do is to sound out the other jarls,' suggested another of the hersir present.

'I agree, then we'll know where we stand,' Lagertha added, unexpectedly getting a dirty look in return for her support from the hersir who'd just spoken.

She knew that she wasn't popular amongst the other hersir and senior bondis. Whilst the skálds might sing of the redoubtable deeds of legendary shield maidens like Brünnhilde, in reality most Vikings believed that women should stay at home and look after the children.

-℣-

Froh paced up and down in the king's hall at Arendal, trying to contain his frustration and anger.

'Where in the name of Hel are they?'

The three Norse jarls who had summoned his call to arms looked uncomfortable. They knew full well that the other three had delayed on purpose because they didn't want to fight against their fellow Norse jarls. Without the missing ships Froh had eighteen longships, but he didn't trust the three Norse jarls who had answered his summons not to hang back when it came to a fight. If they did that he would have to engage the dozen longships the rebels had with ten of his own. Consequently he needed to dissuade them from betraying him.

'I would like you to send me your eldest sons to help crew my own drekar,' Froh told them.

It was supposed to be an honour to crew the king's own longship, but it wasn't. They were hostages for their fathers' good behaviour. The jarls had no option. If they refused then Froh would depose them and place a Swede in their place. So the three sons joined him, even though one was only nine – too young to be a ship's boy by two or three years.

Froh was puzzled. He'd expected the rebels to sail out onto the open sea to fight him. Instead they stayed inside the relatively narrow Lysefjord. The fjord was approximately five hundred yards wide for much of its twenty six mile length, including at the mouth where it joined the Høgsfjord. Although he had their sons as hostages he still didn't trust the three Norse jarls not to hang back, so he signalled for them to overtake the Swedish ships and lead the attack.

As their eight drekar closed on the rebel fleet two things happened. Magnus' ships came together to form three rafts and behind them men on the shores at the entrance to the fjord started to heave on two windlasses, raising a rope boom behind them. Now the leading Norse ships were cut off from Froh's Swedish fleet behind them.

Froh's Norse jarls tried to persuade their men to attack Magnus' ships but their heart wasn't in it. They knew that they would be condemning the boys being held hostage to death, but after the first few men were killed they stopped fighting and rowed their ships clear.

The three jarls watched helplessly as their sons were hauled up the mast of Froh's drekar one by one with a rope around their neck, the eldest first. When he had finished thrashing about, his legs kicking wildly as the air was cut off from his lungs, he was lowered and the next boy was hanged. Finally the nine year old was hauled up the mast to suffer the same fate. As a final indignity the bodies were thrown into the sea.

The Norse jarls' rage was profound. Without any need for communication, they turned their ships as one and headed back towards the mouth of the fjord with Magnus' longships right behind them. The men on the shore hastily lowered the boom and the combined Norse fleet swept on towards Froh's remaining ships.

Outnumbered now by two to one, Froh hastily gave the order to withdraw. Confusion reigned as the ten longships tried to turn in the confined space. Two crashed into each other and another sheared off the oars of a fourth with it bows. Before they could sort themselves out properly the Norse longships reached them.

Lagertha's face was a picture of ferocious joy as her ship came alongside one of the Swedish drekar. Without waiting for the grappling irons to be hauled in to bind the two ships together, she leapt across the gap between them and landed on a rower, sending him sprawling onto the deck. As she came up from the crouching position she thrust her spear into the chest of the oarsman behind the one she'd landed on, then killed the first man.

She re-adopted a crouching stance just as three men attacked her. She used her shield to knock away the spear of one and met the axe of another with the haft of her spear, deflecting it. The third man's eye gleamed with triumph as he saw an opening and aimed his sword at Lagertha's throat. It never reached its target; he fell back with an arrow in his chest shot by one of the archers on her own ship. She had no time to thank him as the other two renewed the attack, but by then more and more of her men were pouring into the Swedish drekar. When another Norse ship grappled itself to the other side of the Swede the outcome was never in doubt.

The remainder of the Swedish crew tried to surrender, but the Norsemen were in no mood to be lenient after watching the murder of their jarls' sons. They were slaughtered to a man and thrown over the side to join the bodies of the innocent boys.

Lagertha ran to the stern to see how the sea battle was progressing, but it was all over. Three of Froh's longships had been captured but the other seven had managed to extricate themselves and had fled. Magnus' ships pursued them but it soon became obvious that they weren't going to catch them before nightfall and he was forced to call off the chase.

-ᛉ-

Froh was furious at the failure of his attack but, for now, there was little he could do about Magnus and his growing power in the north. He contented himself by pillaging the settlements and farms of the three jarls who had betrayed him. Norse bondis and their families were enslaved and Swedish immigrants were given their land. Of course, this did nothing to endear him to the Norse of Agder, who still formed the vast majority of the population.

Unrest was rife and Lagertha continued to attack the halls of the Swedish jarls and bondis. Her reputation grew and, despite the antagonism of many of the Norse jarls and hersirs, she became a heroine in the eyes of the great majority of the warriors.

When Magnus died suddenly the following year Tóki, now sixteen, was chosen to succeed him. However, he was too young to also take over as the leader of the six jarls and Gedda of Rennesøy was chosen instead. This infuriated Tóki, who decided to contest their choice. To bolster his position he proposed marriage to his cousin, Lagertha. She didn't think he was fit to become jarl in Magnus' place, though many bondis supported him just because he was Magnus' son. She certainly didn't want him to share her bed, and scorned his proposal, calling him a puppy still wet behind the ears.

Tóki was not a youth to allow such an insult to pass and he foolishly challenged his cousin to a fight. If he won then, he declared, she would be forced to marry him; if he lost he would stand down as jarl. Lagertha was loathe to fight him, much as she wanted to depose him as jarl. However, she couldn't decline without losing face.

'Don't let him win, Lagertha,' Loptr, one of senior warriors, said quietly. 'He'll make a vindictive bully of a husband, mainly because he is jealous of you.'

'Do you imagine that I don't know that?' she replied with bitterness. 'He's my cousin and he was a ship's boy on my drakar for two years. I know exactly what he's like. Odin won't think him worthy of Valhalla, but I fully intend to send him to Fólkvangr.'

Fólkvangr was the meadow presided over by the goddess Freyja where those who die in combat, but who are not considered worthy of Valhalla, go.

'He may be an arrogant and cocksure young man with few admirable qualities, but if you kill him he'll suddenly become a heroic figure, cruelly slain by a Valkyrie.'

'A Valkyrie? Is that how people see me?'

'They see you as more than mortal, Lagertha. Your luck is attributed to help from the All-father, Odin, and many think that you are one his female warriors. They are simple people, after all. If you win easily they won't think it's a fair contest and their awe of you will turn to fear and loathing.'

'Then I had better let them see that I'm not invincible.'

She entered the circle made by her warriors and the hirdmen of Jarl Tóki wearing no byrnie and no helmet. Her only weapon was a sword and she carried no shield.

'What's this, cousin? Do you treat me with contempt?' Tóki said angrily when he entered the circle wearing byrnie and helmet. He was carrying a shield and spear and wore both a sword and a dagger at his waist.

'Not at all, cousin. I merely wish this fight to be as fair as possible; after all, I have both years and a warrior's skill on my side.'

Tóki was about to make a retort but the lagman held up his hand for quiet.

'I am told that this one to one fight is due to a disagreement over marriage but our laws do not permit a suitor to challenge his intended to resolve the matter by combat, at least not this sort of combat.'

The crowd were silent for a moment; they were unused to their lawgiver making a joke. Then they started laughing, which lightened the mood.

'Therefore this fight is over leadership in the time honoured tradition of the Norse people. If Jarl Tóki loses, he will cede his role as your leader to the victor. If the Lady Lagertha loses, she will submit to her jarl as his obedient subject and pay whatever penalty he deems fitting. This is not a fight to the death, but neither is the first person to draw blood the victor. The loser must submit or be too wounded to carry on.'

The lagman withdrew and the two combatants circled each other warily. Tóki made the first move and feinted with his spear whilst bringing his shield up to deflect the expected counter attack from Lagertha. It didn't come. She neatly sidestepped the spear and her left hand snaked out to grasp it; her sword remained hanging down by her side in her other hand.

Tóki tried to pull his spear back but found that his cousin was much stronger than she looked. It was as if the spear shaft was held in a vice of iron. He felt a fool trying fruitlessly to recover his spear so he let go of it and Lagertha threw it contemptuously aside.

'If this is her showing that she isn't invincible,' Loptr muttered to himself, 'then I'm a witless thrall.'

Next Lagertha staged a series of lightning fast attacks with her sword. Tóki struggled to ward off the blows with his shield and was forced back and back. Eventually, at the edge of the circle, where he faced the spear points of those forming it if he retreated further, he went down on one knee and used his sword in a scything motion to try and cut into Lagertha's legs. She leapt in the air to avoid the blade, but stumbled upon landing.

Initially he had intended to leave her unmarked as far as possible. After all, he didn't want some scarred hag as his wife. However, he had quickly realised that Lagertha was a skilled warrior against whom he had little chance of an easy victory. If he couldn't make her submit and become his wife, he would have to kill her.

Lagertha pretended to have sprained her ankle and hobbled back out of reach as Tóki sprang upright and came after her, a savage grin on his face.

'If I can't have you, then no one shall,' he cried as he banged his sword on his shield.

'Don't be too sure cousin; look, the Valkyries are circling already, waiting for your soul.'

Despite knowing he was being duped, Tóki looked skywards for an instant. It was the moment that she had been waiting for and she charged into him, sending him sprawling onto his back. She stood clear and allowed him to get to his feet. It was only then that he realised that she had wrenched his shield from his grasp whilst he was lying akimbo. Lagertha send the shield spinning away to join the spear.

Now it was sword against sword. Tóki had the advantage of his armour but Lagertha was spared its weight. Her opponent was tiring whilst she still felt as fresh as if she'd just bathed in the fjord. He attacked her and beat her back, feeling a sense of triumph until he realised that she was doing little more than just enough to defend herself. He paused, panting for breath and glared at her.

'You're not trying, cousin. Now why is that?' he said quietly in between pants as he recovered his breath.

'Because I don't want to make your death look too easy,' she replied with a smile.

'Death?' he replied in alarm. 'This isn't a fight to the death. You heard what the lagman said.'

'Oh, but it is, and we both know that. I saw it in your face. If you can't have me as your sex thrall, then you want me dead so no-one else can have me.'

'Sex thrall? Yes, that's exactly what you'll be when I defeat you. Not my wife, just someone to pleasure me, and my hirdmen too if I choose.'

For the first time in the fight Lagertha became angry.

'I'd rather die than let either you or your filthy hird lay your hands on me,' she hissed, gripping the hilt of her sword tightly.

'That's the idea.'

He thrust at her with his sword and she contemptuously beat it away, but he had drawn his dagger with his left hand and now he thrust it towards her abdomen. Caught off balance, all she could do was to twist at the waist so that the point of the dagger didn't penetrate her flesh too far before his arm was fully extended.

She staggered backwards, blood pouring from the wound and staining the bottom half of her tunic and her yellow trousers a dark crimson. The crown grasped. The women had always been on Lagertha's side, and most of the men secretly admired her, even if they called her a völva to each other, believing she cast a spell on her followers.

She hadn't intended Tóki to wound her there, but she had wanted him to give her a flesh wound of some sort. It would gain her a great deal of sympathy so that his death wouldn't be resented. However, she realised that she was losing so much blood that she needed to finish this before she became too weak to do so.

With a roar of feigned rage she attacked the young jarl with a flurry of cuts and jabs with her sword so that he was forced back at speed. When he felt two sharp blows to the back of his byrnie he knew that he had reached the encircling warriors. Lagertha felt her strength draining away so she made to thrust for her cousin's groin, then turned her wrist at the last moment, after he'd committed to blocking it and sunk the point into his throat.

The thrust had all of her remaining strength behind it and the point erupted from the back of his neck. The warrior standing behind Tóki in the circle, against whom he fell, had to jerk his head to the side to avoid being spitted in the chest.

It was over and, as she stood there, bent over with her hands clutching her knees, swaying from side to side, the crowd erupted with shouts of Jarl Lagertha and long life to the shield maiden. She was scarcely aware of Loptr rushing to catch her as she fell. The world went black and she knew no more.

-ᛯ-

Ragnar hadn't fully recuperated, but he wasn't prepared to delay recovering his throne any longer. When he neared the entrance to the fjord that led to Arendal he was astonished to see another fleet of a dozen longships heading towards him.

'Damn it, Froh must have left half his force behind to defend Adger.'

'No, they aren't Swedes. That's my sister, Lagertha's fleet,' Gedda said, appearing by his side.

'Your sister? She has a fleet?' Ragnar asked bewildered.

'Yes, she is Jarl of Lysebotn and leader of the jarls of the north.'

'A jarl?'

'Yes, it's said that she killed the previous jarl, our cousin, in a fair fight and has led the fight against the Swedes for several years. She is called Lagertha the Shield Maiden, amongst other things.'

'Is she now? I look forward to meeting your sister, boy. She interests me.'

'Welcome home, King Ragnar Lodbrok,' Lagertha called across the water, standing at the prow of her drekar wearing a byrnie but with her long fair hair blowing free.

'Not king yet, Jarl Lagertha the Shield Maiden,' he called back. 'I have yet to be acclaimed as such by the thing.'

'You know who I am?'

'Of course, he does, sister. Everyone does.'

'Gedda, is that you, you imp. I wondered where you'd got to.'

Ragnar and Lagertha smiled at each other across the water as her drekar turned and came alongside Ragnar's ship. Gedda studied them and grinned to himself when he saw that they didn't seem able to take their eyes off each other. It was obvious to all that each found the other immensely attractive, if only by repute at this stage. The boy found himself wondering what it would be like to be the brother of a queen.

Chapter Twelve - Aslaug

830 to 835

Ragnar's second marriage was a passionate, if not exactly a romantic, affair. Each enjoyed bedding the other tremendously and Lagertha had two children in as many years – a son, Fridlief and a daughter, Ragnhild. Ragnar sent to Denmark for his two sons by Thora – Eirik and Agnar – so that they could be brought up with their half-siblings.

However, life was never going to be easy for two people who were so strong willed. In particular Lagertha hated being pregnant and didn't have a maternal bone in her body. After Ragnhild's birth she refused to sleep with Ragnar if it meant getting pregnant again. They argued incessantly after that until eventually Lagertha decided she'd had enough; she came to the conclusion that life as a celibate jarl was preferable to that of a fornicating queen. In 835 she returned to the north taking her two children with her and, after a great deal of soul searching, Gedda decided to go with her.

Ragnar watched her sail away with mixed feelings. He truly loved her and he still regarded her as his soul mate, but he'd decided some time ago that she was simply impossible to live with. Moreover, he didn't want to share his life with a shield maiden who could beat him with sword and shield as often as not, however good in bed she was. He was a proud man and he felt that losing to anyone, especially to his wife, damaged his standing in the eyes of others.

What he needed was a woman who would look after his hall and his children, and perhaps give him fewer scars on his back when he rutted with her.

In any case he had other concerns at the moment. His Danish lands had been invaded by Finnulf, Jarl of Gotland, whose father he'd killed several years before. It was rumoured that King Eystein Beli of Uppsala was supporting him, which made the situation even more serious. Eystein was Finnulf's king and

Uppsala was not only the centre of the kingdom which covered much of Eastern Sweden, but it also contained the shrine to the Allfather – Odin, king of the gods. It was the most powerful of the Swedish kingdoms and Ragnar had enough problems without making an enemy of Eystein Beli.

Ragnar prepared to embark on a mission to make peace with Eystein. Meanwhile he sent for Lagertha and asked her to assemble as many ships and warriors as she could from the north.

Whilst he set sail for Uppsala, Lagertha headed for Egholm, the island in the middle of the Limfjord where Ragnar's hall used to be. It was now the base from which Finnulf was operating and it was essential to secure it if she was to eject the occupying Swedes from Jutland.

Evidently Finnulf hadn't expected Ragnar to react so quickly, or in such force. Perhaps he didn't even know that his enemy was now King of Adger. Whatever the truth of it, Egholm was lightly defended and quickly fell to Lagertha's warriors.

Her first priority was to gather intelligence. Apart from finding out where Finnulf and his men were, she was puzzled by King Horik's lack of retaliatory action. Her suspicion was that he was jealous of Ragnar and might even see him as a potential rival for the throne of Denmark. If so, he might even have welcomed Finnulf's depredations in Jutland.

She stopped thinking about what might be and smiled at Gedda as he entered the jarl's hall.

'By Thor's hammer, it's wet out there,' he said shaking the rain off his cloak and going over to the central hearth to dry himself.

'Did you find out anything?'

'Only that Finnulf seems to be making his way north, along the coast, burning and pillaging as he goes.'

'Perhaps he's making for Fladstrand? It used to be Ragnar's base once upon a time and it's where he may well keep a chest or two of silver.'

'Who lives in the hall there now?'

'I seem to remember that its Olaf's younger brother, Vragi. Let's hope we can get there by sea before Finnulf reaches it on land.'

'What about his ships? Where are they?'

'Perhaps he's sent them ahead to Fladstrand. Anyway we'll soon find out.'

It was still raining heavily with the wind blowing strongly from the south east when Lagertha's small fleet left the Limfjord and headed out into the Kattegat. Once they turned to head up the coast they ceased rowing and the ships' boys hauled up the sail with one reef already in it. Lagertha grinned at Gedda as her drekar responded to the increase in pace and carved its way through the spume flecked waves.

'What will you do if the Swedish fleet is at Fladstrand?' he shouted as they both stood in the prow, enjoying the motion of the ship as salt spray hit their faces.

She shook her head to indicate that she didn't want to try and compete with the noise of the wind and the sea and they made their way aft to where the steersman and the ship's captain stood.

'Hopefully we'll find the bastard's ships there. If so, we'll burn them so he's trapped in Jutland. That'll mean he'll be forced to fight us instead of being able to scuttle back where he came from.'

Four and a half hours after setting out Lagertha sailed into the bay below the palisaded hall at Fladstrand. Seven snekkjur, a drekar and a knarr were tied up to the jetty and the hall appeared to be under siege. It seemed that Finnulf had beaten her to the place after all.

'How many do you think there are?' she asked her brother, pointing towards the besieging army.

The rain had stopped and there were now patches of blue sky above them. They were still a couple of miles offshore but Gedda had good eyesight. He called the lookout down and climbed up the mast himself.

'At least four hundred,' he called down. 'There's a few more guarding the ships. They seem to be panicking; they're trying to get the ships ready for sea and the crews are running down the hill to man them.'

His sister smiled grimly.

'It seems we are to have a sea battle then.'

She signalled to the rest of her ships and the rowers rushed to their places. The sails came down as they neared the jetty. Some enemy ships had already cast off but over half were still tied to the jetty as their crews piled aboard.

Lagertha had nine longships but six of those were drekars, so not only did she have bigger ships but they were manned by six hundred and fifty warriors, so her men outnumbered Finnulf's Swedes.

Only five snekkjur faced her as her men shipped their oars and came alongside the enemy, grappling the ships together. In all but one case the Swedes were trapped between two Norse ships; the battle on board the Swedish ships was short and the outcome never in doubt.

Meanwhile Lagertha's own drekar had attached itself to the fifth enemy ship and she led her men on board it, jumping down onto the lower deck of the smaller ship. As she landed she crouched down so that the spear aimed at her went over her shoulder. She thrust upwards with her sword, pushing it into her attacker's rotund belly. He screamed like a stuck pig and fell into the bottom of the ship, trying to stop his intestines from spilling out.

Lagertha ignored him and used her shield to catch a wild blow from an axe aimed at her head. The force of the blow from the axe jarred her arm and it split her shield, sticking fast in the lime wood. Once more her sword snaked out and the axeman fell back with blood spurting from his ripped throat.

The shield was now more of an encumbrance than a help and so she discarded it and drew her dagger with her left hand. Gedda had followed her onto the enemy ship. Unlike his battle seasoned sister, this was his first battle and he was both excited and nervous. He saw the man with the fatal wound in his belly grit his teeth and draw his dagger, intent on stabbing it into Lagertha's leg. Gedda struck downwards with his sword and killed the man just in time. It wasn't much of a victory but now that he had killed his first man he calmed down and moved to his sister's side.

Together they held off the frantic attacks by the Swedes until overwhelming numbers of Norsemen arriving on the enemy ship drove the crew back. Gedda didn't notice until afterwards that he had suffered two flesh wounds during the fighting, one to his right cheek and another to his right biceps. He was rather proud of them, forgetting that the one to his face wouldn't show once he was old enough to grow a proper beard instead of the wispy fluff he now sported.

In less than an hour after sailing into the bay it was all over. The five Swedish longships had all been captured and most of their crews had been killed or badly wounded in the fight. Only a few had been captured and they would soon wish that they had died too; life as a Norseman's thrall was not a pleasant existence.

The other four ships had never left the jetty. As soon as Finnulf had realised that the battle was already lost, he abandoned them and headed inland with his remaining hundred and fifty men.

The arrival of Ragnar Lodbrok at Uppsala hadn't come as a surprise to King Eystein. His capital lay at the northern end of a fjord that was an offshoot of the wide sea inlet peppered with islands that stretched a hundred miles inland from the sea. Messengers had kept him appraised of the progress of the Norse fleet and of the fact that the drekars didn't have their figureheads mounted; the universal sign that they came in peace.

The port, which he assumed was Uppsala, was a much smaller place than Ragnar had expected. Compared to it, his own capital of Arendal was five times the size. The jetty was busy with knarrs unloading and loading and so they moored Ragnar's drekar, and the three snekkjur he'd brought along as escort, further out in the fjord whilst they waited for a vacant berth. He hadn't been there above half an hour when Bjarke drew his attention to a small boat with six oars which had cast off from the jetty and was now heading towards his ships.

'Who are you and what is your business in Uppsala?' a figure standing in the stern alongside the steersman called when the boat was less than fifty yards away.

'King Ragnar Lodbrok of Agder in Norway has come to visit King Eystein,' Olaf called in reply, then said quietly to Ragnar, 'he knows full well who you are from the raven on our sails when we sailed in, if nothing else.'

'Be quiet, Olaf. You're quite right but there is a formality to these things and I must observe them.'

'Bloody waste of time if you ask me,' Olaf snorted.

'I didn't,' Ragnar snapped back.

He was anxious about the forthcoming meeting with the most powerful king in Sweden and Olaf wasn't helping to calm his nerves. Olaf looked surprised and then resentful at the way his friend had spoken to him, but he said nothing further.

'Welcome, King Ragnar. Eystein Beli has been expecting you. He invites you to join him as his guest in his hall at Uppsala.'

Ragnar scanned the settlement in front of him but he could see nothing that might be a king's hall. Still less was there any sign of the fabled Temple of Uppsala, the centre of pagan worship in Scandinavia.

The man standing in the boat laughed when he saw Ragnar looking for the hall and temple.

'This isn't Uppsala, Ragnar Lodbrok. It lies five miles up the River Fyris, the mouth of which is over there.'

He pointed to where a small river flowed into the sea. It looked impassable to all but the smallest craft and he eyed it dubiously.

'Come, a berth has been cleared for you at the jetty, but I fear that there is only room for your drekar. The rest of your ships will have to remain here.'

'How will we get to Uppsala? Walk?'

'No, we have three horses to convey you and two attendants to the king's hall.'

'Two of my hird to guard me? I may have come in peace, whoever you are, but I am not so foolish as to walk into another king's domain with less than an appropriate number of hirdmen, and I will also bring my servants. Keep your horses; we will walk.'

'No, Konungr, I'm sorry but my king would never forgive me. You must ride.'

Ragnar smiled to himself. The young man's attitude had changed as soon as he started to prove difficult. His use of the title Konungr - the formal way to address a king – indicated that he'd become flustered.

'If my men walk, I walk.'

The man shrugged his shoulders.

'Then I must see if I can hire more horses. How many men to you propose to bring with you?'

'Twenty in all, myself, the three jarls who have accompanied me, our body servants and a suitable escort.'

'Twenty?' The young man looked dubious, but then nodded. 'Very well, but it may take me until tomorrow. The horses will have to come from Uppsala.'

'I'm in no rush. We'll stay here at anchor for now. We can come alongside when you've cleared enough berths for all four of my longships.'

The man nodded unhappily and was about to give the order to return to the jetty when Ragnar called out to him one more time.

'By the way, you've neglected to tell me who you are.'

'No, I didn't say, did I? I'm Hákon, King Eystein's nephew.'

On the way to Eystein's hall the next day they stopped at the Temple of Uppsala to worship before the three statues, seated on a single golden throne. The building itself was built like a square timber hall with a pointed tower at each corner. Suspended between each tower and the next was a golden chain. Ragnar couldn't imagine what the chain must be worth; perhaps more than all wealth of the kings of Sweden and Norway put together.

Thor's image sat in the middle with Odin on one side of him and Frey, the god of fertility on the other, his enormous phallus leaving little doubt as to his identity. It was customary that a sacrifice was made to Thor when famine threatened. Before setting out for war or going raiding it was made to Odin. Frey received his sacrifices as part of all marriage ceremonies performed in the temple. However, Hákon suggested tactfully to Ragnar that he might want to appease all three. Ragnar gave the expectant godis, one for each god, a sullen look but he paid for three sheep to be slaughtered and offered to the three wooden effigies. He left thinking sourly that the godis and their acolytes would eat well tonight at his expense.

The king's hall was nearly as impressive as the temple. It was twice the size of Ragnar's hall in Arendal with four fire pits along the central aisle in front of an oversized throne. This sat on a dais three quarters of the way down the hall. Behind it there was a wooden screen which sectioned off the private quarters of Eystein Beli and his family. The main part of the hall had alcoves all along each side which served as both sleeping areas and as places for his hirdmen to eat and drink.

The gaps between the timbers of which the exterior walls were constructed were sealed with dried mud over which hung tapestries, old shields and animal skins. Each fire pit had a flap in the roof above it which could be opened to let smoke out or closed in inclement weather. However, the feature which impressed Ragnar the most was the smooth timber flooring. It all made his own hall, with its hard packed earth floor and bare walls, look primitive.

At first he was so busy admiring the hall that he didn't look at the throne area. When he did he studied the king and dismissed him as no warrior, with his thinning grey hair, wispy beard and large paunch. He looked to Ragnar like a man who enjoyed the good things in life and didn't stir much outside his hall.

His wife sat beside him on a small chair. She was more striking with long blond hair that had no more than a few strands of grey in it and a body, though old, which was still firm and nicely rounded.

Two girls sat on the steps of the dais at their parents' feet. Ragnar experienced a stirring in his loins as he looked at them for the first time. Both were extremely pretty, fair haired and young. He estimated that one was no more than fourteen and the other perhaps a year younger.

Eystein noticed Ragnar's interest in his daughters and he exchanged a quick look with his wife, who let the corners of her mouth curl upwards into a brief smile. Neither of the two girls were the type to look demurely at the floor in the presence of an attractive man. Whilst the elder, Ingeborg, saw a man of twenty seven who was arrogant and thought too much of himself, her sister, Aslaug, saw him as self-confident and handsome.

The King of Uppsala welcomed Ragnar with a feast the like of which his guest had never seen. When he was bloated with food and half-drunk on ale, Eystein raised the subject of an alliance with Ragnar.

'Now that you have regained Adger in Norway and made yourself King of Alfheim, what do you intend to do next?'

'Once my former wife has re-conquered my lands in Jutland, I will set about raising a large enough fleet to raid outside the Baltic.'

If Eystein had anything to do with the former he was too astute to let his face betray the fact.

'Then you don't intent to raid Swedish lands again?'

'No. Now that Froh and Kjarten are dead I have no quarrel with the Swedes; or at least, I won't have once Finnulf of Gotland has joined them in Valhalla.'

Eystein had hoped that Ragnar would diplomatically avoid the matter of Finnulf's invasion, but now he had raised it the matter couldn't be avoided. He gave Ragnar a hard stare, which the Norseman returned until it was the older man who looked away.

'You are obviously aware that Finnulf is one of my jarls?'

'Unless he's acting on your instructions, then I don't hold you responsible for his actions. Is he?'

Eystein bit back the angry retort that sprang to his lips. He wanted this man as an ally, not an enemy.

'Of course not, and I take exception to the suggestion that he is.'

'Then I apologise. I too see an advantage in us becoming allies. You will realise that King Horik of Denmark isn't particularly happy to have a jarl who is also the ruler of two independent kingdoms. No doubt that explains his reluctance to come to my aid when Finnulf invaded.'

'You intend to challenge Horik for the throne of Denmark?'

'Only if he makes it necessary.'

Eystein was beginning to realise that Ragnar was ambitious and likely to be quite ruthless when it came to getting what he wanted.

'I think that only a fool would make you his enemy, Ragnar Lodbrok. I hope that we can be friends.'

'I too would like to see us as allies.'

'You have already given me your word to stop raiding Sweden; however I would like to bind you closer to me. You said that you have put aside the shield maiden?'

'Yes, Lagertha is no more to me now than one of my jarls.'

It wasn't true. He was still felt passionately about her, but he knew that they were not suited as man and wife – and never would be.

'Then I suggest that you marry my daughter Ingeborg to cement our friendship.'

Ragnar thought about it for a moment. The girl was lissom and he lusted after her, but he had was well aware that she didn't feel the same way about him.

'I'm not averse to the idea of marrying one of your daughters – in fact I welcome the idea – but the one I would choose is Aslaug.'

Eystein was both surprised and alarmed. It was the last thing he wanted.

'No, she is too young; Ingeborg is ready to be bedded; her sister isn't.'

'She seems to have already developed breasts, unless my eyes deceive me. In what way is she too young?'

Eystein shifted uncomfortably and wouldn't meet Ragnar's eyes.

'I knew you were coming to Uppsala before my lookouts sent word.'

'Aslaug told you,' he said, now understanding Eystein's reluctance to lose her. 'She's a völva?'

Some fools believed that Lagertha was a völva, but that was because they attributed her success as a warrior to magical powers. That was nonsense. In any case, a true völva could foretell the future and heal the sick. Lagertha could do neither of those things.

Eystein sighed. 'She told me that you were coming and that the Norns had woven your two life threads together.'

Ragnar feared the Norns, as did all Scandinavian people, but he wasn't sure that they controlled his fate. He believed that men made their own destiny, though he did acknowledge that the Norns decided if someone was destined to be lucky or unlucky.

'In that case, I would hesitate to go against the desires of the Norns, Eystein. Do you think it's wise to challenge them?'

Eystein wasn't such a fool that he didn't realise that Ragnar was using his superstitions against him, but he didn't want to lose Aslaug either. He had depended a great deal on the advice of his old völva and, of course, the godis at the temple, but she was getting old and she had told him herself that she wasn't destined to live much longer. She had been training Aslaug as her replacement for the past year.

'We will go to the temple tomorrow and seek advice,' he said, getting up to indicate that their conversation was at an end.

Ragnar's bondis in Jutland had been caught off guard by Finnulf's invasion. Disorganised and leaderless as they were, they had been unable to organise any effective opposition to the Swedes until Lagertha's arrival. Now they flocked to her side and, led by a wealthy young bondi called Grimulf, they set out to corner Finnulf and his remaining Swedes.

Whilst the Danish warriors pursued the Swedes into the interior, Lagertha sailed around the northern tip of Jutland and landed on the coast of the Jammerbugt – the Bay of Woe – an apt name for it as far as Finnulf was concerned. When Finnulf's scouts reported to him that hundreds of Norse warriors blocked his path to the west, he turned north. He would have done better to have turned and attacked Grimulf's small army instead. At least his one hundred and fifty men would only have been faced by two hundred or so.

As it was, the two forces – Norse and Danes – combined and chased him into the narrow peninsula at the top of the Danish mainland called Toppenafdanmark. Lagertha didn't know it, but this was the land originally granted to Ragnar by his uncle eight years previously.

She had been impressed by the rich farmland she had traversed so far - so different to the bleak mountains of Norway – but this part of Denmark was full of sand, coarse grasses and scrub. There were few trees to shelter it from the wind that blew in off the German Ocean and she wondered how anyone managed to make a living in such a barren area. There were some sheep and rather more pigs but few cattle and no crops.

Grimulf explained that there were plenty of fish in the sea and a plethora of wild mushrooms, berries and herbs in the summer and autumn. It was very different to her land in Norway but obtaining enough subsistence for its people seemed to be just as difficult.

Eventually Finnulf was trapped near a small settlement inhabited by fishermen and their families at Skagen. The men, women and children had been killed by Finnulf's men, which only served to enrage the Danes further. The Swedes were tired, hungry and dispirited and Grimulf was insistent on killing them all, but Lagertha was more careful with her men's lives. Although they outnumbered the enemy by four to one, the Swedish warriors would sell their lives dearly and so she was bound to lose a good number of her own men in the process.

Grimulf had consented to Lagertha taking the lead up to that point, but now he was angry at being thwarted by a woman and he refused to accept her decision.

'Very well, Grimulf. Go ahead.'

'What do you mean, go ahead?'

'If you want to lead your men against Finnulf, that's your decision. Neither I nor any of my men will help you, however. My only desire is to take their jarl's head back to King Ragnar.

Those are his orders and, may I remind you, he is your jarl as well as being a king in both Norway and Sweden.'

That gave Grimulf pause for thought. After all, Lagertha had been Ragnar's queen for several years, even if she wasn't now. He didn't want to offend him and wisely decided that the safest course of action was to accept the woman's decision, however much he resented it.

He nodded and so she walked forward and stopped just out of bowshot in front of the Swedes.

'Surrender Finnulf to me and I'll allow you to return to Gotland unharmed. I'll even give you a knarr and a snekkja for the voyage.'

'What will happen to our jarl?' one of the Swedes called out.

'King Ragnar demands his head, that's all.'

'Never!' another man shouted. 'We'd rather die first.'

'Then prepare to enter Valhalla, or perhaps Helheim.'

'Not Helheim, it's only for those who die unworthy deaths or of old age,' someone shouted back.

'And you think that fighting for this devil's spawn who murders Danish women and children for no purpose is a worthy cause?' she asked scornfully. 'Let's hope the Valkyries agree with you.'

She walked back to where her army waited and sent her archers forward as the Swedes formed a shield wall. Most of the first volley of arrows lodged in shields or ricocheted off helmets, but a few found exposed legs and, for one unfortunate youth, the narrow gap between helmet and eyes.

'This is no way to fight,' Grimulf said angrily. 'If they are to die, they deserve a warrior's death, fighting hand to hand.'

'If you want to see your men die, go ahead Grimulf. Do you want me to call my archers back so that you can attack their shield wall?'

'Not on our own, no. But this is the coward's way of fighting. No man would behave like this.'

'Be very careful, Grimulf, or I will kill you too,' Lagertha told him quietly, the cold rage in her eyes chilling him.

By then the third volley had killed or wounded several more of the Swedes and they decided that they had had enough. They started to advance and, in the face of another volley of arrows, the pace quickened and they lost formation.

'Archers retreat, form shield wall,' Lagertha yelled. 'Now you'll get your chance Grimulf. Back to your men.'

He nodded and trotted off to join the other Danes on the left flank. The Swedes never stood a chance. They were seriously outnumbered and their attack was ragged. In contrast their opponents stood firm and held their ground. Try as they might, the Swedes couldn't force the Norse centre back. A man tried to thrust the point of his spear between Lagertha's helmet and the top of her shield but she raised the latter to deflect it, and then stabbed the man's thigh with her sword. He screamed in rage and tried once more to use his spear. It was too unwieldy for close quarter fighting and, seeing an opening, she sunk her blade into her adversary's leather covered chest, killing him instantly.

The heart had gone out of the Swedes by then and, as the wings of the Norse and Danish line curled around the remaining Swedes, they began to surrender. It didn't save some of them as the blood of the Danes, in particular, was up and they wanted revenge for the murder of the unfortunate inhabitants of Skagen.

One of Lagertha's men blew several blasts on his horn and gradually the slaughter ceased. Half of the Swedes had died or were badly wounded and most of the rest had flesh wounds. The only one unscathed was Finnulf, protected as he was by his hirdmen. Casualties on the other side were relatively light with barely more than a dozen killed and a score or so wounded, for which Lagertha was thankful.

She took a bow from one of the archers and took careful aim at the Swedish jarl. The arrow flew straight and true and struck him in the right eye. He collapsed to the ground, twitched once and was still. Everyone was awestruck at the impossible shot and she handed the bow back to its owner in the stunned silence that followed. She hadn't aimed specifically at his eye, of course; it was just a lucky shot.

'You can keep the Swedes as thralls, Grimulf. It'll teach them that they should have accepted my offer instead of fighting.'

'Er, I apologise for what I said earlier, jarl. I can see now that your tactics saved us losing warriors unnecessarily.'

'Thank you, Grimulf. Your apology just saved me the necessity of fighting you to preserve my honour.'

This was said with a smile, albeit a grim one, and the Dane didn't know whether Lagertha was being serious or not. What she said next stunned him though.

'This invasion has convinced Ragnar that he can't realistically remain as the jarl of this area. He needs someone living here to rule and defend his Danish lands for him. He gave me the authority to appoint the man I thought best suited to take over. Provided you swear fealty to him as your king, I will make you the jarl.'

Grimulf was about to accept with gratitude when he thought of a snag.

'I am most grateful and I would like to accept, of course, but I doubt that King Herik would approve.'

'You leave Herik to me. He will accept the situation or he'll lose his throne.'

Grimulf never thought for a moment that Lagertha was boasting.

'In that case, I swear to follow Ragnar Lodbrok as my king and to give him my undivided loyalty.'

-ᛉ-

Ragnar was getting bored watching the godis consulting the gods to decide who he should marry. The temple stank of blood from the sacrifices they had made and which, of course, he'd paid for.

'Why are they taking so long?' he muttered to his own godi, Torstein.

'They don't know who to please, Ragnar, you or their king. They'll probably end up telling you that Thor favours Ingeborg and Frey has chosen Aslaug, a solution to their dilemma which will offend neither of you.'

'What about Odin? Doesn't the All-father want a say?' he asked cynically.

'Careful, Ragnar. The gods have favoured you so far; you don't want to offend them, least of all Odin.'

'You didn't answer my question.'

'This temple is dedicated to Thor, and Frey is the god of fertility. Odin is more interested in war, wisdom and poetry, not matrimony.'

'I know that, you fool,' he replied testily, earning a glare from Eystein.

He realised that he'd spoken louder than he had intended. He nodded in apology then whispered in Torstein's ear.

'Go and ask your fellow priests why it's taking so long.'

Torstein sighed and went up to the godi who was kneeling in front of the statue of Thor, pouring the blood from a black bull he'd just butchered – at some cost to Ragnar's purse – into a large golden bowl.

'Haven't you reached a decision yet?' he asked the godi, who gave him a pained look; you didn't interrupt ceremonies in the temple.

'No, these things cannot be rushed,' the kneeling godi replied tersely, then ignored Torstein.

Ragnar muttered something under his breath and waited impatiently for the man to finish. When he got up another godi moved forward to kneel before Frey, pouring another libation of fresh blood, this time from a ram, into the golden basin at the statue's feet and started to pray.

'Enough of this foolishness,' Ragnar cried, his patience finally at an end. 'If you want me as an ally, Eystein, then I will marry Aslaug; if not, I will return home and find a bride elsewhere.'

'Ragnar, you will antagonise the gods!' his fellow king told him, a shocked expression on his face.

'Well, they are upsetting me, or rather their witless godis are. I have a solution. We'll leave the choice to your daughters.'

Eystein beckoned him and, with an apologetic look towards the affronted temple priests, he led the way into the sunshine outside.

'What if both or neither want you for a husband?'

'If neither, there's an end to the matter. If both, then I will choose.'

Eystein paced up and down whilst he considered Ragnar's proposal. He too had been getting irritated by the protracted ceremony in the temple and this seemed a reasonable idea, much as he didn't want to lose his younger daughter's services as a völva. In the end he reluctantly nodded his agreement.

When Ragnar returned two days later to marry Aslaug, the temple godis almost gabbled their way through the ceremony, wary of another sacrilegious outbreak from the groom.

Chapter Thirteen – The Sons of Ragnar

844

Aslaug proved to have been a good choice. Theirs wasn't a passionate relationship, as it had been with Lagertha. However, she had produced four sons in as many years.

The first had been Ivar, who the other boys at Arendal had nicknamed the boneless because he was a contortionist who could bend his incredibly flexible young body into positions that no other boy could emulate. He was followed in 837 by Bjorn. He too earned a nickname - ironsides - because he did exercises to develop the muscles of his torso from a young age until his body felt as hard as metal to the touch.

Sigurd had been born thirteen months later with a left eye which had a vertical slit instead of a round pupil. Inevitably he was known as snake-in-the-eye. The fourth son, Halfdan, was something of a disappointment in that he had no peculiar distinguishing characteristics. He was just Halfdan.

All Ragnar's sons by Aslaug had been born in the summer when he had been away raiding, having been conceived almost as soon as he had returned each October. It therefore came as something of a surprise to him when, after a break of three years in which Aslaug didn't get pregnant, she told him that she was expecting another baby.

In 844 Ragnar planned to spend the whole seven months plundering the east coast of England. It would be the longest he'd been away from Adger and Alfheim and he decided that the time had come to give two of his sons some responsibility. Thora's sons, Agnar and Eirik, were nineteen and seventeen respectively and so he decided to leave the elder in charge at Arendal and send the younger to Bohus to rule Alfheim.

His son by Lagertha, Fridlief, was now twelve so he was old enough to sail with his father as a ship's boy. Their daughter, ten year old Ragnhild, would stay and help Aslaug, who was already so large this early in the pregnancy that Ragnar was convinced that she would have twins.

At the start of April he set sail for the east coast of England with Lagertha, Olaf and a fleet of twenty longships. Three weeks later his wife gave birth to a baby girl. When he returned it wouldn't take him long to work out that the child must have been conceived in August when he was away raiding in Ireland. She gnawed her lower lip until it bled trying to decide what to do.

'What will you call her?' Ragnhild asked her.

'I thought of Åløf. Åløf Ragnarsdóttir.'

'I may only be ten, Queen Aslaug, but even I know that this baby wasn't sired by my father.'

'Not his? Of course it's his.'

She had always thought of Lagertha's daughter as a sweet, innocent little girl. She was about to find out that she was wise beyond her years.

'I'm not a fool. I can count back nine months as well as the next person. Who's the father?'

The queen's shoulders slumped.

'I don't know. I'm not lying, Ragnhild,' she added, seeing the sceptical expression on the young girl's face.

She paused for a moment, trying to decide how best to explain it.

'You know that I sometimes go into a trance when I dream about the future? Once I dreamt that a man – a stranger – came and lay with me. Perhaps he was responsible.'

'A stranger?' Ragnhild didn't look convinced, then the frown on her forehead cleared. 'Maybe it was one of the gods.'

'It's possible, but even so your father would never forgive me.'

The two were silent for some time, each lost in their own thoughts. Suddenly the girl spoke again.

'Have you had a vision about the future? About what he will do and what will become of you and Åløf?'

'Yes,' the queen whispered. 'I have also dreamt about Ragnar's end, I think, but I don't understand either dream.'

'What happens?'

'I'm with a little girl and we're crossing a lake in winter. It's not anywhere I know. There are mountains but they are grey and barren, not like here, and not like Sweden either. The ice breaks and we sink below it.'

Ragnhild shuddered. 'Are you sure that it's you? How old is the little girl?'

'Not very old, perhaps five or six?'

'So it's not immediately after father returns then. What about him? You said you saw his death?'

'It was a strange dream. He was wearing the animal skin leggings and tunic that caused him to be named Lodbrok, but he told me that he hasn't worn them since he was a young man. I don't even think he has them anymore. In the dream snakes kept biting him but they couldn't get through the hairy clothes.'

'How do you know he dies then?'

'I don't. But he was alone and in a pit. How could he survive?'

'I'm glad I don't have the second sight,' Ragnhild said with feeling. 'What will you do now?'

'I can't stay here. I'm certain that he won't forgive me and he'll probably kill Åløf too. I'll go back to Uppsala, to my father.'

'Will he take you back?'

'I don't know. He valued my gift, though I think of it as a curse now.'

-ᛉ-

'Where's mother?' five year old Sigurd asked his brothers a week later as he came out of the king's hall to join them at the horse trough. He splashed water in his face perfunctorily to wake up properly.

'Probably looking after our wretched baby sister. By all the gods, she can scream louder than any of us and she never shuts up,' Ivar, the eldest replied.

'No, but come to think of it I didn't hear her last night.'

'You're right,' Bjorn cut in, drying his hair by shaking it so water droplets struck the other three.

Ivar punched him the arm and then they both grabbed Halfdan and dunked him in the trough, accompanied by the four-year old's struggles and squeals of protest. By the time that the small boy had got his own back by splashing the others, the four boys had forgotten all about their mother and new born sister. That is, until Ragnhild told them that they'd left.

'Left? For where? Why,' Halfdan asked, feeling bereft.

His mother had protected him from the others' teasing and horseplay before it got too out of hand. Now he felt alone and vulnerable.

'Why didn't she tell us, or take us with her?' Bjorn asked.

Ragnhild thought about explaining but realised that her half-brothers were too young to understand, so she said nothing.

'Does Agnar know?' Sigurd asked.

If the boys weren't depressed enough at their mother's disappearance, the thought that they were now at the mercy of their eldest half-brother sent a chill down their collective spines. He had never liked them, nor had Eirik, and the feeling was mutual.

'If he tries to bully us I'll kill him,' Ivar said, fingering the small dagger at his waist – a present from his father when he'd turned seven.

'He's acting as father's deputy; he could lock us up and starve us to death and we couldn't stop him,' Bjorn said despondently. 'We could kill him first though,' he said suddenly, brightening up at the idea.

'If we did that the Thing would try us for murder and their punishment would probably be worse,' Ivar pointed out, bringing them back down to earth.

'Where has the queen gone?' Agnar asked them, fixing them with what he fondly imagined was a piercing stare.

'We know as much, or as little, as you do, brother,' Ivar replied sullenly.

None of the four boys liked the way that they had been escorted into the king's hall by three of their brother's hirdmen. The fact that Ivar had been deprived of his dagger was even less reassuring.

'You're lying. Don't think that, just because you're little boys I won't have the truth beaten out of you.'

'You can't do that, they're the king's sons, just as much as you are, Agnar,' one of the bondis present called out. There was a murmur of agreement around the hall.

'Who said that?' Agnar snapped.

'I did.'

One of the blacksmiths stepped forward and several men joined him. Agnar had the sense to realise that he was treading on thin ice. Ragnar might have left him in charge, but he was no more than a bondi in status, just as all these men were. His father wouldn't thank him if he returned to find he'd been deposed and the Thing had elected another temporary leader. He would never be trusted by Ragnar again.

'I am determined to find out where Queen Aslaug has gone. She may have been abducted for all we know.'

'She left of her own free will,' another man called out. 'She hired a ship to take her to Uppsala, to her father, and she took the baby with her. I saw them leave early this morning.'

The speaker was the captain of a knarr and Agnar had no reason to doubt what he'd said.

'Very well. Then I shall go to Uppsala and find out why she has gone there.'

-Ⅴ-

Edmund of Bebbanburg was visiting Alnwic when the messenger found him.

'My lord, the Vikings have attacked Whitby in force; some twenty ships with nearly a thousand men, or so the story goes. King Eanred has called out the fyrd and asks you to make haste to defend your coastline.'

'What was the fate of Whitby?'

'The heathens burned the town and sacked the monastery, but the stone buildings still stand.'

There had been sporadic raids by Vikings ever since Lindisfarne was attacked fifty years ago, but nothing on this scale. It would take all of Lothian and Islandshire to equal their numbers, but even then the fyrd were no match for Viking warriors. Edmund's main worry was Lindisfarne. The monastery was still a popular destination for pilgrims and it had been a long time since it was last raided, so it had grown rich again. It had a palisade to defend it but it wouldn't take a thousand men long to breach it, unless it had a strong garrison.

Suddenly he had a thought.

'Was the king there?'

'No, lord. He is in Eoforwīc, making preparations to defend it in case the Vikings attack there.'

And letting the rest of us fend for ourselves, Edmund thought bitterly. Instead of shutting himself away, cowering like a trapped rat in his capital, Eanred should be mobilising the kingdom to fight these raiders. He had never forgiven the king for the death of Ilfrid two years before and now he began to think that the time was coming when Eanred should be deposed in favour of a more able man.

He came round from his reverie to realise the messenger was still standing in front of him, shifting uncomfortably from one foot to the other. He nodded a dismissal to him and then yelled for Laughlin to pack for their return to Bebbanburg.

'First I need to know where these Vikings are now. It shouldn't be too difficult to find such a large fleet,' he told Garr, the captain of his warband.

Garr was getting on in years now. He would like to have appointed Erik to replace him; he found that the Norseman was now his closest confidante and he depended on his advice, but he too was getting long in the tooth. Besides, he wasn't sure that his warriors would accept orders from a man who'd been captured from a Viking ship, even if he was a boy at the time.

The most promising candidate to take over from Garr was Cynefrith, a warrior in his mid-twenties who was respected by his fellows. Perhaps the time had come to test him.

-Ɣ-

Cynefrith cautiously raised his head above the crest of the sand dunes and peered through the marram grass at the beach below him. There were seven Viking longships drawn up in a line in the shallow bay. Three were the larger type which the heathens called drakar and four were the smaller snekkjur. Evidently the raiding party had divided, even so the crews of these ships had to total something like four hundred men – too many for Lord Edmund to take on with the men he had available.

He looked down at the beach again. There were a dozen men and about thirty boys gathered around four camp fires. Nearby a few sheep were standing or lying disconsolately in a pen made roughly out of driftwood; mainly branches brought in on the tide after the recent storm. One of their number had been skinned and gutted and was now being cooked on a spit over one of the fires.

An iron cauldron was hanging over another fire, suspended from a tripod made of crooked branches. One of the boys was throwing something into it from a bag at his feet whilst another was chopping up root vegetables on a flat stone using a dagger.

As far as Cynefrith could see, there were no sentries posted. He glanced back into the hollow behind the dune he was perched on. His thirty men stood with their hands over their horses noses to make sure they didn't make a noise and alert the Vikings. Half of his men were skilled bowmen and all were seasoned warriors wearing mail byrnies and helmets. However, he wasn't contemplating attacking the men and boys left to guard the longships; at least not yet. He needed to know where the rest of the crews were first.

He looked inland and saw a thin plume of grey smoke rising vertically in the still air. As he watched the plume grew thicker and darker. He tried to gauge the distance but it was difficult to tell. However, there was only one sizeable settlement in that direction, although there were a number of individual farmsteads as well.

The plume of smoke seemed to broaden out and Cynefrith grunted. Several buildings must have been fired to make that pattern of smoke and so he was fairly certain that it came from the settlement. It was five miles inland so he calculated that he had at least two hours before the raiders returned with their loot and captives, more if they were driving livestock as well.

He called two of his best warriors to his side and pointed to the two ships that were closest to a dune.

'I want you to fire those two longships. Get into position as close as you can then crawl along the sand until you can climb aboard. Have you both got a flint, striker and tinder? Good. Good luck.'

It seemed like an age but it was probably less than a quarter of an hour before he saw his two men slithering like snakes towards the two longships. Both had discarded their byrnies, helmets and weapons, apart from a seax each had strapped to his back. A short while later they disappeared from view behind the bulk of the two hulls and Cynefrith breathed a sigh of relief. Evidently they hadn't been spotted by the Vikings further along the beach, who were now busy slicing meat from the charred sheep's carcase on the spit and filling their bowls with the vegetable gruel.

Some time later he saw his two men running back towards the cover of the dunes as a spiral of thin smoke climbed heavenwards from each of the two ships. Then Cynefrith saw a bloom of orange erupt from the base of the mast of one, and then the other. By this time his two men had reached the dunes, but they'd been spotted by one of the ship's boys who'd looked up at the wrong moment. No doubt he'd caught the movement out of the corner of his eye.

He called out something in a strange language which caused the rest of the Vikings to look up from their meal and a split second later bowls and haunches of meat were thrown aside as they started running towards the two ships. Cynefrith smiled in satisfaction as he saw them pick up cauldrons and buckets but leave their armour and weapons where they were, stacked near the campfires. A few wore swords at their waists but most only had daggers.

Cynefrith waited until the Vikings were fully engaged in trying the douse the two fires with sea water, using any container that came to hand, then he led his men quietly through the dunes and down onto the beach. The sand had been hard packed by the outgoing tide and, although the going was still on the soft side for the horses, they managed to increase the pace to a slow canter before one of the ship's boys spotted them.

His cry of alarm didn't produce the panic that Cynefrith was expecting. Instead several of the boys climbed aboard the ship nearest the two which were now blazing merrily and started to throw down spears and shields to the others. By the time that the Bebbanburg warband reached them, the Vikings had formed a hurried shield wall and the boys still on board started to send a few arrows towards the oncoming Anglo-Saxons.

Horses didn't like to charge a shield wall and, true to form, they baulked at doing so now. Cynefrith thought quickly and sent a dozen of his men around the flanks of the short shield wall whilst he and the other eighteen dismounted and advanced towards the enemy line.

After a brief exchange of spear thrusts he withdrew just as the rest of his men began hacking at the rear of the Vikings. These were mostly ship's boys who had little military training. It didn't take long before they broke and, leaving a dozen of their number dead, they made for one of the other longships hoping to get away. Cynefrith let them go and surrounded the remaining Vikings.

By the time that the last warrior was dead the boys had managed to get the smallest snekkja afloat and were gamely trying to use the long oars to back her away from the beach. They weren't used to rowing, nor did most of them have the strength to do so. Most of Cynefrith's men, on the other hand, were as adept at crewing a ship as they were at fighting on land. It didn't take them long to get one of the other snekkja manned and they gave chase.

It took them less than half an hour to overhaul the other snekkja and the dejected boys surrendered without a fight. Once back on the beach Cynefrith set a guard on the twenty captured Vikings and fired the rest of the ships. He had lost four men killed and as many again wounded. Against that all twelve enemy warriors and ten boys had been killed. He felt satisfied with what they'd achieved and he made preparations to leave, roping the captured boys together by the neck, tying their hands and hobbling their feet so that they could only shuffle along.

The column had just set off through the dunes when one of the two scouts Cynefrith had sent out to ride point came galloping back, pulling his horse to a halt in a flurry of sand.

'There are twenty mounted Vikings coming this way,' he said, his eyes wide with fear. 'They're no more than half a mile away. They must have seen the smoke.'

-ᚸ-

Ragnar grunted in frustration when his men failed to find much of value in the settlement they'd just pillaged. It consisted of twenty huts, a small hall and a timber church. There was a silver crucifix on the altar of the latter but the candlesticks were made of wood and even the vestments and altar cloth were of poor quality.

The thegn's hall had yielded a small coffer half full of silver hastily buried but, apart from a handful of weapons and a few chickens, there was nothing else worth taking. The people had obviously taken all their items of value and the livestock with them when they'd fled into the hills that rose from the coastal plain a few miles further inland.

He was tempted to follow their trail, but then one of his men called out in alarm and pointed towards the coast. Ragnar could just make out a thin plume of smoke which grew thicker and darker as he watched.

'They're burning the ships,' he called out in alarm. 'Leave everything. We need to get back to the beach.'

Reluctantly his men dumped what they'd found in the settlement and in the various farmsteads they'd raided on their way there and started to run at a steady pace towards the smoke. In all they'd managed to round up a total of nineteen horses during the raid and these now enabled Ragnar and some of his men to travel the five miles back to their ships at three times the pace set by the men on foot.

As he cantered out of the trees that lined the coast at that point he saw a group of Viking boys roped together and standing in the open. He saw with relief that one of them was his son,

Fridlief. He had a cut to his shoulder but otherwise seemed unharmed.

Behind them lay the sand dunes and around them grew clumps of gorse and other shrubs. He pulled his snorting horse to a halt, sensing a trap. Now he could see seven individual clouds of smoke making their way lazily into the still air ahead of him. He suspected that his ships would soon be little more than charred hulks, if they weren't already, and he seethed with anger.

Those behind him went to free the boys, but he called them back to the edge of the trees.

'It's a trap. Whoever has fired our ships wants us out in the open. Our boys aren't going anywhere. Let me think.'

Cynefrith swore under his breath when the Vikings halted at the tree line. He had hoped to catch them in the open where his archers could reduce their numbers before he charged them. He and the majority of his men sat on their horses in dead ground whilst his archers had taken up positions in the gorse bushes on either side of the boys. The latter would have fled but Cynefrith had the sense to tie them together and then secure the end of the rope to a stake driven deep into the ground.

After a few minutes the Vikings split into two groups and circled around the captured boys, obviously looking for the men that they guessed were in the undergrowth. Cynefrith was in a quandary. He daren't wait too much longer because he knew that the rest of the Vikings on foot would be arriving soon. On the other hand he didn't want to lose any more men than he had to dealing with the riders.

He waited until the nine men circling his way had found the first of his archers. As soon as he was spotted, the man sent arrow after arrow towards the nine Vikings, killing one, wounding another and bringing a horse to its knees with an arrow in its chest. Cynefrith led his men out of the hollow and, before the other group could react, he charged into the remainder of the group, taking advantage of their disarray.

'Kill the boys,' he yelled as he fended off a sword thrust with his heavy round shield. He thrust his own sword into the man's leg and his assailant howled in rage and pain. The Viking raised his sword to cut at Cynefrith's head, but he was too slow. As the sword descended Cynefrith thrust his blade into his throat. With a gurgle the Viking fell sideways off his horse.

Ragnar's instinct had been to charge to the rescue of the other group, but the Northumbrians had nearly twice the number of men he had with him. In any case, most of them were dead or badly wounded. He roared in rage, willing the rest of his men to arrive before it was too late.

Instead he headed for the boys, intent on rescuing his son. Suddenly several arrows slammed into the captives and he saw several drop to the ground, including Fridlief. He couldn't believe that the boy was dead – he was barely twelve years old. However, the arrow in his throat and another in the centre of his chest left little doubt. He was so consumed by grief that for a moment he couldn't think.

'Ragnar, we have to get out of here before we're all killed,' Olaf said, grabbing the reins of his horse.

Dumbly the king nodded and looked up. The Anglo-Saxon swine were now reforming to charge his group, so he turned his horse's head away from them and led his remaining men back into the trees.

Cynefrith saw them go and held up his hand to halt his men.

'Let's get out of here before the rest arrive. Make sure none of the heathen devils are left alive though.'

The archers emerged from the gorse and swiftly checked that the fallen Viking warriors and the ships' boys were dead, cutting the throats of those still alive, before retrieving their horses from the hollow. Cynefrith led his men back onto the track that led to Bebbanburg. Five minutes after they had disappeared the first of the panting Vikings on foot appeared and found their king cradling his son's corpse in his arms.

-Ꮙ-

It had seemed a good idea to split his fleet into three and attack different parts of the Northumbrian coast; now Ragnar bitterly regretted his decision. His scouts, who had followed

Cynefrith's trail, told him that the Northumbrians had fled towards Bebbanburg, but he knew he had too few men to do anything against such a formidable stronghold. He could still remember how impregnable it was from the year he'd spent living in its shadow when he was a boy.

Lagertha had been even more devastated than Ragnar. The boy had been her only son and she blamed her former husband for his death. Now the love she still felt for Ragnar turned to hatred. He was used to the close relationship they had enjoyed, even after their break, so he, in turn, bitterly resented her animosity. Not only had he lost a confidante and a friend, but her change in attitude galled his pride.

He had burned the dead on the beach using the charred wood from the destroyed longships. That was another thing she held against him. He hadn't waited for her to re-join him before conducting Fridlief's funeral. When he pointed out to her that the corpse would have rotted and been a stinking pile of putrefying flesh and bone had he delayed, she flew at him in a rage and tried to gouge his eyes out. Only Olaf's quick thinking saved the astounded Ragnar. He smashed his fist into the side of Lagertha's head and she dropped like a stone.

'I should take my ships and leave you here to rot with the ashes of our son,' she hissed at him when she regained consciousness.

'You forget that you are one of my jarls. You have sworn an oath to be loyal to me. Desert me now and I'll hunt you down and kill you. Besides, don't you want revenge on our son's killer?'

She said nothing for a while, merely gazing at him with malice. Eventually she dropped her eyes and nodded.

Until they saw it for themselves, those who didn't know Bebbanburg wouldn't believe that it was as impregnable as Ragnar said it was. When they reached it they realised that, even with hundreds of men, a direct assault wasn't going to work. They could probably starve the garrison out, given time, but that was one thing Ragnar didn't have. Vikings were successful raiders because they struck hard and swiftly. He had no intention of fighting a pitched battle against a Northumbrian army.

'The men are getting disgruntled,' Olaf warned him after they'd been camped outside Bebbanburg for two days. 'They've scoured the land around here and there's nothing left worth taking. They've gained barely enough silver to make a Thor's hammer each and they want to go home.'

A Thor's hammer was the talisman that most Scandinavians wore on a leather thong or a silver chain around their necks. Traditionally they kissed it before going into battle to bring them luck.

'At least there are two drekar, a couple of birlinns and two knarrs down on the jetty. They'll do to replace the longships we lost,' he went on.

'I know. We helped build the drekar if you remember,' Ragnar reminded him.

'Was that here? I'd thought the place was familiar.' He grinned. 'It's only fair that we take them back then, seeing as how we built them.'

Ragnar nodded. It all seemed a long time ago now. Then he was a ship's boy, now he was a king twice over. It made his son's death all the more poignant. He didn't like to admit it, but Fridlief had been his favourite, possibly because he was Lagertha's son.

'Send a couple of ships over to the monastery,' he told Olaf. 'It's deserted, no doubt, but they may have left a few things of value behind; then burn it to the ground. We're going home.'

He didn't tell anyone at the time, but he vowed that someday he would return and kill the Lord of Bebbanburg if it was the last thing he ever did.

-ᛉ-

'What do you want here?' Eystein Beli asked, glaring down at Agnar and Eirik Ragnarson from his throne high on a dais in the hall at Uppsala.

'We want to know the whereabouts of Queen Aslaug,' Agnar replied calmly. 'She has disappeared from Arendal with our baby sister and we are concerned for her safety.'

'You are concerned for her safety? Are you sure you don't mean that she should be concerned about her safety from you two?'

'Why should you say that, King Eystein? Agnar asked him. 'She is our father's wife and he left her in my care when he went raiding this summer'.

'Raiding? Raiding where? Not Sweden?'

'No, England. Why?'

'Because he swore an oath to me not to raid anywhere in Sweden when he married my daughter.'

'Well, I'd say that oath is null and void if she has deserted him, wouldn't you?' Eirik asked nastily.

It was obvious that Eystein wasn't about to tell them anything, so they sent the crew of the two drekar in which they'd travelled to Uppsala into the taverns to find out what they could. It didn't take them long to discover what had happened.

'She arrived here on a knarr with a baby girl and two thralls,' one of the men reported. 'Her father told her to return to Ragnar, but she refused so he banished her. A Norseman from Orkneyjar – a man named Ingólfr Arnarson - was visiting and the rumour is that she seduced him and he took her back with him. I'm sorry, Agnar.'

The two brothers were stunned. They wouldn't want to be Ingólfr when Ragnar caught up with him.

'What do we do now?' Eirik asked when they were alone again.

'Leave Aslaug to our father; at least we've found out where she's gone,' his brother replied.

After a few minutes Eirik broke the silence again.

'We can't go back empty handed. Our four hundred men will expect to get something out of this voyage.'

Not only had they brought a drekar each, but there were five more longships beached a few miles away. They hadn't wanted to venture into Swedish waters without a fleet to protect them, but it would have looked somewhat belligerent to have arrived at Uppsala with so many warriors.

Agnar smiled slyly.

'Do you remember Gotland, Finnulf's island? I gather that his cousin rules there now. We could plunder it on our way home.'

'Finnulf? The jarl that Lagertha killed with an arrow into his eye from a hundred yards?' He thought for a moment. 'Why not?'

-Ꝟ-

Edmund stood on the parapet at Bebbanburg and thought about Joscelin. It had been two years since he had last seen her but scarcely a day went by when he didn't think of her. His greatest desire was to sail back to marry her but, after the death of his brother, he'd been too busy to embark on such a journey.

He sighed and his eyes swivelled from the far horizon, beyond which his love lay, to the other side of the bay where the smoke rose into the sky from the burning monastery on Lindisfarne. He hit the wood beneath his hand in frustration. Against the strength of the Vikings he could do nothing with the numbers inside the fortress. He hadn't even been able to stop them taking his ships. It would take a long time and a lot of money to replace them he thought bitterly.

The only good news was that the Norse fleet had sailed away after venting their frustration on the island. Fortunately he had had enough warning and the inhabitants of both Lindisfarne and the vill of Bebbanburg had time to take refuge inside his stronghold with their livestock before the Vikings had arrived to besiege it.

The king arrived with nearly two thousand warriors two days after Ragnar had left and was furious to discover that he was too late.

'Why didn't you attack the pirates?' Eanred demanded as he dismounted.

Without waiting for a reply he threw the reins at a stable boy and stomped off into the ealdorman's hall. Edmund stared after him in amazement, then followed him, beckoning Cynefrith to accompany him.

'Well?' Eanred said after he'd seated himself in the chair where Edmund normally sat.

'Er, well for a start there was a thousand of them and I only had a fraction of their numbers. Even if I had sallied out against them I'd have risked them capturing this fortress; I'm sure you wouldn't have wanted that. In any case,' he went on before the king could say anything in response, 'we did attack them and managed to destroy a third of their fleet. Cynefrith discovered ...'

'But you then let them take your own ships so burning a few of theirs was immaterial, wasn't it?' the king asked derisively.

Edmund pursed his lips and tried to contain his anger at the way that Eanred was treating him.

'I had a choice; either sail my ships out of harm's way or man this fortress. I didn't have the men to do both.'

'And where were the ealdormen of Lothian? Why didn't they come to your aid?'

'Why don't you ask them that? Perhaps they were worried about their own shires? One of the problems in countering these Viking raids is they strike swiftly and then they are gone. Unless you create a fleet capable of fighting them at sea, I can't see how we can ever bring them to battle on land.'

'But your captain did, didn't he? Except that he ran away.'

Cynefrith stiffened at the king's scornful tone. He wasn't about to let the snide remark pass without comment.

'Thirty men against over ten times that number, Cyning? I would have been throwing my men's lives away for nothing. Besides, my orders were to locate the enemy, not fight them.'

'I'm disappointed in you, Edmund,' Eanred continued, ignoring Cynefrith's outburst. 'You were given the whole of Islandshire specifically to prevent these raids and you've failed. Not only that, but you allowed the holy monastery on Lindisfarne to be pillaged and destroyed. I knew it was a mistake to pardon you after your brother tried to kill me. I should have gone with my first instinct and killed you too instead of listening to my son. The Witan has been summoned to meet here in three weeks' time to try you for cowardice and incompetence.'

Before he could protest, four of the king's gesith seized both him and Cynefrith and disarmed them.

'You will be kept chained until your trial. My men are already disarming your warband and expelling them from Bebbanburg. This used to be a royal fortress and now I'm reclaiming it.'

Edmund couldn't believe what was happening but, before he could say anything else, he was half dragged and half carried out of the hall and thrown into an empty hut with Cynefrith. Ten minutes later the blacksmith entered and, with a muttered apology, placed manacles on both their wrists and ankles. The man couldn't look his ealdorman in the eye and sobbed as he completed the distasteful task.

That evening they were given some bread, cheese and an apple each by two of the king's gesith and Laughlin brought them a wooden pail in which to piss and shit. Edmund hoped that when he came to empty it he would be able to tell him what was happening, but a scruffy stable boy smelling of horse dung came to change the buckets over the next morning and he refused to say anything.

They couldn't hear much of what was going on outside, but the hut was near the main gate and so they were vaguely aware of comings and goings. On the afternoon of the second day they heard an argument between the guards on the gate and Kendric, the Ealdorman of Dùn Èideann.

'Only members of the Witan are allowed inside, lord.'

'Where I go my captain, servant and an adequate escort accompany me,' Kendric retorted. 'Now stand aside.'

'I'm sorry, lord. It's the king's orders.'

'Does Eanred seek to alienate all the Witan? He's already a good way down that route by arresting Edmund on trumped up charges. Where is he? I want to speak to him.'

'I'm here Kendric. I'd advise you to keep a rein on your tongue if you know what's good for you.'

Inside the hut where Edmund was chained up the voice sounded nearby and so he assumed that the king had come out of the hall and was standing on the wall overlooking the gates.

'If you challenge me you may find yourself joining your friend,' he continued.

'Which is exactly what I'm afraid of, Eanred. I don't trust you and so no, I'm not going to accept your invitation to stay in this place. I'll camp with my men and I think you'll find most of your nobles will do the same. The Witan will meet in the thegn's hall.'

'You'll meet where I say,' Eanred yelled, losing his temper.

'No, we'll meet where the Witan decide. It's your choice whether to attend or not.'

Edmund heard several horses ride away to the accompaniment of threats yelled after Kendric by the king.

Presumably Kendric did his best to dissuade his fellow ealdormen and the senior churchmen from joining the king inside Bebbanburg, but it seemed that several of them had ignored his warning as the sounds of arrivals continued for three more days.

'What do you think the king will do with us?'

'I've really got no idea. From what he said I suspect that I'll no longer be an ealdorman but, other than that, I don't want to speculate. I'm sorry that you are locked in here with me. None of this is your fault; the king should be praising you, not seeking to blame you. I'll do my best to make sure that you're not punished.'

'This is so unfair,' Cynefrith cried out in despair, hitting his hand on the beaten earth floor.

He knew that he sounded like a spoilt child but he was past caring.

'Kings are not known for their fair dealings. I suspect that Eanred is being blamed for the depredations of the Vikings and so he seeks to shift the responsibility elsewhere.'

On the fourth day the two men were escorted out of the hut and taken into the king's hall. Without the means of washing and still wearing the same clothes they looked unkempt and filthy.

'Shame on you, Cyning, for keeping a noble in such degrading conditions. At least allow him and his captain to wash and change their clothes before they appear in front of the Witan. And for God's sake get rid of those chains.'

Edmund noted with pleasure that the speaker was Rædwulf, the Ealdorman of Cumbria. His quick glance around the room revealed that none of the Lothian ealdormen nor Ecgred, Bishop of Lindisfarne, were present, but the rest of the Witan seemed to be. Did he only have one friend present?

'Very well. Take them away and get them cleaned up. We have other matters to discuss in any case, such as the disloyalty of Kendric and Ecgred.'

-Ӽ-

Agnar and Eirik sat on stolen horses looking down at the bay where they'd beached their ships. They'd arrived with seven longships but now there were at least twenty more on the yellow sands. Warriors were disembarking and gathering on the beach. Eirik looked towards where the ships boys and the guard they had left to watch the ships had been and he saw several bodies lying on the ground. The rest of them were sitting in a circle being guarded by a score of spearmen.

'It seems that Eystein has outguessed us,' Agnar muttered laconically to his brother after a few choice oaths.

'Do we fight him? He's got twice the number of men we have.'

'What choice do we have? The only way off this island is by ship and he's just captured ours.'

'There are ships at Visby.'

The brothers had pillaged much of the island but they had left the fortified port of Visby alone. Now it seems they had little choice but either face him in the open or attack Visby and capture its ships in order to escape Eystein's clutches. Visby was not an inviting prospect; the palisade was twenty feet high.

'We could try negotiating, I suppose.' Eirik suggested.

Agnar snorted in derision.

'In order to negotiate you must have something the other person wants. I suspect that the only thing we have that Eystein wants are our heads. At least we hold the high ground,' he went on. 'And we have archers. Come on we had better explain the situation to our men.'

At first it looked as if the two brothers might stand a chance. The Swedes advanced stolidly up the hill on which Agnar and Eirik had decided to make their stand. It was difficult to advance uphill whilst keeping one's body protected by your shield and scores of the attackers were wounded or killed during the advance. However, as there were nearly a thousand Swedes the loss of a few of them only served to anger the rest.

As the first men of the Swedish shield wall reached their enemy they tried to stab upwards with their spears but found that they were at a considerable disadvantage. The Norse held their shields low to protect their legs and stabbed downwards at the faces, necks and torsos of the Swedes.

When Eystein called off the first wave of the attack the Swedes left behind a pile of dead and wounded all along the Norse front rank. In contrast only about thirty of their opponents were casualties. Eystein might want to punish those who had had the effrontery to raid his lands, but he wasn't prepared to lose hundreds of men doing so. At this rate of attrition he would lose half his warriors before nightfall.

His solution was to send three hundred of his best warriors around the hill to attack up the far side whilst he assaulted the front of the hill again. That way the Norsemen would be fighting on two fronts.

'You command the rear, I'll hold them off here,' Agnar shouted to his brother as the two halves of the Swedish army advanced again.

This time the Swedes held their shields above their heads as they advanced and used their spears to stab at the exposed legs of the man standing next to their immediate adversary. This tactic was much more successful and the numbers of casualties were more evenly matched. The Swedes main problem was the wall of dead between them and their enemy.

Agnar thrust his spear into the neck of the man in front of him. The Swede collapsed but the spear point remained stuck in his neck. Agnar struggled to free it for a second or two before realising how vulnerable he was. He let go of the spear haft and went to pull out his sword, but it was too late. The Swede to the rear of the one he'd just killed took advantage of the moment and brought a battle axe down on Agnar's shoulder, slicing into the chain mail and the leather jerkin below it before breaking his collar bone and three of his ribs. One of the broken ribs pierced Agnar's right lung and he fell to his knees.

The warrior next to Agnar in the shield wall thrust his spear into the axeman's chest, but it was too late. The wound that Agnar had suffered was fatal. Word spread that he had fallen and the heart went out of his men. Eirik continued to fight on with his warband but defeat was only a matter of time now. When he was struck on the helmet by a sword, knocking him unconscious, his men surrendered along with those of Agnar's who had not already done so.

Eystein now found himself in something of a quandary. As king he'd been forced to defend the territory of one of his jarls or he'd have looked weak. However, he was loathe to antagonise Ragnar. Both men were powerful but he secretly thought that, if it came to war, Ragnar would probably win. Agnar was dead, and that couldn't be helped, but Eirik was his prisoner and he didn't know what to do with him.

If he released him he could expect Ragnar to be grateful, but his own jarls would consider it the action of a weak man. If he killed him in cold blood he would rise in their estimation, but would alienate Ragnar even further and that was the last thing he wanted. Agnar's and Eirik's men had fought hard and bravely until the last and his Swedes had suffered a lot of casualties, including the death of three of his jarls. He was in no position to fight Ragnar at the moment, despite the losses the man's sons had suffered.

As rain began to spit down he surveyed the battlefield. His men were stripping the enemy corpses of anything of value and killing their wounded. His own dead were loaded onto carts ready for burning on pyres, but that would have to wait until the rain stopped. Their armour and weapons would go to their relatives and they would die fully clothed. In contrast, the enemy would be buried in a pit naked and then covered in lime before it was filled in; all except Agnar who would be cremated separately as befitted his rank.

Leaving his men to their grisly task, he took Eirik with him and returned to Uppsala.

-℣-

Edmund stared gloomily out over the calm sea as the knarr made its slow progress over the German Ocean. The Witan had been a farce. It turned out that Bishop Ecgred had suffered a heart attack and died in the night; thus he had escaped whatever punishment the king had in mind. No appointment had been made before Edmund left but he expected it to be Eanbehrt, the Prior of Hexham, who was a second cousin of King Eanred and who could be depended upon to support him.

Kenric had decided that it was better not to attend the Witan and had shut himself away in his fortress at Dùn Èideann, daring the king to cross into Lothian and try to evict him. Eanred was no warrior and he had listened to those who cautioned him that a war with Lothian would merely be an open invitation for the Picts, the Britons of Strathclyde and the Scots of Dalriada to invade. He had therefore decided to pardon Kenric.

Edmund wasn't so fortunate. At least his fellow nobles had prevented Eanred imposing any greater punishment than exile on him and he was banished to the Continent. The king had confiscated everything of his at Bebbanburg, including his coffers of silver and gold, but he was allowed to take his warband and servants with him.

Fortuitously a knarr and its escorting birlinn had arrived at Bebbanburg from Paris in time for him to embark with his men and sail away, leaving his home in the possession of the king.

He was headed for Caracotinum before going on to his base in Paris. It had been nearly two years since he last saw Bastiaan and, more importantly, his sister Joscelin. He wondered how much she had changed over that time and his excitement at the thought of seeing her again mounted the nearer he got. He was therefore unprepared for the shock that awaited him when he docked.

Caracotinum was far busier that it had been the last time he'd been there. The port was positively bustling and the number of huts ashore seemed to have grown too. As soon as the ship's boys had secured the mooring lines, a self-important official accompanied by three burly looking guards bustled up to the two ships and haughtily demanded to know their business.

Edmund was about to say that he was the Ealdorman of Bebbanburg come to visit the viscount when he realised that he was no longer entitled to call himself that.

'I'm Edmund of Bebbanburg, the betrothed of Joscelin, the sister of Viscount Bastiaan.'

The man looked at him suspiciously before replying, somewhat impatiently.

'I don't take kindly to jokes, whoever you are.'

'I'm not joking, now go and tell Bastiaan that I'm here,' Edmund said, getting annoyed.

'You do know that the Lady Joscelin was married to the Count of Amiens seven months ago.'

'What? Married?'

Edmund was stunned. He knew that he should have returned, or at least send a messenger, but he'd been so busy since the killing of his brother that time had flown by and now he'd left it too late. Not only had he lost his home and his shire, now it seemed he'd lost his love as well. He sat down heavily on the deck with his head in his hands. After a few moments he was gently lifted up by Cynefrith and Laughlin and helped into his small cabin.

'What's going on,' the official demanded, bewildered by the effect that his news had had.

'If what you say is true,' the captain told him, 'I suspect that we won't be staying, but you had better inform the viscount that Edmund of Bebbanburg is here.'

When the information that Edmund had arrived eventually reached Bastiaan he rushed down to the port, only to see the two Northumbrian ships heading back out to sea.

'Do you know where Lord Edmund is going?' he asked the port reeve.

'The captain of the knarr told one of my men that he supposed that they'd now head for Paris.'

Bastiaan sighed. He had liked Edmund and would have far rather that he had married his sister instead of that elderly oaf, the Count of Amiens. However, his father had insisted on the match. Louis of Amiens was a powerful man and he was close to the king.

'Why didn't you come back sooner, Edmund,' he muttered to himself as the two ships receded into the distance.

-ᛉ-

Ragnar was in a foul mood when he arrived back at Arendal. Not only had the raiding season provided little in the way of plunder when divided amongst his jarls and warriors, but his eldest son and his wife weren't waiting on the jetty to greet him as they should have been. Instead little Ivar and Bjorn stood side by side with their two younger brothers standing behind them. Where were Agnar and Aslaug?

Then a horrible thought struck him. Perhaps Aslaug had died in childbirth? But that didn't explain Agnar's absence. As his drekar nudged the jetty and the ship's boys secured her, he jumped ashore and strode towards his young sons. It was only then that he noticed Edda, the thirteen year old son of the jarl of the region surrounding Arendal, standing next to his boys.

As Ragnar reached them and was about to demand an explanation the two youngest boys, Sigurd and Halfdan, threw themselves at him and hugged his legs. He was astounded. Vikings didn't display affection in public, at least not like that. A hearty punch on the arm between friends was about as affectionate as they got. Even children were taught that at a young age.

'Welcome home, father,' Ivar said formally whilst Bjorn told his brothers to let go with anger in his voice.

Sigurd and Halfdan muttered sorry and returned to their places behind the other two. Ragnar was about to ask what in the name of Hel was going on when his daughter, Ragnhild, said quietly that he had better come up to the hall and they would explain what had happened since he'd been away.

Around them the usual greeting between the returning warriors and their families carried on as normal but Ragnar sensed that the welcome was more subdued than usual.

As he walked away Olaf heard others talking about what had happened and for a moment he thought of going after his friend, but his own wife and children demanded his attention and he let him go. He would visit him later and they could get drunk together. Then would be the appropriate time to discuss how to take revenge on Eystein and Aslaug.

Lagertha hadn't followed Ragnar back to Arendal. She and the other jarls from the north of the kingdom had gone directly to their respective bases so they were unaware of the death of Agnar and the betrayal of Aslaug until they got home.

When she did eventually hear the news Lagertha's hostility towards Ragnar softened somewhat. She even thought of sailing down to Arendal to see him, using the excuse of seeing her daughter, Ragnhild, but she hardened her heart against it.

'What will you do?' Olaf asked Ragnar that evening after they had drunk several horns of ale together.

'Do? Go and see Eystein, of course. Agnar and Eirik were fools and I can understand that the old king had to protect Gotland, but I can't forgive him, especially if he has given sanctuary to Aslaug.'

He said her name as if it was something nasty he'd eaten.

'However, it would be folly to turn this into a blood feud unless he's murdered Eirik. I'll demand my son back unharmed together with my wife and her bastard child. In return I'll continue our alliance.'

'And if he refuses?'

'Then I'll kill the old goat, regardless of the consequences.'

He looked across the table at Bjorn and Ivar, who'd been allowed to stay and drink a little ale with their father.

'They did well in my absence. There's not many seven and six year olds who could take command of things. There was a real danger than some ambitious jarl or wealthy bondi could have seized the throne.'

'With the help of Edda,' Olaf pointed out. 'Besides all but the greybeards and boys were either away with us or had accompanied Agnar.'

'Yes, I was sorry to hear that Edda's father had died with my fool of a son. He's too young to be accepted as a jarl, yet but he shows real promise.'

'I'm not so sure – about him being too young, I mean. He's a strapping lad for thirteen and those of his father's men who came with us seem to respect him,' Olaf said pointing across the hall to where Edda and a group of warriors were getting uproariously drunk.

'Maybe; it's up to the bondi to elect their new jarl in any case. I don't want to interfere. In any case, we have Eystein to worry about and I haven't finished with Northumbria yet. Ealdorman Edmund must pay for the death of Fridlief.'

'You're not thinking of going back there next year?'

'No, I need to give my warriors a place to raid which will give them a chest full of gold and silver first or they won't want to come raiding with me again.'

'So where are you thinking of going next year? Frankia?'

'Yes; I have Paris in mind. If all I've heard about it is correct, we'll make every bondi richer than his wildest dreams.'

Chapter Fourteen – Invasion of Frankia

845

Edmund had sunk into depression when he found out that Joscelin was lost to him. It was Cynefrith who took charge and got them to Paris. Once there he arranged to rent a suitable house for Edmund and himself and accommodation for the rest of the crew.

'You're going to have to rouse yourself, lord,' he told Edmund after they'd been there for a few days. 'You can't stay locked away in your room.'

'I'll do what I bloody well want, Cynefrith, and stop calling me lord. Here I'm no more than a simple merchant.'

'Not even that if you don't get a grip on things. Besides, Charles wants to see you.'

'Charles? Charles who?'

'Charles the Bald, King of West Frankia, the son of Louis the Pious. That Charles.'

'What on earth does he want with me?'

'I've no idea. A messenger arrived from Aix la Chappelle this morning with the royal summons, though it's worded like a request.'

Edmund sighed. A request from the king was a politely worded order, especially as he was now a resident of that part of the Frankish Empire ruled by Charles. He had succeeded his father when Louis had died, but his brothers had rebelled against him.

The civil war had lasted for three years and ended up with the partition of the empire created by Charlemagne. Charles had kept the valleys of the Rhine and the Rhône, including the regions of Lorraine, Alsace, Burgundy, and Provence as well as the coastal regions of Frankia. But the civil war had reduced his political influence significantly and had weakened him militarily.

He'd also lost the title of emperor, which had gone to his brother Lothair. He was now known as the King of West Frankia.

'How far is it to Aix?' Edmund asked, now resigned to having to travel there.

'Overland? Nearly three hundred miles; but it's probably more convenient to travel by ship. I'd made some enquiries and we can go back into the German Ocean and down the River Meuse. Aix La Chappelle lies on an offshoot, the River Wurm.'

Edmund felt rejuvenated once he was back on board again. He had shrugged off his lethargy and the wind in his hair and the sea spray in his face made him glad to be alive again. They had to row much of the way down the Seine and he joined his men pulling on an oar for a time. His hands soon blistered and the muscles in his back made him feel as if it was on fire, but he ignored the pain. Even a sudden heavy shower of rain did little to dampen his spirits. It was if he'd been reborn again.

The only thing which clouded his new found enthusiasm for life was the niggling worry about why Charles the Bald wanted to see him. It made no sense. In Paris he was just another merchant, albeit a relatively wealthy one. Perhaps Eanred had changed his mind? Exile wasn't enough and he now wanted him dead. But in that case he would have been arrested in Paris and sent back to Northumbria if Charles had acceded to Eanred's request.

The more he pondered the reason for the summons the more in the dark he was. In the end he gave up worrying and concentrated on enjoying the journey.

It took ten days to reach Aix. As soon as they docked the port reeve came down personally to greet them.

'The king is expecting you, Lord Edmund. You are to be his guest. An escort is on its way with horses for you and two companions.'

Edmund thought that this was mildly encouraging. If he was to be incarcerated he would have been taken away on his own, and on foot. Aix wasn't as big as Paris, but it wasn't small by any means. However, the palace complex lay to the north of the city and proved to be much larger than Edmund was expecting. He was so overawed by the scale of the buildings that he scarcely noticed when a groom and two boys came running to take the horses away.

Cynefrith and Laughlin accompanied him and together they entered the palace via a gate adjoining the palace chapel. Edmund thought that it looked enormous, more like a cathedral than a chapel. However, it wasn't built in the style he was used to; it was round with a domed roof like a basilica. Other buildings adjoined it, including accommodation for the monks and priests and, on the other side of the entrance hall to the chapel complex, the king's private rooms.

They walked along a long covered walkway and entered another building which the captain said was the barracks for the guards on duty. Edmund noticed that the palace was full of people scurrying about: courtiers, scholars, nobles, merchants and even beggars and poor people who had presumably come to ask for charity or to submit pleas to the king.

Beyond the barracks lay an even longer walkway which ended at a large building which housed the council chamber and the treasury. Both were built of brick, rather than stone and the council chamber was larger than any building Edmund had ever seen, measuring some one hundred and twenty feet long by seventy feet wide.

'There are other buildings outside the palace complex,' the captain told him. 'These include the main barracks, quarters for the courtiers, officials and servants and a hospice. There is also a hunting park and a menagerie where various exotic animals are kept for the amusement of important visitors.'

Edmund thought of the king's hall at Eoforwīc, which was like a poor shepherd's hut by comparison to Charles's palace. The brick buildings particularly fascinated Edmund. Some of the Roman ruins in England were built of brick, but no Anglo-Saxon builder had mastered the art of turning wet clay into hard-baked bricks. He thought it looked a simpler, and cheaper, way of building than stone and determined to find out more about the technique.

The council chamber was full of people milling about waiting their turn to be called forward to speak to the king. The chamberlain's assistants moved amongst them, finding people who were lucky enough to be granted a brief audience and taking them forward to where King Charles sat on his throne. There they waited their turn to move to the base of the dais and go down on one knee. Once they had submitted their plea or concluded their business, they got to their feet, bowed low and backed away from the royal presence.

Edmund had to restrain a laugh. He couldn't imagine any Northumbrian being so obsequious to Eanred. However, he was faced with a dilemma. He still had no idea what he was doing here but he wasn't about to scrape and bow to the Frankish king, whatever the reason for his summons.

Thankfully he didn't have to. The captain left the three of them and went to have a quiet word in the chamberlain's ear. The man, who was standing at the foot of the dais with those patiently waiting in line for a word in the royal ear, banged the end of his staff of office on the stone floor and the buzz of conversation died away.

'That concludes today's business. You may return tomorrow at midday if you so desire.'

The chamberlain said this with such an air of disdain that it was obvious he wished they wouldn't bother. Charles got up from his throne and everyone, except the three Englishmen, bowed low as he left though a door behind the dais. One of the men who had been standing in a small group chatting together at the other side of the dais from the supplicants followed him out.

'Come with me, the king will see you privately,' the captain said when he re-joined them. 'Your two men can wait here for now.'

'Ah, Lord Edmund, thank you for coming,' Charles greeted Edmund in Latin with a smile as soon as he was shown through the door.

The room was quite small and only contained the king and the man who had followed him. It was richly furnished with tapestries on the walls, a table covered with papers and a chair. There were two other chairs in front of the desk but both the other occupants of the room were standing and so Edmund walked across to join them.

'Princeps, I am honoured to meet you, but I have to confess that I am ignorant of the reason,' he replied in Latin.

'We don't use the term princeps, Edmund,' the other man said in heavily accented English. 'Highness is the correct form of address.'

'Forgive me, Highness,' he replied in Franconian, ignoring the other man and addressing the king.

Charles frowned at the man who'd corrected Edmund and turned back to his guest with a smile.

'I do apologise, I haven't introduced my companion. This is Count Louis of Arras.'

Edmund was stunned. This then was Bastiaan's father; the man who had ruined his chances of marrying Joscelin. For a moment he just stared at the man, then he realised that both men were looking at him, puzzled by his reaction.

'I'm sorry, Highness. Am I correct in thinking that you are the father of Bastiaan and Joscelin?' he said, turning to the count.

'Er, yes,' the latter said, taken off guard. 'Do you know them?'

'Yes,' he replied tersely before turning back to the king. 'Highness, how can I help?'

Charles looked at him curiously and then at the count, who was clearly mystified by the peculiar exchange. Edmund came to the conclusion that the count had arranged Joscelin's marriage whilst ignorant of Edmund's betrothal to her; but surely his children would have mentioned it? More likely he had been told but ignored it as unsuitable and had failed to even remember Edmund's name.

'My agents have reported that the Viking leader, Ragnar Lodbrok, is amassing a large fleet. The rumour is that he intends to attack Paris,' Charles was saying. 'I have placed the count in charge of our defences against these pirates, but I understand that you have fought them before. Not only that, but you are more experienced in naval warfare than any of us are. I'm hoping you can help us to come up with a strategy for defeating them.

'We don't believe that we can tackle them at sea,' Louis went on. 'We are going to have to stop them once they are in the River

Seine. I thought that perhaps a chain across the river might stop them and we can then bombard them from the shore.'

'Do your agents have any idea how large Ragnar Lodbrok's fleet is? When he attacked Northumbria last year he brought twenty ships and a thousand men with him.'

'If the threat was the same size this time, then I feel we could deal with him easily; however, I have spies in all the main Scandinavian ports and they tell me that Grimulf the Dane and a fleet from Uppsala in Sweden have agreed to join the ships from Adger and Alfheim. The best estimate I have is that he can bring some three thousand warriors in some fifty longships against us.'

'How many men do you have for the defence of Paris, Highness?'

'I can probably muster five thousand, given enough warning.'

Edmund didn't like to say that a Viking warrior, trained from boyhood to fight and kill, was probably a match for two or even three Franks. Instead he returned to the idea of barring access upriver.

'A boom won't work. They'll merely land downstream and kill the men defending the windlasses and then lower the chain.'

'What would you suggest, then?' Count Louis asked, not trying to hide his resentment at the offhand way that Edmund had dismissed his idea.

'You have enough ships, they are just not as fast, seaworthy or as agile as the Viking longships. However, if you raft them together across the river and build turrets at the bows, you can prevent them rowing upriver and inflict significant casualties using archers and rock throwing catapults, if you have them. They can't break the line or capture your ships easily because the towers will be too high to assault from the deck of a longship.'

'Alas, we have no catapults, but we do have archers, of course. What do you think they will do then?' Charles asked warming to the Englishman's idea, whilst Louis tried to think why the idea wouldn't work.

Edmund shrugged. 'Probably leave their precious longships and advance on Paris overland. If so, you can then meet them in the field and crush them with superior numbers.'

Charles smiled broadly and clapped Edmund on the shoulder in congratulation whilst Count Louis gave the young man a sour look. He felt his influence with the king slipping away and tried to think of a way to discredit Edmund's plan.

-ᛉ-

Ragnar watched from the crowded jetty at Arendal as yet another fleet of longships anchored out in the fjord. The largest drekar detached itself from the rest and made its way to the jetty where Ragnar's havnesjef was hastily trying to make room for it to tie up. Thirty two longships and eight knarrs were already there and the new arrivals made the total up to forty two plus ten knarrs. It was the largest Scandinavian fleet ever assembled.

The leading ship had been displaying the golden lion before the faded blue sail had been lowered but, even without that confirmation, Ragnar was well aware that the last contingent was from Uppsala. Eystein hadn't come himself, or course; it was led by his younger brother, Osten.

'Greetings, old man. We've come to show you how to fight,' did nothing to endear him to Ragnar. At forty two he thought of himself in his prime. True, he was starting to grow the odd grey hair, especially in his beard, but he had his favourite thrall pull them out as soon as they appeared.

'You are welcome, Osten, but you will treat me with the respect to which I am entitled, not only as your senior in years and experience, but as a king twice over.'

'I meant no offence, Ragnar,' the young man said with a grin. 'Now where are the drink and the women?'

'A feast has been prepared in your honour, of course, but you will leave my thralls alone if you know what's good for you.'

Since Aslaug had left him he'd decided that wives were too much trouble. He had several nubile young female thralls to look after his needs, in bed and out of it, and he had no intention of sharing them with this brash young Swede.

'Did you find my wayward niece?' Osten asked as they walked up to the king's hall together, followed by a scowling Olaf and an equally irritated Eirik.

Ragnar looked at him sharply.

'No, do you know what happened to her?'

The other man nodded. 'I heard that she's living with a Norseman called Ingólfr Arnarson on Westray.'

'Then Ingólfr is a dead man as soon as the raid on Paris is over.'

'If you want to kill him you'll have to be quicker than that. My informant told me that he is planning to join a hersir called Ráðormr who is putting together an expedition to capture the Land of Ice and Fire.'

'The Land of Ice ....? I've never heard of it.'

'It's an island on the edge of the world currently inhabited by monks who worship the nailed god.'

'The White Christ? What are they doing there?'

'I gather that they live there because they seek solitude away from the world in order to worship.'

'How do they live, if there is nothing but ice there?'

'I don't know. Perhaps it's only a name?'

By this time they had reached the hall and sat down with Olaf and Eirik at a table in one of the many alcoves that lined both sides of the hall. Two thralls, a boy and a young girl, brought them four horns of ale and platters of bread and cheese. Osten leered appreciatively at the girl, who couldn't have been more than twelve.

'Forget it, Osten. She's too young and she's my property in any case,' Ragnar told him, noticing the lust in his eyes.

'Will you seek him and my niece there?' Osten said, returning to the original topic.

'Perhaps, but not yet awhile. After Paris I've got a score to settle with a Northumbrian called Edmund whose men killed my son, Fridlief.'

-ᚡ-

'I can't hire any more carts or knarrs, Lord Edmund,' Amalric, his agent in Paris, told him with a note of despair in his voice.

The news that the Vikings had reached the Seine estuary had engendered panic amongst the population of Paris. Whilst

Edmund was fairly confident that the defence measures he had eventually persuaded the Count of Arras to adopt would stop the Vikings from getting as far as Paris, he wasn't taking any chances. All of his wealth was now tied up in his warehouse or on his ships out at sea.

Furthermore he had borrowed from business colleagues to expand his trading operations. If he lost the goods in his warehouse to the raiders he would owe more than the cargo currently at sea was worth. Consequently he would be bankrupt. It was imperative that he transported his merchandise to safety, just in case the worst happened.

'Take the most valuable goods to Châlons-sur-Marne and then get the knarrs to return to collect what else they can. They should have enough time for two trips, if not three, before the wretched Vikings can get this far - if we can't defeat them first, that is. The carts won't have enough time to return but the knarrs can carry more in any case.'

The confluence between the Seine and the River Marne lay near Paris and was the start of the navigable route to Châlons. It lay one hundred and twenty miles away and Edmund was sure as he could be that the Vikings wouldn't stray so far away from their target of Paris. It had cost a considerable amount to rent a warehouse there in the present situation, and to hire men to guard it, but it was money well spent if it enabled him to save the majority of his goods.

The scene on the quayside was chaotic as merchants constantly outbid each other for the services of labourers to load their ships and carts. Men would start to load one ship and then abandon it as soon as someone offered them more. However, that wasn't a problem that bothered Edmund. The men loading his ships were from the warband who had travelled with him from Northumbria; they'd been in his service for years and he was as confident as he could be of their loyalty. Nevertheless, Edmund thought it prudent to offer them a bonus, payable once the cargo was safely under lock and key in Châlons.

Not all his warriors were employed loading goods; many a fight had broken out between rival gangs of workers as merchants tried to get their hands on various means of transport by fair means or foul. Edmund therefore had his best fighters arm themselves and dress in chainmail byrnies and helmets. Just the sight of them looking for a chance to blood their spears was enough to deter anyone from chancing their arm.

Three days later a messenger arrived to tell Count Louis of Arras that the Vikings had reached Rouen and had besieged it for three days. Rouen was well defended, unlike Paris which depended on the river and defensive gateways at the end of its bridges to keep out attackers. The Seine was seen by the Franks as a line of defence, not as a weakness.

Having sacked the surrounding countryside, the raiders had moved on and were now no more than a day away from the little surprise that Edmund had in store for them.

'It won't work,' Count Louis had told him contemptuously.

'I see. What is your plan, count?'

'To shadow them on land and prevent them landing.'

'To do that you'll have to split your forces to cover both banks. You have, what? Eight thousand men in total, most of them farmers and tradesmen with a spear. Split in two, your four thousand will face some three thousand Vikings, if your scouts are correct. Your men won't stand a chance.'

Louis glowered at him before stomping out of the room in a rage. Edmund sighed. He needed at least fifteen hundred men, principally archers and crossbowmen, if his plan was going to work; and he also needed all the ships he could get his hands on. Without the count's support he was helpless.

Ragnar was concerned. His supplies of food and ale were running low yet he risked a battle if he tried to plunder the countryside through which the Seine ran. Two and a half thousand men and several hundred ship's boys defecated daily into buckets that were tipped over the side into the river; that same river from which the ships later drank. It wasn't surprising that an increasing number of those on the rearmost ships now suffered from dysentery.

He cast a jaundiced eye at the thousands of Franks trudging along both banks keeping pace with his longships. He could see that many weren't that well-armed nor did they have proper protection. Nevertheless there seemed to be a lot of them and they were accompanied by hundreds of mounted warriors.

Finally they came to a section where the road alongside the river diverted inland for a while and Ragnar decided to seize the opportunity to disembark his men unopposed. There was a length of shingle between two low hills which could take ten ships at a time and, as one went to anchor mid-stream, another took its place until all his warriors were on dry land; although dry wasn't quite the word as rain was falling and it wasn't long before the whole bank became a sea of glutinous mud.

Count Louis watched the Viking disembarkation impotently through the rain from the other bank. There was nothing he could do to warn the other half of his army as the enemy set off at a slow trot, heading inland.

Ragnar's scouts didn't take long to locate the marching column of Franks. They were trudging along with the horsemen in the lead and the baggage train at the back. Osten and few of the others were all for a straightforward attack all along the length of the column but, luckily for them, wiser counsel prevailed.

It was the Danish jarl, Grimulf, who suggested cutting the column in half, using a shield wall of a thousand men to keep the front half of the Frankish army at bay whilst their main force slaughtered the rest and captured the much needed provisions in the carts. Ragnar nodded his agreement and grinned wolfishly at Osten.

'You and your men can have the honour of holding off the vanguard and the horsemen. Do you think that you can manage that?'

The young Swede scowled. He knew that, being outnumbered two to one and fighting against cavalry was the most dangerous part of the plan. He could lose a lot of men in the process, but to demur would make him look like a coward. Reluctantly he nodded but he vowed to himself that he would get even with Ragnar one day.

The road, such as it was - more of a muddy track in reality - emerged from a wood onto a meadow that sloped down towards the river half a mile away. About two hundred yards above the track there was a dip before the slope continued up to the ridgeline. The last of the Vikings made it into the dip just as the leading horsemen emerged from the trees. They made a brave show, two counts, three viscounts and a dozen barons led with their banner men immediately behind them. Resplendent in knee-length byrnies with splits in front and rear, polished helmets, gaudily painted shields and lances with fluttering pennons, they looked invincible.

Behind them came a long column of riders, some wearing chain mail, but most in stout leather jerkins or padded linen gambesons. All wore helmets, mainly pots with a nasal guard, and carried shields. They were armed with an assortment of spears, long-handled horsemen's axes or just swords. The leading footmen were similarly attired and equipped, presumably the lords' personal war bands, but they were followed by hundreds and hundreds of men wearing everyday clothes and carrying an assortment of weapons from crossbows to hunting spears and from swords to woodmen's axes.

Most had a shield of some sort but only about a tenth had the expensive lime wood shields banded in iron or bronze with a metal boss that every Viking carried. Many were made of woven wickerwork or looked as if they had been made from an old door or table.

They walked in ranks of five or six, although there was no real order to them. Some walked in pairs and there were gaps between various groups. None looked about them, intent on keeping the rain out of their eyes, and there were no scouts out as far as Ragnar could see.

He waited until he thought that perhaps two thousand had passed him, then he and the young warrior carrying his raven banner stood up. Ragnar nodded at the youth and he waved the banner to and fro. At the pre-arranged signal the Vikings emerged from their hiding place almost as one. They ran down the hillside, sliding and skidding on the wet grass, yelling and waving their weapons in the air, quickly closing the gap between them and the Frankish column. A few lost their footing and took a tumble, but not enough to affect the charge.

The noble in command gawped at the thousands of Vikings hurtling towards the column some half a mile behind him and was so stunned he couldn't think what to do for a moment. The delay was fatal. By the time he had collected his wits, Osten's Swedes, reinforced by Grimulf's Danes, had sliced the column in half, killing a hundred Franks in the process, and formed a shield wall four deep across the track. He watched in horror as the rest of the Vikings proceeded to attack the half-trained tradesmen and farmers that formed the rear of the column.

Leaderless, the Franks found themselves being slaughtered until at last someone managed to organise them. Crossbowmen and a few archers raced away from the track and formed up, sending a hail of bolts and arrows into the Vikings. This enraged the latter and they turned their attention to the bowmen.

Whoever had taken command knew his business. Whilst one third of the crossbowmen kept up a steady fire the rest laboriously reloaded their crossbows. The next third stepped forward and fired. This, coupled with the archers, who could get off four arrows to every crossbow bolt, produced a steady rate of fire which slammed into the Vikings as they tried to get to grips with them.

Of course, it couldn't last and the Franks broke and ran once the Vikings got close. Some made it to the safety of the woods but the majority were cut down as they fled; not just cut down but butchered. The furious Norsemen killed the wounded and hacked at the dead bodies, mutilating them by beheading them and cutting off limbs and genitals.

The blood soaked ground turned to pink as the rain diluted it. The Vikings had killed four hundred Franks but they had lost half that number of their own in the process. Furthermore, their preoccupation with the crossbowmen had left Ragnar with a mere seven hundred men to tackle twice that number of Franks. He soon came to the conclusion that this wasn't going to be the easy victory he'd envisioned.

Meanwhile, the Swedes and Danes faced charge after charge by the horsemen in their centre whilst their flanks were attacked by the Franks on foot. Osten calmly waited for the first horseman to reach him and, as the rider leant forward to aim his spear point at the Swede's eyes, Osten calmly thrust his spear into the horse's chest. It toppled sideways, spilling its rider onto the ground where he was quickly dispatched by an axe blow from a Swede standing a little further down the line.

However, Osten didn't have time to extract his spear before the next horsemen was upon him. He threw up his shield in a panic and yelled in relief as he felt the point glance off the boss. He fumbled for his sword and managed to draw it before his adversary stabbed at him again. He slashed wildly at the horse's head and felt the jarring blow as the blade connected with it.

In pain the horse reared up, its fore hoof catching the rim of Osten's helmet. He felt as if he was choking and then the pressure eased as the strap holding it in place broke and the helmet went spinning away. Osten was congratulating himself on surviving when the other fore hoof struck his temple, cracking his skull.

Word that their leader had fallen spread through the Swedish line like wildfire. The next time the Frankish horsemen charged they managed to break the shield wall in the centre and poured through the gap. However, the Danes, who had been relegated to the rear of the Swedish line, were ready for them and moved to meet them, chopping at the horses with their axes. The tactic was so effective that the gap was soon plugged with dead animals and the Danes set about slaughtering their dismounted riders.

The remaining Franks withdrew and regrouped. The number of horsemen had been halved and their commander now sent his footmen forward again. Grimulf and his Danes advanced clear of the pile of dead and he signalled for the Swedes to do likewise. They hesitated for a moment or two, then one of their jarls led his men forward and the rest followed. Now the combined force formed into one long shield wall three deep. They were outnumbered by the Franks, but not by that much, and the Vikings were experienced fighters, whereas less than a third of the Franks had fought before.

The Franks battled away against the shield wall but they couldn't make much impression on it and they suffered significant casualties. Eventually they lost heart and the Vikings started to advance, a movement that became relentless. Gradually their enemy began to slip away until the number fleeing became a flood. The Franks' rout was complete when the horsemen turned and followed the rest back towards Paris.

Ragnar surveyed the scene of his victory. Any euphoria he might have felt was tempered by the scale of his losses. Whilst the Franks at the rear of the column had been defeated fairly easily and he had captured the baggage train, putting paid to the immediate need for provisions, the other part of the column had put up much more of a fight. The Franks had lost over a thousand men and, although his losses were perhaps only half that, it wasn't a rate of attrition he could sustain for long.

He had also captured over a hundred prisoners.

'Kill them,' Olaf urged him. 'They are only more mouths to feed and if we keep them they'll need to be guarded.'

'No, I want them kept alive for now.'

'Why? They are common soldiers, no-one will pay a ransom for them. What's the point in keeping them as captives?'

'I'm not sure but I have a feeling that they may be useful to me.'

Olaf shrugged and went off muttering to himself.

Although the Franks on this side of the river had virtually been destroyed as a fighting force, four thousand Franks remained on the opposite bank. However, although his losses had been significant, he took some comfort from the fact that one of the dead was Osten.

He suspected that the Swedish prince would have proved even more troublesome in the long run, but without him the rest of the Swedes might decide to return home. He racked his brains trying to think how best to convince their jarls that they should remain. The most influential of their number was now Esbjörn, the current Jarl of Gotland – the very island his two eldest sons had invaded. He thought that he wouldn't be inclined towards co-operation, but he was wrong.

To his delight, Esbjörn agreed to remain and the other jarls had followed his lead. Ragnar might have been less sanguine about retaining him and his men if he had known his motivation. Esbjörn's younger brother had died in the battle on Gotland and the Swede had been furious when Eystein had let Eirik go free. The jarl was determined that, if the Franks didn't kill Ragnar's son, then he would do so himself.

Chapter Fifteen – The Capture of Paris

Summer 845

Having effectively lost nearly half his army, Louis of Arras decided to let Edmund have the men he needed. True, the Viking army had been weakened by the battle on the left bank of the Seine, but the rout of their comrades had disheartened his own men and they were convinced that the Vikings were invincible. Consequently, he daren't risk meeting Ragnar in the field again.

However, if he allowed the Vikings to capture Paris, the king would never forgive him and he would most probably be executed.

'Let the Northumbrian try,' one of his aides had suggested. 'What have you got to lose? If he succeeds you can take the credit and if his plan doesn't work you can blame him for failing to defeat the Vikings.'

A broad grin lit up the count's face.

'You're right. Send for him straight away.'

-Ⅹ-

Ragnar was standing at the prow of his drekar with his arm around the base of the dragon's head as it rounded yet another bend in the Seine some forty miles from Paris. At that point the river ran in a large U shaped loop and, although the wind would have helped them along one part of the bend, it was against them for the rest so the men had to row. It was early afternoon and they were getting tired, however the light wind would be almost behind them once around the bend and the ship's boys prepared to raise the sail. The sight that greeted them as they cleared the bend made Ragnar swear and Olaf came running forward to see what had happened.

The river had narrowed and now it was blocked by an assortment of ships tied together gunwale to gunwale so that they stretched from bank to bank. Near the bows of each vessel the Franks had built an ungainly wooden superstructure. Ragnar could see men standing behind a parapet at the top of this tower, for want of a better word, protected by wickerwork shields spaced so as to leave a narrow gap through which archers and crossbowmen could fire.

'Cease rowing,' Ragnar called out as soon as he had recovered from his surprise but, of course, the ships behind him couldn't yet see the barrier and the whole fleet started to bunch up, some ships crashing into others before their rowers could back water and stop.

'What will you do?' Lagertha called across from her drekar.

'Wait,' he called back, annoyed at being pressed for a plan, especially by his former wife, before he had time to think.

It was Eirik who came up with the solution. The two outside ships in the Frankish line were moored to the bank by stout cables tied around tree trunks. He suggested that all they had to do was to cut one of them.

An hour later the majority of the Viking ships advanced slowly towards Edmund's barrier. The longships had reefed sails and they closed slowly on the barrier as the light breeze gave them just enough momentum to overcome the current.

Hidden back around the bend several others made for the two banks. Esbjörn led one group and Lagertha the other. Eirik had begged to be allowed to go with them and so Ragnar had sent him across to Esbjörn's ship. It was a decision that he was to regret.

Now that the object of his enmity was aboard his longship, Esbjörn was tempted to kill him out of hand, but that would only bring Ragnar's wrath down on his head. He needed to make it look as if the Franks had slain him.

Eirik wasn't a sensitive man and he completely missed the hostility of the Swedish jarl. He was so wrapped up in the excitement of what they were about to do that he even forgot that Esbjörn was the Jarl of Gotland. He was a man who always looked to the future and forgot about the past.

The task of both groups was to chop through the cables so that the Franks were carried downstream out of control. As soon as their enemy were on the move, the longships would then turn and row ahead of them until they reached a wider part of the river where they could get past the Franks and continue on their way to Paris. Ragnar realised that the Franks could cut themselves free of each other once they were cast adrift, but that didn't matter. As individual ships they were no match for a longship and the towers would make them unstable and unwieldy in any case.

It didn't quite work like that. Edmund had foreseen the move and had hidden several hundred men in the woods that lined the river. Half of these men were equipped with a crossbow, a weapon that didn't require the strength or skill needed for a normal bow. The four longships beached on the north bank and, as their crew -, including Eirik and a few of his friends - leapt ashore they were met with a hail of bolts. At short range a crossbow bolt could penetrate even the most expensive chain mail and, if close enough, they would go straight through all but the best made shields.

The hail of bolts from the edge of the trees was completely unexpected and almost fifty Swedes died in the first volley. The rest stood there stunned for a moment and then, screaming their rage, they hurled themselves towards the trees. A second volley sent another thirty odd tumbling to the earth, but most of the first group of crossbowmen hadn't had time to finish re-loading.

'Those who are loaded, fire at will,' their commander yelled, drawing his sword and hefting his shield. 'The rest of you forget your crossbows and pick up your spears and shields.'

A few more bolts struck down a few more Vikings but then the remainder reached the line of Franks. By then there were only a hundred and twenty of them left whereas Edmund had allocated four hundred men to each bank.

The Vikings had lost all semblance of order in their maddened bloodlust. Outnumbered by more than three to one they found their desire for vengeance soon changed to panic as their enemies engulfed them and forced them back. They were now fighting for survival. Esbjörn hacked the point from the spear of the man facing him and grinned in triumph as the man realised that all he now held was a useless lump of wood.

Just at that moment he realised that Eirik was fighting alongside him. He forgot about the Frank and, using his sword overarm, Esbjörn forced the point into Eirik's neck. He yelled in triumph as blood spurted out all over the two of them. He had managed to kill Eirik so that it would seem that he had died in battle, but he forgotten about the Frank with the useless spear.

Seizing the moment's respite, the man threw down the useless spear haft and drew his dagger. He knelt down and thrust it up under the jarl's byrnie and into his groin. Blood poured down Esbjörn's legs but he managed to slay his killer before he fell to his knees and lost consciousness. His men dragged him to the rear, but in vain. Within minutes he died from loss of blood.

All they could do now was to make a fighting withdrawal to the longships. As they did so the Franks slowly disengaged and then made a mad dash back to where they'd left their crossbows. The Swedes only had enough warriors left to man two of their longships, so they were forced to abandon the other two. As they made their escape Edmund's men sent a parting volley of bolts their way and killed several more.

On the other bank Lagertha had been quicker to realise that she had walked into a trap. She had taken the precaution of putting out a rear anchor from each of her drekars so that they could haul their ships back out into the river quickly, should it prove necessary, and she sent twenty men ashore first.

The Franks should have melted back into the trees and waited until the rest had disembarked before springing their trap. As it was, as soon as the crossbow bolts started to fly and the scouts were cut down, she ordered a swift retreat. Apart from the loss of the scouts, the only casualties were minor wounds to two of the rowers.

Ragnar was distraught at the death of a third son and blamed the Swedes. However, he had other problems. He had a choice: a direct assault on the floating barrier, which would cost a lot of men to break, or disembark a large enough force to defeat the Franks guarding the mooring ropes.

The trouble was the shingle beaches on either bank were too small to allow more than a few longships to beach at a time. He eventually decided to sail back to where it would be possible to disembark without facing opposition.

The next day he set off on foot along the right bank with a thousand men to cut the mooring ropes on that side of the river. His original army of over two thousand five hundred had been reduced by casualties in battle and, more worryingly, by dysentery. Cases were increasing daily and a number had died from the disease.

However, the Franks guarding the mooring ropes stood no chance against so many Vikings, especially as they had been caught unawares watching the river, not the land. When the ropes apparently mooring the barrier to the right bank had been cut, Ragnar had been puzzled, then his puzzlement turned to fury. He'd been outwitted. He had expected the rafted ships, which were still tethered to the left bank, to swing around in an arc, pushed by the current, until they ran aground. Instead they had stubbornly remained in place. It was only then that he noticed the anchor cables running fore and aft from each ship. The mooring lines had either been a ruse to lure his men into an ambush, or had merely been a second method of securing the raft of ships in place.

He decided that the only sensible course of action was to push on to Paris on foot. His men grumbled and quite a few asked how they were meant to carry away all the plunder and thralls that they anticipated collecting without their ships. By the time that they camped for the night quite a few were feeling mutinous; none more so than the Uppsalan Swedes.

'We've had enough, King Ragnar,' their senior jarl, a man named Villner, told him.

This was greeted by a muttering of agreement from the rest of the Swedes, who had followed their jarls to see Ragnar and who now crowded around him.

'We have lost the prince, one of our jarls and too many men, and for what?' Villner continued. 'The Norns have tricked you into making this ill-fated voyage. No doubt they think that you have grown too mighty and self-important and need cutting down to size.'

Ragnar was stunned. Paris was all but within his grasp and the words of the Swede were not to be borne. He reached for his sword, intent on chopping the insolent man's head off, but Olaf put a restraining hand on his right arm.

'There are too many of them and they are between us and the rest of our men. They'll kill you if you raise a hand against them,' Olaf whispered urgently in his ear.

Ragnar still attempted to draw his sword, hissing at Olaf to unhand him, until he heard some of the Swedes draw theirs. He looked around him; Olaf was right. He was surrounded by Swedes with only a few of his own men nearby. However, they had become alarmed at seeing Ragnar surrounded by angry Swedes and started to push their way through their ranks to the king's side.

Ragnar had the sense to see that the situation was growing ugly and there were still enough Uppsala Swedes left to further weaken the number of his followers to no good purpose if fighting broke out. He nodded and threw off Olaf's hand, letting his own hand fall to his side.

'Very well. Scuttle back to Uppsala if you must. When we sack Paris the skálds will sing of our heroic deeds and call you craven.'

There was angry muttering at this sally and the Swedes began to argue amongst themselves. Several of Ragnar's own Swedish warriors from Alfheim tried to dissuade their fellow Swedes from leaving, but to no avail. As they headed back to where they had left the fleet Ragnar was left with less than fifteen hundred warriors, and many of those had dysentery.

-ᛉ-

Edmund smiled in satisfaction when he saw that his plan had worked. He had captured the two longships abandoned by the Swedes during their abortive attempt to capture one of the windlasses, and now he planned to destroy the rest of the fleet.

The Vikings were afoot. If they could be defeated in the next land battle they would be left with no means of escape.

Once the enemy had departed, heading south east along the river bank, he set off with five hundred men to find the rest of their ships. However, when he and his men reached them he found that they were moored in the middle of the river. He turned round and made his way back towards his own fleet intending to sail downstream to capture them now that they had so few defenders. However, one of the Franks at the rear of his column came running forward before he got very far to say that a large party of Vikings were coming up behind them.

'How many,' he barked at the man, then regretted taking out his frustration on the hapless messenger. It wasn't his fault that Edmund had been wrong footed.

'Difficult to say, lord. Several hundred anyway.'

'Not the whole Viking army then?'

'No, lord. Hundreds not thousands.'

'How far off are they? How long before they get here?'

The Frank thought for a moment before replying.

'Not long; perhaps a quarter of an hour, maybe less.'

Edmund's first thought was that they were going to increase the guard on the ships.

'What are you going to do?' Cynefrith asked quietly.

'If I let them reach their ships it will make it more difficult to capture them. I'd like to destroy them before they get there, but the problem is not knowing their strength.'

'If we take up ambush positions we can catch them unawares or, if there are too many of them, let them pass.'

Edmund nodded in agreement and quickly briefed his captains.

-ℽ-

Villner was in a foul mood. He had lost nearly half his own men and he knew that, of the three longships he had personally brought, he would be lucky if he had enough warriors left to man two of them. Furthermore they would return home with nothing to show for the summer, and that made him personally vulnerable. Men wouldn't follow a jarl they considered unlucky or incompetent and the fact that he was merely answering the king's summons to join Osten wouldn't matter one iota. Any bondi could challenge him at the Thingstead. All they had to do was tell the lagman that they contested Villner's position as jarl. Of course, he could decide to fight his challenger but usually it was just a matter of a vote amongst all the bondis.

He had to find somewhere on the voyage home where he could raid and gain sufficient plunder to make them forget about the disastrous attempt to capture Paris. He was sunk in thought, and his men were plodding along dejectedly under a sullen sky that matched their mood when the first crossbow bolts tore into them. It was an elementary precaution to put scouts out ahead and on the flanks but Villner hadn't bothered. Now he would pay dearly for his oversight.

Edmund had a hundred Frankish crossbowmen with him in addition to the twenty in his own warband who were trained archers. There was only time to get one bolt away but the archers managed to release three arrows apiece before it was time to charge into the stunned column of Swedes.

A tenth of their number had been badly wounded or killed within that first minute. However, the Swedes were all experienced warriors. They quickly recovered and reacted swiftly to Villner's command to form a shield wall. Their problem was that the dead and wounded lay in their way, preventing them from forming into one line three or four deep. Instead they organised themselves into four separate groups.

Edmund realised that it would be easier to attack the smaller groups even as he led his men forward.

'Cynefrith, lead your men into the gap over there and cut the end group off.'

The captain of his warband nodded and headed towards a pile of the dead and dying that Edmund had indicated. He found it difficult to make his way through the Swedish casualties and, when one of them found the strength to slash at the legs of one of his men as he stepped over him, he gave the order to stab each corpse, just to make sure.

The Swedes at the other side of the piles of casualties tried to get to grips with Cynefrith's Northumbrians, but they could only do so by breaking formation. Once they did that they would lose the advantage they had and it would become a wild melee where the superior numbers of their enemies would tell.

Meanwhile Edmund led the Franks in his troop around the Swedish flank. When the Swedes moved to intercept him, his banner man waved it to signal his men to change direction and they managed to insert themselves between two groups of Swedes. As each was about eighty strong and Edmund had nearly three hundred men with him, he had no fears about fighting on two fronts. His men slowly encircled both of the Swedish groups and started to crowd them so that they had no room to manoeuvre.

By this time Cynefrith had found himself in some difficulty. He had managed to split the remaining group in two, but now he risked being enveloped as the Vikings tried to encircle his group. However, the Swedes didn't have enough men to contain the Northumbrians effectively and the latter broke through the encircling Viking line in several places.

Cynefrith found himself facing a large Viking with a long-handled axe. The man was several inches taller than he was and his bare head revealed a face with a scar from his left ear to his mouth which gave him a permanent leer. The Swede hefted his axe ready to chop the blade down onto Cynefrith's head but this was far from the old Northumbrian's first fight. As the blade descended he stepped to the left so that the descending axe missed him completely and left the over-confident Viking unbalanced.

Cynefrith stepped in close to his opponent so that he had no room to swing his axe and he jabbed at the distended belly with his seax. The first attempt broke a few of the chain mail links of the Viking's byrnie but didn't penetrate his flesh. He jabbed again, panic lending strength to his arm as the taller man grabbed Cynefrith by the throat, cutting off his air supply.

The tip of his seax forced the links to break and, just as he felt himself blacking out, Cynefrith thrust the blade home, expecting it to cut through the leather under-jerkin and into flesh. But the

Viking was quick for such a large man. He let go of his throat, leaving Cynefrith sucking in a great lungful of air. The man then kicked him in the right knee, causing Cynefrith to stumble. Before he could recover, the axeman swung his weapon again, chopping deeply into the shield, which Cynefrith had only just managed to raise in time.

He felt his left arm go numb so that he had little or no control over it. His shield had split but, thankfully, the axe had stuck fast. The Viking tried to yank it out, but to no avail. Cynefrith tried to strike his adversary again, but his shield arm was jerked this way and that. So violent were the Viking's attempt's to free his axe that Cynefrith had trouble in keeping his balance and he lost his grip on his seax.

Just as the Swede managed to free his axe fate stepped in and another Northumbrian stepped up beside Cynefrith and thrust his spear into the Swede's neck. Blood spurted everywhere and the man dropped to his knees. The wound was fatal and with a muttered word of thanks, Cynefrith stepped back to gauge how the melee was going.

About half of the Swedes were dead or wounded and his men had surrounded a hundred or so who were making a desperate last stand. The remainder, who had been at the front of the column, decided to cut their losses and fought their way clear before making off in the direction of the longships.

Cynefrith and a few of his men made after them but he gave up after a while. If the Swedes decided to turn and fight they would outnumber their pursuers. By the time they returned to re-join Edmund it was all over. The former ealdorman was sitting on a fallen tree whilst Laughlin sewed up several minor wounds to his arms and legs with catgut.

The next morning a few mounted Frankish scouts arrived to report that the Viking Army was some twelve miles away and still heading for Paris. Edmund therefore ordered his captains to untie their ships from one another and sail downriver to where the enemy fleet was moored. The Swedes who'd escaped had apparently left, but the ships' boys and the wounded who had been left to guard the other longships put up a stiff resistance before Edmund's men overcame them. A few managed to up anchor and escape under sail but the majority of the ships were captured.

Edmund toyed with the idea of keeping them and giving them - or perhaps selling them - to Charles the Bald, but he didn't have the crews to man both the Frankish ships he'd borrowed and the two Swedish longships he'd already captured. On the other hand he daren't leave them there in case the Vikings returned. If they got their ships back they could raid elsewhere; without them they'd be stranded. Edmund therefore beached the longships and left them burning before heading upriver to Paris, taking just the Viking's knarrs with him, intending to use them as trading vessels once peace was restored.

-ᛉ-

Ragnar stood with Olaf, Lagertha and the Danish jarl, Grimulf, on the bank of the Seine looking across at the island called the Île de la Cité on which Paris was built. There were only two bridges which gave access to it: one from the right bank and one from the left. The bridge on their side of the river was defended by a small fort at their end and a gateway with a tower on each side of it at the far end.

A couple of arrows had landed a few yards short of them when they had first appeared, but the garrison in the fort didn't waste any more once they had established the fact that the Vikings were out of range. If they were out of arrow shot, they would certainly be too far away to reach with crossbows.

'We need our ships,' Olaf grumbled.

Indeed it did seem that the only way into the city was from the river, unless he wanted to lose a lot of men trying to capture one of the bridges. Then Ragnar had a stroke of luck. Four knarrs appeared from upriver and, evidently oblivious to the presence of the Viking army on the far bank, moored alongside the Paris quayside. Immediately men appeared and proceeded to load the four merchant ships with cargo from one of the warehouses.

'Olaf, go and pick out two dozen strong swimmers.'

'You want to cut the knarrs out tonight and use them to ferry our men across the river?' Olaf guessed.

Ragnar nodded.

'They are to only take their daggers. This needs to be done quietly. If the alarm is sounded they will be killed before they can row the ships over here.'

Olaf, even at thirty seven, was one of the strongest swimmers there was and he decided to lead the foray. He didn't tell his friend because he was certain that Ragnar would forbid it. He'd been Ragnar's right hand man from the day they first met and, although they weren't as close now as they had been, the Viking leader depended on his advice and delegated much to him.

Of course, Ragnar had been generous when it came to lavishing rewards on his friend, but, apart from a small farm near Arendal, these gifts had always been hack silver and arm rings, just like any other warrior. Officially he was still a bondi whilst others had been rewarded with promotion to jarl. Officially jarls were elected by those they led, but if Ragnar supported someone it would be a foolish man who opposed his candidate.

He knew why Ragnar had refrained from making him a jarl; it would take him from his side. Well, that was too bad. Some jarls had already fallen during this summer's campaign and more would do so in the taking of Paris, of that he was certain. After he brought Ragnar the ships he needed to make the crossing he determined to ask to be made jarl as his reward.

Æthelred had disagreed with his father increasingly as he grew older. Now Eanred and he had argued violently. The Strathclyde Britons had invaded Cumbria once more and this time they had captured most of it. Rædwulf, its ealdorman since the death of his father, had fled south into Luncæstershire and was trying to raise an army to retake his shire. Of course, he had appealed to Eanred for help, but the king had done nothing. He seemed content to lose Cumbria from his kingdom, something that had appalled his son.

'Why aren't you at least summoning the Witan to discuss the situation?' he almost yelled at his father in his frustration.

'Don't shout at me, you impudent boy,' Eanred had replied calmly. 'I am doing something. I pray to God daily to keep the rest of the kingdom safe. What you don't seem to understand is the precarious position we are in. Beorhtwulf of Mercia has forged an alliance with Wessex because of the Viking raids on both their coasts and Northumbria stands alone in England as an independent kingdom. Æthelwulf of Wessex is the dominant partner and he's made no secret of his desire to unite all of England under his rule. We need to keep our men ready in case of trouble on our southern border.'

'That's all you think about – Deira. What about Bernicia and the rest of your kingdom. Letting the men of Strathclyde run amok in Cumbria sends the wrong message to the Picts. They may have been quiet in recent years but now that Drest mac Uurad has won the struggle for the throne, he may well be tempted to invade Lothian to match Dumnagual of Strathclyde's advance in the west.'

Eanred shrugged. 'The Lothian nobles are an unreliable lot. They still oppose my choice of Anson as Ealdorman of Islandshire. Let them guard the north against the Picts. At least, it'll stop them plotting against me.'

'Expelling Edmund of Bebbanburg and putting Anson in his place was a stupid idea, and all because you tried to exhort money from his brother and failed. I'm not surprised that they feel little loyalty to you. Especially as you have never visited the northern part of your kingdom, nor given them anything in exchange for the taxes they pay you. I'm just surprised that they haven't deposed you from the throne of Bernicia and re-established it as a separate kingdom once more.'

'Be very careful what you say,' his father hissed at him, rising from his chair, purple in the face with rage. 'Most would regard that as treason. By rights, I should have you thrown into a cell until you learn some respect.'

'Respect has to be earned and you have failed in that regard for many years, now, father.' Æthelred spat back. 'Perhaps it's time you retired to a monastery. After all, you spend most of your time in the one here or at Whitby. You should have been a monk, not a king.'

Eanred raised his hand and slapped his son hard across the face. The young man looked shocked for an instant. He lifted his fist to strike the king down but recovered control over himself just in time. The penalty for striking the king was death, though he doubted that the Witan would impose it in his case. He abruptly turned on his heel and strode out of the room and through the hall beyond, calling for his gesith to saddle their horses.

'Where are we going, Æthelred?' the captain asked, alarmed at the look of fury on the ætheling's face.

'North, to raise an army to defeat Dumnagual and recover Cumbria.'

This announcement was greeted by cheers and several of the other warriors in the hall rushed to get ready to accompany Æthelred. No one thought to ask if the king had sanctioned war against the invaders or, if they did, they refrained from voicing the question. His failure to act had lost Eanred most of the support he'd enjoyed hitherto and, though he might continue to sit on the throne, it was Æthelred that the warriors of Northumbria now looked to as their leader.

Olaf swam slowly and silently towards the far side of the Seine, his movement through the water scarcely making a sound as he led his twenty men towards the four laden knarrs. He'd been afraid that they might leave when the labourers had finished loading them just as dark fell, but their captains had evidently decided to wait until dawn before sailing.

The clouds obscured the moon and it was only thanks to the candles and oil lamps inside the few taverns along the quayside that silhouetted the knarrs partially against the darkness that guided him in the right direction.

Each of the men following him was tied to the next man by a thin cord to make sure no one went off course. As each man reached Olaf as he trod water under the lea of one of the ships, he untied the cord.

Olaf swam to the wooden pontoon to which several small boats were tied. From there some wooden steps led up to the quayside. A few minutes later all his men joined him and lay flat on their bellies on the cold cobbled surface of the quay. Once he was satisfied that there was no one around, apart from the few men keeping watch aboard the laden knarrs, he sent his men off in small groups to capture the ships.

He slithered over the gunwale of the knarr he had picked and landed on the deck, crouching down, his eyes darting about him. The ship's guards were huddled together aft playing some game of chance under the light of the storm lantern mounted on the stern rail. They were so intent on their game that they didn't hear the five Vikings moving slowly towards them until a cry from another ship alerted them.

By then it was too late. Olaf and his men seized them and cut the throats of the four men before they could add to the cries of alarm from the other knarrs. Olaf cursed and had to think quickly. The noise would soon bring the city watch running to see what was amiss and men were already spilling out of the tavern a hundred yards away.

One of the unfortunate Franks had been armed with an axe and Olaf now pressed this into the hands of one of his men.

'Cut the mooring lines of all the ships, quick as you can. Then go and row the small boats tied to the pontoon out into the river and tow the knarrs over to our side. Now move!'

Luckily for the Vikings only one of the ships had put up a fight. Although normally four seamen would be no match for five Vikings, the odds were against the latter - armed as they were with just daggers - once the Franks had picked up their weapons and shields. One enterprising soul threw a rope around the bow post of the ship on which the fight was still raging, then he and his friends towed it away from the jetty.

Olaf's ship came alongside it and he leaped onto it carrying a Frankish shield and a sword he'd picked up from the deck of the ship he'd captured. In the darkness the Franks thought that his shield meant that he was one of them, which made it easy for him to cut the first man down. By this time two of the Vikings had been killed and another was seriously injured. However, they had also killed one of the Franks, which evened up the odds a little.

Two the Franks tried to spear the remaining Vikings whilst the third turned to face Olaf. He was armed with a heavy axe and, once he had tried to chop Olaf down and failed, his fate was sealed. The Viking thrust his sword through the base of his throat whilst he was still off balance. He collapsed onto the deck, where his blood stained it black under the yellow light of the lantern.

The outcome was now a forgone conclusion. The two Franks threw down their weapons but Olaf didn't have time to deal with prisoners. The Vikings threw the two of them over the side, together with the dead bodies.

Now that all four knarrs were nearing the far bank the boats let go the towing cables and those on board laboured at the oars to propel them the last few yards. Olaf collapsed as he felt the keel ground on the shingle of the far bank, partly from effort, but mainly with relief.

The next morning the captured knarrs, filled to capacity with warriors, made the return trip. As soon as they had discharged their human cargo they returned to bring the next few hundred across.

Ragnar had expected resistance to his landing but the city remained ominously silent. He led the first few hundred men into the city but found it virtually deserted. Those who had remained after the initial exodus had fled as soon as they heard that the Viking horde had captured the four knarrs.

However, some poor souls were unable to flee. As Ragnar threw open the door of the first hut he came to his nose was assailed by a stench which he couldn't identify at first. Then he made out the dead family of five lying on their cots in the gloom. It wasn't until one of his men lit a torch so that he could see better that he realised that the corpses were of a couple and three small children; all bore the unmistakable buboes and blackened feet and hands that characterised bubonic plague.

Chapter Sixteen – From Disaster to Victory

Paris 846

After the hasty abandonment of the city, Ragnar ordered it to be burned to the ground. However, a few of his men had already been infected by the dead and dying and the plague began to spread amongst the others.

The one positive occurrence was the discovery that the monastery of Saint Denis to the north of Paris hadn't been abandoned. Some of the monks put up a futile resistance and were slaughtered but many, including the abbot, were captured. Such was the latter's faith in the protection of Christ that he hadn't even bothered to send the monastery's treasures to a place of safety.

However, the spread of the plague amongst the Vikings, coupled with the dysentery that some still suffered from, vindicated the abbot's belief in the retribution of God. Unsurprisingly, Ragnar was worried that the abbot's incessant preaching about the White Christ and the vengeance he was visiting upon the heathens was undermining his men's morale. He therefore threatened to cut out the old man's tongue unless he kept his mouth shut.

The warning seemed to have little effect; indeed the abbot seemed to relish the thought of suffering for his beliefs. Ragnar was about to carry out his threat when news arrived about the advance of the Frankish King, Charles the Bald, with an army six thousand strong towards the Viking camp on the Seine just to the north of Paris.

-ᛉ-

At just fifteen Jarl Edda had been proud to have been chosen by Ragnar to look after things at home; though he would far rather have been allowed to accompany the raiders to Paris. Like many youths, he had a greater faith in his own abilities than was warranted. When the Swedes who had managed to escape made it safely back to Uppsala a few months earlier, they had maintained that Ragnar's campaign had ended in failure. Of course, they made it sound worse than the reality to explain why they had fled. They maintained that Ragnar was dead and most of his warriors with him.

Edda's first reaction had been panic. Most of the bondis and their sons over the age of sixteen had gone with Ragnar, leaving mostly boys and old men to defend Adger, Alfheim and Jarl Grimulf's lands in Northern Denmark. However, he soon came to see that this presented him with a golden opportunity. The eldest of Ragnar's surviving sons, Ivar the Boneless, was not yet nine and far too young to rule. As the only jarl left in Adger he saw himself as the new king.

'You've heard the rumours?' Bjorn said to Ivar and Sigurd.

'Tales spread by treacherous Swedes,' Ivar replied, spitting onto the earthen floor of the king's hall in Arendal. 'They deserted him; there is no proof of father's death. For all we know he has captured Paris and will return a hero laden with treasure.'

'I overheard Edda talking to the old bondis. He seems to believe the stories are true,' piped up Sigurd Snake-in-the-Eye.

This was said tentatively in his high boy's voice. At only six his two elder brothers tended to ignore him, classing him with the youngest, five year old Halfdan. At this Ivar's eyes narrowed.

'If he really thinks that father is dead, that would leave him as the ruler of Adger.'

'What difference does that make?' Bjorn asked. 'Father left him in charge anyway.'

'Yes, but if he doesn't think that the king or any of the other jarls will return, he may well seize the throne and promote his friends to replace the missing jarls,' Ivar explained impatiently.

'But if father isn't dead, he'll come back and depose Edda, so what's the problem?' Bjorn asked, puzzled by Ivar's evident concern.

'We are growing older day by day and Edda will want to get rid of us before we grow up to challenge him; that's the problem.'

'Oh, you think he plans to kill us?'

'Well, I would if I was in his position,' Ivar replied bluntly.

'So, what do we do? Flee before he can murder us?' Sigurd asked, his eyes wide with fright.

'No, we kill him first.'

That night Edda crept into the chamber at the back of the king's hall that the four brothers shared. Three of his closest friends, all of whom he had promised to make jarls once he was king, followed him in. Silently they stood above the four sleeping boys, who lay under wolf skins to keep them warm, their eyes on Edda. When he nodded, they stabbed down with their swords. The points sank into the boys and, in their trepidation at what they were doing, they stabbed again and again until it occurred to them that the bodies were remarkably unresistant.

Edda pulled back the skins covering the boy he'd been stabbing to find nothing underneath except a couple of rolled up sheepskins. He cursed and whipped around as the door crashed open.

Torgny the lagman stood there with Ivar and Bjorn standing on one side of him and one of the elderly warrior who guarded the king's hall on the other. Behind them Edda was vaguely aware of other old men carrying spears and shields.

'Jarl Edda you are accused of attempting to murder...'

He got no further as Edda launched himself at the two boys with a scream of rage. The jarl raised his sword, intending to bring it down on Ivar's head but Bjorn was too quick for him. The young boy thrust a long dagger into Edda just under his belt and the jarl doubled up as the shock of the abdominal wound momentarily paralysed him. His momentum knocked Bjorn from his feet and he fell with the fatally wounded jarl on top of him. Edda would die in due course, and a stomach wound was a painful way to go, but in the meantime he was still dangerous.

Edda struggled to get up but, before he could regain his feet, Ivar thrust his own dagger into the young jarl's right knee, causing his leg to collapse under him. The savage glint in the young boy's eye was a good indication that he hadn't finished with his attacker, but the men who'd entered with Torgny pushed Ivar and Bjorn to one side and two of them grabbed Edda.

Others swiftly disarmed the other three without further injury and they and Edda were dragged outside. Edda was left to die in excruciating agony whilst his accomplices were thrown into a pit to await judgement by their fellow bondis at a meeting of the Thing.

The next morning the Thing was quick to condemn the dead Edda and his three friends. Their status as bondis was revoked and they would become classed as thralls. However, their sentence was deferred for twenty four hours. If they were still in Agder at the end of that period they would be enslaved. Perhaps their fathers would have pleaded for a lighter sentence, but they were all away taking part in Ragnar's raid on Paris. They had kept their lives, but little else. Inevitably they became exiles with no means of existing except as mercenaries.

With Edda dead that only left two other jarls, and both were Swedes who lived in Alfheim. With the memory of Froh's rule still in their minds, few of the Norse bondis wanted to appoint one of the Swedes to replace Edda as ruler of Ragnar's three kingdoms. Whilst the fate of the other would-be assassins was quickly decided, it took the Thing over three hours to decide who should rule them pro tem. In the end they appointed Ivar and Bjorn to rule jointly with Torgny the lagman. It wasn't a satisfactory long term solution, but everyone hoped that Ragnar had survived; everyone, that is, except the ambitious Ivar.

Æthelred looked around the hall, meeting the eyes of every noble and churchman present at the meeting of the Witan in turn, before he spoke.

'Whilst Wessex, Mercia and even East Anglia to the south gain in power, prestige and prosperity, Northumbria has become a backwater,' he stated, then paused waiting for anyone to disagree.

No one did.

'Once the rulers of this kingdom were bretwaldas, not only of much of England, but also of the kingdoms north of Northumbria – the Land of the Picts, Strathclyde and Dalriada. Since then we have only hung onto what we have by luck. The struggle between Wessex and Mercia in the south and between various contenders for the Pictish throne in the north have left us in peace. Only Strathclyde threatened us, but now the Norse settlers threaten to take our lands in the west and Danes increasingly attack us in the east.'

He paused briefly in his tirade and took a deep breath before continuing.

'It is to my eternal regret that my father has been able to do little or nothing to defend our kingdom over the past two decades.'

Here he looked at the elderly man who sat on the throne on a raised dais, glaring balefully at him.

'I agree,' Rædwulf of Cumbria said, getting to his feet. 'Perhaps it's time that the father retired to a monastery and allowed the son to take the throne.'

There was a murmur of agreement around the hall but Æthelred held up his hand just as his father leapt to his feet, his face puce with rage. Before he could vent his spleen his son reassured him.

'I have no intention of replacing my father as king whilst he still lives and wishes to remain on the throne. No, my proposal is that I help him to rule more effectively. I request that you appoint me as King Eanred's sub-regulus and also as the hereræswa.'

At this Eanred subsided onto his throne but he still looked angry. He gnawed his lower lip, drawing blood, but contented himself with glowering at his only son. Æthelred waited calmly for the hubbub that followed his announcement to subside.

'How will this arrangement work? Will you rule jointly?' Rædwulf asked. 'I can't see that working very efficiently. We need a strong leader, not a bickering couple.'

'My father will remain as king and be treated with all the respect that his position requires. I will take over responsibility for the day to day governance of Northumbria.'

'And how will you deal with the pirate menace that stalks our shores?' another of the ealdormen asked.

'By building longships to equal theirs, just as Eafa of Bebbanburg did twenty five years ago. Only this time I'll build a secure harbour protected by a fortress to keep them safe when they are not at sea.'

'You mentioned a harbour; you mean just one haven, presumably on the east coast?' Wigmund, Archbishop of Eoforwīc queried. 'Where will it be located? The coastline must be at least two hundred miles long. I suggest Whitby; from there it can protect the most populated part of the kingdom.'

This caused an uproar with the ealdormen of Bernicia and Lothian demanding that it be located much further north and Rædwulf asking about Cumbria and Luncæstershire.

Æthelred made no attempt to intervene; instead he waited patiently for the tumult to die down.

'Obviously we will need to discuss the details calmly and reach a logical solution,' he said, once he could be heard. 'I am not so foolish as to think that we can defeat every attempt to raid our lands. The important thing is to be strong enough to dissuade these pagans from thinking we are a soft target. My aim is to make it so hazardous for them that they go elsewhere where the pickings are easier.

'What I ask of you now is your formal recognition of me as sub-regulus.'

After that had been agreed unanimously, much to Eanred's displeasure, Æthelred had one more announcement to make before the Witan broke up for the day.

'I will need the help of one man, currently in exile, to help me build my fleet and to take charge of it as my admiral. No-one is more suited to that role than Edmund of Bebbanburg.'

Anson, the man to whom Eanred had given Bebbanburg and made Ealdorman of Islandshire, got to his feet, his face white.

'You cannot take away what is mine,' he spluttered.

'Ealdormen are royal appointments, Anson, I am sorry to have to do this, but the interests of the kingdom have to come first. You were a thegn in Deira before my father elevated you, I think. So at least you won't be homeless, as we made Edmund for no good reason.'

He glared at his father who shifted uncomfortably on his throne. Æthelred had never reminded him that Edmund's brother, Ilfrid, had died because of his father's greed, but what had happened that day had clouded the relationship between father and son.

'You'll regret this, Æthelred,' Anson hissed at him.

'Are you threatening me? I would tread very carefully if I were you - that is if you wish to avoid a charge of treason.'

Æthelred was sure of his ground. Anson had never been a popular choice to replace Edmund. The latter's family had held Bebbanburg for two centuries and had become the unofficial leaders of the north of the kingdom. Kendric, the ealdorman who held the border along the Firth of Forth, including the mighty fortresses of Dùn Barra and Dùn Èideann, had nearly risen in revolt at the time, but luckily his fellow ealdormen of Lothian had persuaded him otherwise.

Now the announcement of Edmund's reinstatement was applauded by the majority of the Witan, including Eanbert, the newly appointed Bishop of Lindisfarne.

Anson subsided, defeated for now, but he exchanged a look with Eanred which boded trouble for Æthelred in the future.

Edmund was with King Charles the Bald, Count Louis of Arras and several other nobles when the messenger came.

'I maintain that paying these Vikings seven thousand livres in silver and gold to go away is merely rewarding them for the carnage and destruction that they have wrought. Pay now and they will return again next year demanding more money,' Louis said, vehemently opposed to what Charles had proposed.

'You are forgetting two things, Louis,' the king replied calmly. 'It is partly a ransom for the release of the saintly Abbot of Saint Denis and those of his monks who have survived and, secondly, they may be pagan pirates, but they have a reputation for keeping their oaths. If Ragnar Lodbrok swears to cease from raiding Frankia for a period of three years, we will have that time to improve our defences and build up our forces once more.'

'Don't forget, Louis,' another count added, 'the king's brothers are still causing trouble in the south and the east. These Norsemen and Danes are formidable fighters and, even if we could defeat them – something which is far from certain given your past performance against them in the field – it would weaken us and leave us vulnerable.'

Louis looked at him angrily. He didn't like to be reminded of his incompetence, which had led to the loss of Paris. He had tried to blame Edmund but the king was well aware that the Northumbrian was the only one who had scored a measure of success against the Vikings.

'Good. It's decided then. I will negotiate with Ragnar along the lines we have agreed. Excellent.'

As Edmund stepped outside the royal pavilion a tired and travel worn man holding an equally exhausted horse stepped into his path.

'Ealdorman Edmund of Bebbanburg?' he enquired hopefully in English with the unmistakeable accent of a man from the north.

'I used to be. Who wants to know?' Edmund asked puzzled by the presence of a stranger from Northumbria so far from home.

'I have a letter for you from Sub-regulus Æthelred, lord.'

'Sub-regulus?'

'Yes, Lord Æthelred now rules Northumbria on behalf of his father.'

'Really? So Eanred is still king?'

'In name only, lord.'

'I see. Go and get some food and get some sleep. Come and find me when you are awake to see if I have a reply. My camp is over in that direction. Tell Cynefrith, the captain of my warband that I sent you.'

As the man trudged away Edmund broke the seal and unrolled the parchment.

To my trusty and faithful Lord Edmund, in whom I have great faith it began.

I have long regretted the injustice that was done to you and to your brother Ilfrid. It is only now that I can do something to make some sort of amends. I realise that nothing I can do will bring Ilfrid back, nor can I make up for the time that you have spent as an exile. However, I can at least restore your home at Bebbanburg to you and re-appoint you as Ealdorman of Islandshire. The bearer of this document also carries with him the necessary deeds to restore your property and status. Anson has been ordered to quit your lands by the end of March and so I would be grateful if you could take possession then.

I have it in mind to build a fleet to counter the Viking marauders and I would count it a great favour if you would construct as many longships as you consider necessary to guard my eastern seaboard. You will, of course, take command of this naval force as its admiral.

I look forward to renewing our acquaintance as soon as possible after your return to Northumbria. There are many things for us to discuss, not least the programme for ship building and the training of their warrior crews. We will also need to decide on a safe haven for the fleet when it is not at sea. Budle Bay will not serve, I fear. It's too exposed and perhaps a little too far north.

The letter ended in the usual verbose way and Edmund was interested to note that Æthelred described himself as Sub-regulus and Hereræswa of Northumbria.

Edmund walked off, heading away from the vast camp, to find some peace and quiet where he could reflect on the offer which Æthelred had made to him. His initial reaction had been one of joy that he was being allowed to return home, but princes seldom act out of altruism. Evidently the effective ruler of Northumbria wanted him to defend it from Viking attack. He knew from experience that it was an impossible task. The most he might be able to do was to dissuade all but the boldest Vikings from preying on such a long coastline.

If he failed, no doubt he would shoulder the blame. Æthelred would only be guilty of choosing the wrong man to be his admiral. And what about the western coast, which was nearly as long as that in the east? Æthelred's letter had said nothing about that.

Still, what did he have to lose? His home and his warehouse in Paris had been torched and it would be some time before he could operate out of Paris again. His temporary base at Châlons-sur-Marne, to where most of his goods had been shipped, was not somewhere to conduct trade from very easily.

His one regret was that he'd always promised to revenge Ilfrid's death and, if he took up this offer, he would have to accept the detested Eanred as his king, even if only in name.

He sighed. Was he really about to reject reinstatement as an ealdorman because of his hatred of an old man who no longer had any power? Hopefully, he'd soon be dead anyway.

All in all it was an easy decision to make. He'd leave a competent manager to sort everything out and return to England. His mind made up he retraced his steps and went to find Æthelred's messenger.

PART FOUR – THE RAVEN VERSUS THE WOLF

THE FINAL CONFLICT

Chapter Seventeen – The Return Home

Autumn 846

Ragnar set sail for Norway in the late summer. By then his army had shrunk to no more than fourteen hundred. Many more had died of the plague or dysentery and others had found wives and had decided to settle in Frankia. Knowing how well they fought, Charles had encouraged them to stay, granting farms to them in the area that later became known as Northman's Land or Normandy. However, he insisted that the settlers become Christians; a stipulation which reduced their potential numbers considerably.

The rest were forced to delay their departure until they could build new longships. Ragnar also kept the four knarrs that Olaf had captured and at the end of July they and the eighteen new longships set sail for home.

Once more he was greeted by Ivar and Bjorn standing together on the jetty at Arendal to welcome him. He had liked Edda and was saddened by his betrayal. He was, however, inordinately proud of how the boys had defeated the traitor's scheme to replace him.

Five new jarls were required to replace those killed in Frankia and, with Edda's perfidy in mind, he ignored the custom whereby the regional Thing elected their jarl and he appointed those he trusted, including Olaf who took Edda's place. There was some opposition to this change from the traditionalists, but the wealth brought back from Frankia had increased Ragnar's standing even further and no one openly challenged his decision.

Olaf had long held ambitions for advancement and seeing others become jarls had started to rankle. It was frustrating that he, effectively the second most important man in the two kingdoms, remained a mere bondi, as his wife was quick to point out at every opportunity. His advancement therefore came at the right time for him. It did mean that he wouldn't be so close to Ragnar now, but he could see the king's sons, especially Ivar, taking that position soon in any case.

He was even more convinced of this when, even though they were well below the usual age for such an honour, Ragnar made both Ivar and Bjorn members of his council.

The ultimate result of the campaign to capture Paris might have been a success, but it had cost Ragnar too many fine warriors and he was sensible enough to realise that he would have to wait a few years until boys grew into men in order to replenish his numbers. Unfortunately the time necessary for this wasn't something that the Norns gave him.

It was Yingvi, newly created jarl of Adger's easternmost lands, who brought him the news. Eystein Beli had been incensed by the death of his brother and the loss of most of the men he'd sent with Osten. It seemed that the truce between the King of Uppsala and Ragnar was over.

Anson had been reluctant to cede Bebbanburg to Edmund when he eventually arrived in September 846. Keen as he was to return to his homeland, Edmund had been forced to remain in Frankia until Charles released him, and the king wasn't going to do that until after Ragnar had sailed.

Edmund used the time to build a longship of his own, paying a Norse shipwright to do the work alongside a drekar the man was constructing for Ragnar. He rebuilt his warehouse in Paris, this time in stone, and moved his goods back there once he was convinced that the Vikings were on the point of leaving without any further trouble.

Stone was expensive - more so as Charles was building a wall to defend the city against any further attacks from the river – but Edmund thought the expense worthwhile if it saved his merchandise from being burned. It would also make pilfering more difficult.

The next problem was who to leave in charge. He could have appointed a Frank, but he preferred someone he knew he could trust. In the end his unexpected choice fell on his servant, Laughlin.

During the years he had spent in Paris the man had become as much of an assistant as a personal servant and he knew the business as well as Edmund did. Plus he knew that he could trust him. He was loyal and extremely grateful for the appointment. Furthermore it meant that his new manager could now marry the Frankish widow he had been visiting whenever his duties allowed.

When Edmund finally arrived in Budle Bay in his new longship, accompanied by three knarrs that he proposed to fill with goods for export to Paris, he found Anson's bull's head standard still flying over the fortress. As Edmund only had the hundred men and a dozen boys who had crewed his ships any assault was out of the question. He didn't know how many men Anson had inside, but he suspected that it might be as many as fifty or sixty. Enough to defend the walls at any rate.

Edmund wasted no time. Having been prevented from entering Bebbanburg peaceably, he hired horses and sent messengers to Kenric at Dùn Èideann in the north and to Æthelred. Meanwhile he besieged the stronghold. His warband couldn't guard both entrances on their own without the danger of being overcome by a sally, so he called out the fyrd to reinforce his warband and sat down to wait.

For a time nothing happened and it began to look as if he might have to starve Anson out. That being the case, he could only hope that his arrival had been unexpected and that there was only enough food already in the store huts to last for a month or so.

In the end he didn't have to wait as long as that. Kenric and the ealdormen of Lothian had only just joined him with several hundred more men when a messenger from Æthelred arrived. The missive was addressed to Anson and the man read it out at the top of his voice before the main gates.

'To the Thegn Anson and all occupants of the fortress known as Bebbanburg,' he began pompously. *'The fortress and all of Islandshire now belongs to Ealdorman Edmund, by the will of King*

Eanred. All those who continue to oppose the decision of the king and his vice-regulus, Æthelred the Ætheling, one hour after the reading of this proclamation will be deemed traitors and their lives shall be forfeit, as shall the lives of any sons over the age of fourteen. The rest of their families will be sold as slaves.

By God's grace,

Eanred, King of Northumbria.

The messenger rolled up the scroll and put it back inside the leather cylinder before handing it to Edmund.

'Let's hope that works, lord. I wouldn't want to be the one to have to assault that place,' he said as he went to wash and get something to eat.

Edmund, Kenric and the other nobles waited patiently but there was no sign of the gates opening after the passage of what they estimated was most of the allotted hour. Then Bishop Eanbert arrived from Lindisfarne with three monks.

'It's good to see you back where you belong, my boy,' he greeted Edmund, nodding to the other ealdormen before raising his right hand to bless them.

'Not yet, Eanbert. Anson seems determined to hold Bebbanburg against me.'

'Hmmm. Let's see what I can do to change his mind.'

The bishop strode towards the gates and halted well within bow range before raising his staff topped with a golden cross. His monks gathered around him holding bell, book and candle - the accoutrements necessary for the act of excommunication.

'Anson, you have sworn an oath before God and the king that you would relinquish these lands and return to the vill from whence you came. By denying the rightful ealdorman entry to this stronghold you have broken your sacred oath,' he began. 'Unless you repent I shall be forced to pronounce a sentence of excommunication upon you, your family and all those who assist you in your rebellion. As you will also be sentenced to death, you will be executed unshriven and will go to Hell.'

The bishop paused for a moment.

'To all those within the walls, you can only save yourselves if you immediately repent and throw open the gates.'

After another pause he continued.

'Very well, I am forced to commence the act of excommunication.'

'Bishop, I'm not certain that Anson understands what excommunication means; indeed I'm not sure that I do,' Edmund muttered in his ear.

'Really? It means that a person or persons are no longer members of the Catholic Church, they may not partake of the body and blood of Christ during mass, nor marry or receive a Christian burial. They are outcasts. It is a sanction more prevalent in the Eastern Church than in the West, but even our blessed Saint Columba was excommunicated in 562 for allegedly praying for the help of Christ for one side in an Irish War. The sentence was later lifted, of course.'

'I see; perhaps you could explain what it means in more detail to Anson and his men, so that they understand the full import of the penalty that they are about to suffer.'

The bishop did so in graphic terms and almost immediately afterwards they heard the faint sounds of a fierce argument coming from the other side of the main gates. A little while later the massive oak gates swung open and Anson rode out with a man carrying his banner flying above his head.

He glared at both Bishop Eanbert and Edmund before bowing his head stiffly.

'Bebbanburg is yours, boy. Allow me time to prepare and we will vacate the place within the hour.'

'You will call me lord, Thegn Anson,' Edmund said impassively. 'You may have your hour, but no longer.'

Anson stiffened but said nothing further. Just over an hour later he departed followed by his warband. The exodus continued for some time with carts piled high with possessions bringing up the rear.

Edmund walked into his old home and wept at the destruction left behind by Anson and his men. The furniture had been broken up and the grain and other foodstuffs spoiled. Many had evidently defecated in his hall. Even the wine barrels had been broached and their contents spilled. He was only thankful that no one had thought to pollute the two wells.

No one remained in the place. Even the lowest slave had been taken with him by Anson.

Edmund fought to contain his fury and to think clearly. He had counted less than forty warriors with Anson, many more than he would be able to afford as a thegn. They would be seeking new masters before long no doubt and he wondered whether they would fight for Anson.

'How many riding horses are there in the settlement?' he asked Ordric, the thegn of the local vill.

'Perhaps a dozen, lord, why?'

'I want them rounded up now. I'll pay for their hire of course.'

'What are you going to do?'

'Get Anson to return and clear up this mess and to give me back the slaves that belong here.'

'With a dozen men?'

'I'm sure that they'll be enough,' he replied grimly.

As Ragnar's ships sailed into the fjord that led to Bohus he could see the smoke rising from several places inland from the fjord. He ground his teeth in anger. Eystein Beli would pay dearly for this.

In fact the King of Uppsala had been too old and infirm to conduct the war against Alfheim himself, so his army was commanded by Hákon, his nephew and the son of the dead Osten. He had been fourteen and too young to accompany his father as a warrior when he left to attack Paris. Now he was sixteen and he was determined to wreak vengeance on the man he blamed for his father's death.

His fleet had landed on the same beach that Ragnar had used all those years before when he had captured Alfheim. Like Ragnar before him many years previously, Hákon found the fortress at Bohus too formidable to capture by direct assault. He therefore left men to besiege it whilst he and his army lay waste the surrounding farms and settlements.

Ragnar's forces were depleted after Paris and the bondis living in Alfheim were dispersed, having been caught unawares by Hákon's attack. Nevertheless, he had more than enough warriors to deal swiftly with the Swedes left to continue the siege of the stronghold.

'What will you do with the prisoners?' Bjorn had asked excitedly after the fighting was over.

He'd been upset at being left aboard his father's drekar under the care of Leofstan, now its captain, but he had been allowed to go to find Ragnar as soon as it was safe to do so. He had set off at a run like a young colt through the dead and dying, pausing only to thrust his dagger into the neck of any Swede who still showed any sign of life.

'I'm not sure you should be here, Bjorn. There are still Swedes wounded but alive who would kill you given half a chance.'

'Not any more, father. I killed half a dozen of them on my way to your side.'

Ragnar laughed and ruffled his son's hair.

'Spoken like a true Viking.'

'Now I'm blooded, can I be a warrior?'

'No, Bjorn. You're only nine and it's a very different matter facing a fully armed man. He wouldn't care how young you are and you'd be dead within minutes. Don't be in such a hurry to grow up; your time will come soon enough.'

Bjorn pointed to the dejected group of Swedes who'd surrendered.

'Can I have one of them as a thrall, father?'

'I need to chase down the rest of the Uppsalan invaders, Bjorn. I can't afford to take prisoners; they are all to be hanged.'

'Even the boys?'

Ragnar sighed. He didn't like killing children but even they would be a liability when he marched inland to confront the main Swedish army.

'Very well. If there is a suitable boy your age or younger, you may take him as your thrall, but you are responsible for him. If he gives any trouble it will be you who has to kill him.'

'I understand. Thank you.'

There were several boys with the Swedes, mainly ship's boys but one was eight, the son of a jarl who'd been brought along to witness what his father had thought would be an easy campaign with little danger. It's what Hákon had told him, naively thinking that Ragnar would be too weak after the debacle of Paris to oppose his invasion in any strength.

'What's your name, boy,' Bjorn asked him.

The lad looked down at the ground and refused to answer, so Bjorn pulled out his dagger and pressed the point up under the young Swede's chin. A thin trickle of blood ran down his neck and he was forced to look up into Bjorn's eyes.

'I asked you a question. Now stand up. You'll either answer me of I'll kill you.'

The boy licked his lips nervously and carefully climbed to his feet looking Bjorn in the eye the whole time. Bjorn kept his dagger at his throat and, inevitably, the point drew a little more blood as he got up.

'I'm Erling,' he said reluctantly. It meant son of a chief.

'And are you the son of a jarl?'

'Yes, my father died during the fighting. He was Jarl of Östra Aros, to the south west of Uppsala itself.'

Bjorn could see that Erling was trying hard to stop from crying over the loss of his father. He pulled the point back from the young Swede's neck, but kept the blade pointing at him, whilst he took his upper arm in a firm grip and led him away from the other captives. Ragnar watched with approval. It seemed that his son had a head on his shoulders wiser than his years would indicate.

'Now, Erling, I'm going to give you a choice. You can become my personal thrall and serve me faithfully, or I'll kill you with this dagger now. I'll try and make your death as painless as possible but I can't promise it won't hurt. Now which is it to be?'

'I'd rather die than serve Norse scum like you,' Erling said, trying to keep the tremor out of his voice.

'Very well, your choice.'

He went to stab the boy in the neck but Erling ducked and the blade went over his head. He tried to run but his hands were tied and it didn't take Bjorn more than a few seconds to catch him and kick his legs from under him.

Ragnar's son flipped the winded boy onto his back and knelt either side of his torso, pushing the blade into his neck again.

'You're a fool. What did you think you were doing? Trying to escape? Now, I'll give you one last chance. Become my thrall or die.'

Erling broke down in tears, all the fight knocked out of him.

'I'll serve you.'

'I'll serve you, lord,' Bjorn corrected him, pressing the point a little further into the Swedish boy's neck.

'I'll serve you, lord.'

'Right, get up so I can cut your hands free. Then you can strip off those fine clothes and go and wash in the fjord. I'll find you something more appropriate to wear as befits your new station in life.'

'You trust me not to try and escape?' Erling asked as his hands were freed.

'Yes, you've given me your word and, besides, runaway thralls die a long and painful death.'

-ᛉ-

It didn't take Edmund long to catch up with the slow moving column, but he rode past the carts and the people on foot, ignoring them as they scuttled to the side of the road. However, when he reached the front of the line of people on foot he found just five mounted warriors and no sign of Anson.

'Where is he?' he barked at the man at the head of the dejected procession.

'He's abandoned us, lord. He said that he couldn't afford to keep so many servants and warriors now that he only had the income from his vill to sustain him. He took his family and ten warriors with him, along with two chests of silver strapped to a packhorse.'

'What made you decide to stay with the servants? And where are the other warriors?'

The man shrugged. 'I don't know where the others have gone, probably to seek service elsewhere, but we are heading for Hexham to see if the abbot will employ us. The servants and slaves followed us, but I'm not sure why.'

'I see. Very well; I'll offer you employment if you swear to serve me loyally. If anyone breaks that trust he will hang.'

All five warriors immediately sat taller in the saddle and assured him that they would be faithful to him.

'Good; but you will swear an oath before Bishop Eanbert when we return to Bebbanburg. Meanwhile you can tell these people that they are to return to the fortress. I'll forgive them if they clear up the mess that was left behind'

'You are not coming with us, lord? How will the garrison know that we are now your men?'

'I'll send one of my warband with you to inform them. Now, in which direction did the other warriors head?'

'Due south, lord.'

'Hmmm, it sounds as if they might be heading for Eoforwīc.'

'That makes sense, Edmund,' Cynewise said, speaking for the first time. 'The word is that Æthelred is hiring mercenaries, though I've no way of knowing if that's true or not.'

'Why would he be hiring? Mercenaries are expensive and I'm not aware that he is planning war.'

The leader of the five former members of Anson's warband, a man called Aldin, coughed politely to attract Edmund's attention.

'I believe that it's Rædwulf of Cumbria who is hiring men, lord. He wants to build up his forces because he's still threatened by Strathclyde and the Norse invaders.'

'Then surely they would have headed west, not south?' a puzzled Edmund asked.

'I've heard that Rædwulf is at Eoforwīc at the moment, conferring with Æthelred,' Aldin explained.

'Thank you. How much of a head start do they have?'

Aldin looked up at the sun's position. Although it was hidden behind a wispy cloud at the moment he could still make out its position in the sky.

'Probably about three or four hours, lord, but they weren't moving in a hurry. They will need to hunt game or gather wild fruit as they travel if they want to eat this evening. Anson took all the supplies with him.'

'Then I suggest that you halt here and do the same. You can retrace your steps to Bebbanburg tomorrow.'

It took Edmund two days to find the other thirty former members of Anson's warband. When he did they were only too willing to exchange the uncertainty of being recruited by Rædwulf for guaranteed employment by Edmund, especially as a few of them had women and children they'd been forced to abandon. Mercenaries might attract camp followers but they weren't encumbered by families as a general rule.

Now Edmund had enough men to garrison his stronghold and fully man his longship. It was a start, but he would need to recruit many more warriors, train them to fight at sea and build more longships for them to crew. It would take a long time before he was ready to tackle even a small flotilla of Viking raiders.

Chapter Eighteen – The Land of Ice and Fire

847

Ragnar stood at the prow of his drekar with the wind blowing his greying hair around his face as the ship ran down the far side of another huge wave. It struck the bottom of the trough and the spray from the impact stung his exposed skin as the ship shook itself free and started to climb up the next huge wave.

The water streaming down the king's face was icy cold, but he relished it. His small fleet had left Orkneyjar four days previously, having been told that it normally took around a week to complete the journey to Snæland, where Aslaug had fled with her daughter, Åløf, or so it was said.

Ragnar had been undecided which old score to settle first – revenge on his former wife for betraying him, or on Edmund of Bebbanburg for the death of his only son with Lagertha. She had urged him to kill Edmund first but his jarls and their men were exhausted after the war to conquer Uppsala and so he resolved to find Aslaug first.

The voyage to the island of Snæland, called the land of ice and fire by some, was taking longer than he'd hoped. Space on a longship with a full crew was limited and normally they only carried provisions and water for a few days. By the end of the first week out from Orkneyjar both food and drinking water were running low and there was still no sign of land.

Their course was north-west and so they had been able to use the wind from the south-west much of the way. It had died on the third day, but the following morning a cold wind from the north-east began to blow, increasing in strength hour by hour until the ship was flying along, heeled over and powered by the fully reefed mainsail.

Just when Ragnar thought that they would have to lower the sail and start to row to keep the ship heading into the violent sea, the storm blew itself out. They all breathed a sigh of relied and Ragnar thanked Ran for their survival. The storm left behind a heavy swell with scarcely more than a light breeze to fill the sail. However, the wind was now laced with snow and, increasingly, hail.

At first he couldn't see the other five ships that had sailed with him, even from the crest of the waves, but as the day wore on four hove into view. The fifth one never did reappear and Ragnar was forced to the conclusion that it had been lost in the storm.

On the seventh day they had to go onto half-rations, but at least they had been able to harvest the snow and ice to partially refill the water casks. As the sun rose behind them in the east the following morning a smudge on the horizon gradually resolved itself as a mountainous land with snow on the peaks, one of which was belching out fire and black smoke high into the air.

'The Land of Ice and Fire,' Olaf muttered as he came to stand beside Ragnar in the bows.

'Indeed, it has to be Snæland. Where else could it be?'

As they approached the island from the south east they could see more of the dramatic landscape: steep cliffs topped by barren hills and mountains and wide sweeping sandy bays with a mixture of grasses and fir trees growing in the bottom of the valleys behind them. There was, however, no sign of habitation.

'What do you know of this place Ragnar?'

The latter shrugged.

'Not many have visited here. There was a trader I spoke to who told me that the first people to settle here were Irish monks who worshipped the White Christ. It seemed they sought a place of tranquillity away from the world where they could pray and meditate in peace.'

'They sound like a load of old women,' Olaf scoffed.

'When the Swede Garðar Svavarsson discovered the island a few years ago he killed or enslaved the monks but he didn't stay himself when winter threatened. One of his men, Náttfari, stayed on with a few thralls. Word spread about this new land and, over the decade that followed, others followed, attracted by the prospect of free land. One of these was the hersir Ingólfr

Arnarson, the Norseman who fled here with Aslaug and her bastard daughter.'

'It seems a large island,' Olaf commented as they turned west and started to row into the teeth of the prevailing wind.

'The main settlement is at Reykjavik, just around the south-western extremity of the island.'

'You think that's where we'll find Ingólfr and Aslaug?'

'If not, someone will know where they are. The population is no more than a couple of hundred, including thralls, or so I'm led to believe.'

Even discounting the snekkja which had been lost in the storm, Ragnar had nearly three hundred men with him.

'Do we plunder this place, Reykjavik?'

'I have no quarrel with the Norsemen who have chosen to live here,' Ragnar replied with a shake of his head. 'I'm paying our men in silver, but we may well raid the west coast of Ireland on our way home,' he added with a grin.

The icy weather from the north had given way to more a milder climate as they rowed westwards along the coast. The temperature wasn't that different from southern Norway in the middle of May, although they were much further north. The main difference was the hours of daylight. Whereas nights in May were twice as long as the days at Arendal, here it was the other way around and, even then, the night time skies seemed lighter.

Twilight was approaching as they rounded the point and hauled up the sail. They beached the ships for the night shortly afterwards. The next day Ragnar decided to go hunting to replenish their depleted food stocks before heading for Reykjavik.

Although they scoured the land for five miles from the coast, they saw nothing apart from a species of white fox and a few rodents.

'What in Odin's name do the people here live on?' asked a puzzled Yingvi after a fruitless morning.

'I suspect that it must be fish. It's not animals at any rate. Let's head back,' another dispirited warrior suggested.

Glumly the rest of the hunting party agreed and traipsed back to the ships.

'We'll eat the rest of what we have and drink the last of the ale tonight,' Ragnar decided. 'We can buy more when we get to Reykjavik.'

'Well, I hope so,' Olaf replied. 'But I suppose the people who live in this place must find something to eat.'

'Probably fish and eggs,' Torstein the godi suggested. 'There are plenty of sea birds and doubtless there are fish in the sea.'

'That's true,' Yingvi said. 'We've seen lots of dolphins and a few whales too in the last few days.'

'You can't hunt whales in a longship,' another man scoffed.

'Perhaps the people here have built ships which are better suited to doing so,' Ragnar suggested. 'Where else would they get the oil for their lamps from?'

As dawn broke the next day the bleary eyed Norsemen hauled their longships back through the surf and sailed onwards to the west. With nothing to eat they were beginning to get worried when the ship's boy up the mast of Ragnar's drekar called down that he could see huts dotted along the shoreline about three miles ahead.

The sight of the longships produced a flurry of activity in the settlement. At first the sight of three drekar and two snekkjur caused consternation. Traders normally arrived in one or two knarrs and occasionally a longship would call, but not a fleet like this.

However, as the ships drew closer the absence of the fierce dragon's heads from the prow, signalling that they came in peace, reassured the men, women and children gathered along the jetty to watch their arrival.

Ragnar had noticed a dozen or so boats heading out to sea as they approached. Two seemed like small knarrs but with a lower freeboard and what appeared to be cranes mounted just behind the mast. The others were much smaller boats propelled by four oars aside. There was no mast, unlike most fishing craft, but some sort of structure was built onto the prow. Later Ragnar was to discover that these boats were used to harpoon and then tire out dolphins and whales before their prey was lifted aboard the larger craft.

There wasn't room for all five ships to tie up alongside the jetty and so two of them were beached further up the coast. The stench which hit Ragnar as he stepped ashore surprised him, then he noticed the mixture of guts, blood and oil that coated a slipway beside the jetty. Presumably this was where the dolphins and whales were butchered for their meat and oil.

'Greetings stranger, what brings you to Reykjavik, and with so many warriors,' a tall man with a large belly asked him as Ragnar looked around.

The man was dressed in leather trousers and jerkin so presumably the settlers had some domestic animals.

'I seek Ingólfr Arnarson, do you know him?'

The man's eyes narrowed and he licked his lips nervously.

'What business do you have with Ingólfr?'

'That's between me and him. Now where can I find him?'

'We don't want any trouble, another, smaller man, standing nearby called out, eyeing the large number of armed warriors piling onto the jetty. 'You're speaking to him,' he added, nodding towards the other man.

Ragnar whipped out a dagger and thrust the point into the soft, puffy flesh under the large man's chin.

'Is that so? Well, Ingólfr Arnarson, let's go and find your whore shall we?'

'Whore? I have a wife. Is that who you mean?'

'Aslaug used to be my wife. My name is Ragnar Lodbrok.'

'Aslaug? No, my wife is called Astrid. Aslaug some time ago with her daughter, Åløf.'

'Died how?' he asked, still keeping the point of his dagger pressing into the jowls of the other man.

'Look, she was never anything to me,' he said quickly, trying to keep the tremor from his voice. 'She merely sought passage here, no more. She paid some of the men to build a hut and lived there quietly with her daughter. She had money to pay for food, but in the winter she and Åløf used to cut a hole in the ice through which to fish. One winter the ice was thinner than usual and they both fell into the freezing water. Someone saw them go in but we never found the bodies.'

'He's telling the truth,' one of the other men called out. 'I was the one who saw them fall through the ice.'

Ragnar felt deflated, although in a way the news had come as something of a relief. The Norns had deprived him the pleasure of confronting Aslaug, but at least he wouldn't have to tell Ivar and his other sons that he'd killed their mother.

'When was this?'

'This past winter.'

'Very well. It seems our journey here has been wasted. We'll stay tonight and return home tomorrow, but we'll need to buy provisions from you. What have you got to sell?'

'Smoked fish would be best.'

The prospect of eating nothing but that for ten days didn't appeal but it was better than starving.

-ᛟ-

When they got back to the area where they had encountered the storm the sea was relatively calm and the sun blazed down on a deep azure sea. It would have been almost pleasant had it not been for the icy wind.

Around midday the lookout called down that there was a group of islands on the port bow. As they came closer it looked as if there was one large island with two smaller ones to the south of it. The islands were mountainous but they were not nearly as high as those on Snæland and none spouted out fire, but the landscape was less barren. As they got nearer they could see that there were a number of islands, not just three – perhaps a dozen in all.

'What are they called?' Olaf asked Ragnar as they sailed around the coast of the largest island looking for somewhere to land.

'I suspect that they must be the Faroe Islands. A few Norsemen from Orkneyjar are said to have settled here fifty years ago but no-one seems to know whether any of them still survive.'

'Look, there are a few sheep on that hillside. Perhaps they brought them with them.'

'Good. I could do with some real meat for a change. The only problem is finding somewhere to land.'

Ragnar was right. The coast seemed to consist of steep cliffs. Even when a stream flowed into the sea it did so as a waterfall. At one point the hills sloped down to the sea but the shoreline was rocky with no place for a ship to land safely.

Eventually they found an inlet with a shingle beach at the end. The ships' boys leapt ashore to moor their respective vessels to one of the large boulders that littered the shoreline. Several hunting parties set off to bring back sheep, both for that evening's feast and to cook and stow in casks for the remainder of the journey home.

Olaf led the group from Ragnar's drekar as they ascended the steep slope out of the valley. Once they reached the summit they saw a small flock of sheep on the far side of a large shallow depression. They had thought the island was deserted, the original settlers having died out but, to their surprise, they saw a boy sitting on the hillside above the flock with a large dog by his side.

'Not uninhabited after all,' a warrior called Porsi muttered to Olaf.

'So it would seem,' Olaf replied before gesturing for his men to remain where they were.

As he walked towards the boy, the latter stood up and watched Olaf nervously. At one point it seemed that he would turn and flee but the dog's growl seemed to steady him. Olaf dropped his spear and unbuckled his sword belt, letting both drop to the ground.

'We mean you no harm,' he called across to the young shepherd. 'Where do you and your family live?'

The boy pointed behind him and, evidently deciding that Olaf posed no threat to him, he stood calmly and waited for the man to reach him. The dog was still growling so the boy stroked his neck and said something to him. Whatever it was seemed to calm the dog and it lay down, never taking its eyes off Olaf.

'We are Norsemen sailing from Snæland to Orkneyjar. We need meat, can we buy a few sheep from you?'

'Snæland? I've never heard the name before but my grandfather came here from Orkneyjar a long time ago. But you can't have any of my sheep, we need what we've got to keep us fed.'

'There are no other animals on the islands?'

'No, none. Birds, yes. More than enough but their meat tastes awful. We eat their eggs though.'

'How many of you are there?'

'About twenty of us live on this island and perhaps another fifty in total on some of the other islands.'

'If there are no wolves or other animals to prey on your sheep, why guard them?'

'Because raiders come from the other islands to steal them.'

'Ah, I see. But you knew we weren't from the other islands?'

'Yes, everyone on the islands wears sheepskins like me. I've never seen clothes like yours before. How do you make a shirt out of metal?'

Olaf started to explain but the look of incomprehension on the lad's face caused him to stop.

'Look, we don't want to hurt you but we need some of your sheep and I don't want to kill you, so be a good boy and let us take a few, all right?'

'You said you came in peace!' he yelled. 'You lied.'

Before Olaf realised what was happening the boy had pulled out his dagger and thrust it up under the hem of his byrnie and into his groin. Blood spurted down his legs as Olaf collapsed onto the ground. With a roar of rage the other warriors started to run towards the boy as he reached for a horn that lay where he'd been sitting. He put it to his lips and blew three long blasts. Then he turned and ran, the dog at his heels.

He was fleet of foot and the Vikings had no chance of catching him. Porsi gave up the chase and knelt by Olaf to take care of the wound, but it was evident that he was dying.

'Curse this place,' he cried, tears running down his cheeks.

Like all Ragnar's hirdmen he admired Olaf almost as much as he did Ragnar himself.

'Two of you go back and let Ragnar know what has happened. Someone stay with Olaf until his body can be collected; the rest of you come with me.'

The boy had foolishly run straight back to his home, so it wasn't long before the dozen Vikings led by Porsi came across the collection of huts where the Faroese lived. There were few trees on the island to provide timber and so their dwellings were built of stone packed with mud to fill the gaps and had turf roofs. A dozen men and boys of various ages had already assembled clutching spears, axes and shields, whilst the women and small children ran away into the hinterland.

Porsi and his eight Vikings didn't hesitate but, armed with spears and swords but no shields, they moved into wedge formation and descended on the Faroese. The latter had formed a shield wall but they were no match for Porsi's experienced warriors. Without hesitating Porsi and his men charged straight at the shield wall which, parted as they hewed their way through it, killing four settlers as they did so. The fight descended into hand to hand combat which the Vikings won without suffering more than the odd minor flesh wound. The only surviving Faroese was the shepherd boy; they wanted him alive so that he could be made to suffer for killing Olaf.

It took two days for Ragnar's men to scour the island and round up the women and children. Those who would be useful as thralls were bundled on board and the rest, including the younger children and old women, were killed out of hand.

Ragnar was distraught over the loss of his oldest friend and the boy who'd killed him was made to suffer, being slow cooked over a low fire so that his legs sizzled like roasting pork and then, when Ragnar was sick of his screaming, he cut open his belly and let his entrails spill out. It took another hour for him to die but, mercifully for him, he had lost consciousness when he'd been gutted.

Ragnar had extracted a brutal revenge for the death of his closest companion, but it didn't make him feel and better. He sailed away, his belly and the ships' casks full of mutton, but it was a poor exchange for Olaf's life.

Chapter Nineteen – The Struggle for Supremacy

848 to 858

When he returned to Agder Ragnar was even more determined to kill Edmund of Bebbanburg. He had to pay for the death of Fridlief. However, that would have to wait. In his absence Eystein Beli had died and his nephew and successor, Hákon, had seized the opportunity presented by Ragnar's absence to invade Alfheim once more.

Ragnar drove the Swedes back across the border in the summer of 848 and went on to invade Uppsala, determined to kill Hákon; but the war reached stalemate and the Swedes re-conquered part of Alfheim before the year ended. In the following years the Norns favoured one side and then the other. Ragnar had finally recovered all of Alfheim in 853 but then Vestfold had entered the fray on Hákon's side.

Aided by the Danish Jarl Guthrum, son and heir of Grimulf, Ragnar had conquered Vestfold in 854 and Hákon sued for peace. The truce hadn't lasted. Once both sides had – at least partially – recovered from their losses in manpower and refilled their empty money chests by raiding far and wide, Ragnar launched what was to be his final assault on Uppsala in 857.

The following year the final battle took place just outside the sprawling settlement of Uppsala. By then Ragnar was approaching fifty and had slowed down to the extent that his sons refused to allow him to fight in the front rank. This had caused a blazing row between them and their father but, in the end, Ragnar had seemed to accept that his place was in the rear.

However, when the fighting began he forced his way to the front, accompanied by the cheers of his men. His exasperated sons gathered around him, determined to keep him safe, but he was struck in the right shoulder by an arrow and was carried to the rear.

His men lost heart when their heroic king was wounded but Ivar and Bjorn rallied them and, assisted by the nineteen year old Sigurd Snake in the Eye on the right flank and his brother Halfdan, who was two years younger, leading the left, they managed to hold the line.

When word spread that Ragnar wasn't badly wounded, his army surged forward and overwhelmed the Uppsalan Swedes. Bjorn killed Hákon and his men broke. It was only later that the truth emerged. Sigurd had spread the lie that his father only had a flesh wound. The truth was that the arrow had a barbed point and had carried steel, leather and linen deep into the wound. By the time that Bjorn, assisted by his servant Erling, had managed to cut the arrowhead out and cleaned the wound as best they could, Ragnar was feverish and delirious.

He kept asking for Olaf, but of course his old friend and companion had been ashes scattered on a Faroe Islands hillside for many years. As time went on the wound became infected and it was only Erling's insistence that they cut away all the putrefying flesh that saved Ragnar's life. Ragnar's delirium continued, however, and his fever got worse.

The situation was critical. Hákon might have been killed but there were other claimants to the throne of Uppsala and the King of the Geats to the south was known to be mobilising to take advantage of the power vacuum.

'We need to act now to consolidate our hold on what we've gained, not just Uppsala, but Vestfold as well,' Ivar began, once the four brothers and the senior jarls had gathered in the king's hall at Uppsala.

'Not only that, but several jarls were killed in the battle and they need to be replaced,' Lagertha added. 'Otherwise you could find dissention spreading throughout the ranks of this disparate army as men struggle for power. Strong leadership is needed to hold us all together.'

She was no longer the young shield maiden she had been when she'd been Ragnar's queen, but in her early forties she was still a striking figure of a woman.

'Thank you, Jarl Lagertha. What you say is true but I suggest we need to agree on a leader to act on our father's behalf until he is recovered. That must be our immediate concern,' Ivar responded, earning himself a glare from Lagertha.

'Fine, she said curtly. 'But then turn your attention to replacing the jarls. Two men have already fought over who is to replace one of them. As a result Ólaug is dead. Ragnar won't thank you for allowing that to happen.'

No one had been aware of the tragedy and the hall buzzed with concern over the news. Ólaug had been Olaf's eldest son and, as such, had been a favourite with Ragnar.

'I'm sorry, we didn't know.' Bjorn was the first to speak. 'I agree that it is something we need to resolve here and now, once we have sorted out the question of leadership.'

'Thank you, Bjorn.' Lagertha smiled at him, acknowledging his support, whilst Ivar scowled at both of them.

'I'm the eldest and so it is natural for me to assume the role of king of all our father's territories until he is well again,' Ivar stated.

'Do you think that's a good idea, Ivar?' Jarl Guthrum interjected before Ragnar's other sons could vent their disagreement.

'Why? What do you mean?'

'King Ragnar now rules a vast swathe of Southern Norway and all of Sweden apart from Kvenland in the north, which is sparsely populated, and the land of the Geats. The combined kingdoms are made up of diverse peoples - Gepids, Goths, Heruli, Rugii, Scirii, Vandals, Finns and the Warin – and is governed by nearly seventy jarls. Only his reputation as an outstanding Viking leader enabled him to achieve this. With all due respect, Ivar, you may be his eldest surviving son, but you are only twenty two years old and still have to make a name for yourself.'

'I won the Battle of Uppsala after my father was wounded,' Ivar pointed out with some spleen.

'No you didn't, Ivar, we all worked together to win that battle. Most importantly, it was Sigurd's quick thinking that steadied our men. He had the presence of mind to circulate the false story that father was only slightly wounded,' Bjorn said calmly.

Ivar subsided into a sulk, glaring at his brother.

'It doesn't help if we fall out, Ivar,' Sigurd put in. 'Halfdan and I are too young to rule anywhere yet, so you and Bjorn need to agree how to govern father's old kingdoms and this new one. Whatever you decide, we'll help you.'

Ivar thought for a minute or two and, just when the silence was becoming uncomfortable, he nodded, as if having just resolved a conflict within himself.

'We may have captured the capital of Uppsala and killed its king, but we are a long way from having secured the kingdom,' he began. 'It will take time and effort to pacify the rest of the country and, as Guthrum pointed out, we may face a threat from the Geats to the south of us and the Kvens to the north. Furthermore we will need to capture the Åland Islands in order to dominate the Gulf of Bothnia.'

'That's all true, but meanwhile we have been absent from our homeland in Norway and Western Sweden for too long,' Bjorn pointed out.

'I'm coming to that. My proposal is that I return to Agder and take over the rule of our lands to the west whilst you remain here as the new King of Uppsala to consolidate our conquest.'

There was a great deal of detail to resolve, but in the end Ivar's proposal was accepted by the others present. He and Halfdan returned home with half the fleet, Guthrum went back to Denmark, and Bjorn was enthroned as King of Uppsala. Sigurd elected to remain with him to help him conquer the rest of Sweden. Ragnar was stretchered aboard his drekar and taken back to Agder. He was still delirious and feverish but the sea air seemed to do him good. Gradually he improved, but he remained very weak and he could scarcely move his right arm. Even if Ragnar eventually made a good recovery, it seemed as if his days as a Viking warrior were over.

-ᛉ-

'What is it, father?'

Edmund's daughter, Osgearn, was only nine but she could tell that her father was upset by whatever news the messenger had brought.

Edmund had married Burwena, the younger sister of Rædwulf of Cumbria, in 848. It wasn't the love match that it would have been had he married Joscelin of Arras, but they were happy enough together. Their first child, a girl, had been born in 849 and she had been followed by another girl in 850, however the baby had died shortly after it was born. Burwena had been distraught and for a time refused to have another baby.

She had eventually relented and their son Ricsige had been born early in 852. It had been a difficult birth and, although she had agreed to try for another child, it would be a long time before they had one.

Edmund didn't reply to Osgearn's question but he showed the letter to Burwena, who put her hand to her mouth and went white.

'Why? Why would he do this?'

'Because Æthelred is ill and he seized the opportunity presented to him, I presume.'

Æthelred had been formally crowned in 854 when his father had eventually died, but he'd been the de facto king for some time before that. Now he was very ill and it was said that he'd lost his wits. The letter clarified the situation, but it wasn't good news as far as Edmund was concerned.

Burwena handed the letter back to her husband and Edmund read through it once more. It had come from the archbishop, Wulfhere, who had succeeded Wigmund in 854.

To the noble Edmund, Ealdorman of Islandshire, greetings,

As you will be aware, King Æthelred has been unwell since his horse threw him whilst he was out hunting three months ago. At first he could remember nothing but slowly his memory is returning, thanks be to God. However, it is the opinion of those members of the Witan who have been consulted so far that the government of Northumbria cannot continue for much longer without a strong hand at the helm.

We have invited the Ætheling Rædwulf to take the throne as he is nearest in blood to the present king. I regret that there wasn't time to call a full meeting of the Witan, but we hope that you will support the action that we have taken. Æthelred will be moved to the monastery at Whitby where he can be looked after. In due course he may well decide to become a monk there, but time will tell.

'Rædwulf is no more an ætheling than I am,' Edmund said angrily. 'We can both trace our descent back to Ida, the first King of Bernicia, but only through the female line. I'm sorry, Burwena, but your brother is a usurper.'

'I agree, but perhaps we should continue this discussion in private.'

She gave a meaningful glance towards Osgearn, who was looking tearful, and six-year-old Ricsige, who just looked bewildered.

'What does this mean, father? Is Uncle Rædwulf now the king?' Osgearn asked.

Edmund sighed. 'It would seem so. But don't worry about it. It won't change anything up here. Thankfully we are remote from the court at Eoforwīc.'

However, that was all about to change. Rædwulf had been Æthelred's hereræswa, the most powerful position in the kingdom after the king and the archbishop, and that had given him the status and reputation to challenge for the throne. Now he had written to Edmund summoning him to Eoforwīc and offering him the post of hereræswa. It was a logical decision. Edmund had some experience of fighting Vikings in Frankia and, as admiral, he'd had considerable success in reducing the number of raids on the east coast to a handful each year.

'What will you do?' his wife asked when the invitation arrived.

'I don't really have a lot of choice. We'll set sail for Eoforwīc tomorrow.'

'We?'

'Yes, as hereræswa my place is at your brother's side. That means living at Eoforwīc and travelling around the kingdom with the court. I don't intend to live the life of a bachelor so I'd like you to come with me, if you will, and the experience will be good for the children.'

'Though I disagree with his usurpation of the throne, it would be good to see my brother again. Of course we'll come with you.'

-ᛉ-

Ragnar hobbled into his hall at Arendal leaning on a staff. He had made a good recovery but his right arm was crippled and he was still very weak. Every day he set off with determination to walk further than he had managed the day before but he was always exhausted by the time he returned.

It galled him that he was so feeble; made worse by the knowledge that Ivar and Halfdan were away raiding Frankia again. This time they avoided the area of the Seine, which was now well defended, and headed westwards to the peninsula called Brittany, where the Britons who had fled from the Anglo-Saxon advance into their homeland centuries before, had settled.

As soon as Ivar had sailed Ragnar had seized back the governance of Agder, Vestfold and Alfheim. He'd made those jarls who'd not sailed with his sons reaffirm their oaths to him as their king. He'd no intention of allowing Ivar to usurp his throne, even if it meant confrontation when he returned.

He had sent messengers to Bjorn to discover what progress he was making in Uppsala. He was pleased to hear that he had not only pacified the rest of the kingdom, but he was now engaged in a war to subdue the Geats to the south.

He wasn't worried about Bjorn, he had always been loyal, but Ivar was a different matter. He was ambitious and Ragnar had a feeling that his eldest son had secretly hoped that his father would die of his wound. He might not be able to wield a sword in his right hand anymore, but he could hold a shield with it.

Not only was he walking as far as he could each day to build up his strength again, but he was training to fight left handed. His training partner met him in a remote spot on his walk where they had hidden two swords and shields. The young man, whose name was Agði, was another he trusted completely as he was another of Olaf's sons.

Ragnar knew that he would never be as proficient with his left arm as he was with his right, even if he fully regained his strength, but he believed that he would be able to hold his own in a fight against most warriors in due course.

When Ivar and Halfdan returned that September they were greeted by the sight of their father standing tall and proud on the jetty waiting to welcome them home. Ragnar looked just as he had before the Battle of Uppsala apart from two things. His hair and his beard were no longer streaked in white, he was totally grey and, secondly, he wore his sword on his right hip.

'Greetings, father,' Ivar called as the ship's boys jumped ashore to secure the mooring lines. 'It's good to see you looking so well.'

'Thank you Ivar. I trust you came back laden with spoils? Next year it will be my turn to go.'

'Go? Go where? Raiding Frankia?'

'No, now that Uppsala has been dealt with, I am free to settle an old score with Edmund of Bebbanburg, the man responsible for your brother Fridlief's death.'

Both Ivar and Halfdan regarded their father sombrely. They worked well together and had got used to making their own decisions. Now that Ragnar had reasserted his authority they would be relegated to doing as they were told, something neither relished. Besides, from what he had just said, their father intended to go raiding next year whilst they stayed behind with the old men and the women. It was not to be endured.

Chapter Twenty – The Fall of Eoforwīc

Summer 858

Edmund had brought back four skeid from Frankia - the correct name for drekars which didn't display a pagan dragon figurehead – two of them were the original ships built by Thorkel and Ragnar at Bebbanburg decades before and he had kept one of those captured from the Swedes near Paris. The fourth had been built before he left and was the largest of all with space for seventy two oarsmen.

In addition he had built two smaller snekkjur back in Northumbria. The latter had twenty oars a side and needed a crew of fifty. Two more skeid were under construction and he hoped to have them in service by the start of the following spring.

To house them in safety he had constructed a fortified harbour at the mouth of the River Wansbeck some forty odd miles south of Bebbanburg. He had also installed a chain boom across the entrance and towers each side to defend it.

The five hundred warriors, sailors and ships' boys needed to crew his fleet lived in a hall near the harbour with another twenty warriors too old to do anything other than man the harbour defences. With the families of those who were married, tavern keepers, whores, merchants and artisans, shipwrights and labourers, the settlement's population topped seven hundred.

The whole enterprise cost a great deal of money to maintain but the king thought it was worth it if it kept the Vikings away. Unfortunately, not all his nobles, bishops and abbots, on whom the greater part of taxation burden fell, were of the same mind. Even with the support of the royal treasury Edmund still had to find a proportion of the cost.

From the new port his longships patrolled the whole of the east coast. Usually three would head north and the rest south and spend two or three days at sea at a time. The patrols weren't infallible at deterring raiders but, after they had caught and defeated two snekkjur, hanging those of the crew who weren't killed in the fight, word soon got around. After that other Danish raiders – and along the east coast they were mainly Danes rather than Norse - chose the more vulnerable coastlines of Pictland, East Anglia and Kent to raid.

His new position as hereræswa took Edmund away from the sea and so he appointed Cynefrith as commander of the fleet with a man called Uxfrea as his deputy. One would command the northern patrol and the other the ships that covered the southern coast of the kingdom.

Uxfrea wasn't a universally popular choice. He was the son of a poor fisherman but he had proved to be a skilled sailor becoming in turn, helmsman, captain of a skied and now the fleet's deputy commander.

Life was quiet for the first four months of Rædwulf's reign. The only ripple on an otherwise calm sea was the rapid recovery of Æthelred at Whitby. Now that he had recovered his memory, he was apparently getting increasingly agitated by the usurpation of his throne, as he saw it, by his distant cousin.

'I'm not quite sure what to do about him,' Rædwulf confessed to Edmund one evening during an all too rare visit to his former shire of Cumbria where his son was now the ealdorman. 'Many of the nobles and churchmen who were keen enough to support me during Æthelred's illness now seem to favour his return to power. I fear my days are numbered unless I can somehow get rid of him. The increased taxation to fund your fleet hasn't helped, of course.'

'You don't mean...' Edmund's words trailed off.

He didn't want to mention the possibility of assassination and, indeed, he was totally opposed to it. He liked his brother-in-law, but it was Æthelred who had brought him back from exile and had re-instated him as an ealdorman, despite his father's opposition. Obviously Burwena sided with her brother and so Edmund's loyalty was divided between the two rivals. Whatever happened, he wanted Æthelred treated with respect.

'No, if I killed him it would be like prodding a wasp's nest with a stick. Others would seize the opportunity to accuse me, if only to make a bid for the throne themselves.'

Edmund had a feeling that he was referring to two brothers who were also distant cousins of Æthelred: Ælle and Osbehrt.

'The alternative is to exile him, I suppose,' Edmund suggested.

'What? And give him the opportunity to raise an army abroad? I don't think that's a good idea.'

'The only other option would be to keep him closely confined but treated well so as not to give anyone an excuse to raise trouble over his treatment. He could easily escape from where he is at the moment.'

'Yes, I suppose you are right, Edmund. Thank you.'

However, all thoughts about the troublesome Æthelred were forgotten when, shortly after their return to Eoforwīc, news reached Rædwulf that three of Edmund's longships had encountered a Viking fleet off Bebbanburg. As there were sixteen longships, Uxfrea had taken the sensible decision to return to their base in the estuary of the Wansbeck and leave the monastery on Lindisfarne to its fate.

In the face of a Viking army of around a thousand there wasn't much the garrison of Bebbanburg could do except alert the surrounding shires and call up the fyrd. By the time that sufficient numbers had assembled the Vikings had long since departed, leaving the burning and pillaged monastery behind them.

-Ӿ-

'What will you do now father?' Ivar asked as Lindisfarne faded into the distance.

Ragnar had intended to leave Ivar behind with Halfdan and Sigurd, but over the past winter he had become suspicious of his eldest son's ambitions. In the end he had decided to take him with him; better to keep him close than to allow him to make himself king in his father's absence. Halfdan would look after

Agder and Vestfold and Sigurd Alfheim. That way neither would become too powerful.

They had sacked the monastery once more, but Ragnar still had no idea how to capture Bebbanburg. He stared at it malevolently as they sailed past it and wondered if Edmund was hiding behind its walls.

'I think we'll see if the Norns still look kindly on us and attack the city they call Eoforwīc,' he said in reply to his son's question.

'Do you think that's a good idea, father? It'll be heavily defended,' Ivar said doubtfully.

'Perhaps, but there is every chance that, by the time we get there, their king will have sent his warriors – or at least some of them – north in response to our attack on Lindisfarne.'

Eoforwīc lay surrounded by marshland on the River Ouse. Ragnar's small fleet lay just over the horizon until after sunset and then, in the pale moonlight, his eighteen ships followed his drekar into the Humber estuary. An hour later they reached the confluence of the Ouse and the Humber and turned north. The area to the south of the old walled city was marshland and so their passage was unlikely to be detected until dawn. By then they had reached the small vill of Acastre built on the site of an old Roman fort.

There was a small jetty but it was only big enough to allow two longships to moor at a time. The river was quite wide at this point and so the rest of the Viking fleet moored two abreast in the middle of the waterway. Whilst a few ships patrolled upstream to prevent any passing boats from reporting their presence, Ragnar's crew landed and sacked the place, not that there was much plunder to be had. Captives for sale later as thralls would have been an encumbrance and so the unfortunate inhabitants were killed, even the small children, and their bodies were thrown down the well.

As darkness crept over the land once more the Viking fleet set off again. This time there was no moonlight to guide them. The sky was overcast and a light rain had been falling since mid-afternoon. As the surrounding land was flat and the swamp merged into the water in the gloom, some care was needed if their ships were not to run aground near the banks.

Consequently Ragnar kept their progress down to a few miles an hour.

Eventually they rounded a bend and the beacons on top of the ramparts that surrounded the old Roman city appeared, illuminating the quayside between the river and the walls. Obviously they couldn't tie up alongside the quay as they would be seen. Instead the fleet was beached two miles or so short of the city, the keels squelching into the soft mud that lined the river.

It took a long time to disembark. The warriors, most wearing chainmail and helmets and carrying heavy shields, sunk into the mire and a few had to be extricated by their fellows. Even when they managed to get away from the riverside they found themselves on marshy ground. By the time that they reached dry land they were exhausted. At his age Ragnar was one of those who were practically dead on their feet, but he wasn't about to show it. He was everywhere, encouraging others in hushed tones and even pulling others along to help them through the mire.

By dawn they had reached a small wood near the walled city. From there Ragnar could see the dilapidated state of the eastern wall. It had been allowed to fall into disrepair over the four centuries since the Romans had left. Attempts had been made to patch it up but whole sections of it had been replaced by a timber palisade.

Initially the Anglo-Saxons didn't have the skills to build in stone and so filled gaps in the original stonework with timber. Now that stone buildings were becoming much more common in England, the walls could have been properly repaired with stone blocks, but the fact that they hadn't done so worked in the Vikings favour.

The Vikings had spent the day quietly making ladders out of timber found in the wood. They did as little chopping as possible because of the noise involved and, in consequence, the four ladders that they'd made were very rough and ready; but they would serve.

The sun was obscured by clouds as it set in the west, which helped the Vikings as the night was pitch black when it came.

The torches set at intervals along the east wall were more of a help to the invaders than a hindrance as it showed them where the walls lay without lighting up too much of the area below. The Vikings split into four groups, each with a ladder, and headed for one of the pools of darkness below the wall.

The first four men had gained the walkway along the top of the fortifications before the alarm was given and by the time that the defenders had reached the parapet, the Vikings had killed the sentries and taken possession of the whole wall.

Ragnar paused to regain his breath when he reached the top of one of the ladders and was pushed out of the way by Ivar, who had followed him up.

'Let me past, old man,' his eldest son grunted at him as he run to engage one of the Saxons who had just emerged from the steps leading up from the interior of the city.

Ragnar bellowed in rage and followed Ivar yelling for his hirdmen to follow him, not his son. By the time they had driven the defenders back into the city Ivar had disappeared, but Ragnar didn't have time to worry about him. He and the fifty warriors with him found themselves beset by over a hundred of the city's garrison. These weren't members of the fyrd but professional soldiers and Ragnar and his men found themselves hard pressed.

There were near on a thousand Vikings somewhere inside Eoforwīc and he doubted if the garrison numbered more than a few hundred. It should have been a simple matter to capture the city, once inside the walls, but instead he was in danger of being overwhelmed.

The problem he realised later was that the place was a warren of tiny streets. Doubtless most of his men had found no-one to fight whilst other groups, like his, were fighting for their lives. It was something that Ivar would remember and use to his advantage a decade later.

Ragnar had an advantage in using his sword in his left hand. It was not something that an opponent was used to. However, that arm was now tiring and he'd already suffered a couple of minor wounds. He shook himself to drive away the fatigue which threatened to overwhelm him before moving to his left to fill a gap left by one of his hirdmen. The man had been cut down by a giant of a man wielding an axe and Ragnar guessed that he was a blacksmith; certainly there was no finesse or skill to his fighting, just the application of brute force.

As the man raised his axe once more to bring it down on Ragnar's left shoulder, the latter twisted away so that it struck the shield on his right hand side. The blow numbed his whole arm and split the lime wood down to the centre boss, where the axe stuck. As the giant struggled to free it Ragnar twisted back, jerking the man forward. As he did so he thrust the point of his sword into the man's right armpit, twisting the blade so that it cut through the muscles and severed an artery.

The arm was useless and blood was spurting everywhere. Still the Saxon tried to free his axe with his left hand until Ragnar pulled his sword out and thrust the tip into the man's throat.

As he fell away Ragnar looked for his next opponent but the men of Eoforwīc were in full retreat. Later Ragnar learned that Ivar had killed their king – Rædwulf – and the heart had gone out of the defenders.

The Vikings spent three days sacking and pillaging Eoforwīc, but when his scouts informed Ragnar that an army over two thousand strong was approaching from the north and another thousand were closing in from the west, he decided that it was time to go.

Ragnar had wanted to sail north again and make one more attempt to capture Bebbanburg. His feud was with Edmund, not Rædwulf, and although it was satisfying to have killed their king and looted his capital, it was not what he'd come for.

Ivar and his men took a different view. They had plundered the king's hall, the monastery and the city and they had come away with a great deal of treasure as well as over a hundred captives to be sold as thralls. All they wanted to do now was to go home, regale their friends and families with tales of their exploits and celebrate their new found wealth.

Ragnar was king because men followed him. He couldn't persuade them to attack the fortress in Northern Northumbria again if they didn't wish to do so, still less could he order them to, so they sailed back to Norway leaving Ragnar's thirst for revenge unquenched for another year.

-ᚸ-

As it happened Edmund wasn't at Bebbanburg when the Viking fleet sailed past on either occassion. He was at sea with all six of his longships, including the two new skeids, and four birlinns looking for Ragnar's fleet. He had to rely on some of his fyrd to complete the crews of many vessels, but they were rapidly becoming used to life at sea and could give a reasonable account of themselves in a fight. He had no illusions that they would be a match for an experienced Norse crew though.

It wasn't until they called in at Whitby that he learned about the capture of Eoforwīc and the death of Rædwulf. Archbishop Wulfhere had managed to flee and was reportedly somewhere in Mercia, but most of his monks and priests had been killed or captured.

Edmund sniffed. It sounded as if Wulfhere had been intent on saving his own skin and left his fellow clergy to their fate.

'What will you do?' the abbot asked. 'The ealdormen have taken their warbands and those of the fyrd they could muster in time and marched south.'

'They will be too late,' Edmund stated, shaking his head. 'The Vikings will have left after sacking the city.'

'Perhaps you can cut them off at sea.'

'I have ten ships of war in all, many of them smaller than a Viking drekar, and they have a fleet over twice my size. Furthermore, most of my men aren't as well trained as their warriors. It would be suicide to try.'

At that moment a gust of wind rattled the shutters that kept most of the wind out of the abbot's house. Edmund strode outside and looked at the storm clouds approaching from the west.

'Unless we have our Lord's help, that is,' his said, his eyes lighting up with excitement. 'Abbot, pray for us and hope that we can locate the enemy ships.'

-Ṿ-

The storm drove Edmund's fleet eastwards under reefed sails at a fast pace. His problem was not so much overcoming the superior Viking fleet, but in finding them in the first place. The German Ocean was a vast stretch of water but the Ealdorman of Bebbanburg had a feeling that he knew the course that the Vikings would take if, as he suspected, they were heading for the entrance to the Skagerrak.

The scudding grey clouds obscured the sun but the wind was heading due east so, as long as he kept the pennon at the top of his mast pointing the same way as his bows, he was confident that he was heading in that direction too. The wind was strong but he had taken in one more reef than he had to for the conditions in order to ensure that the smaller birlinns could keep up. If his ships got dispersed it wouldn't matter if he found the Vikings or not.

He was losing hope that he would come across them before dark when the boy at the top of the mast called out that he could see two ships dead ahead.

'No, there's more. I can see five now,' he called down excitedly.

'Are they together?' Edmund asked, shouting as loud as he could to make himself heard over the wind.

Even so the boy indicated that he couldn't hear him. Edmund realised that he was shouting into the wind and ran aft before repeating his question. This time, with the wind behind him, the boy understood him.

'No, several hundred yards apart,' he replied, shaking his head as he clung precariously to his perch whilst the masthead dipped and sprang back.

Edmund smiled to himself. He hadn't heard the reply but he'd seen the boy shake his head. The enemy ships were dispersed. That gave him a chance.

On the nearest Viking ship, a drekar with thirty five oars a side, there was no boy up the mast as lookout. Unlike Edmund's ships, who were flying before the wind with the waves behind them, Ragnar's ships were rolling as they made their way north east. Their masts were moving about so much it would have been suicidal for anyone to have sat up there.

Instead the lookout was in the bows and he was concentrating on looking ahead and on maintaining contact with the rest of the fleet. The first he knew of the approaching Northumbrian ships was when his steersman spotted the yellow sails displaying the black wolf symbol of Bebbanburg just before they were lowered. As the sails came down the rowers ran their oars out. By that stage they were only three hundred yards from the closest drekar.

By this time about a dozen of the Viking longships were in sight, but they were scattered over a large area. Edmund knew that there would be more just over the horizon but they wouldn't be aware of the situation. Even those in sight but further off might have difficulty in seeing what was going on, given the poor visibility and flying spray.

Edmund's captains knew what to do. They paired off, each heading for one of the nearest longships. They needed to capture them and sink them before the rest could come to their aid. It was risky but it would take the other Viking ships time to reach the Northumbrians, given fact that they would be rowing against the wind and the storm-tossed sea.

Edmund's ships quickly reached their respective targets. Whilst his own ship ran down one side of the large drekar Cynefrith grappled his to the other side. The drekar had over seventy warriors on board but the combined crews of the two Northumbrian ships totalled a hundred and twenty, most of them warriors.

Edmund led his boarding party onto the Viking deck as soon as the two sides touched. The Norsemen were experienced and hadn't made the mistake of leaving their oars out for too long. By the time that Edmund landed on their deck they had pulled in their oars and picked up their weapons and shields. However, there hadn't been time to don byrnies or helmets.

Edmund found himself facing two Norsemen as he rose from the crouch he'd adopted on landing. One was armed with an axe and the other with a sword. He fended off the axe with his shield and blocked the other man's cut at his head with his own blade. As the axeman swung again Edmund ducked and slashed out at the man's legs, cutting into his left knee. With a howl the axeman collapsed onto the deck clutching his shattered patella.

Edmund had scarcely time to draw breath before his other opponent thrust his sword at his throat. He jerked his head to the side as the Norseman's blade nicked the side of his neck. The man was slow to recover his balance and Edmund thrust the point of his own sword into the man's stomach. He followed up with a blow to the man's skull to make sure he was dead.

When he looked around him he saw that his men and Cynefrith's had driven the Vikings back into such a tight group that most were unable to use their weapons. Five minutes later it was all over. Those of the enemy who had survived were thrown over the side to sink or swim. There was little time left as two other Viking longships were closing in on them.

'Stave in the hull,' Cynefrith ordered as the Northumbrians made haste to re-board their own ships.

As they rowed back into the storm they saw the dragonhead on the prow of the drekar rise high in the air before it followed the rest of the ship down into the depths of the German Ocean. As they headed westwards Edmund looked around him. Four other Viking longships had been sunk and all ten of his fleet were rowing as hard as they could away from the six longships who were now pursuing them. The rest were either continuing on course for Norway or were still over the horizon.

Edmund debated with himself for a few moments and then gave the order to turn and face the oncoming ships. It took time for the rest of the fleet to understand his intention as only Cynefrith's ship was within hailing distance. Even then his captain had trouble hearing Edmund's shouted orders. But within a few minutes every captain realised what their ealdorman wanted them to do.

As the six longships and the four birlinns turned and started to close on their pursuers the Vikings panicked. They had already seen five of their fellows sunk and they lost their nerve. Edmund watched as they tacked and turned back onto a north easterly course. He let them go, well satisfied with the day's work.

-ᚷ-

The Witan was in uproar. The fall of Eoforwīc and the slaying of King Rædwulf had shaken the whole kingdom. Recrimination was rife with various nobles blaming each other for what had happened. Even Edmund had come in for criticism for not doing more to fight the Vikings at sea. He had a feeling that only his defeat of part of Ragnar's fleet had saved him from being formally censured.

'Quiet, silence I say,' Ealdorman Osberht of Loidis bellowed, struggling to make himself heard above the din.

The capital had moved to Loidis whilst Eoforwīc was being rebuilt and Osberht was supposed to be chairing the meeting of the Witan. Archbishop Wulfhere banged the ferule of his crozier on the stone floor and Osbehrt drew his dagger and banged the hilt on the table in front of him. Gradually the staccato noise restored some semblance of order.

'Thank you. This is getting us nowhere. We need to elect a new king as the first matter on the agenda. I submit that, as the senior ætheling, I should be elected to the throne.'

When the renewed tumult that greeted this announcement had died down Edmund stood up and quietly reminded the Witan that they didn't need a new king.

'Rædwulf was my friend, but he was a usurper. Æthelred is now fully recovered from his unfortunate illness and he should be restored to his throne.'

'You only say that because you hope to receive favours from him,' Ælle, Osbehrt's brother, sneered.

'No, I say that because it's true. Æthelred is our king and, by the sound of it, the only choice if we wish to avoid civil war between you and your brother.'

Ælle flushed at that. Both he and Osbehrt had put themselves forward as contenders for the throne. Everyone knew that they couldn't stand one another and both had already declared that they wouldn't accept the other as king.

Wulfhere got to his feet to support Æthelred and Bishop Eardulf of Lindisfarne and the other senior churchmen did the same. After that the vote was a foregone conclusion and Edmund was dispatched to Jarrow, where Æthelred now lived as a monk, to give him the good news.

Chapter Twenty One – The Fate of Kings

858 to 862

Ragnar had returned home to a mixed reception. Whilst those who had survived were wealthy by comparison to the average bondi, nearly three hundred men had been killed in the sea battle. On top of the fifty who'd died during the assault on Eoforwīc; that meant a lot of widows and orphaned children, as well as parents who blamed Ragnar for the death of their unmarried sons.

It gave him another reason to hate Edmund of Bebbanburg. He had been on one of the ships over the horizon when the attack happened, but as soon as he'd heard from one of the few men rescued from the sea that the device on the sails had been a black wolf's head he knew who the architect of his misfortune was.

By now Ragnar was over fifty and he looked it. He was increasingly isolated. His favourite son, Bjorn, was ruling Uppsala and he rarely saw him. Ivar, on the other hand, made no secret of the fact that he thought it was about time his father handed the eastern kingdoms over to him. Halfdan did whatever Ivar told him and, although he tried to be loyal to Ragnar, he was no fool. His father's time on this earth was limited and his eldest brother was the coming man.

After Bjorn, Ragnar was closest to Sigurd Snake-in-the-Eye, but he too was still in Sweden. Now that they were older, and perhaps wiser, it wasn't surprising that Ragnar turned increasingly to Lagertha for advice and support. She hadn't quite forgotten her antipathy towards her former husband but they had come to an understanding years ago. If the passion had died, they each respected the other as a leader and a warrior. In any case she shared his desire for vengeance. She also blamed Edmund for the death of her only son.

However, for a few years Ragnar was content to stay behind at Agder in the summer months whilst Ivar and Halfdan went raiding. Their targets were the land of the Rus across the Baltic, Frankia and Ireland. Although they raided East Anglia and Kent once or twice, they avoided Northumbria - a fact which did much to restore Edmund of Bebbanburg's standing in the eyes of both his fellow nobles and King Æthelred.

However, Ragnar had not forgotten his oath to kill Edmund and wreak his revenge on Northumbria. In time his dead son Fridlief had grown in his affection as his feelings for his living sons diminished. Nevertheless, he had trouble in putting together a large enough expedition; especially as all the young men wanted to sail with the ever more successful Ivar.

'I'm your king; I decide where and when we raid.'

It wasn't until the spring of 862 that events conspired to give him the chance to put together a large enough fleet.

In 861 Bjorn had finally come to an agreement with the Geats in the south. He then turned his attention to Kvenland in the north. After he had defeated them and killed their king he finally felt safe on the throne of Uppsala and Sigurd was able to visit his father at Agder. He brought five longships and two hundred and fifty warriors with him. However, when Ragnar invited him to join him and raid Northumbria, he declined, asking instead to be given Vestfold to govern. It was a blow, especially as Sigurd was the son he trusted the most.

With Lagertha and two other jarls, the old king managed to put together a fleet of a dozen ships manned by nearly eight hundred men. Against Edmund's fleet it should be more than enough and in April 862 he sailed for Northumbria once more.

-Ỿ-

When Æthelred had returned to the throne in 858 he had forgiven all those who had deposed him when he was ill and set about reuniting the kingdom. He had improved the defences of Whitby and began repairing the Roman walls of Eoforwīc. He had also agreed to pay for two more longships to replace Edmund's four birlinns.

All of this had cost money; money he didn't have, so he increased taxation which made him unpopular, especially with the Church and his nobles, on whose shoulders the burden largely fell.

'I've had enough of being bled dry by Æthelred,' Osbehrt complained to his wife one evening.

'Well, what do you propose to do about it?' she replied tartly. 'You're always moaning about him but you do nothing.'

He glared at her and stabbed his knife into a piece of mutton, putting it into his mouth. She watched, noting with distaste the grease running down his chin. Theirs was far from a love match. She was the daughter of his richest thegn and half his age. The attraction for him had been a large dowry and the pleasure of bedding a young girl. Her father had, of course, been flattered by the offer of matrimony from his ealdorman.

Osbehrt stabbed at another piece of meat.

'I mean, all this tax goes towards defence against the bloody Vikings. What's the advantage for us? Loidis is as far from the sea as you can get; we're never likely to see a Norseman or a Dane.'

'So, if you were king you'd abandon those who live on the coast to the depredations of the pirates, would you? That's hardly likely to make you popular with Edmund and the other ealdormen whose shires are bordered by the German Ocean.'

'Bugger Edmund. Do you know he now has five hundred warriors which we pay to maintain? It's a bigger warband than that of the king himself. How is that right?'

'But he keeps the Vikings away.'

'So you say. He uses his damned longships to guard his knarrs as they trade with Frankia more like. He's filling his chests with gold and silver at our expense.'

Although it was true that two of Edmund's longships did act as escort to his trading knarrs, they were ships he had paid for and maintained himself. The ships maintained by the royal treasury were only used to patrol the coast, but that was a truth that Osbehrt chose to ignore.

In March 862 a messenger arrived at Loidis to inform Osbehrt that the king would be visiting him for a few days in early April. Of course, he would be accompanied by the court and he would expect them all to be housed at Osbehrt's expense.

'It's not to be borne,' he yelled at his long suffering wife. 'Not only does he tax us to death but now he expects me to feed his fawning courtiers and clerks and lay on a hunt.'

'You are always saying that you wish you were king instead of him; well, now is your chance,' his wife said slyly.

'What? You mean kill him whilst he's here?'

'There is a wise woman in the town who sells poisons for the right price.'

He wondered how his wife knew that and, in truth, she'd been tempted to poison her oafish husband on more than one occasion.

'Would you like me to pay her a visit?' she continued.

If she had to endure being married to Osbehrt then being queen would help; and it would make her father so proud of her.

He couldn't bring himself to reply so he just nodded and swallowed hard. What had he allowed himself to be talked into?

-ᛉ-

Æthelred's mysterious death was put down to a reoccurrence of the illness he'd suffered years before and, at first, nobody suspected poison. When the Witan met at Eoforwīc in May the choice for his successor lay between Osbehrt and Ælle. Neither was popular with their fellow nobles: Osbehrt was a self-indulgent oaf who few thought would make a good king, but his younger brother wasn't much better.

One or two knew that one of Edmund's ancestors had been the King of Northumbria for a short while and the fact that he was married to the previous king's sister helped his case. However, Edmund made it clear to those who'd approached him in secret that he had no wish to be a candidate for the throne. In view of what happened later his decision was regrettable.

In the end the Witan chose Osbehrt and Ælle stormed out of the hall declaring that he would never swear allegiance to his brother. Whether he or another started the rumour that Osbehrt's wife had poisoned Æthelred wasn't clear but, once the thought was planted in people's minds Osbehrt's reputation suffered a severe blow.

In August the wise woman was dragged before the shire court, now presided over by a new ealdorman who had replaced Osberht when he'd been crowned. He owed loyalty to the man who'd appointed him, but the old woman had confessed to supplying poison to the queen and there was nothing he could do but condemn her to be hanged.

'What will happen now?' Burwena asked her husband as they stood together on the battlements of Bebbanburg watching three knarrs and their escorting longship sail towards Frankia.

Edmund put his arm around her waist and pulled him closely to him and kissed her neck.

'The Witan will be asked to depose Osbehrt and that evil bitch he's married to will be tried for regicide.'

'Good! Hanging's too good for her.'

'Oh, I doubt that she'll hang. She is the queen after all. No, my guess is that she'll spend the rest of her life as a nun.'

Edmund's guess proved to be correct and in late May Ælle was crowned. Osbehrt, following his brother's earlier example, refused to pay him homage and disappeared. When next Edmund heard about him he had taken refuge in Cumbria and was trying to raise an army to take back his throne.

Civil war threatened but then something happened to take Edmund's mind off the brothers' struggle for power.

-X-

Edmund's ten year old son, Ricsige, was visiting Lindisfarne with his mother and elder sister when the alarm bell was rung. The bishop had finally conceded that the monastery wasn't defensible and a fort had been built on top of the crag at the south-east tip of the island. It dominated the surrounding landscape and had sheer cliffs on every side. The only approach to the summit was via a narrow path cut into the southern face of the rock.

As soon as the alarm was given the monastery's treasures were piled into carts and everyone fled to the small fort. There weren't enough provisions to withstand any sort of siege and the only water available was what could be carried up the path in small barrels. However, it was only intended as a short term refuge until the fyrd could be called out to come to its relief.

This time Ragnar had every intention of waiting for the fyrd to arrive. The keels of three drekar slid into the soft sand of the bay below the monastery and the Vikings took their time looting the place as well as the farmsteads scattered over the island. He hoped that Edmund would see one hundred and seventy Vikings as a less than formidable threat and would come to the relief of the besieged fort with his warriors and the local fyrd.

If he did so, he would be walking into a trap as nine more longships lay just over the horizon waiting for Ragnar to light a signal beacon. It was unfortunate for Ragnar that Edmund was away at a meeting of the Witan at Whitby called to discuss how best to bring the renegade Osbehrt to justice. He also had a personal reason for seeing King Ælle. The latter had written to him privately asking for his daughter Osgern's hand in marriage. She was now thirteen and, to Edmund's surprise, she hadn't been too averse to the idea.

Perhaps the idea of being queen sweetened the pill of marriage to an older man, he mused. From Ælle's point of view it would bind Edmund, and consequently the whole of the north east of the kingdom, to his side in his dispute with Osbehrt over the throne.

Edmund had travelled down to Whitby on one of the three longships which patrolled the southern coast of Northumbria – so killing two birds with one stone. So when a knarr arrived with a messenger sent by the garrison commander at Bebbanburg, he already had one hundred and seventy warriors with him. It was fortuitous and bad luck for Ragnar.

It wasn't the only reason that the Norns appeared to be looking unfavourably on the Viking king. As Edmund sailed north making good progress thanks to a strengthening wind out of the west, further out to sea the rest of Ragnar's fleet were struggling to maintain position. When the rain arrived Lagertha, who'd been left in charge of the main fleet, decided that it was futile to stay where she was and she headed for the safety of the mouth of the River Twaid.

Her fleet couldn't head directly there with the gale force winds pushing them westwards, so she headed north with the intention of turning onto a south-westerly course once she calculated that she had sailed far enough. The other longships followed her but, of course, they had little clear idea of what she intended.

The rain was now coming at them in horizontal sheets, making it difficult for those ships further out to sea to keep Lagertha's drekar in sight. After several hours, and with darkness descending, one of the other jarls had had enough and he changed his heading to head west. Let Ragnar continue with his campaign against Northumbria; he was going to head for the Continent and raid there instead.

The next morning, as the sun rose above the German Ocean to the east, Lagertha counted with dismay the ships who had made it to safety in the Twaid estuary. There were only five in total. Four had vanished in the storm. She didn't know if they'd been sunk or had deserted her; not that it made any difference. Ragnar's force was now reduced to five hundred men. The original eight hundred had been few enough when it came to capturing Bebbanburg and killing Edmund; now the task seemed impossible.

Chapter Twenty Two – The Final Battle

August 862

Lagertha decided that it was unwise to stay where they were. A sizeable settlement existed on the north bank of the Twaid a mile inland from the mouth and now armed warriors were gathering along the shoreline and making threatening gestures towards the Viking longships. Various craft were being assembled at the jetty and she knew it wouldn't be long before some fool decided to lead an attack on her ships.

She was confident of beating them off, but she would lose warriors in the process to no good purpose. She gave the order to haul up the anchors and the small flotilla sailed lazily out to sea, pushed along by a gentle westerly.

Once clear of the estuary the swell left behind by the previous day's storm made for a lively motion under the hull as the boys raised the sails and the ships made their way south east, back towards Lindisfarne. She needed to talk to Ragnar as she saw little point now in sticking to the original plan of ambushing the relief force. As their small army had been severely weakened it was stupid for their forces to remain divided.

All night Ragnar had worried about the fate of his other ships in the storm and, as Lagertha came in sight, his concerns grew. There were four longships missing and all had all been drekar with crews of seventy or more.

Ricsige stood beside a grizzled old warrior, one of a dozen who lived in the small fort on Lindisfarne. Like the others, the man was an experienced archer and so far they had managed to keep the Vikings away from the steep approach to the only entrance; not that the Vikings seemed that keen on capturing the place, which puzzled him.

'Look,' Edmund's son cried with dismay. 'There are more Viking ships approaching from the north.'

'Perhaps that's what these scum have been waiting for?' the archer said, spitting at the rocky ground below the palisade.

An hour or so later the newcomers beached their ships in the bay below the monastery and the crews joined their fellows in the camp that encircled the small fortress.

'I hope help arrives soon or we'll be eating each other,' the archer said gloomily.

'What do you mean,' Ricsige replied with some alarm.

'Not literally, Ricsige. What I meant is provisions are running low. The storerooms only hold enough to feed this lot for a few days and the only water is in the barrels over there. They're nearly empty and even on half rations we'll run out of food in two days' time.'

'Oh! My father is still away at Whitby and Godwine the reeve is too timid to do much.'

'Except we saw a knarr leave Budle Bay and head south two days ago so hopefully your father is on his way back by now.'

Ricsige brightened up and anxiously scanned the sea to the south, but it remained depressing empty.

--

Uxfrea was immensely proud of the trust that Edmund had displayed in him when he made him the deputy commander of the Northumbrian fleet. Those who had been captains for far longer had resented the appointment of the young man at first but, as time went on, they grudgingly admitted that Uxfrea was a good sailor, a fair commander and a doughty warrior. Not all accepted him, but the few that didn't were too few to pose much of a problem.

He wasn't a brawny man by any means, he was slim, shorter than most and had trouble growing much of a moustache. Few Anglo-Saxons sported a beard like the Vikings did, but most cultivated a luxuriant growth of hair on their upper lip which drooped down either side of their mouths. Uxfrea saved the problem by remaining clean shaven, which made him look even younger than his twenty seven years.

He might still be in his twenties, but his eyesight was deteriorating, not something he admitted to. When the lookout called down that three longships were approaching from the south he peered in vain in the direction the ship's boy had indicated but he could see nothing but a blur where sea met sky.

'Can you make out the sails?'

'No, they're too far away and, in any case their sails will be hard over to catch the westerly wind.'

Uxfrea felt a fool. He glanced at his own sail which was held almost exactly fore and aft so that the wind from the west pushed the ship southwards. Of course, it also meant that with only a shallow keel they made a great deal of leeway, but it was better than rowing all day.

The same would apply to the other ships, of course. They too would be crabbing out to sea. He needed to know if they were on course to intercept one another.

'Where will their heading take them, to windward of us or to leeward?'

'I'm not sure. Either way they'll pass quite close to us.'

Uxfrea thanked the boy and, as soon as he could make out the other ships, he had the sails on all three of his own ships lowered and the oars run out in preparation for a fight. The archers made for the bows and the rowers donned their helmets and leather jerkins. Few wore byrnies; they were expensive and the weight would drag even the strongest swimmer down into the ocean depths.

'I can make out the sails now,' the lookout called out. 'They're yellow but I still can't see their device.'

At that moment the other longships lowered their sails but then the boy up the mast called out again.

'They've got crosses on the prow, not dragons' heads.'

Uxfrea took a deep breath and released it slowly in relief. It had to be Edmund's flotilla. He was surprised though. He'd expected him to still be at Whitby.

'You've not heard about the Vikings then?' Edmund called across once they were within hailing distance of each other.

He knew that Uxfrea was patrolling the northern half of the coastline but evidently he didn't know about the attack on Lindisfarne.

'No, we've seen nothing except for a knarr on the horizon heading south two days ago.'

'That must have been the one that brought the news to me. They've landed on Lindisfarne in force and are besieging Lady Burwena and our children in the fort.'

'How many Vikings?'

'Less than two hundred, or so I'm told.'

'Then our combined strength of nearly four hundred should suffice.'

'I hope so, yes, but the knarr has gone to fetch out the two birlinns to join us.'

It was unfortunate that the other two birlinns belonging to Edmund were away protecting his knarrs en route to Paris with a cargo of wool, weapons and jewellery.

Uxfrea rubbed his hands together in expectation of teaching the bloody Vikings a lesson. However, when they came in sight of Lindisfarne they saw eight longships on the beach. That meant that there were probably more like five hundred Vikings on shore.

-Ɣ-

When Ragnar was told that a fleet of longships had been sighted at first he thought that the rest of his raiders had re-joined him but, when he climbed the rise to the south of his camp and looked out to sea he saw the yellow sails with their wolf's head. He bared his teeth in a fierce grin. Now at last he could settle his score with Edmund of Bebbanburg.

'Is it him?' Lagertha asked as she joined him.

'That's his device and, if he was at sea, it explains why no-one from the fortress over there has come to attack us.'

'Man the ships!' he roared at the men who'd come to gawp. 'He mustn't get away.'

Ricsige watched with his mother and sister as the Vikings abandoned their camp and rushed back to the bay where their ships were beached.

'I knew you'd come, my love,' Burwena said, almost to herself.

'But father doesn't have as many ships,' Ricsige pointed out.

'And the Vikings are more adept at fighting at sea,' Osgearn added.

Burwena looked at her two children in alarm.

'Yes, you're right. We must pray for him. God will bring him victory over the pagans,' she said piously.

'Perhaps,' Ricsige muttered sceptically under his breath.

He was convinced that God always remained impartial when it came to earthly conflicts. Look how many times Lindisfarne had been raided by the pagans with no divine intervention to stop them, no matter how hard the monks prayed.

However, it seemed that his father had no intention of fighting the Vikings at sea. As soon as the last drekar had been launched, the Northumbrian fleet went about and headed on a south by south easterly course back down the coast.

When the last ship disappeared over the horizon it appeared that the distance between the two fleets was about the same as it had been when the pursuit had started. At least Ricsige hoped that was the case. He watched the empty horizon until his mother called for him to come down and get ready for the journey back to Bebbanburg.

Thankfully the Vikings hadn't killed the horses; presumably keeping them in case they needed them for a foray inland. A quarter of the livestock on the island had been slaughtered for food though; and once more the monastery would have to be rebuilt. Ricsige did wonder about the wisdom of keeping it in such a vulnerable place. If it was up to him he thought that he'd probably relocate it well away from the coast.

He mounted his pony and joined his mother and sister for the sixteen mile ride across the sands and back home around Budle Bay.

-Ꮙ-

Edmund stood beside the steersman looking aft at the Viking fleet just over two miles behind them. He could just make out the red and white striped sails with the black raven emblem on several of the drakar that confirmed his suspicion that he was facing his old adversary, Ragnar Lodbrok.

He turned and studied the land, trying to calculate where exactly they were. The coast was featureless at this point; just miles of golden sand with the odd streak of black coal dust and occasional outcrops of limestone. Behind that were low sand dunes with marram grass growing on the uneven ridgeline above the beach.

He was just beginning to worry because his rearmost ship was slowly being caught up by the two leading drekar, when the lookout called down that Coquet Island lay just ahead, fine on the larboard bow. He knew then where he was. His goal, the mouth of the River Tyne, lay some twenty five miles further on. If the wind held he estimated that they should reach Jarrow just as darkness fell. That was where his two birlinns would join him, giving him another seventy men.

It was a close run thing. The last of Edmund's longships tied up alongside the jetty at Jarrow just as the sun sank behind the hills to the west. The Vikings followed them, rowing into the mouth of the Tyne and up towards the monastery on the south bank, but then turned and beached their ships two miles downriver and on the opposite bank.

Edmund strode along the jetty towards Siferth, the Ealdorman of Jarrow. He was a young man he was acquainted with, but who he didn't know that well. He knew his father rather better, but the old man had died a year ago and Siferth had succeeded him. After the usual greetings he asked him how many men he'd managed to muster.

'In the short time available I've gathered three hundred of my fyrd in addition to my own warband of nearly fifty. How many do you have?'

'Four hundred and twenty. Ragnar has some five hundred but they are all hardened warriors. Against them your farm boys and townsmen won't stand much of a chance. I suggest we leave them as a reserve. They outnumber our warriors so I'm certain that we will need many more men before we dare to face them in battle. Have you heard anything from King Ælle?'

'No, nothing. Why?'

'When I left Whitby he was about to return to Eoforwīc and gather his men before riding here.'

'How long ago was that?'

'Three days.'

'Then I doubt he will get here much before the day after tomorrow, even if his men are all mounted. It'll take him a day to get back to Eoforwīc and probably the best part of four days to travel north.'

Edmund nodded his agreement before pacing up and down, lost in thought.

'As I see it we have two alternatives,' he said eventually. 'We can retreat into the hinterland and hope that we can avoid being forced to fight until the king can get here, or we can attack the Viking camp tonight and hope that we can kill enough of them to even up the numbers.'

'If we abandon Jarrow they will plunder the monastery and the settlement,' Siferth pointed out, chewing at his lip in agitation.

'I'm sure that they won't do that until daylight. That gives you time to cart everything to safety.'

'No. It doesn't. We only have a few carts. The library here is nearly as extensive as that at Whitby. It is full of priceless and irreplaceable books. We lost many of those at Whitby the last time it was raided and I won't let Jarrow suffer the same fate. There are just too many of them to move in a few hours.'

'If the Vikings have camped on the north bank, then we might have time to ferry the library by ship down the coast to your associated monastery at Wearmouth. Of course, that will only work if we can slip past their camp in the dark.'

'But Wearmouth is only six miles south of here. What's to stop them pillaging both monasteries?'

'They will if we lose, but Ragnar is waging a blood feud against me because my men killed one of his sons years ago. I'm sure that he'll want me dead before he does anything else.'

'Very well, but what about the people and their possessions?'

'They will have to make their own way to Wearmouth. We don't have the ships or the time to move everyone with their valuables by sea. At least they can now make use of the carts. Then we'll see what Ragnar does tomorrow.'

'He'll use his own ships to cross over but, with any luck, we'll be in position to oppose his landing. That might give us a chance.'

'You've just given me an idea; whilst you supervise the evacuation here I'll take a few of my men and see what I can do to upset the Vikings' plans.'

Lagertha was with Ragnar and her fellow jarls discussing how to defeat the Northumbrians without losing too many men when the alarm was sounded. They had camped above the beach in an area of grassland and scrub. The rain from the recent storm had quickly disappeared into the dry soil and the area remained dry and parched. Because of the danger that the area could be set alight, the Vikings had dug a series of fire pits in which to cook their evening meal. The one problem they had was a lack of fresh water so they had to make do with what they had on board.

They had imagined that their campsite was secure with the river as a barrier between them and Edmund's forces. In any case no one thought that he would dare attack them. It was a serious miscalculation.

What had caused the sentries to sound the alarm was the crackle of flames to the west – the direction from which a stiff breeze was blowing. Then a crescent of fire sprang up and smoke began to blow towards the camp. There would have been enough men to douse the flames but for two things – the lack of water nearby and the volley of arrows that came out of the darkness behind the flames.

Edmund had split the ninety men he'd taken with him into three groups: one led by him, one by Cynefrith and one by Uxfrea. Whilst Cynefrith had been given command of the fire setters, Uxfrea had taken his group down to the beach to kill those left to guard the longships and set them adrift. That left Edmund with the archers.

As the smoke grew thicker the Norsemen illuminated by the flames disappeared, but Edmund kept his men sending volley after volley blindly into where the camp was. Eventually a few brave Vikings ran through the flames to get to grips with their tormentors. The first few were killed, but as more and more burst through, Edmund decided that the time had come to withdraw a little.

He moved back two hundred paces and joined up with Cynefrith's men. The sixty warriors now waited for the enemy to appear. They did so in dribs and drabs and were so intent on pursuing the Northumbrians that they were easy to pick off one by one. In time one of the Vikings realised what was happening and they formed a shield wall before advancing again; by that time Edmund and his men had melted away into the darkness.

Meanwhile Uxfrea and his group had caught the warriors and the ship's boys left to guard the Viking fleet by surprise. They were so intent on watching the fire a few hundred yards to the north of them, and trying to puzzle out what the screams and shouting was about, that they forget that they too might be a target.

Many of them stood, craning their necks, by the cooking fires on the beach. Illuminated as they were, nearly twenty of them died or were wounded by the first volley of arrows. A second volley followed but that caused fewer casualties. Nevertheless many of the thirty six ship's boys were casualties and even the wilier warriors lost nearly half their number.

They were still scrambling for their shields and weapons when Uxfrea led his men into their midst. The remaining men and boys gave a creditable account of themselves, but they were unprepared and demoralised by the unexpected attack. Although numbers on both sides were equal, ship's boys were no match for the Northumbrian warriors and many died in the first ten minutes, leaving Uxfrea's men with an advantage in terms of numbers.

Before long the remaining Vikings were surrounded and, though a few tried to surrender, no prisoners were taken. The sounds of the skirmish on the beach must have reached the main camp, but they had their own problems and no one came down to investigate until it was too late.

By then Uxfrea's men had cut the anchor ropes and pushed the longships, one at a time, out into the river. It carried the ships along with the ebbing tide until they disappeared into the darkness. Two of them ran aground on the far shore near the entrance to the estuary but the others were carried out to sea. The Vikings might be able to recover some of them, given time, but Edmund only needed them out of action for two or three days at most. His aim was to maroon the Vikings on the north bank of the river.

A little later Uxfrea met up again with the other two groups and they crossed back to the south bank in one of Edmund's longships.

The next morning a furious Ragnar strode along the river bank until he was opposite Jarrow Monastery. Edmund had drawn up his men in front of the buildings to taunt Ragnar. His ships were moored alongside the jetty but he was certain that they were safe there. Ragnar might try sending swimmers across to try and cut them out but, after Paris, Edmund was well aware of that danger and had placed a strong guard on each of them.

The Vikings took their revenge out on the nearby settlement and a few farmsteads, much to Siferth's dismay, though it was hardly unexpected. Edmund and Siferth had succeeded in buying a little time, but at a cost. However, buildings could be replaced. The nearest crossing place was at Wylam and so, whilst messengers headed off to find Ælle and appraise him of the situation, the small army led by the two ealdormen set off westwards along the south bank of the Tyne.

-ᛉ-

The ford upstream at Wylam was a good day's march from the mouth of the river for men on foot. It took until the middle of the afternoon for Ragnar's men to finish pillaging what they could find and consequently they didn't get far upstream before nightfall forced them to camp. This time they set more sentries and patrolled further out from the camp, but they were left in peace.

The Northumbrians had arrived opposite the vill of Wylam on the north bank several hours before the Vikings were expected. That gave them time construct a concave earth rampart topped by wicker breastworks to give their archers protection. It was designed to block off the exit from the ford and make it into a killing area. To hinder their passage through the water, Edmund's men sank sharpened stakes into the bed of the ford.

When the Vikings hadn't put in an appearance by mid-afternoon Edmund began to worry.

'We should send scouts out to find them,' Cynewise suggested.

Edmund looked at Siferth, who nodded his agreement.

'Did you find them?' Siferth asked the scouts when they returned, just as dark was falling.

'No, lord. We found their trail though; it wasn't difficult to see the marks left by so many men. They by-passed the ford a mile north of Wylam and carried on to the west.'

Edmund and Siferth looked at each other in consternation. Their plan had been to hold them at the ford until the king came up to support them. Now they had no idea where they were, and Ælle was heading for the wrong place.

-Ꮙ-

Ragnar was still furious about the surprise attack on his camp but that didn't affect his cunning and tactical ability. He'd guessed that his enemy would plan to hold the ford at Wylam against him, so he'd pressed on to the west making for the next ford some eight miles further on. By the time that Edmund had realised that he'd been tricked he would have crossed to the south bank. With any luck he'd catch the Northumbrians by surprise.

'The men aren't happy,' Lagertha told him that night as they camped, ready to cross the ford at dawn.

Ragnar had been so focused on his vengeance against Edmund that he hadn't noticed how disgruntled his followers were. He supposed that it wasn't surprising, given the fact that they'd lost their ships, also losing the little plunder they'd taken from Lindisfarne. Moreover they were hungry. They'd moved at such a fast pace that there had been little time to hunt animals and the fruit, berries and the like that they had managed to gather weren't food fit for warriors.

'I suppose I'd better talk to them then,' he muttered.

He wandered from camp fire to camp fire for the next four hours, sitting and talking to individual groups. He reassured them that, once they'd defeated the Northumbrians they would take their ships and, not only collect the plunder they'd taken from Jarrow, but carry on down the coast raiding and killing.

It was what his men needed to hear and, by the time he dropped off into a dreamless sleep, Ragnar was confident that he'd restored his warriors' morale.

The next day it took little more than an hour for the five hundred Vikings to cross over to the south bank of the Tyne. They were now eager to get to grips with Edmund's army, slaughter them and seize Edmund's longships. A Viking without a ship was like a fish out of water.

They reached the defensive works opposite Wylam in the early afternoon but found them abandoned. They lost time crossing back over to pillage the settlement but it didn't yield much in the way of plunder, and what they did find they had to carry, so all it did was to slow them down. As they left, heading east on the south bank, two scouts watched them leave from a low rise a few hundred yards to the north of the river. As the dust cloud which marked the passing of the Norsemen disappeared in the distance, they mounted their horses and splashed across the Tyne heading south.

That night Ragnar and his men camped halfway between the ford at Wylam and Jarrow. They were tired and hungry, but they looked forward to plundering the rich monastery the next day and that made up for much.

-V-

Ælle halted at the old Roman fort at Concangis for the night. It was situated on a high bluff, overlooking the valleys of the River Wear to the east and the Cong Burn to the north. From there it was only fifteen miles to Wylam, a distance he and the two hundred horsemen he had with him could cover in a few hours. However, he didn't know whether to delay his advance until the rest of his men on foot could catch up, or press on to the River Tyne at dawn the next day.

It was dark by the time that Edmund's two scouts found him. They had taken something of a gamble that he would be there, but it seemed the logical place to stop overnight. The hall of Heremond, the Ealdorman of Weardale, was located there and the old ramparts and palisade, much repaired, would provide protection for the king's forces.

'Where does Lord Edmund propose to make his stand against the Norsemen?' Ælle asked, once he had been told the latest situation.

'At the mouth of the River Derventio, where it runs into the Tyne, Cyning,' the elder of the two scouts replied. 'There is a stretch on the east bank about seven hundred yards long between the Tyne in the north and extensive marshy ground to the south.'

'And how wide is this Derventio?'

'Not wide, Cyning, perhaps fifty yards?'

'Ummm. Is it deep then?'

'It varies, as it's tidal at that point. At the moment with no rain to feed it for a while it's probably knee deep at its shallowest and chest deep at high tide.'

'Thank you, you've been helpful; you may both go.'

'It doesn't sound much of a defensive line,' Wulfnoth, the Ealdorman of Eoforwīc, said disdainfully.

He had accompanied the king north with twenty horsemen of his own, as had two other ealdorman who he'd collected on the way.

'You don't know the ground, Wulfnoth,' Heremond put in quickly. 'The ground is fairly flat at that point and, as a place to take up a defensive position, it's as good as any and better than most.'

His fellow ealdorman gave him a sharp look but said nothing further.

'How many mounted men can you raise overnight, Heremond?' Ælle asked, frowning at Wulfnoth.

He was a foolish man who believed that he was cleverer than anyone else: a dangerous combination. Ælle would have replaced him but he needed his support and that of the man's family against his brother.

'Well, I've a warband fifty strong but I only have eighteen riding horses; not that it matters. I don't have eighteen men who can fight on horseback.'

'Oh, I'm not talking about using them as cavalry. We just need to arrive before it's too late; then we'll fight on foot.'

The king left at dawn with his horsemen, the scouts and two of Heremond's huntsmen acting as guides. They headed north-west to ford the Derventio two miles south-west of the place where the battle was to be fought, then headed along the far bank.

As they neared the confluence between the Tyne and its tributary they heard the sound of battle. Ælle prayed that he would be in time.

-ᛯ-

Ragnar had reached the west bank of the Derventio two hours previously. He might have been obsessed with obtaining his revenge upon Edmund, but he was no fool. As soon as his scouts came back he knew that he was walking into a trap. Not only was the far bank held in force by warriors behind a rampart but Edmund had anchored his longships out in the Tyne parallel to the shore from where his archers could inflict severe casualties on his men without fear that they could be attacked. He had to admire Edmund's strategy, but he wasn't about to do anything so stupid as to assault the Northumbrian's position.

Instead he turned south westwards out of sight of Edmund's position and then followed the Derventio until he found a place beyond the marshy area where he could cross the river. Then he retraced his steps along the other bank until he was in a position to attack the Northumbrians in the flank.

Except that they weren't there anymore.

Hrothwulf and Drefan were two brothers who were constantly up to mischief. One was fifteen and the other fourteen. Their father was one of Edmund's warband and officially the boys were too young to be there; they were both still training to be warriors. However, they had two attributes useful to Edmund: they were good climbers and they were skilled trackers and hunters.

The boys had watched from the upper branches of two oak trees on the west side of the Derventio as the Vikings came to a halt below. They watched the Viking scouts return to tell their leaders about Edmund's defensive works, then they saw the army disappear to the south-west. Hrothwulf, the elder of the two, signalled for his brother to go and tell Edmund what was happening whilst he climbed down and proceeded to follow the Vikings.

Once Drefan had reported to Edmund, he made his way stealthily down the east side of the river until he heard the unmistakeable sounds of a large group of men making their way towards him. Then he swiftly retraced his steps.

'Thank you, Drefan. You've done well. Now get back up into one of those trees over there and stay there. You're too young to fight,' Edmund said with a smile.

'But, lord, I can use my bow to good effect from up there,' the boy pleaded.

'Do as you're told,' his father barked at him. 'I only agreed to you two scamps coming with me on condition that you didn't fight.'

Sullenly Drefan nodded and darted away to climb the largest oak he could find. As he did so Edmund had a hasty discussion with Siferth and Cynefrith. Three minutes later the whole army was on the move into the woodland some hundred yards back from the river bank. At the same time a small fishing boat put out from the banks of the Tyne to brief the longship captains about the change of plan.

As Ragnar stood wondering where the Northumbrians had gone, the ships out in the Tyne weighed anchor and started moving slowly downstream powered by a few rowers. Fortunately for them the tide was on the turn and had just begun to flow seawards. The Vikings couldn't believe their luck as the ships headed towards a beach just to the east of where they were and they started running towards them.

Both Ragnar and Lagertha sensed a trap and yelled for their men to stop, but to no avail. The trees came down to within fifty yards of the beach where the first longship had just run into the shingle strewn sand. The Vikings were a disorganised mass as each man ran to be the first to climb aboard. Suddenly a volley of arrows struck them from the treeline and, at the same time archers appeared all along the side of the beached longship.

The other ships threw their anchors overboard before they reached the beach and the ships slewed around with their bows facing upstream. More archers appeared along the sides of each ship and the Vikings faced volleys of some three hundred arrows every ten seconds or so.

Ragnar watched in dismay as scores of his men were hit before they could swing the shields they carried on their backs around to protect themselves. By the time they had formed a shield wall over a hundred of them had been killed or seriously wounded.

Ragnar yelled at them to close up so that one shield could be placed above another; that way they would be protected from head to foot. This shielded them from the archers on the ships, but those in the trees kept up the attack on their flank.

'Every alternate man turn and face the trees,' Lagertha shouted as three more men were hit. Edmund didn't have many archers in the trees – most were on the ships – but what few he did have were being very effective.

Suddenly, whilst one half of the Vikings remained facing the ships, the other two hundred ran towards the trees, intent on avenging themselves on their tormentors. It was too much for Drefan to resist. He strung his bow and pulled an arrow from the quiver on his back. He wet the feathers with his lips and checked that the arrow was straight; then studied the mass of warriors as they approached the treeline.

Edmund's archers retreated and warriors armed with swords, axes and spears waited in the gloom twenty yards inside the wood for the Vikings to reach them. The charge had been led by what Drefan originally had thought was a young man, but he now realised it was a woman. Her long hair streamed out from under her helmet and, even disguised by a byrnie, he could tell the shapely body was female.

Her helmet was banded in gold and her upper arms were covered by silver and gold arm rings. He had never heard of a shield maiden, but he knew that this woman had to be one of the leaders of the accursed Vikings.

He took careful aim and, allowing for her movement and the slight breeze, he released the arrow. To Drefan it seemed to fly towards its target too slowly and for an instant he thought he'd miscalculated; then it hit.

One moment Lagertha was running, the adrenalin pumping through her body as she screamed her rage at the enemy then, just five yards short of the tree line, she felt a tremendous pain in her neck. Her steps faltered and, as the blood spurted out of her jugular, she fell to the ground and lay still.

Her men faltered, seeing their jarl fall, but then they recovered and cursing their enemies, they charged into the trees. In the woods it wasn't a matter of fighting together as a group. The trees made that impossible and the charge deteriorated into a series of individual combats. However, the Vikings were now outnumbered by the experienced members of Edmund's and Siferth's warbands. Gradually the Northumbrians gained the upper hand.

Meanwhile Ragnar had realised that staying where he was achieved nothing and he gave the order to retreat towards the trees whilst keeping shields facing the arrows coming from the ships. The volleys were now slower as the archers on board got tired and their supply of arrows ran low. As he neared the treeline Ragnar gave the order to form a line and advance into the trees to support Lagertha's men.

It was only then that he saw her body lying, her limbs akimbo, just short of the treeline. From the angle of the arrow protruding from her neck he knew that the archer must have been high up in one of the larger oaks and, urging his men on, he swiftly decided which tree the shield maiden's killer was likely to be hiding in.

Drefan had been tempted to try and kill more Vikings but then they had disappeared from sight below him. Then he saw the second group advancing towards the wood and he selected a second arrow. He scanned the ranks of warriors, looking for a leader.

Ragnar stood out from the rest. His helmet was plain but his byrnie was polished, unlike the dull and sometimes rusty chain mail worn by most of the Vikings. His beard was grey and, like the woman, his upper arms were covered in rings. A man with a red banner tied to his spear followed him and Drefan recognised the device on the banner. It was a spread-eagled raven – the same as that on several of the Viking longships.

Of course, Drefan didn't know that his target was the infamous Ragnar Lodbrok, but he knew that he had to be an important man. Once again he took careful aim and let fly. However, this time the wind gusted just as the arrow darted towards Ragnar and it was blown slightly off course. Instead of striking the Norse king's neck it lodged in his thigh just below the hem of his byrnie.

The leg gave way and Ragnar collapsed, clutching his leg as the pain began to build. Drefan couldn't resist a whoop of triumph and that was his downfall. The Viking warrior standing immediately below the tree he was in had just killed two of Edmund's men and was looking around for a new adversary when he heard the sound from above him. Looking up, at first he saw nothing but as he circled the tree he caught a glimpse of a boy with a bow.

Dropping his shield and axe and putting his dagger between his teeth he leapt up and grabbed the first branch. Slowly he hauled himself up the oak. He wasn't as young and agile as

Drefan, but the boy had nowhere to go so the young Viking took his time. Drefan wasn't aware of his predicament until he heard leaves rustling below him. He looked down and yelped in dismay when he saw a fierce bearded face grinning up at him.

For an instant Drefan was paralysed by fear, then he pulled himself together. He had the advantage of height so he waited as calmly as he could until the Viking was just below him. Then he grabbed the branch above him in both hands and swung his legs back before kicking forwards with them locked together. His leather shoes connected solidly with the Viking's head, driving the blade held between his teeth back and cutting deeply into his cheeks.

The young man was knocked from his perch and he went tumbling earthwards, his body striking several thick branches on the way down. By the time he hit the ground below several of his ribs had been broken and one of these was driven into his right lung as he landed. He lay there unconscious until he died.

Drefan was left shaking, but euphoric. He was just fourteen and he had killed two of the enemy and badly wounded another. He couldn't wait to tell Hrothwulf.

By the time the king arrived the battle was all but over. Only eighty of the Vikings had survived and they had seized the beached longship, killing its crew of archers. They pushed it clear of the mud and sailed away pursued by the rest of Edmund's fleet. As the latter were mainly manned by members of the fyrd with a handful of ships' boys and experienced rowers to help them, it wasn't long before the last of the Vikings made good their escape. No quarter had been given to the rest and Ragnar had only been spared because he was a Norse king.

When Drefan had claimed to have killed the shield maiden and another Viking as well as wounding Ragnar, he wasn't believed at first. However Edmund changed his mind when Ragnar confirmed that the arrow that had laid him low had come from the top of the trees.

Suddenly the boy was hailed as a hero and his father stood proudly with his hand on his shoulder whilst King Ælle congratulated him. Flushed with pride, Drefan glanced at his brother, expecting Hrothwulf to share his delight. The two had always been close, but now Drefan saw that Hrothwulf was scowling. When his brother noticed Drefan looking at him, the stare he gave him was full of malice. Then he turned and stomped away.

It was a salutary lesson for the younger boy. Hrothwulf evidently hated to be eclipsed. Of course, he knew that Hrothwulf could be jealous at times, but those moments didn't last, nor did they harm their relationship. This time it was different, his brother had tarnished his moment of glory and Drefan was furious with him.

'What do you want to do with him, Cyning?' Edmund asked, gesturing towards Ragnar as he lay on the ground being attended to by one of the monks skilled in healing. He had arrived from Jarrow with several of his fellow monks to deal with the Northumbrian wounded and bless the dying. The Norse wounded didn't need their ministrations; they'd already been killed.

Ragnar had suffered the removal of the arrow and the cauterisation of the wound in silence, though he passed out as the red hot blade was applied to the wound. His byrnie had been removed, along with his blood soaked trousers, but at least they'd left him his goatskin jerkin to cover his nakedness.

As Ælle contemplated how to answer Edmund's question there was a disturbance a short distance away and four men carried Hrothwulf into the space around Ragnar, pushing others out of the way in their haste.

Full of anger at Drefan's sudden fame, Hrothwulf hadn't been paying attention to where he was going. He didn't notice the viper sunning itself in his path until he stood on it. The sudden pain in his right leg, just above the ankle, caused him to cry out and luckily a few men standing nearby realised what had happened. One chopped the snake in half with his axe whilst several others rushed the boy to the monk.

'Quick, give me a dagger.'

When one of the warriors did so, the monk cut across the two angry marks left by the snake's fangs and sucked at the wound, spitting out blood and venom and then returning to suck again.

'I've got as much out as possible, now leave him to rest. He'll either die or recover, it's in God's hands. Someone please give me some water to rinse my mouth out.'

Drefan forgot his brother's animosity and cradled him in his arms, trying to comfort him. Hrothwulf stared at him for a moment, then gave him a weak smile before dropping into unconsciousness.

The king had ordered that Ragnar's wound should be attended to because he didn't want him to die from loss of blood. He would be the arbiter of his fate and the incident had given Ælle an idea. He sent some of his men to gather as many of the venomous snakes as they could find, whilst others dug a pit eight feet deep. They came back with eight of the creatures in sacks which wriggled and hissed as the vipers struggled to get out.

When the pit was ready the men held the sacks over the pit and shook them until the last snake had dropped into the bottom of the pit. Their anger at their treatment was all too apparent. They tended to avoid humans and were not normally aggressive, unless attacked. However, these eight were now extremely agitated. By this time Ragnar had regained consciousness and, spotting the Northumbrian king, he struggled to stand, leaning on a length of wood the monk gave him.

'My sons will pay a large ransom if you are prepared to let me go. I give you my oath not to attack Northumbria again.'

'A heathen's oath is worth nothing; no you are going to die, Ragnar Lodbrok.'

'Do you think that will save you from my sons? The squealing of the piglets will deafen you when they hear of the death of the old boar. I tell you that they will visit your land with fire, rape and pillage until you wish with all your heart that you had spared me.'

'Bleat all you like, Ragnar, it won't help you. They say that you sacked Paris but, Charles the Bald must have been a weakling to have allowed it.'

'I had five times the number of warriors then that I brought here with me. My sons will come for vengeance with twice the number of men that I took to Paris.'

'Let them come. I don't fear them.'

'Then you are a fool. At least give me a sword to grasp whilst you kill me so that I may enter Valhalla and dine with Odin tonight.'

'I don't hold with your pagan beliefs. You will die and go to hell.'

Ragnar knew something of the religion of the White Christ. Hell was a place of fire and torment where those who had led an evil life were sent, whereas Ragnar believed that Helheim was a cold world reserved for those who died of old age or illness.

Ragnar shook his head.

'No, my fame is too great for me to wait until Ragnarök in Helheim with the elderly and the feeble. Whether you give me a sword or not, the Valkyries will take me to Odin.'

'Pah, what utter nonsense.'

So saying Ælle pushed Ragnar so that he toppled backwards into the snake pit. At first the angry vipers tried to bite through Ragnar's goatskin jerkin, but without success. He succeeded in strangling two of them before one fastened its fangs into his calf. Then another bit him on the hand and a third struck at his wounded thigh.

Ragnar stopped moving and Ælle told his men to fill the pit in again. As they did so Edmund threw a discarded sword into the pit and he thought he saw Ragnar grab it before he disappeared under the soil. Ælle gave him an angry look, but Edmund just shrugged. It was the least he could do for a worthy adversary.

Afterwards no one could be certain whether Ragnar had died from snake venom or because he had been buried alive.

Epilogue

Autumn 862

As soon as the longship sailed into Arendal the news spread like wildfire. Those Vikings who had escaped on Edmund's snekkja couldn't be certain what had happened after they'd fled, but they were afraid of being branded as cowards, and so the tale they told was worthy of any skáld.

They had seen both Lagertha and Ragnar fall, they said, surrounded by hundreds of enemies, many of whom they had killed between them. Of course, this was a long way from the truth: that they had both been brought down by a fourteen year old boy up a tree.

They claimed that they had only escaped themselves after heroically fighting their way through a thousand Northumbrians and capturing one of their ships. At least the last bit was true.

Eventually merchants and others arrived with a more accurate tale and the survivors were revealed as the cowards and liars that they were. Some were killed by the distraught relatives of those who had died and the rest were either banished or fled. They would have done better to stay and die with their comrades.

'Did you hear father's comment about the piglets squealing when they heard of the death of the old boar?' Sigurd Snake in the Eye asked Ivar the Boneless when he heard the story.

'Yes, you may like to think of yourself as a piglet but I certainly don't.'

'I don't think he meant it like that. He meant that we would avenge him.'

'Perhaps.'

'At any rate the whole of Scandinavia is talking about his death. It's a disgrace that he was thrown in a snake pit without a sword to defend himself.'

'I heard he was buried alive.'

'Either way we must avenge him. Everyone one expects us to.'

At that moment Halfdan entered the hall and joined his brothers, yelling for a thrall to bring him some ale.

'Sigurd's right. We'll be called cowards if we do nothing.'

'Oh, I don't intend to sit on my arse. It gives us the perfect excuse to gather a mighty warband and invade England.'

'Excuse? I don't understand,' Sigurd asked, a little bewildered.

'Our father was a fool to go to Northumbria with so few men. Even then he managed to lose a third of them at sea. No, when I land it will be at the head of a great army. Given time and luck we should be able to gather perhaps three thousand warriors.'

'Three thousand? Why do you need so many to avenge father's death?'

'I don't. Revenge is merely the pretext. What we're really going to do is to conquer the whole of England. Here the land is poor, the winters long and we need to raid just to survive. Wessex, Mercia, Kent, much of East Anglia and the southern half of Northumbria is rich and fertile farming land.'

'You intend to settle?' Sigurd asked incredulously.

'Why not? Other Norse have settled around Duibhlinn in Ireland.'

'Yes, and others in Orkneyjar and the Land of Ice and Fire,' Halfdan added, getting enthusiastic.

Ivar gave him a pitying look.

'Both of those are worse than here. The only people who settle there are outlaws and folk too poor to make any sort of living here. No, England is a land where we can thrive and prosper, once we have killed or made thralls of the Angles, Saxons and Jutes.'

'Three thousand warriors?' Sigurd mused. 'We'll need fifty drekar or more to transport us.'

'Which is why we have to be patient. In five years many of today's young boys will be warriors and we need the time to build the extra ships to carry them. Then we'll set sail with the largest Viking army the world has ever seen.'

The End

The Kings of Northumbria Series will conclude with

Sons of the Raven

due out later in 2018

AUTHOR'S NOTE

Kings of Northumbria

Very little is recorded about Northumbria during the ninth century. It appears to have been somewhat of a backwater where little of what happened was recorded.

What we do have is the names of the kings, but in some cases even their regnal dates are uncertain. I have set out below a precis of the facts that we are aware of:

Eardwulf ruled from 796 to 806, when he was deposed and went into exile. He may have had a second reign from 808 until perhaps 811 or 830, records vary.

Ælfwald appears to have been a usurper who ruled from 806 to 808 before Eardwulf was restored.

The only reference in the Anglo-Saxon Chronicle to Eanred, Eardwulf's son, is the statement that *in 829 Egbert of Wessex led an army against the Northumbrians as far as Dore, where they met him, and offered terms of obedience and subjection.* Eanred appears to have succeeded his father in 810, 811 or 830. He may have ruled until 854.

Æthelred II was the son of Earnred but his regnal dates are uncertain. All that is known is that he was king in the middle of the ninth century. Once source sates that he ruled from 840 to 848, when he was killed, with an interruption in 844 when Rædwulf usurped the throne. However coinage surviving from the time indicates that Æthelred's reign was from c.854 to c. 862, with Rædwulf's usurpation in 858. The latter was only on the throne for a few months before he was killed in battle by Viking raiders.

Little is known about the reigns of Osberht and Ælle. Whilst Ælle is described in most sources as a tyrant and not a rightful king, one source states that he was Osberht's brother. What seems certain is that Ælle became king after Osberht was deposed. This is traditionally dated to 862 or 863 but evidence about Northumbrian royal chronology is less than clear about dates prior to 867and it may have been as late as 866.

It is possible that a civil war over the disputed crown raged between the two until they agreed a truce in 867 in order to face the threat posed by the Great Heathen Army.

Ragnar Lodbrok

Ragnar is the archetypal Viking hero, but his story is so mixed up in myth and folklore that it's difficult, if not impossible, to sift the truth from the legend. The various accounts even differ on who he was married to when and who his sons were.

Part of the problem lies in the fact that much early Scandinavian history was recited by the skálds - poets who entertained at the courts of Scandinavian leaders during the Viking Age and Middle Ages with sagas that mixed history with fable. Skaldic poetry forms one of two main groupings of Old Norse poetry, the other being the anonymous Eddic poetry. Such tales were verbal in the main and were altered to make them more entertaining or to flatter the king or jarl in whose hall the skáld was staying. Only later were some of the sagas written down.

Most of what has been recorded about Ragnar Lodbrok was written much later and it is entirely possible that what survives relates to more than one man. He is variously described as a Dane, a Swede or a Norseman (Norwegian). Some accounts say that his father was King Sigurd Hring of Sweden, but then they give different names for his mother. In some tales he is a king of Sweden who ruled for sixty one years, which seems somewhat unlikely.

What is known is that Paris was captured by the Vikings in 845 and that their leader was a Norse chieftain named "Reginherus", or Ragnar, who is traditionally associated with Ragnar Lodbrok.

There is also evidence in the Anglo-Saxon Chronicle that the sons of Ragnar fought under a war banner depicting a raven. It therefore seems reasonable that was also Ragnar's emblem.

I have tried to take the various sources and combine them to produce what is, I hope, a credible story.

About the Author

H A Culley served as an Army officer for twenty four years during which time he had a variety of unusual jobs. He spent his twenty first birthday in the jungles of Borneo, commanded an Arab infantry unit in the Gulf for three years and was the military attaché in Beirut during the aftermath of the Lebanese Civil War.

After leaving the Army he spent twenty one years in the education sector. He has served on the board of two commercial companies and has been a trustee of several national and local charities. His last job before retiring was as the finance director and company secretary of the Institute of Development Professionals in Education. Since retirement he has been involved in several historical projects and gives talks on historical subjects. He started writing historical fiction in 2013.

He lives between Holy Island and Berwick upon Tweed in Northumberland.

Printed in Great Britain
by Amazon